Suicidal Samurai

Suicidal Samurai

MEIJI MYSTERIES BOOK ONE

SARAH G. ROTHMAN

Published by Rozfire Productions.
www.rozfire.com

ISBN-13: 9780998964713
ISBN-10: 0998964713

Cover image by Gene Mollica Studio, LLC
genemollica.com

Editing by Alison Williams
alisonwilliamswriting.wordpress.com

Printed in the United States of America.

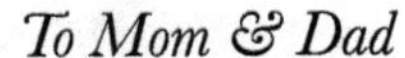

To Mom & Dad

Prologue

A cool, summer night descended over the sleepy port town of Yokohama, a perfect night for murder. Dangling stern lanterns swayed with the bobbing ships in the harbor. Adjacent to the waterfront, newly installed street gaslights illuminated European-style hotels, offices, and shops. A few blocks inland, the state-of-the-art gaslights gave way to dim, paper lanterns. And just beyond the modern, European part of the city stood a small, old-fashioned inn. Its traditional architecture blended well with the other native buildings but contrasted sharply with the new brick structures nearby. Softly glowing lanterns dotted the entrance of the inn, while the guest rooms were all lit with oil lamps. One guest room on the second floor suddenly went dark as its lamp was extinguished.

In that room, a pair of hands savagely wrenched out a blade. Blood poured from the gash and dripped onto the hard, reed *tatami* mats, which covered the floor. The old man looked down in horror at the mortal wound to his abdomen. The blood formed a large, dark stain on his bright blue *haori* jacket. He staggered back and tried to draw the long sword at his side. However, his strength left him as he grasped the haft. He clutched the wound and crumpled backward onto the floor, letting out a weak gasp of air. He looked up once more to glare at the face of his killer before his eyes rolled back, and he let out his final gasp. Looming over him, the killer carefully placed a knife in his hand. Carved in the wood of the handle was a red, circular flower. The assassin gave a low chuckle.

"So begins a new age."

Chapter One

On a humid, summer morning in 1878, a giant steamship pulled into Yokohama harbor. An oversized American flag fluttered over the stern and beneath it, the ship's name, *Abraham Lincoln,* was painted in large, gold lettering. The ship's massive hull kept it steady, while the neighboring ships bobbed up and down in the choppy waves. The dockworkers scrambled to maneuver a gangway long enough to reach the deck. Dozens of onlookers gathered to gawk and stare at the ship and its foreign passengers. Once the gangway was connected, the passengers began descending in a single file to the pier and walked down a clearly marked path, leading straight to the newly constructed, brick customs office.

Inside the office, a tired customs official looked over and stamped the papers of these newcomers while his bored colleague pawed through their luggage, searching for contraband. A fresh set of papers were handed to the clerk by the next person in line, and he briefly looked them over.

"Let me see…" he muttered in strained English, "coming from San Francisco?"

He looked up at the man in front of him and jolted, grabbing his desk to avoid falling out of his chair. The man before him had the straight black hair and facial features of a typical Japanese man, but was far taller than most and wore the distinctive garb of an American cowboy. The visitor's long, black duster reached below his knees, revealing a pair of black boots underneath, and on his head sat a black, broad-brimmed hat. His face was expressionless.

The clerk switched from surprise to suspicion. He looked down and saw the name "David Wong" in English and frowned. The man in front of him could easily pass as a Chinese-American, but something about him seemed off. The clerk glanced toward his colleague who was looking through the man's Gladstone bag. Its rectangular shape and brown leather seemed like luggage appropriate for a prosperous merchant or gentleman explorer, not for this black-clad cowboy. The inspector pulled out a mid-sized wooden box covered in squares, a folding chess set. He gave it a rattle and opened it up to see the metal chessmen inside. Not finding anything objectionable, he closed the set and tossed it back into the bag where it landed with a clatter. The inspector struggled with the weight of the heavy bag as he handed it back to its owner, although the cowboy grabbed it effortlessly with one hand.

The cowboy stood silently, waiting for the clerk to approve his papers. The clerk scanned the documents one more time to try and find something to nitpick but gave a relenting sigh and stamped the papers. He handed them over and waved him through. The cowboy tipped his hat toward the official and walked through the crowds of lingering foreigners, who were perusing advertisements along the wall for various tourist locations and hotels. As he passed, the clerk gave the cowboy one last glance and was confused when he saw a white crane spreading its wings painted on the back of the cowboy's coat.

***

After scanning the advertisements, Mori Makoto glanced down at his forged papers. He was impressed they'd managed to fool the customs officials in both San Francisco and Yokohama, but he wasn't too fond of his fake Chinese-American alias. But that didn't matter now, because after fifteen years he was finally back in Japan. Back home. He stuck his forged documents into one of the many pockets in his duster and headed for the exit.

As he stepped from the customs building, Makoto was greeted by the hustle and bustle of the international port. The smell of sea salt and freshly caught fish permeated the air. Burly stevedores hefted crates, barrels, and bales between the docked ships and the waterfront warehouses. Small stands offered local wares: ornate fans, handcrafted flower hairpins, erotic woodblock prints, and delicacies like fried octopus and grilled eel. The docks had been completely renovated and some of the Western-style buildings stood almost four stories tall, far taller than the ones Makoto remembered. Despite these changes, there was something in the air that felt familiar and welcoming to him. He breathed in deeply before stepping into the crowd.

Travelers from Europe and America crowded the booths, seeking great finds and curios to amaze their friends back home. In the distance, Makoto saw the wooden ribs of several small and mid-size ships still under construction. He navigated his way around the clusters of people, but the crowd grew thicker as more gathered to see the *Abraham Lincoln*. The mob of people soon became near impassible, and Makoto had to shove his way through. In one over-enthusiastic push, he bumped into a dark-haired, middle-aged Caucasian woman clad in a bright purple dress, hat, and matching umbrella. She let out a squeal, which nearly turned into a curse, and tumbled backward. Before she hit the ground, Makoto reached out, grabbed her arm, and yanked her upright.

She stumbled forward a few steps and stood upright, dusting off nonexistent dirt before shooting Makoto an angry look. "What's the big idea you-" She looked at his clothes and face and gawked. "What in the world? They say the apparel oft proclaims the man, but what are you supposed to be?" Her face shifted from bewilderment to fascination. "Wait a moment. That's a cowboy getup, isn't it? Did you just come from America? Have you heard any news about-"

"Helen!" The woman turned at the familiar voice of her husband, John Arkwright. He was dressed in the stylish suit of a prosperous robber baron, his graying hair complementing the dark suit, which bulged a bit in the middle and emphasized the heavy gold watch chain decorating his vest. Arkwright trotted up to Helen, already out of breath. "Where the devil were you?"

"You should see this John! A cowboy, right here in Yokohama! He's right over-" Helen turned back and was startled to see the cowboy had vanished. She stared in slight confusion for a moment but regained her poise. "Never mind. It was nothing."

"I hope you're not bothering some poor sap with your theater talk."

"Well, it worked on you, didn't it?" Helen gave a smug smile to John, who shrugged. She waved the crook handle of her umbrella near his face. "Besides, the theater was my past life. Detective stories are all the rage now. Haven't you heard about that interesting fellow in London?"

"No," John replied. "And I don't wish to be educated on the matter. I'm not sure if you've noticed, but the *Abraham Lincoln* has finally arrived. We need to go meet her!" John and Helen turned toward the ship, which had attracted an admiring crowd as it towered over the entire harbor. John gave a proud smile. "Magnificent, isn't she?"

Helen gave a bored sigh. "Yes, dear. Just like all your other ships."

***

After a significant effort, Makoto broke through the crowd and walked toward the warehouse district. The tourists and vendors were slowly replaced by trading company offices and seedy hotels that catered to sailors. The cobblestone streets gave way to muddy alleys, populated by run-down bars frequented by brawny, unfriendly looking patrons. Makoto tightened his grip on his bag as he passed a large group of tattooed men leaning against a wall. They gave dark stares, which Makoto returned. He saw four of the men point toward his bag and whisper among themselves.

Makoto continued forward but gave the occasional glance back over his shoulder, and he noticed a couple of the men break from the group to follow him. He scanned the surrounding area and spotted a small alley between two dilapidated buildings. After he turned into the narrow alley, Makoto heard the sound of running footsteps heading his way. He looked ahead and saw a wooden fence at the back end of the alley. It would have been too tall to scale for someone of average height in Japan, but not for Makoto. He tossed his bag over the fence and with a swift leap upward, grabbed the top and heaved himself over in one smooth motion. He landed on the other side and crouched low, just as the footsteps stopped on the opposite side of the fence.

"Wha-? Where'd he go?"

"Come on! This way!"

Makoto kept his attention on the fence until he could no longer hear the sounds of their footsteps. Once they were out of earshot, Makoto reached for his bag, but when he grabbed at nothing, realized it was gone.

He looked up to see a short man dressed in a loose *yukata*, his bare feet in worn-down *geta* sandals, and his head topped with a Western-style straw hat. He was dragging the bag out of the alley, but he struggled with its heavy weight. Makoto stood upright and with a couple of steps caught up to the thief. He reached down, grabbed the handle of his bag, and yanked it from the thief's hands.

"Hey! I saw it first!" the thief squawked.

Makoto glared.

The thief flinched. "But by all means take it! I'll just, uh, be going now!" The man bolted.

Makoto knew the bag would continue to be a tempting target for thieves. He had to get rid of it. He looked around to see if he was alone. The shadows of the two-story buildings made it hard for passerby to see inside the alley, which was perfect for Makoto.

Satisfied he was unobserved, he placed the bag on the ground and kneeled to open it. Inside were a few items of clothing, a shaving kit, his folded chessboard, some Japanese coins he got before leaving San Francisco, and a small bag containing half a pound of tiny gold nuggets. He reached inside and pulled out a canvas duffel bag he had purchased from a sailor on the long voyage to Yokohama and opened it.

He slid his possessions into the duffel bag and set it aside before he reached into the Gladstone bag and ripped out the bottom. This revealed a thin, hidden compartment that contained the twenty-eight-inch blade of a cutlass with a flattened haft and no handle. He carefully picked up the blade of the sword and ran his finger along the edge. Satisfied there were no nicks or damage, he slid it into the duffel along with the two halves of its wooden grip. He knew swords were illegal to carry in public, but this blade was special. They had been through too much together for him to leave it behind in San Francisco, hence his need for a bag with a hidden compartment.

He returned to the bag's hidden bottom and retrieved the frame and cylinder of the 1851 Navy Colt revolver he had brought along as well. Firearms were also illegal to possess in Japan, but Makoto knew he would need the gun for the dark tasks ahead of him. He placed the revolver components into the duffel. After one last glance over his empty Gladstone bag to make sure he hadn't forgotten anything in the hidden compartments, Makoto stood up and swung the duffel over his shoulder. He picked up the empty bag and left the alley.

It didn't take him long to find a pawn shop whose owner was happy to buy the expensive leather bag, though Makoto received a fraction of the price he'd paid when he'd bought it. At least he had a few more Japanese coins in his pocket and didn't have to worry about his shabby duffel being a tempting target for thieves. As Makoto continued to walk through the warehouse district, he heard cheerful, drunken shouts.

He glanced toward a flimsy, two-story wooden building with colorful banners fluttering on both sides of the entrance. Makoto glanced up and saw a rotting sign precariously balanced on the roof that read "*Sakénomi*

No Izakaya" or "Drunkard's Bar." Makoto reread the surprisingly honest name. There was no door at the entrance, but instead, there were three strips of brown fabric that together showed the Japanese symbol for "*saké*" in white paint. Next to the entrance was a wooden sign that spelled out "alcohol" and "bar" in several different languages. After another round of raucous cheers erupted from the tavern, Makoto stepped inside.

The first thing he saw was a hulking man with the build of a sumo wrestler standing next to the entrance. He and Makoto just about matched in height, but the man was significantly wider and more muscular. The sumo stared at Makoto but didn't stop him from stepping further inside. In the bar, boisterous, laughing sailors chatted away in their native tongues and tattooed Japanese gangsters spoke in whispers while huddled around the teetering, uneven tables. The reek of alcohol and sweat hung heavy in the air.

Makoto made his way between the tightly packed Western-style tables to the bar, a simple wooden counter with several large cracks and stains. He sat on one of the stools, placing his duffel at his feet. As he scanned for the bartender, he saw rows of shelves housing a disorganized arrangement of liquor bottles from around the world. Along the ground below the shelves were several large saké barrels. One was open and had a wooden ladle jutting from the clear liquid.

At the end of the counter, he caught sight of the bartender, a slender, clean-shaven, European-looking young man. His short, dirty-blonde hair was carefully combed, and he wore a loose white apron over a European shirt and pants that seemed far too fine for the seedy bar. The young bartender was conversing with a giggling Japanese woman dressed in loose, bright pink yukata robes common for a lower-class girl, but she wore the sickeningly sweet perfume of a high-class woman. "Oh please," she said in Japanese, "say something to me in French."

The bartender gave her a warm smile. "*Quelque chose en français.*"

The woman lovingly sighed and resumed her giggling. Makoto didn't understand what he'd said and turned away in mild annoyance. On the adjacent wall, were dozens of woodblock, *ukiyo-e* prints, ranging in content from mundane to obscene.

As Makoto stared he heard an intoxicated, laughing sailor come up behind him. "What've we got 'ere?" he asked in drunken English with an American accent. "A slant who thinks he's a cowboy? Ain't that a riot?

Hey cowboy! Look at me!"

Makoto ignored the sailor and focused on the prints instead. But he felt the burly man's hand grab his collar and yank him so he had no choice but to look at the sailor.

"Pay attention ya filthy-"

Before he could finish, Makoto reached up, grabbed the back of the sailor's head, and slammed him face-first into the counter with a loud *thunk*. This caught the attention of everyone at the bar. The sailor let go of Makoto's collar, reeled back in pain, and nearly fell to the ground. He bent over, gasping for breath and rubbing the darkening bruise on his forehead. Everyone else in the room stared at the two with interest, which quickly morphed into encouragements and jeers for both parties. A fight was always good entertainment.

The bartender and the woman at the end of the counter also looked on with interest. "Aren't you going to stop them?" she asked.

The bartender checked the counter and once satisfied it had sustained no further damage than it had before the fight, leaned back without much care. "They're big boys, mademoiselle. They can take care of themselves."

In the midst of the cheers, the sailor shook off the pain and reached into his vest. Makoto stepped off the stool and braced himself.

"Why you lousy-! I'll kill ya!" The sailor pulled out a folded gully knife hidden in the pocket of his vest, flicked the blade out, and charged toward Makoto.

Chapter Two

As the sailor hunched down into a fighting stance, he extended his knife forward and charged.

"Hey! No knives! You might scratch the counter!" the bartender called out.

The sailor ignored him, while Makoto crouched down and braced for the attack. The sailor kept his blade low, aiming to strike Makoto in the gut.

"Tora!" The bartender pointed toward the sailor.

In a single motion, the sumo, who had already situated himself nearby, reached down and yanked up the sailor by his collar with one hand and forced the knife out with the other.

"What the- Hey! Lemme go!" The sailor thrashed around, trying to regain his footing, but Tora held him just above the ground as though he was a misbehaving cat.

Tora handed the gully knife to the bartender, who carefully snapped it shut. With a sigh of annoyance, the bartender bent down behind the counter, pulled out a crate filled with confiscated weapons, tossed the knife inside, and kicked the crate back under the counter. The sumo walked the swearing, flailing sailor toward the front entrance and heaved him into the street. After pausing at the entry to make certain the sailor didn't return, he resumed his post near the front as the bar patrons stared.

"I trust there won't be any further commotion?" the bartender asked in English, French, Japanese, German, and Russian.

Some of the customers nodded while others grumbled affirmations under their breaths. Makoto returned to his seat, both relieved and disappointed. It was unusual for others to handle fights for him.

With an overly dramatic sigh, the woman by the counter pulled away, rearranging her yukata to be more presentable. "I must go. Otherwise, the innkeeper will punish me again."

The bartender returned to the woman and made a gracious, Western-style bow, which made her giggle. "Such a shame, mademoiselle. You know, I could teach you a few things myself."

"Oh?" The young woman smiled and batted her eyelashes. "Like what?"

"French, of course." The bartender smiled. "You keep asking to hear it, why not just learn it?"

"Oh." The woman deflated a little. "I see. I'll … think about it." She scurried out one of the side-entrances, ignoring the wolf whistles and stares from the other patrons.

The bartender saw the seated Makoto from the corner of his eye and walked up to him. "Welcome to Sakénomi's," the bartender recited in monotone Japanese, "I'm Jean Dubois, and assuming you pay promptly and don't cause any trouble…" Jean glanced at the entrance. "Well, if you don't cause any *further* trouble, we'll take good care of you. What'll you be havin'?"

"Whiskey," Makoto replied in English.

Jean blinked a couple of times and raised an eyebrow. "You speak English?"

Makoto nodded.

"Nobody's asked for whiskey in a while. I've got both rye and bourbon. We've also got single malt scotch, brandy, grappa, schnapps, and rum."

The bartender reached up on the back shelf and pulled down two bottles, Old Overholt and Old Crow, high-quality brands compared to the coffin varnish and red eye that was more typical saloon fare. The bartender ran a quick calculation in his head. "It'll be three yen for a shot."

Makoto was startled at such a high price. Three yen could buy ten full-quart bottles of either of those brands in San Francisco. "That's … expensive."

"Probably why nobody's asked for it recently. But between shipping it halfway around the world, the tariff, the tax, the blackmail, and the bribes, the costs add up. But I guarantee you won't find it better or cheaper anywhere else in the country."

"Blackmail and bribes?"

Jean shrugged. "Just a cost of doing business. Let's just say that some of my patrons aren't just here for the spirits." Jean motioned his head toward the tattooed gangsters sitting at the table. "Though at least they're upfront about their protection rackets. Unlike the police. Those clowns aren't even allowed to drink on duty, but for some reason, they keep managing to find excuses to harass my establishment. The only way to get 'em to back off is to pay 'em off."

Makoto shook his head. Some things were the same as in America after all. "Do you have any less expensive brands?"

"No. Cheap stuff would be just as expensive after all the costs. It's not worth carrying anything except the best. So, do you want any?"

Makoto preferred whiskey, but he had no intention of wasting all of his money. "What do people usually drink here?"

Jean pointed toward a stack of square, wooden *masu* boxes. Makoto noticed most of the patrons were drinking from similar boxes. "Saké. Three sen per box."

Makoto nodded. That was a hundred times less expensive and a much more reasonable price. He fished into his coat and handed Jean three large, sen coins. The bartender pocketed them with a smile, grabbed a *masu* box from the stack, and walked over to one of the open saké barrels. He used a bamboo ladle to stir the clear liquid a couple of times, lifted out a full ladle of the wine, and poured it into the wooden box, filling it to the brim. After depositing the ladle back into the barrel, he handed the box to Makoto. "Here you go. Let me know if you want anything else."

"There is one thing." Makoto reached into one of his inner pockets and pulled out a small, carefully folded piece of paper. He unfolded it, showing a pencil drawing of the crane symbol painted on the back of his duster. He handed the paper to Jean. "Have you seen this?"

Jean looked over the paper, scrutinizing the symbol before shaking his head. "I don't think so … but maybe…" Jean rubbed his chin in thought and snapped his fingers in recollection. "The old lady! She'll probably know."

"Old lady?" Makoto asked.

"The innkeeper of the Yasumi Inn. That old broad knows just about everything going on in the port. You'll know her by her dark *kimono* and even darker scowl."

"Where is this inn?"

"Just a little further into the neighborhood. In fact, the young mademoiselle works … *zut alors*, she just left didn't she? Well, you can't miss it. The building's almost as old as that dour innkeeper." Jean chuckled as he handed Makoto back his paper.

"I understand. Thanks." Makoto pulled out a couple more sen coins and handed them to Jean, who grinned, pocketed the extra coins, and walked away to serve other customers. Makoto looked down at his box of rice wine and picked it up, carefully handling it so none of the saké spilled out. He took a sip. It wasn't as strong as whiskey, but the taste was decent and he felt a satisfying warmth. He took a second sip.

Makoto heard the sound of the creaking floorboard as someone forcefully pushed the entrance curtain aside and strode in. He glanced back to see if the troublesome sailor had returned. The person in the entranceway was a round, boisterous man in a dark blue police uniform with a baton dangling at his waist. He strutted into the bar like a gamecock and glanced up at Tora. He was a foot shorter than the bouncer but almost as broad. Though by the way his uniform pulled and his stomach overhung the belt, it was clear the policeman's mass was mostly fat, not muscle. Frowning at the sumo's larger stature, the policeman sucked in and puffed out his chest as he walked into the middle of the bar. The patrons grew quiet at the sight of the policeman and averted their gazes. Growing irritated at this purposeful lack of attention, the policeman placed himself in the middle of the room at the point of easiest visibility.

"Criminals beware! For I am the great and powerful Yamada Kotaro! Savior of Osaka!" With his loud declaration, the entire bar fixated on him, save for Makoto, who turned back to his drink. The drunken sailor would have been less obnoxious.

Satisfied he had a proper audience, Kotaro continued. "Osaka once had the reputation as a hive of criminal scum, much like some of the people I see here." Kotaro loomed forward and looked over the patrons of the tavern. "But after I was *begged* to join the force by none other than the superintendent himself, I single-handedly wiped out the ten most dangerous gangs in Osaka! Just me and my handy baton!" Kotaro pulled out his short nightstick and started randomly pointing it at the patrons. Most of the sailors stared with confusion and fascination, especially since his Japanese words were lost on the Americans, Germans, French, and Russians. Meanwhile, the gangsters who could understand him snorted and struggled to contain their laughter.

"But because my superiors feared that I would wipe out all crime and leave them out of a job, I was transferred to Yokohama, a hotbed of crime and villainy! Well, before you even think about committing any crimes, know the great and powerful Yamada Kotaro is always watching!" Kotaro slid his baton back into the notch on his belt and puffed out his chest, satisfied with his little speech.

He swaggered his way up to the counter and sat on a rickety stool next to Makoto, who lowered his hat to obscure his face. He knew better than to deal with policemen, especially loud ones. The bar resumed its previous volume of chatter, though most conversations were about the policeman. Kotaro impatiently drummed his fingers on the counter while waiting for the bartender.

Jean appeared, but a distrusting glare replaced his warm smile. "Yes?" he asked through gritted teeth.

"Give me saké. In a *big* box!" Kotaro held out his arms and moved them in the shape of an invisible box larger than his head. "Actually, you can just save us all some trouble and get me one of the barrels!" Kotaro laughed at his own joke, and Jean rolled his eyes.

"That'll be three sen."

Kotaro balked. "You want me to pay now!? Get me my drink first!"

"First pay. Then drink."

Kotaro grumbled and pulled out three sen coins from his pocket and tossed them on the counter. Jean picked them up and scrutinized the coins. Once satisfied they were genuine, he slid them into his pocket and served Kotaro a standard masu box filled with saké. Kotaro grabbed the box and downed the contents in one swift gulp. His face turned several shades redder, and he waved the empty box at the bartender. "Give me another!"

"Won't you get in trouble for being drunk on duty?" Jean asked.

"Ha! I'm from Osaka. There we drink saké like water. And you dare think I'm drunk? Bah! I'm twice the man of anyone in this town!"

"I can see that," Jean said.

Makoto thought he heard a distinct snort of disgust from the sumo near the entrance.

"That's why I need twice as much saké!" Kotaro said.

"And that's why you have to pay twice. Three more sen," Jean replied.

"This swill's so expensive!" Kotaro complained while yanking out three more coins and slamming them on the counter. Jean picked them up and refilled the masu for Kotaro. As he waited for his next box, Kotaro looked over at Makoto, who was still sipping from his first. Kotaro leaned back a little, his chair straining from the movement, to look at the large, white bird symbol painted on the back of Makoto's duster. Kotaro's chair nearly fell backward, but he grabbed the counter, pulling himself back up to the bar just as Jean brought the refilled box. Kotaro eagerly grabbed the saké and cast Makoto a leery glance, trying to make out his face.

"Feh. Foreigner," Kotaro muttered. He downed the second box almost as quickly as the first. He turned several shades redder still and started waving the box around again. "This saké's so weak! I need another!"

"Three more sen."

"Just put it on my tab," Kotaro said. "I'm good for it!"

"We don't do that here," Jean replied.

"Why not!?"

"Our customers aren't very reliable."

"You saying I'm not reliable?"

"Something like that." Jean left Kotaro to tend to another customer.

Kotaro grew annoyed and leaned over the counter, waving his box around frantically. The chair groaned in its new position. "Blasted foreigner! Gimme another!" With a sharp *crack*, one of the legs of Kotaro's chair gave out. Kotaro flailed about as he tipped backward and downward, grasping at anything he could. His hand grabbed the top of Makoto's duffel and dragged it down, spilling most of its contents, including the sharp-edged cutlass blade.

The bar quieted down at the sudden crash. Kotaro landed squarely on his back. Realizing that everyone was staring, Kotaro sat upright and tried to scramble to his feet, but couldn't quite manage it and tumbled back down, which caused snickering among the patrons. As Kotaro struggled like a turtle on its back, Makoto quickly descended from his stool and started scooping the spilled contents back into his duffel.

"Blasted sickle weasels!" Kotaro cursed. He looked around him and saw Makoto sliding his things back into his bag. Kotaro's eyes landed on the metal blade. He jolted upright and managed to scramble to his feet. "What the-? How'd a foreigner like you get your hands on a sword!?"

Makoto did not reply and continued carefully placing items into his bag, accounting for each piece.

Kotaro grew impatient, pulled out his baton, and pointed it directly at Makoto. "Listen, you stupid foreigner! It's illegal to carry swords in public!"

Makoto remained silent. Kotaro grew angry and slammed his baton into the counter, startling many of the patrons. The blow left a large, new crack in the already weak wood. Within a second, the bartender descended on him and started cursing at Kotaro in a torrent of French. Kotaro was first startled by Jean but started shaking his baton toward him as well. "Police business! You want to be arrested, too?"

Tora stepped forward, but Jean put out his hand, took a deep breath, and shook his head. "Not worth getting arrested."

Tora stopped. Jean glared toward Kotaro but shifted his glance toward Makoto. His glare changed to an annoyed frown. "You seem to be good at attracting trouble."

Kotaro ignored the bartender and pointed his baton toward Makoto. "In the name of the Emperor, I, the great and powerful Yamada Kotaro of the Yokohama police, arrest you for carrying a bladed weapon in public! Hand over your bag and sword right now!"

Makoto sighed, stood upright, and swung the bag behind his back. Makoto stood a solid foot taller than the policeman. Kotaro's hands and knees began to wobble. Makoto tilted his hat up and looked Kotaro dead in the eye. "No."

Kotaro stepped back after getting a look at Makoto's face. "Wait. You're Japanese? Never mind, it doesn't matter. Surrender! If you know what's good for you!" Kotaro's hands were shaking now. All eyes in the bar were on the two and everything had gone quiet. Unable to bear the stares and silence any longer, Kotaro let out his best attempt at a war cry and charged at Makoto, swinging his baton back and forth, hoping to strike something. Makoto remained still until Kotaro was less than a foot away, and in one movement, stepped to the side. Unable to stop his lunge, Kotaro tripped over his own feet, spun around in mid-air, and landed backward on one of the tables, causing it to collapse under the sudden extra weight.

Jean balked at the collapsed table. "Who's going to pay for that!?"

Kotaro tried to heave himself upward but fell backward again. "Blasted sickle weasels!"

The bar rattled with laughter at the policeman's plight. With another heave, Kotaro was able to sit upright but flinched in pain. He groaned and clutched his head, which only further amused the drinkers. The laughter of the bar was cut short when several police officers rushed in with sabers dangling by their sides.

Chapter Three

The bar grew silent as the police officers entered. There were a half-a-dozen men in blue uniforms with various rankings pinned to their hats. Each was ready to draw his sword. The most senior of the officers, his lieutenant's insignia prominent, stood ahead of the other officers and scanned the room for danger. Nobody dared move, much less attack.

Satisfied none of the patrons posed a threat, the lieutenant called the other officers to attention. The commanding officer pushed aside the ragged cloth at the entrance and stepped inside. He stood significantly taller than his fellow officers and wore the same dark blue uniform, but his hat displayed the golden star and bars of a captain. Unlike the standard saber of the other officers, he wore a Japanese-style *katana* at his side. As the captain approached the end of the line, the lieutenant saluted. "The area is clear, sir."

The captain nodded and returned the salute. He scanned the room, clearly not pleased to be there, and his eyes fell on the dazed Kotaro, who still sat on top of the collapsed table. Stepping away from the lieutenant, the captain stalked forward and loomed over Kotaro. "Patrolman Yamada, why am I not surprised to find you here?"

Kotaro flinched at the captain's acid tone of voice. "C-Captain Fujita!" He scrambled upright and gave an overenthusiastic salute, which the captain did not return.

Captain Fujita's glare grew icy as he stared toward the counter and the bartender. Jean folded his arms and returned the glare with interest.

"We were informed of a disturbance involving a police officer in this sewer of a bar," Fujita said.

"Sewer!?" Jean leaned over the counter, scowling at the captain.

Fujita ignored him. "In my foolishness, I thought an *officer* required assistance, not a lowly *patrolman*. A patrolman who *should* be at his post." Fujita shifted his scowl toward Kotaro, who dropped his salute.

"Well, I have a good reason, sir. You see-"

"I'm not interested in your reasons," Fujita growled, grabbing Kotaro's collar and heaving him up onto his toes, despite Kotaro's significant weight.

"S-Sorry captain!" Kotaro squawked.

"Don't you realize your drunken wallowing in this pigsty interrupted important preparations for the ceremony this week!?" Fujita shouted, his face twisted in fury.

"Pigsty!?" Jean slammed his fist on the counter, making the new crack in the wood even larger.

Fujita looked at the bartender, his face easing back to a cold glare. "You're right. A pigsty has higher standards and better customers than this place." Fujita let go of Kotaro's collar, causing him to stagger back.

"What!?" Jean looked ready to leap over the counter and smack the captain over the head with one of the expensive bottles in the back, but Tora stood in front of him and shook his head. Jean spat out a few French curses before breathing in and out. He sighed, crossed his arms, and leaned against the counter. When Tora determined Jean's anger was under control, he stepped aside. Jean mumbled even more French curses.

"B-But I was gathering information, sir!" Kotaro said, regaining his footing and rubbing his neck. "L-Looking for dastardly criminals! And I found one carrying a sword, a man dressed in black! He was very suspicious. He's over there!" Kotaro pointed toward the counter, but other than the bartender, who was still glowering, there was nobody there.

"Is that so?" Fujita said, straining to maintain his composure.

"Well, uh," Kotaro stammered, "but he was there, sir! I'll search for him right away!" Kotaro was about to make a dash for the door, but he felt the captain's hand clamp down on his shoulder with an iron grip.

"No, Yamada. You've caused enough trouble for one day. You are to report back to the main station … immediately."

Kotaro deflated. "The usual punishment, sir?" he asked.

Fujita let out an exasperated sigh. "You're lucky I owe your family a debt of gratitude. Otherwise, you wouldn't get such a light punishment as guarding the evidence room."

"Yes, sir," Kotaro groaned at the thought of the menial and mind-numbing job that had become his de facto punishment since arriving in Yokohama. He sulked as he walked out of the bar, and the officers followed. Fujita gave one last icy glare toward the patrons and left.

***

After sneaking outside via the side-entrance during the commotion, Makoto kept his hat low, his duffel over his shoulder, and his pace quick. One policeman was bad enough, much less a swarm. After getting a few blocks further into the harbor area, Makoto slowed down and glanced around at the mix of traditional and Western-style buildings. Small to mid-sized warehouses also peppered the area. As Makoto passed by a warehouse with a large "four" painted on its side in both Arabic and Japanese numerals, the door swung open and two policemen stepped out, grabbing large crates sitting by the door and hefting them inside. Makoto stiffened, wondering if they were going to stop and question him, but they didn't seem to notice him.

Once he passed the door, Makoto turned away from the harbor and into the neighborhood. He briefly wondered why policemen were doing the grunt work of stevedores but reminded himself he had more important things to worry about. He reached into his pocket and pulled out the sheet of paper on which he had written down rough directions from the bartender, but as he looked around the unfamiliar neighborhood, he had serious doubts he would be able to find the Yasumi Inn.

As Makoto delved further into the Yokohama neighborhoods, the Western influence quickly disappeared. Dirt pathways replaced paved roads, and brick buildings gave way to wooden ones. It was as if the Western buildings formed a thin mask covering the true Yokohama. Makoto felt a tinge of familiarity. In his youth, he had explored every hidden path and alley of Yokohama, the old Yokohama at least. Many of the roads now twisted in new ways.

After a few hours filled with wrong turns and backtracking, the orange glow of sunset signaled to Makoto he didn't have much daylight left. Dark clouds began forming overhead, a sign of a rapidly approaching summer storm. He looked over the vague directions and mentally calculated his location from the bar. He should have found the inn by now. In fact, he should be standing in front of it.

A familiar strong perfume filled his nostrils. He glanced at a shabby two-story building to his right and was surprised to see the young woman in the yukata from the bar. She had her sleeves rolled up, and was carefully lighting multi-colored paper lanterns near the entrance.

Makoto recalled the bartender mentioning that she knew something about the inn and moved to ask her, but looked up to see *Yasumi Yado* scrawled in a nearly illegible font on a paper sign hanging from the entrance. The woman lighting the lanterns noticed Makoto staring, hopped in front of him, and made a quick bow. "Welcome to the Yasumi Inn! Please come in!" She didn't seem to recognize Makoto from the bar and pulled open a sliding door at the main entrance. She beckoned him inside.

As Makoto stepped in, the woman stepped back outside, slid the door shut, and resumed her lamp lighting. The immediate entrance was a patch of dirt that led to the raised wooden platform of the lobby, which was covered with tatami mats. Resting on the mats were several low tables with cushions surrounding them. Scattered newspapers covered a couple of the tables. Makoto scanned the inn and saw, seated at one of the newspaper-covered tables, an old woman, her gray hair tied up in a well-kept bun; she was wearing a very clean, dark kimono. Her grim and sour demeanor was a sharp contrast to the upbeat young woman outside. She looked up at Makoto and made a small bow, not bothering to get up.

"Welcome," she said in an unenthusiastic tone of voice.

Makoto raised his leg to step up onto the wooden platform, but a loud, purposeful cough from the old woman stopped him. Makoto gave her a confused look and she pointed toward his feet.

"Shoes," she said in a croaky voice.

Memories of being scolded for running inside with his sandals on came to Makoto's mind. He reached down and yanked his boots off with some effort. He considered leaving them in the wooden shoe rack populated with sandals, but after remembering an unfortunate shoe-stealing incident in America, decided against it. And with the policemen out there, he needed to be prepared in case he had to make a quick escape. He stepped up to the platform, boots in one hand, duffel in the other, and walked toward the woman. Makoto glanced down at the newspapers the woman was reading and noticed two prominent stories: "Suicide or Murder? Home Minister Ōkubo's Mysterious Death!" and "New Battleship to Arrive! The *Hiei* Makes its Grand Debut!" Makoto shook his head. It seemed the newspapers in Japan ran the same type of sensationalist nonsense popular in the States.

The woman interrupted Makoto's staring by taking a long, loud sip of tea from the stone cup next to her. When she finished and placed the cup down, Makoto spoke. "You're the innkeeper, correct?"

The old woman paused, took another long sip of tea, and nodded.

"I need information," Makoto said. He glanced back to one of the open windows, saw it was dark outside, and heard the rumbling of thunder above. "And a room."

"Thirty sen for the room. We require payment upfront."

Makoto frowned. It had been a long time since he had stayed at a Japanese inn, but he recalled payment was usually due at the end of the stay, not the beginning. He thought back to Jean's comment about unreliable customers and wondered if it was a common problem in Yokohama.

Resigned to the request, Makoto reached into his pocket and pulled out a couple of coins. He looked them over and realized there weren't enough. He slid them back into his pocket and reached into a different one. He pulled out a tiny nugget of gold and held it in front of the innkeeper. "Will this do?"

The woman frowned at the nugget but held out her hand to take it. Makoto placed it in her hand, and she carefully looked it over. She laid it out on a piece of paper and hit it with a wooden pestle. It immediately flattened into a small disc. She nodded. "Yes. This will do. But I have no change."

"Keep it. But tell me what you know about this." Makoto pulled out the carefully folded piece of paper from his pocket and spread it out for the innkeeper to see.

She leaned forward and scrutinized the crane on the paper. "Isn't this the crest of one of the branch families of the Mori clan?"

Makoto nodded. "What do you know about them?"

"It's a tragic case really. All killed about fifteen years ago. But nobody knows why." She leaned back with a knowing smirk. "Though there are interesting rumors."

Makoto stiffened, and the dark memories of coming across the bodies of his family swirled around his mind. "What kind of rumors?"

The smirk grew to a dark smile. "The land is cursed. Once the family was gone, nothing grew right. Even the animals started dying." The woman took another sip of tea. "Once the emperor retook power, the land was converted into a Shinto temple to appease the spirits. Practically abandoned now."

"Where is this temple?" Makoto asked.

"Deep in town. It'll take a while to walk there. It's at the top of a hill, I believe. Though some say it's haunted by the angry spirits of the Mori family." She took another sip. "That's all I know. Your room is the first one upstairs."

She waved her hand toward a narrow staircase not too far from the table. Makoto picked up his paper, folded it, and returned it to his pocket. He tipped his hat toward her. "Thanks."

The innkeeper sipped her tea as she watched him walk toward the stairs, noticing the white crane on his back. There was a flash of lightning, a crack of thunder, and rain started pounding the roof. The sliding door slid open and the now drenched young woman squeaked as she flung herself inside the dry room. As Makoto made his way up the narrow wooden stairs, he could hear the innkeeper scolding the young woman for getting mud and water into the inn. Makoto had to dip his head as he climbed in order to avoid hitting the low ceiling, and his shoulders rubbed the walls of the cramped staircase.

When he finally made it to the top, he tried to stretch upright, and nearly clunked his head against the low ceiling. He looked around the hallway, faced with many paper *shoji* sliding doors. He could hear the babble of conversations and arguments through the paper walls. The innkeeper said his room was the first one upstairs, but there were two rooms across from each other, sliding doors at each entrance. Makoto noticed the translucent paper of the shoji to the left flickered yellow, most likely from a small candle or lantern within. The shoji to the right was completely dark. He pondered for a moment and figured the room with the light must be occupied, and the other one not. He slid open the door to the right.

"Is anyone-" Makoto began to ask, but paused mid-sentence. There was just enough light from the hallway for him to make out the interior of the room. On the side stood a large closet to hold bedding. Toward the back was a small table with an extinguished oil lamp, from which wafted wisps of smoke. Along the back wall, there was a partially open window letting in rain from outside. And sprawled on a tatami mat in the middle of the room was a man in a bright blue coat, lying in a pool of blood.

Chapter Four

After a moment, Makoto recovered from the shock of seeing the bloody body sprawled on the floor. The dim light from the hallway palely illuminated the body and floor around it. The man had receding gray hair, a wrinkled face, and wore plain, dark robes, with the exception of a bright blue haori summer coat with white, triangular trimmings along the sleeves.

Something about the blue coat seemed eerily familiar, but Makoto dismissed the thought and cautiously entered the room. Not hearing or seeing any other guests nearby, he approached and crouched down next to the body, which gave off the rusty, iron stench of blood. Makoto pressed the fingers of his left hand on the man's neck to check for a pulse and hovered his other hand over the man's mouth to check for breathing. He found neither. The blood was fresh from a large, stabbing wound in the man's gut, and his clothes were saturated with blood. His body was still warm; so he must have only died moments ago.

Makoto glanced toward the man's lifeless hands and saw one of them loosely held a bloody knife. He reached down to pick up the blade, but his hand paused just above it. Makoto knew this was none of his business, and it would make more sense to simply inform the staff downstairs. But a combination of experience, curiosity, and pity for the dead man overcame him and he picked up the knife and held it in front of him.

The blade was a short *tantō* sword with a black lacquer handle, the kind often used to commit *seppuku*, ritual suicide. Makoto glanced back at the dead man's gut and remembered a deep slash along the stomach was common to seppuku, the preferred suicide method of the *samurai* class. But Makoto felt something was off. He turned his attention back to the blade. Engraved into the handle was a small red flower, but he couldn't make out its details in the dark room. As he brought the handle closer for a better look, an ear-piercing shriek jolted him.

Makoto spun around to see the young woman wearing the pink yukata from downstairs, staring at him. Her yukata was still dripping water on the floor, and she was shaking. She took a step back and stammered out nonsense at the sight of the dead man. Her eyes darted back and forth between Makoto and the dead body. She breathed in sharply when her eyes landed on the bloody knife in Makoto's hand.

"Wait-" Makoto started, recognizing what her eyes believed.

"Murderer!" she screeched.

The woman fled down the stairs before Makoto had a chance to explain himself. Her scream echoed throughout the inn, and with the thin paper walls, Makoto figured he had less than a minute before others came to see the cause of the commotion. He could already hear the stunned mumblings of guests in the adjoining rooms. Makoto spat out a curse. He knew if he stayed and tried to explain himself, the police would naturally arrest him. They already tried to arrest him earlier that day just for possessing a sword, and if Japanese police were even remotely similar to American police, Makoto knew they wouldn't listen to reason.

He yanked on his boots, glad he brought them with him, grabbed his bag, and rushed for the window. When he slid open the paper screen, pouring rain greeted him with a splash to the face, and he could see the occasional flash of lightning, brightening the entire town.

Makoto turned back once more to look at the body. He knew he'd seen the blue coat before but couldn't quite place it. The sound of stomping footsteps and sliding doors interrupted his thoughts. He cautiously stepped out the window, balancing on the thin ledge below it, and became drenched in the downpour. The wet wood creaked under his weight. Not waiting for it to break, Makoto made a small jump down to the slanted roof of the one-story shop next door, slipping on the wet tiles. He shot his arm out instinctively and grabbed the ridge of the roof to stop his fall. Makoto slowly made his way down the angled roof, using the curved edges of the traditional *kawara* tiles to avoid slipping.

As he descended, he could hear the shouts of people inside the dead man's room. Makoto reached the bottom edge of the roof, swung himself over, and hung on the eaves by his fingers, which was made difficult by the weight of his bag on his shoulder. He released his grip, made the short fall to the ground, and landed on his feet. His boots sank into the mud. Thanks to the heavy rain, any potential bystanders had already retreated indoors.

Makoto stepped under the roof overhang of the empty shop for a temporary shelter and looked toward the window he had just escaped. Somebody must have lit the oil lamp since light poured from the previously dark window. He felt bad there was nothing he could do for the old man, but he remembered he had his own problems to deal with and didn't have time to take on anyone else's issues, especially the problems of someone who was already dead. Besides, even if it didn't feel right, the old man probably killed himself, which made it none of his business.

He heard more shouts and commotion coming from the room and realized he had to get moving. While he considered his options, the heavy downpour lightened to a moderate drizzle. The darkened hills in the distance reminded Makoto of the temples frequently built there, and he thought perhaps the priests might be willing to accept travelers. Having made up his mind, and despite feeling as wet as a drowned rat, Makoto stepped into the lighter rain and walked further into the neighborhood, heading for the first hill he saw. Perhaps he could even find this so-called "haunted temple" the innkeeper had described. If so, it would be the first piece of good luck he'd have since arriving in Yokohama.

***

Making her best effort to ignore the noise of the thunderstorm outside, Helen Arkwright focused on her book in the fancy multi-room suite her husband reserved in the Grand Hotel just off the harbor. She'd already changed from her form-fitting dress into a loose nightgown, this one a lighter shade of purple. A young Japanese woman in a long, Western-style dress and pinafore apron of a maid was undoing Helen's hair, pulling out pins and brushing through it.

"Aha!" Helen chuckled and lightly tapped her book. "So that's how he did it! I knew it all along."

"Really, ma'am? You were able to figure out the killer in your book?" The maid leaned over Helen's shoulder to look at the text, though she could not understand it.

Helen gave a smug smile. "Of course, my dear. This is child's play for a proper actress. When you live for the stage, you can see the masks people wear. Even in books."

The maid nodded, though she didn't completely understand what Helen was talking about. Helen closed her book and looked at the maid in the mirror. "You really must learn to read English, Aki. Then I can share these books with you. They are quite enjoyable."

Aki smiled at the mirror and nodded. "That would be nice, ma'am! Though speaking is all I need to do my job and -oh! Another pin!" Aki interrupted herself to pull out the last of the hairpins. She happily showed it to Helen.

"Yes, thank you," Helen said dryly. "You know, you don't have to show me every pin you pull out."

Aki smiled and placed the pin at the top of a small pile on a nearby table.

There was a knock at the door. "Come in," Helen said, glad for the interruption.

The door opened with a *creak*, and John Arkwright peeked in. Once he made eye contact with his wife, he smiled, opened the door, and entered the room.

Helen returned her attention to Aki. "That's enough. You may go Aki. Oh, and how do I say, 'thank you' again?"

"*Arigatou*!" Aki said over enthusiastically.

"Yes. Of course. Ar-ri-ga-tou."

Aki grinned and made a quick bow. She scurried out the door, giving John a quick bow as she walked by. John closed the door after her as she left. "Reading those flights of fancy again?"

Helen stood up and tossed her loose hair back. She used her book to point toward her husband. "I'll have you know they are not flights of fancy! They're collected from the Strand Magazine. It's important to be aware of current events."

"Yes, yes, of course," John said. "Anyway, I have good news!"

Helen set her book on the nearby table and raised an eyebrow. "Oh?"

"Tomorrow, I'll be meeting up with Watanabe to finish up our transactions, and then in a couple of days we can be on our way back home on the *Abraham Lincoln*!"

Helen blinked. "What? Home? Already?"

"Of course!" John said. "We've already been here a month, and at long last, we can finally leave this primitive place."

"But we barely saw anything. We didn't even leave the harbor!"

"Why would we want to do that? The only decent food is here at the hotel."

"But John, this trip has been so dull. No mysteries. No scandals. No adventures. No nothing!"

John chuckled. "That's the only thing this blasted country's got going for it. And if we're lucky, in the time we've been gone the neighbors will have forgotten your little fiasco."

Helen scoffed. "Fiasco? I saved our lives!"

"From Mrs. Jones' pudding?"

"She tried to poison us!"

"Maybe with bad flavor, but did you really have to dump it on her?"

"*That* was an accident. Even so, she was acting very suspiciously."

John shook his head. "This is what I'm talking about with those blasted flights of fancy. You're tilting at windmills."

"They're not flights-!" Helen stopped and sighed. She was in no mood to have this argument again. "Can we at least go to a theater or do something fun before getting back on a lousy boat for three weeks?"

John looked a bit taken aback. "It's not a boat. It's a magnificent ship. *My* ship. And being on it *is* fun."

Helen groaned. Before she could continue their argument, they were interrupted by a knock at the door. John went to the foyer, where Helen saw him open the door. A steward stood in the hallway carrying a tray with a note on it. After taking the note and dismissing the steward, John opened and read the note. The color drained from his face. Helen stepped out of her boudoir into the sitting room. "What's that?"

He looked up at her. "Nothing important. Just business. Though I'm afraid it's urgent, and I have to go. But I'll be back soon, my dear." He kissed her forehead and placed the note in his jacket. Then he seemed to change his mind, opening a drawer in the fold-down desk by the entrance and throwing the letter inside. He locked the drawer and took the key with him as he left the room.

After the door shut, Helen frowned. She knew whatever was in the note, it was certainly more important than just "business" to make John turn pale. It may have been something interesting, even something *mysterious*.

The pudding incident flashed through her mind. Not wanting to make mountains of molehills again, she tried to ignore the locked drawer, picked up her book, and started slowly flipping through the pages. She paused when she found herself on a page where the detective had to pick a lock to find stolen documents. Helen felt her eyes drifting to the locked drawer.

She knew she shouldn't. But with each passing moment, she rationalized her husband's business was her business as well. Though deep down, she knew she was just being nosy, but she was unable to resist.

"What was the saying? The game's afoot, I believe." She chuckled under her breath. A light tug on the handle confirmed the drawer was locked, and she glanced back at the pages where the detective explained to his companion how he picked the lock. She'd need some thin pieces of metal, something like … hatpins. She dashed back to her room and grabbed a couple of the hatpins by the mirror. She bent one of them to act as a lever and stuck it in the bottom of the lock.

She dug the other hatpin into the lock and moved it around. The sound of light metal scratching continued as she poked and prodded. Wondering if she was doing it right, she pulled out the metal hatpin and saw it was bent out of shape. As she stuck the pin back in, she accidentally scratched up the outside of the lock. She mumbled a distinctively unladylike curse and was starting to get frustrated, but then she heard the satisfying *click* of the lock giving way.

She smiled. "Ha! So much for flights of fancy! Then again, something like this is mere child's play for a proper actress."

She realized she was talking to herself and felt silly. Focusing her attention back on the desk, she opened the drawer and extracted the folded letter. On the front of the letter was a small, red flower. She unfolded the paper and read the contents. "Plans changed. Meet me at the usual place immediately." And it was signed, "Watanabe."

Chapter Five

As darkness enveloped Yokohama and the heavy rain faded, the usually quiet Yasumi Inn bustled with policemen. Muddy roads didn't deter the onlookers and gossipers from crowding outside and getting as close as the policemen would let them, hoping to catch sight of something grotesque. Every lamp inside and outside the inn shone brightly, as guests grumbled about being confined to their rooms throughout the night and forced to answer intrusive questions about their activities.

Downstairs at the inn's entrance, several policemen combed the area, looking for clues and picking up loose items. The innkeeper, chagrined at the inconvenience to her guests, glared from her table as the policemen made a mess of her lobby. Meanwhile, the now mostly dry young woman wearing the pink yukata sat at one of the low tables in the traditional kneeling position with her legs tucked underneath. Her demeanor was polite as would be expected of a maid in a traditional inn, though red eyes and frequent sniffling betrayed her efforts to hold back tears. "Oh, poor Mr. Watanabe," she sobbed.

Patrolman Yamada Kotaro sat across from her taking notes with glazed-over eyes and trying his best to avoid breathing in her insufferable perfume. He made another tick mark for each utterance of "Poor Mr. Watanabe." "Yes. Yes. You've said that already, Miss. Many times. When you saw Mr. Watanabe, the killer was kneeling over him with a knife, correct?"

The maid nodded, unable to contain the tears any longer. "It was horrible. Just horrible. Poor Mr. Watanabe."

Another tick mark. "Was he alone when he came in?" Kotaro asked.

"I-I don't know," she replied.

"He was alone."

Kotaro turned toward the innkeeper, who was still sitting at her newspaper-covered table directly behind him. She took a long, loud sip of her tea while giving dirty looks to the other policemen.

Kotaro nodded and turned back to the young woman. "Did you recognize the killer?"

She shook her head. "No. I only knew Mr. Watanabe. He usually stayed here when he had business in Yokohama. He was so kind. To suffer such a terrible … poor Mr. Watanabe!" The young woman continued her sobbing session. Another tick mark.

"Yes, I know. You can be certain justice will be served, since I, the great and powerful, Yamada Kotaro, am on the case!"

The young woman calmed down a little but continued to sniff.

"Could you at least describe the killer?" Kotaro asked. "Without mentioning Mr. Watanabe?"

She thought for a moment. "He was very tall. I think he might be a foreigner. He wore a long, black coat. Oh, and a hat too."

"Let's see. Tall. Black coat. Hat … Wait! Are you sure?" Kotaro leaned forward, and the young woman leaned back uncomfortably. She nodded.

"Did he have a white bird painted on the back of his coat? Well? Did he?" Kotaro demanded.

She leaned further back. "I-I don't know."

"There was a man who came in with a white crane painted on the back of his coat," the innkeeper said, between sips of tea.

Kotaro turned once again to the innkeeper, stood up, and approached her. "Are you sure?" he asked with a disbelieving tone.

The innkeeper gave him an annoyed look and nodded. "Of course. As sure as I see a fat fool in a police uniform standing in front of me."

"Then it must be him! I've got to tell the captain!" Ignoring her insult, Kotaro bolted up the stairs, leaving the innkeeper and the puzzled maid behind. He reached the top of the stairs, panting hard from his short sprint, then took a deep breath to regain his composure before stepping into the room that contained the crime scene.

Many high-ranking police officers filled the room as opposed to the lowly patrolmen investigating down in the lobby. One officer carefully scrutinized the body, examining the dead man's clothes, wound, face, and other body parts, while another officer, kneeling across from him, took meticulous notes. Or at least that's what it looked like to Kotaro. Another officer picked up the bloody blade from the ground with a piece of cloth and carefully set it handle first in a designated evidence bag. Though Captain Fujita directed the entire operation, at the moment, he stared intently at a letter splattered with blood.

Kotaro cautiously approached him. "Uh, sir?"

Fujita's head snapped up, and he quickly folded up the letter and faced Kotaro. His expression soured. "Yamada. Any news from the witness?"

"Yes, sir!" Kotaro saluted. "The killer is the man from the bar!"

"Who? The bartender?"

"No, sir! The man in black I told you about. The innkeeper and the maid saw him. He was towering over the body with the weapon in his hand. He must have killed him!"

"That's impossible," Fujita replied.

"Huh?"

"Because this man killed himself." Fujita motioned toward the police officer bagging the knife to come over. "Sugimoto, come here."

The young police officer with first lieutenant rankings walked over to them. Kotaro knew him as one of Fujita's most trusted subordinates.

"Give us a report, Sugimoto," Fujita commanded.

Sugimoto nodded. He pulled out the blade, using a cloth, and showed it to Fujita and Kotaro. "Based on the weapon and the depth and type of wound, the man most likely committed seppuku." Sugimoto pointed to the body. "The cut was from the upper right of the abdomen to the lower left. It was a remarkably deep cut, which slashed through his stomach and intestines. He would have been paralyzed and dead within minutes."

"Right to left?" Kotaro asked scratching his head. "Isn't that the reverse of the usual cut?"

"He was probably left handed. Besides-" Sugimoto responded.

"But what if it was a surprise attack?" Kotaro interrupted.

Sugimoto glared at him in annoyance at the question. "Are you proposing he just stood still while someone else carved into his stomach?"

"Uh, no, but what about-" Kotaro started.

Sugimoto cut him off. "He couldn't have been attacked from the rear either. The wound is one large cut, which would have been impossible to do from behind. He even used the traditional tantō sword." Sugimoto displayed the bloody blade for the two to see, and after a nod from Fujita, he returned the tantō to the evidence bag. "Also, there's no sign of a struggle. Look at the walls; they're made of wood and paper. If there was a fight, the other guests would have heard something."

"But the maid!" Kotaro protested. "She saw the man in black standing over poor Watana- I mean the victim, with the knife!"

"Man in black?" Sugimoto turned to Fujita in confusion.

Fujita rubbed his face in annoyance. "Clearly the patrolman has a very active imagination."

"But-"

"Even if this mysterious man actually existed," Sugimoto interrupted again. "He most likely would have been the victim's second, to finish him off and end his suffering."

"But there wasn't a suicide note!" Kotaro finally got in. When Sugimoto and Fujita gave him annoyed glares, Kotaro glanced around the room. "There wasn't, was there?"

Fujita sighed and unfolded the bloodied paper and showed it to Kotaro. It contained writing, but it was heavily smudged with ink and blood to the point of being illegible; though this letter seemed to be different from the one Fujita had been staring at earlier. "Since the writing is obscured, we can't completely confirm this was his death poem, but given the other evidence, that seems to be the most likely option."

"B-But..." Kotaro stammered, hoping to come up with some other reason.

"Enough, Yamada," Fujita said. "You raised similar objections when the home minister committed suicide a couple of weeks ago. You need to realize most deaths in Yokohama are not elaborate murders to solve."

"But I still don't think-"

"Thinking has never been one of your strong points Yamada. If you insist on indulging in a pastime for which you are *clearly* not qualified, guarding the evidence room will be your new *permanent* station. At least there you can't cause as much trouble. Am I understood?"

Kotaro deflated. "Yes, sir."

"Speaking of the evidence room, your shift will be starting soon. You're no longer needed here."

Kotaro deflated even further. "Yes, sir."

Fujita turned to Sugimoto. "Accompany Patrolman Yamada to the evidence room to make sure he doesn't get 'lost' at any more bars. And make certain that," Fujita pointed to the bag containing the blade, "doesn't get lost either."

"But sir," objected Sugimoto, "wouldn't it make more sense for me to-"

"Now, Sugimoto."

"Yes, sir."

Sugimoto and Kotaro both bowed to Fujita and went down the stairs. They reached the lobby, where the maid still sat at the table, trying to dry her tears. She rocked back and forth on her knees repeatedly moaning, "Poor Mr. Watanabe." Kotaro refrained from adding additional tick marks to his notes. Meanwhile, the innkeeper looked on, still displeased with everyone around her. Kotaro and Sugimoto left the inn and headed for the police station.

***

Makoto was exhausted. Having wandered the residential district for hours, his legs ached and he no longer knew which direction to go. Each time a road seemed to head for the hills, it veered off in a different direction. Makoto passed many small roadside shrines, but none of them seemed to lead him toward the "haunted temple," or any temple for that matter.

He contemplated just lying out on the dirt road and sleeping for the night. He'd done it many times in the desert back in America, but then again, the desert sand and dust was much drier and there weren't any nosy residents who would report him to the police. Fatigue was starting to interfere with his thinking, and he could feel his vision starting to blur.

As he walked, he noticed a stone *torii* gate, a common entranceway to temples and shrines, by the side of the road. The gray rock made the gate nearly black in the dark, so Makoto didn't notice it until he was standing before it. He peered through the gate and saw stone steps leading up a small hill. He wondered if there was a temple at the end of the path.

Makoto was so tired, he hesitated to make the climb, but he finally decided to follow the path since it might lead to a place where he could lie down and sleep, away from prying eyes. The path was choked with weeds, some of which had cracked the stone steps. He nearly tripped over a couple of roots but managed to force his way to the top of the hill. A dark building came into sight.

As Makoto stepped closer, he could make out the details of the temple. The structure was in shambles. Its slanted roof was broken in many places and the wood pillars holding up the building were rotted as if it had been abandoned a long time ago.

Two stone structures stood in front of the broken wooden steps leading to the entryway, but it wasn't until Makoto stood right next to them that he could make out what they were: *komainu*, the lion-dogs which frequently guarded temples from evil spirits. One of them was broken in half and the other was covered in cracks, but they gave Makoto a sense of relief that he had finally found a temple, even if it was abandoned. At least he wouldn't have to explain himself to potentially nosy monks or priests. He just wanted to sleep and put everything else off until the morning. Right before Makoto stepped into the temple, he saw a large stone behind the half-broken komainu. A symbol at the top caught his eye.

He stepped back and approached the stone. He kneeled down and brushed away the parts covered with moss. There was writing, but it was so faded he couldn't make it out. However, he definitely recognized the symbol at the top, a white crane.

There was more writing carved lower on the stone that was legible. At first, Makoto struggled with the *kanji* symbols he had not seen for fifteen long years, but then he realized they were names. As he racked his memory he saw the familiar symbol of three small trees, the character of his family name, Mori. The writing on the stone listed the names of his family members. He saw the names of his father, mother, two older brothers, and older sister. His eyes fell on the last name: his. This must have been the "haunted temple" he was looking for. He reached out to touch his own name.

However, the instincts that had kept him alive in the California goldfields kicked in and his hand jerked upright, catching a *bō* staff aimed squarely at his head. Makoto felt a sharp twinge of pain in his hand as the staff was yanked backward. Makoto rose to face his attacker, an older man, wearing the white robes of a Shinto priest. The priest raised his staff again and charged toward Makoto.

Chapter Six

The attacking priest lunged toward Makoto, bō staff at the ready. Makoto stood up and braced himself, fists in front, never taking his eyes off the priest. As the older man swung his staff toward Makoto's side, Makoto threw out his hands and caught the staff. He gave a sharp tug and with his superior strength, yanked it out of the old man's hands.

The priest staggered backward in shock, looking desperately around for another weapon. Not able to find any, the priest stood up with as much dignity as he could muster and pointed an accusatory finger at Makoto. "How dare you desecrate this temple, you foreign Jesuit scum!"

Makoto nearly dropped the staff in shock from this bizarre accusation. After trying and failing to remember what a Jesuit even was, he quickly brushed off the insult, planted the bō staff into the ground with one hand, and with the other, pointed toward the stone bearing the names of his family. "What can you tell me about the memorial stone?" he asked in Japanese.

The priest scoffed and crossed his arms. "I don't speak with foreigners."

"I'm not a foreigner."

"Well, you're certainly not a true Japanese!" The priest pointed another accusatory finger toward Makoto. "With those weird clothes, you're already set in the filthy ways of the *gaijin*, even if you can speak the one true language. You're a Jesuit traitor, which is even worse than a regular Jesuit!"

Makoto glanced down and pulled at his duster, wondering if his clothes were really that strange. Nobody seemed to find them odd in America, but then again, he hadn't seen anyone else in Japan wearing them. Though he could hardly tell why his clothes made the priest call him a Jesuit. "But … I'm not a Jesuit."

"Same difference! All you foreigners and foreign-lovers are all the same. So quick to abandon the ways of tradition and honor!"

Makoto contemplated trying to force the old man to tell him about the stone, but couldn't think of any way that didn't involve hurting him, since the priest didn't seem the type to cave into empty threats. Even though the priest did attack first, Makoto guessed this was his temple and it would only make sense for a priest to defend it from intruders. And technically, Makoto was trespassing. Makoto sighed and tossed the priest back his staff. The old man, surprised by this sudden motion, instinctively stumbled backward and caught it. The priest looked on with confusion as Makoto made a respectful bow. "I am sorry for disturbing you and your temple. But this stone…"

Makoto turned toward the memorial and placed his hand on top of it. Despite the darkness, the priest caught sight of the white crane painted on the back of Makoto's coat. His eyes grew wide with recognition. "Wait. That crest. It couldn't be? Are you…"

The priest wobbled forward. "Are you part of the Mori family?"

Makoto stared at the priest in confusion and cautiously nodded.

The priest let out something between a laugh and a sob. "By the gods! It's a miracle!" The priest fell to his knees and bowed deeply toward Makoto. "Please forgive me, Master Mori! I never realized!"

Makoto shifted back uncomfortably, not used to this kind of treatment. "Do I know you?"

The priest's head popped up. "Ah! Forgive my rudeness! I am Inzan, the head priest at this temple, though before that I was but a humble and loyal servant of the Mori family!" Inzan's head bowed back down low.

Makoto grew even more uncomfortable at being bowed to and being called master. He vaguely recalled there being servants in his old family home, but he had just assumed they had perished with his family on that fateful night.

Makoto stepped forward and extended his hand toward Inzan. "Stop bowing."

Inzan looked up at the command, and Makoto motioned for him to take his hand. After a moment of hesitation, Inzan took the extended hand, and Makoto pulled him upright. Once back on his feet, Inzan stepped forward and scrutinized Makoto's face, which was still mostly in shadow. "Forgive my rudeness, but which esteemed member of the Mori family are you?"

Makoto tipped back his hat, letting the moonlight hit his face. "Mori Makoto. I am the third son of Mori Norio."

"Ah!" Inzan said in recognition, "That explains why you look so much like the late master! Please come in, we can talk inside. Better than standing out here with another rainfall heading this way! Though I must apologize for the temple's condition. Unfortunately, after two typhoons, three fires, and limited donations, the temple is not in the best of states. Some people even have the audacity to say it's haunted!"

Inzan laughed and gestured toward the old, dark temple. A flash of lightning lit up the shadows of the temple, making it look even more ominous than when it was pitch black. Makoto heard the accompanying rumble of thunder, nodded, and followed Inzan toward the living quarters behind the temple.

***

A crack of thunder and a flash of lightning startled Helen as she looked over the letter. She glanced out the window to see heavy rain pouring down the closed window, and she pulled the curtains shut. Even if she couldn't stop the sound of the thunderstorm, she at least didn't have to see it.

She moved closer to the oil lamp perched atop the folding desk to study the letter once more. The main things that stood out to her were both the red flower at the top of the page and the name on the bottom: Watanabe. She remembered her husband mentioning going to see Watanabe for some sort of business transaction, which was hardly anything scandalous. She slowly started to realize this "secret letter" she had made such a fuss about was really just business like her husband had said. She let out a disappointed sigh and placed the letter back in the drawer.

As she closed the drawer, she flinched when she realized the lock was completely ruined and covered with scratches due to her picking. She hoped her husband wouldn't notice. But if he did, it would be simple enough to convince him it was like that the entire time. Helen tried to return to her book, but couldn't stop thinking about the message and Mr. Watanabe. She wondered if she had met this Watanabe fellow before and if he was also staying at the Grand Hotel. Maybe he'd know of something to do in this dull port, or at least he might know of a nearby theater. He certainly would be more likely to know than her husband.

Unable to sit still, Helen tossed aside her book and put on the first few layers of her street clothes. She struggled greatly with her petticoat, bloomers, stockings, and camisole as she was unaccustomed to dressing without the assistance of a maid, and she had to only look at the corset before giving up on trying to put it on. But she was able to throw on enough layers to no longer be indecent to the public eye.

Her straight, purple skirt reached to her ankles and matched her purple high-collared long-sleeved blouse. She quickly wrapped her hair into a rough ponytail and slid it into a mesh hair net and tied it all off with a purple ribbon. It had been a while since she put up her hair without assistance, but she hadn't forgotten several years of costume changes between acts. Her hair wasn't as fashionable as the high-class Gibson Girl hairstyle Aki set for her each morning, but it was certainly less scandalous then running around in public with her hair streaming wildly behind her.

Helen headed down to the lobby and noticed it was mostly empty with a few late-night stragglers coming in from the rain and heading to their rooms. The lobby was furnished with the finest Western-style furniture and carpeting. Two large staircases twisted around the lobby leading to the second floor, and hanging above it all was a massive gaslight chandelier, which sparkled in the light of its many flames. Helen looked around and saw a single receptionist behind the marble-coated counter. Helen approached him, and he quickly plastered on a smile. "Welcome!" he said cheerfully in English, "Checking in?"

"No," Helen replied, "I'm already checked in. I was wondering if you have information on someone named Watanabe."

The receptionist gave her a confused look. "So … not checking in?"

"No. I already said I'm looking for Mr. Watanabe. Have you seen him? Or Mr. Arkwright? He's my husband."

The receptionist's confused look deepened. "Sorry. Could you repeat?"

Helen groaned. "Don't you understand English for crying out loud?"

"Unlikely," said a male voice with a British accent.

Helen turned toward the voice behind her to see a tall man carrying a medical bag. He was dressed in a knee-length brown coat and matching bowler hat, which were both drenched from the rain outside, and he left a trail of water behind him on the floor.

"What do you mean?" Helen asked.

The doctor gave an annoyed sigh and removed his hat, revealing a young face and a mass of dark hair with the slightest tinge of gray around the temples. "He's only been taught some puppet phrases so the tourists feel welcome. This isn't America. Try learning the language. Excuse me."

The doctor moved past her to the receptionist and asked something in Japanese. The receptionist perked up in understanding and eagerly responded to the doctor's question while pointing up the stairs. The doctor nodded and started to walk in that direction. However, before he could get to the stairs, Helen grabbed his wet coat, stopping him. He turned back and gave her an exasperated look. "What do you want? I have a patient."

Helen stubbornly hung onto his coat. "I only need a moment of your time. Could you please ask the receptionist if he knows anyone named Watanabe? The quality of mercy is not strained."

The doctor gave a bewildered look of recognition at the Shakespeare quote, but his annoyed glare returned. He gave a sigh, yanked back his coat, and spoke to the receptionist again. The receptionist paused at the question, giving it some thought, remembered, and spoke. The doctor turned to Helen. "He's seen him. This Mr. Watanabe claimed to be the assistant of the home minister and demanded the receptionist give a letter to a Mr. Arukorito."

"Aruko-?" Helen questioned. "Oh! He must mean Arkwright! My husband! Does he know where they went?"

The doctor rolled his eyes. "Blasted Americans are so demanding."

He turned back to the receptionist and spoke with him again. When the receptionist responded, the doctor blinked in confusion. "The shipbuilding district?"

"Shipbuilding district?" Helen repeated. "John builds ships, so it would make sense he'd go there. Where is it?"

The doctor shook his head. "That's a rough area. It's not a suitable place for anyone, least of all an unescorted lady."

Helen put her hands on her hips. "I'll decide what's 'suitable' myself."

The doctor shrugged and sighed. "Do as you see fit. It doesn't matter to me. Now excuse me." The doctor headed for the stairs once more.

"Oh! One more thing!" Helen said.

The doctor turned back, very annoyed. "What do you want now?"

"Thank you. I really appreciate your help." Helen smiled and nodded toward the doctor.

He was a little taken aback by the sudden gratitude, and after a moment, reached into his coat pocket and handed her a card. "If you ignore my advice and get yourself banged up there, here's my card. My fees are high, but I'll understand what you're saying and won't try to saw your arm off when all that ails you is a stomachache."

Helen took the card and looked it over. One side said, "Dr. Clement Halifax" with an address printed below it. The reverse side was written in Japanese, which she presumed had the same information as on the English side. As she read, Dr. Halifax hurried his way up the stairs. Helen held onto the card, making a mental note to herself to put the card in her purse back in her room. She went up the opposite staircase of the doctor and headed toward her room. After passing the large chandelier, visible from the railing, she opened the door to her room and entered.

After closing the door behind her, Helen remembered the letter in the drawer and decided to take a look at it once more. She pulled open the drawer and peered inside. She gasped. "What!?"

The letter was gone.

Chapter Seven

Inside the dimly lit Yokohama police station, Lieutenant Sugimoto dumped a huge pile of papers on Kotaro's small desk. Kotaro took one look at the mountain of papers and groaned.

"Don't complain," Sugimoto warned. "Once you're done organizing these case reports, it's straight to the evidence room."

"But what good does sorting these papers do when there are dangerous criminals out there? Including Watanabe's killer!"

Sugimoto sighed. "Without organization, the police would quickly fall into disarray. And while you, Patrolman Yamada, may thrive in that kind of environment, most of us require structure and steadiness."

"But if I can't bring criminals to justice, how will I get promoted? And if I can't get promoted how will I..." Kotaro looked longingly at the saber by Sugimoto's side. "Get my own sword?"

Sugimoto stifled a laugh. "Promoted? Patrolman Yamada, you will not need to worry about being promoted for a long time. You are far too attached to worldly vices for anyone to take you seriously. An officer needs to remain calm and maintain inner peace, especially while facing adversity." Sugimoto clapped his hands together in meditation, closed his eyes, and deeply breathed in and out.

"But I am calm! And inner peace is just a saké box away! Besides, Buddhism isn't required or even sanctioned by the government anymore. As long as you're a capable officer, who cares about things like that?"

Sugimoto gave Kotaro a glare and dropped his pose. "And I suppose that little demonstration today, when you fell on the table in a drunken stupor, was a prime example of your capabilities as an officer?"

Kotaro flinched at the reminder. "Well, uh, you don't understand. I was ambushed by the man in black. And he had the entire bar on his side. I was outnumbered but had I been fully prepared, he would be in custody right now! Just wait until I catch him, then you'll see!"

"If you know what's best for you, you'll let go of this imaginary 'man in black.' Holding onto such foolish fantasies will only destroy any hope you have of advancing your career."

"But I saw him! And so did the innkeeper, and the maid! We can't all be wrong."

Sugimoto sighed and shook his head. "The issue isn't whether or not he exists. The issue is whether it matters. And-"

"Of course it matters! We have to find the truth and make sure evil faces justice! Then I'll get promoted and show those doubters back home not to underestimate the great and-"

"You speak like a child, patrolman," Sugimoto interrupted. "Our job is not to ensure justice; it's to keep the peace. And the last thing we need is the populace panicking because you, an old woman, and a young girl are seeing phantoms. Especially so close to the *Hiei's* arrival."

Kotaro cocked his head in confusion. "The *Hiei*? You mean the battleship? What does that have to do with anything?"

Sugimoto's eyes grew wide for a moment, but just as quickly his face returned to a neutral expression. "Never mind, patrolman. It's not important. Just focus on those papers." Sugimoto looked away and stuck one of his hands in his pockets to fidget with something.

"But-"

"No more but's patrolman! I swear you would make the Buddha himself lose patience. If you continue to insist on these idiot theories, you'll infuriate the captain enough to transfer you to Abashiri prison."

Kotaro shuddered at the name. Nobody wanted a position in that Hokkaido prison, which was an icy hell for both prisoners and guards. Kotaro turned his face back to the papers and tried sorting them. Relieved to finally have some silence, Sugimoto went to his significantly larger desk and started making notes for his own reports. As Kotaro sorted the papers, he came across a crime report. It was a report on the death of Home Minister Ōkubo Toshimichi from a few weeks ago, which caused quite a stir in the political world and forced the preceding home minister to return and take the office again.

Kotaro's eyes darted to the cause of death: suicide by seppuku and the cut was reversed. Just like Watanabe. But unlike Watanabe's case, there was no weapon found at the crime scene. Instead, there was only the body and a single fan with a flower design covered in blood. That didn't stop the police from declaring it a suicide, but Kotaro had seen sensationalist stories in the newspapers questioning whether the home minister actually committed suicide. Kotaro knew what he believed. "Sir, do you remember Minister Ōkubo's death?"

"Yes, patrolman, what about it?" Sugimoto replied, not looking up from his papers.

"Why were the officers in charge so quick to call it suicide? They never found the weapon, right?"

"It is not my place nor yours to question police procedures. It was declared a suicide because there were no weapons and no suspects. Let the home minister's soul rest with his ancestors and focus on your paperwork." Sugimoto failed to hide the anger growing in his voice.

"But the lack of a weapon is even more suspicious! Why didn't they find it?"

"Enough patrolman, the next time you speak, you'll be sent early for guard duty in the evidence room, am I clear?" Sugimoto snarled, giving Kotaro a malicious glare.

Kotaro wanted to raise an objection but decided against it, realizing Sugimoto would make good on his threat. He turned back to the papers and made a haphazard attempt to sort them. But he couldn't get the cases out of his mind. He wondered how in the world the weapon couldn't be found in the case of the home minister's death. There was always the possibility of a hidden blade, though those kinds of weapons were rare these days. However, he had a nagging feeling the two deaths were connected somehow.

Kotaro rocked back on his chair, lost in thought. Sugimoto gave him an annoyed glance. "Have you finished already, patrolman? Would you like to be sent to the evidence room right now?"

"Uh, no sir!" Kotaro rocked his chair back to a normal position and grabbed more papers, making an attempt to look busy.

Sugimoto stood up and approached Kotaro from behind, looming over him as Kotaro pretended to work. After a few awkward seconds, Sugimoto placed a small bag next to Kotaro. "When you head to the evidence room, file this under the 'Suicide' cases. Understood?"

Kotaro glanced at the bag, which he recognized as being the one that carried the tantō from that night's incident, and nodded. Sugimoto returned to his desk and pulled out a new set of papers to complete.

After Sugimoto seemed to become engrossed in his papers, Kotaro quietly pushed aside his case reports, removed the tantō from the evidence bag, and stared at the blade. The metal was caked with dried blood, and the handle was a blackened wood. But in the center of the wood was a small, red, circular flower. Kotaro could have sworn he'd seen it somewhere before. He racked his brain, trying to remember, but to no avail.

"Patrolman! Paperwork," Sugimoto nearly shouted, which startled Kotaro, and he shoved the tantō back into its bag.

However, rather than getting back to the paperwork, Kotaro continued to ponder the possible connection between the cases and the significance of the flower.

"Ah! That's where I've seen it!" Finally remembering, Kotaro grabbed the bag and bolted from his desk, scattering a flurry of papers to the ground and ran down the hallway at an impressive speed.

Sugimoto stood up. "Wha- Wait, patrolman!"

Kotaro dashed down the maze of hallways, which led past cabinets, interrogation rooms and holding cells. He stomped down the stairs toward the evidence room, the dark corridor swallowing up what little light the oil lamps provided.

This didn't faze Kotaro as he yanked open the door labeled, "Evidence Room." In the room were tall cabinets of wooden drawers each with their own labels and a small table and chair in the middle. Seated there dozing was another patrolman, who jerked awake at the sound of the door being opened. The moment he caught sight of Kotaro in the doorway, he sneered. "You're here early, Yamada. Upset the captain again?"

Kotaro ignored him and went up to the drawers, searching for the "Suicide" section.

The other patrolman stood up from his chair and stretched. "Well, since you've been sent, I guess my shift is done. So I'll just be on my way." The patrolman opened the heavy door but jolted when he saw Sugimoto standing there with a grave expression. The patrolman threw up a quick salute with one hand and held the door open with the other for Sugimoto to enter.

Sugimoto gave a curt nod, and the policeman scrambled out the door. Sugimoto walked up behind Kotaro. "What are you doing?"

Kotaro remained focused on his task and didn't respond. "Let's see. Ah ha!" Kotaro pulled open one of the drawers and dug inside. He yanked out a black fan and walked toward the table in the middle of the room, which was lit by a solitary oil lamp on the table.

Sugimoto loomed behind him and focused in on the fan. "That fan … wasn't it evidence in the home minister case? I thought it was discarded after the case was closed."

Kotaro looked toward Sugimoto and held up the fan. "That's because the captain changed his mind and gave the order to hang on to it. And look!" Kotaro showed Sugimoto the bottom of the fan where a small red flower was engraved in the wood. "The flower!"

Sugimoto gave Kotaro a confused look. "A red chrysanthemum. What about it?"

Kotaro held up the small blade found beside Watanabe's body at the inn and pointed to the red flower engraved on its handle. "They're the same!"

Sugimoto leaned in and slowly nodded, Kotaro smiled since he knew Sugimoto would have to admit that, side-by-side, both the blade and the fan had the same symbol, proving a connection. But the nod quickly turned into a frown as Sugimoto stood up straight and shook his head. "It's hardly important. They were probably made by the same blacksmith."

Kotaro balked. "What kind of smith makes both a fan and a knife?"

Sugimoto pointed toward the fan. "Look closer. The handle of the fan is metal."

"It is?" Kotaro felt the fan in his hand and realized it was a combination of wood and wrought iron, the same type of metal used to weaponize fans into bludgeoning tools.

"Besides," Sugimoto continued, "it could just be a coincidence. The blacksmith and the fan maker might have just chosen the same symbol. Chrysanthemums are the flower of the royal family. Of course, that symbol would be popular."

Kotaro tried to flick open the fan, but it was sealed shut. He tried prying it apart by force, but it wouldn't budge.

Sugimoto snatched the fan from him. "You're going to break it! It won't open because of the dried blood. It was found next to a dead body after all!"

"But sir, what if the fan was the murder weapon?"

Sugimoto let out an annoyed sigh. "Of course we checked that. But the home minister was stabbed, not bludgeoned. For all we know, the fan belonged to the home minister himself." Sugimoto looked at the fan, his frown deepening. "I don't even know why we're retaining such a useless piece of evidence. We should just get rid of it."

"But sir, the captain said not to-"

"Yes. Yes. I know." Sugimoto handed the fan back to Kotaro. "Put it back in its drawer."

Kotaro took the fan and looked it over, trying to figure out its secrets. "If there was a hidden blade, then maybe…"

Before Sugimoto could stop him, Kotaro turned the bottom of the fan in one direction and the top in the opposite way. There was a *click*, which shocked both Kotaro and Sugimoto. Kotaro slowly pulled the bottom away and out came a short, sharp blade. The gleaming steel was stained with darkened, dried blood. After a moment of stunned silence, Kotaro laughed and lifted the blade into the air. "Ha! You see, sir? I, the great and powerful Yamada Kotaro, have found an all-important clue! And look!"

Kotaro picked up the blade from the inn and compared it to the fan blade. Both the steel blades were the same length and showed the wavy *nioi* pattern produced by traditional Japanese sword makers. "They match! There's got to be a connection! Very suspicious. And I know just who's responsible … the man in black!"

Sugimoto gaped at the hidden blade. He reached out to take it from Kotaro, but stopped and pulled back. "By Buddha's tree. How? How could *you* of all people have found that?"

Kotaro grinned. "One time my older brothers showed- I mean, it's my natural genius, of course! This ought to get me a promotion for sure!" Kotaro slid the blade back into the fan and locked it into place. He also picked up the tantō knife from the inn. "I have to inform the captain immediately!"

Kotaro started forward, but Sugimoto put out his hand to stop him. "You've been assigned to look after the evidence room tonight. I don't think the captain would be too pleased to see you away from your post."

"But I … my promotion and…" Kotaro looked down at the fan in his right hand and at the blade in his left.

"However," Sugimoto started, "I agree this is important. I'll inform Captain Fujita. Hand me … No, it makes more sense to leave the evidence here where it's safe. Keep an eye on it, and I'll return with the captain."

Sugimoto turned to leave and opened the door. Before stepping out he looked back at Kotaro. "Keep up that kind of work, and you may just have what it takes to be an officer after all."

Sugimoto left and let the door shut behind him. Kotaro carefully placed the blade and the fan down on the table and pulled out a small flask from his pocket and sat down, grinning. "This calls for a celebration!" Kotaro shook his flask, which was half-empty and took a swig. His face started to turn red. He glanced toward the blade and the fan on the table. "Just you wait, man in black! The great and powerful Yamada Kotaro is coming for you!"

Chapter Eight

Inzan led Makoto to the small *chosuya* fountain near the memorial stone. He used a bamboo ewer to rinse first his left, then his right hand. Makoto looked on, not understanding. "This is your home Master Mori, but it's also sacred ground. Please purify yourself so you don't offend the god of the shrine." Inzan pointed at the ewer and basin. Makoto gave a light shrug and copied Inzan's washing ritual.

When Makoto had finished, Inzan smiled and beckoned Makoto to follow him toward a small, single-story structure behind the temple. It was in significantly better condition than the temple, though the slanted roof had many cracks in the tiles and the wooden beams were at odd angles.

"This is the lodging area, please follow me, Master Mori."

Makoto nodded and followed him inside, yanking off his boots and taking them in with him. The interior of the priest's lodging was sparse. Drops of water leaked onto the ragged tatami mat floor. A single, square paper lantern sat on the low table and gave off a dim, flickering light. Inzan motioned for Makoto to sit on one of the old cushions on the floor as he went to a back room. Not long after Makoto sat down on the cushion, Inzan returned with a teapot and two stone cups.

As he poured the tea, Makoto shifted about uncomfortably on the cushion. He sat cross-legged and balanced his boots precariously on top of his duffel, which he placed on a dry part of the floor. Makoto pulled out his sword from the duffel and rested it on his lap, attaching the two halves of the wooden handle to the tang of the sword with small screws.

Inzan gave Makoto's boots a disdainful look. "Master Mori. It's customary to leave shoes outside."

"I know. I prefer to keep them close at hand." Makoto didn't elaborate further, and Inzan didn't bring it up again.

After inserting the screws, Makoto tried to weave some silk over the wood haft in order to form the traditional crisscross pattern of a *tsuka* grip. However, thanks to the dim light and his fatigue from the night's activities, Makoto was having a difficult time of it. Back in America, he'd just wrap wet rawhide to form a grip around the wood. As the rawhide dried, it shrank making a tight grip. However, neither Makoto nor Inzan had any idea where to find rawhide in Yokohama. It was Inzan who found a spare bit of silk in the back and suggested using it to wrap the katana handle.

Inzan took a sip of his tea and stared as Makoto struggled with binding the handle of his sword. "You haven't touched your tea, Master Mori."

Makoto glanced up and noticed the cup for the first time. He took a quick sip and winced at the chalky flavor, placing it back down on the table.

Inzan let out a light chuckle. "If I recall, you didn't care much for tea when you were younger either."

"I prefer coffee," Makoto replied.

"What's that? Some Jesuit devilry?"

"It's not important." Makoto resumed his work on the handle.

Inzan stared at Makoto's sword and shook his head. "It's such a shame all the family's weapons were taken by the government. Then you wouldn't be forced to use such an inferior blade."

Makoto simply nodded and continued his work.

There was an awkward silence that made Inzan shift uneasily. "Forgive me Master Mori for being so bold, but … how did you survive all this time? I thought the entire family was lost in the raid and the subsequent fire. Where have you been these last fifteen years?"

Makoto stopped working on the handle and stared at his sword in silence for a moment. "I wasn't there … I mean *here*, when it happened. But I saw the aftermath. I…" He gripped the loose silk strips tightly. "I ran away. There was nothing I could do."

Inzan nodded. "I understand. That would have been a terrible sight for one so young. You must've been ten at the time. Where did you go?"

Makoto loosened his grip on the silk. "I ran to the harbor. It was dark. There were no gas lamps back then, but I saw some men down there."

"What were they doing?"

Makoto shook his head. "I don't know. I decided to hide from them, but I got lost and ended up crawling under some fishing nets and falling asleep on one of the boats. When I awoke…" Makoto thought he heard a light shuffling sound, but after pausing and only hearing the rain pound on the roof, he dismissed it and continued. "The boat went out to sea to meet a whaling ship from America. I woke up when they moved the nets and found myself in the middle of a smuggling operation. When I was discovered, the captain of the smugglers put me on the American ship, which put out to sea."

"What!? They just took you? They should have brought you back!"

"Why? They had heard about the fate of the Mori family and told me that if I went back, the killers would finish the job. Handing me to the whalers was an act of kindness."

"But what about the main family? They could've taken you in."

Makoto shrugged. "They always looked down on our branch family, and my presence would have put them in danger. But in the end, it didn't matter. The sailors had no intention of turning the ship around. And once I was out to sea, the *shogun* would have put me to death if I tried to return."

Inzan grumbled something about Jesuits under his breath. "But why have you chosen to return now?"

"I only found out recently the laws had been changed so I could return. Then I saved the money for the voyage and arrived today."

"But where did you go, Master Mori?"

"It was an American ship, so I went to America."

"I see. What was it like there?"

"You'd find it very big and very … Jesuit."

Inzan frowned at the thought, but he shook it off and smiled. "Never mind that. I'm just glad you've returned to reestablish your family once more."

"That's not why I'm back," Makoto said.

Inzan balked. "It's not?"

"I didn't come back to reestablish the family. I came back for retribution. To find the ones responsible..." Makoto glanced in the direction of the courtyard where the memorial stone was located. "And make them pay."

"But think of your responsibility to the family! To continue the family line!"

"Revenge *is* my responsibility to the family."

Inzan stared down at his tea. "I understand your feelings Master Mori, but your desire for revenge is impossible to fulfill."

"Why?" Makoto asked.

Inzan shifted around. "Because the ones responsible are all gone."

"You know who's responsible? Tell me!"

Inzan looked up at him with wide eyes. "You didn't know? No. That makes sense. You were only a child at the time. The ones who wiped out the Mori clan were the *Shinsengumi*."

"Shinsengumi?" The name sounded familiar to Makoto but he could not quite place it.

"The elite fighters for the shogun."

"Then they are…"

"They acted on orders from the shogun to raid the Mori home and killed…"

Inzan trailed off, not wanting to go into detail.

"Why?" Makoto asked.

"I don't know. We'll probably never know since all who were involved are dead, even the shogun who gave the order."

Makoto gripped the silk. "That's … unacceptable."

"I know you're upset," Inzan said. "I was too. But sometimes the gods act in ways we can't understand."

"It wasn't the gods who murdered my family."

"Maybe not, but the ones that did are all dead. The Shinsengumi were disbanded after the emperor took over, and any which remained died in the revolt last year."

"Revolt?"

Inzan nodded somberly. "In the Satsuma region, led by those who longed for the old days of the *daimyo* and samurai, before these blasted Jesuit Westerners came in and ruined everything. So many young men cut down in their prime."

Makoto leaned forward. "The Shinsengumi fought in the revolt?"

Inzan nodded again. "The remnants of them — they wanted the old ways back as well. But most of them either died in battle or committed seppuku when defeat was inevitable."

Makoto was not satisfied with that explanation. "Some must have survived. They can't all be gone."

"I suppose it's possible, but how would you even find them? If any survived, they'd be in hiding. It's not like the old days where they would throw on their blue haori coats and strut down the street."

"Blue?" Makoto tensed up when he remembered the blue coat of the dead man.

"That's right. And since no one can carry swords in public anymore, you won't be able to find them that way either. And-"

"The coat. Did it have white, triangular trimming along the sleeves?"

"Yes," Inzan replied. "It's a bright shade of blue with white trimmings. Why do you ask?"

"I saw it."

"Saw what?"

"The coat. At an inn. On a dead man."

Inzan jolted back. "A dead man? Who?"

"I don't know. The maid came in just as I found him and she screamed that I killed him."

"Killed him!?" Inzan gave a horrified look. "D-Did you?"

Makoto's face grew dark. "No. But if he was Shinsengumi…"

Inzan shifted back a little. Makoto noticed the fear in his eyes. He eased back to a neutral expression, slid his unfinished sword into his bag, and stood up. Makoto held his boots in one hand and slung his bag over his shoulder. "Thank you for your hospitality. I won't intrude on you any longer."

"What!?" Inzan stood up, knocking over his cup of tea. "But you can't go! You just got here!"

"As you said, I desecrate this place with my 'Jesuit' ways."

"What? No! Of course, *you* don't Master Mori. Please at least stay the night. It's still raining outside."

Makoto hesitated as he listened to the rain pounding on the roof and the thunder rumbling outside. "I'll manage." He heard the shuffling noise again, and he noticed a shadow by the paper sliding door behind Inzan.

"But-" Inzan started.

"Shh!" Makoto reached into his bag, pulled out his blade, and motioned Inzan to be quiet. "Is there anyone else here?" Makoto whispered.

"I don't think so," Inzan replied in a whisper.

Makoto approached the door, keeping close to the walls to avoid being spotted through the paper door. When he reached the door, he could hear light shuffling on the other side. He pushed the paper door open rapidly, sword ready to slash.

He nearly dropped his sword when he saw the person on the other side of the door - a very surprised and very beautiful, young Japanese woman. She was sitting on her knees and was dressed in the loose white and red robes of a *miko* shrine maiden, her long, black hair was cut in the traditional, straight *hime* style. She was startled at the sight of Makoto but then smiled demurely at him. Makoto lowered his sword.

Inzan looked in and recognized her. "Oh! Emiko! I wasn't sure if you were coming back tonight."

Emiko bowed deeply, lowering her head to her hands on the ground. "Forgive my late intrusion, the rain slowed me down." She sat back upright and gestured behind her, where Makoto saw a *mino* hung near a sliding door toward the back. The straw raincoat was dripping wet.

"Would you like me to make a fresh pot of tea for you and your guest, Master Inzan?" Emiko asked.

Makoto glanced toward Inzan's knocked-over cup and his own still-full cup but found his eyes wandering back to Emiko.

"That won't be necessary," Inzan replied. "But please come in. Allow me to introduce you."

Emiko stood up and entered the room, keeping her head low as a sign of respect. Makoto couldn't help but stare. He had seen many beautiful women in America before, but he had never seen someone who was quite as stunning. Emiko noticed him staring and smiled at him again.

Inzan introduced the two. "Emiko, this is Master Mori Makoto. He is one of the esteemed sons of the late master, the former lord of this land. Master Mori, this is Hayashi Emiko, the shrine maiden at this temple."

Emiko's eyes grew wide, and she stared at Makoto, almost in disbelief. "But I thought the Mori family was-" She stopped abruptly and looked away. "Forgive my impertinence. It's not my place. I'm glad you're here to join us, Master Mori."

She gave a deep bow. Makoto opened his mouth to try and say something, but couldn't seem to find the words. Emiko raised her head. "Will Master Mori be spending the night?"

She turned expectantly toward Makoto, who was still having trouble speaking. "I…"

Inzan clasped Makoto's shoulder. "Of course he will! Emiko, would you be so kind as to lay out a futon for him?"

Emiko nodded, bowed deeply, and walked back to the door. After sliding the door open in a delicate manner, she stepped into the other room, knelt down and bowed once more before closing the door. Inzan gave Makoto a sly smile. "You know, Emiko would make a fine bride, certainly one worthy of the Mori family," Inzan whispered.

Makoto stared at Inzan, flabbergasted. "What?"

"Emiko's a fine girl, and she's from a noble samurai family. Like you, she's alone in the world." Inzan's enthusiasm faltered a bit. "Her family died last year in Satsuma. A terrible loss."

Makoto remembered Inzan mentioning the rebellion in Satsuma and briefly wondered on which side Emiko's family fought.

Inzan shook his head and perked up again. "Think about it, Master Mori! You would honor your family by continuing the Mori line! I think they would want you to do that rather than pursue this futile quest for vengeance-"

Makoto gave Inzan a dark look. "*I'll* decide how to honor my family."

Inzan took a step back. "Of course Master Mori. Please forgive my boldness." Inzan bowed and turned to leave.

Makoto realized he overreacted and sighed. "It's fine. Don't worry about it. Where will I be sleeping tonight?"

Inzan brightened up and motioned at the sliding door. "This way."

Makoto stood up and gathered his things, including his half-assembled sword. Inzan led him to a room in the back of the living quarters. There was a single futon spread out in the small, empty room.

"Ah, I don't know what I'd do without Emiko," Inzan said. "She is so reliable. She's even taken it upon herself to work at one of those accursed Jesuit hotels to help provide money for the temple."

Makoto looked at him in confusion. "Jesuit hotel?"

"One that caters to foreigners, but never mind. Please, make yourself comfortable. Emiko laid out a yukata if you would like to change." Inzan bowed before closing the door.

Makoto put his things down and held up the yukata. It was clearly way too small and far too short for him. He tossed it aside, collapsed into the futon, and drifted off to sleep.

Makoto slept deeply, and he awoke as the sun hit his face from a small window along the wall. He arose and checked on his belongings. The clothes from his bag were laid out, neatly folded on the tatami. His coins and gold nuggets were stacked next to them along with his chess set and simple toiletries. His boots had been cleaned from their accumulated dust and mud. Everything was present and in perfect order save for one thing. His sword was gone.

Chapter Nine

A couple of hours after the early summer dawn, Helen Arkwright sat in the boudoir of her hotel room with her book on her lap, tapping her foot impatiently. She was properly dressed in a different purple dress from the one she wore the day before, and her hair was done up in a stylish Gibson Girl style thanks to the assistance of Aki. However, her husband never came back last night. Helen wondered where he might have gone and tapped her foot even faster.

She knew the most logical course of action would be to wait for him to return, but the strange note and the doctor telling her about the shipbuilding district the previous night, set her imagination reeling into all sorts of conspiracies. She knew gallivanting off into a mostly unknown city without an escort would be risky, and even worse, improper for a woman of her class. But she stood up and decided it was her responsibility, no her *duty* as a proper wife to investigate whatever nonsense her husband had gotten himself into. It was up to her to get him out of it, even if it would be considered improper, and afterward, she would give him a piece of her mind for keeping her in the dark. Besides, she used to be an actress, and it once was her job to try new things and act in new roles. She grabbed her umbrella by the door and proceeded out of her room, down the staircase, through the lobby, and out the front entrance.

When Helen stepped outside of the hotel, she was greeted with the hustle and bustle of the early morning harbor. The distinct smell of dead fish attacked her nose, and she guessed the morning catch was being laid out in the nearby marketplace. It reminded her of the wharves back in San Francisco. Several guides and translators loitered around the entrance of the hotel. They crowded around and offered their services to her. She made her way through them, using her umbrella to push overly aggressive importuners aside as necessary.

She knew she had enough money to pay for transportation but not enough to pay a guide for the day. Besides, she didn't need one since she already knew her destination. Next to the coins in her purse were extra hatpins Helen borrowed from Aki, since they had proven to be so useful before. She approached a rickshaw man and showed him a coin. "Take me to the shipbuilding yard."

The man gave her a confused look. She pulled over one of the translators. "Tell him I want to go to the shipbuilding yard," she said, handing the translator a small coin.

"Yes, ma'am." The translator spoke in words Helen didn't understand. The rickshaw man nodded. The translator turned back to Helen. "He'll take you there. Do you want a guide, ma'am? I can show you-"

"No, thank you." Helen stepped up, took a seat in the rickshaw, and handed the man a coin. "Go on." She waved toward the rickshaw man who got the idea and took off at a fast trot, leaving behind the chaos in front of the Western-style hotel.

***

In the evidence room, Kotaro woke with a start, rubbed his eyes, and looked at his empty flask. It was still dark in the windowless room, save for the flickering oil lamp that had burned all night, but the familiar sounds of the footsteps and voices of his colleagues told him it was sometime in the early morning. He heard the sound of someone walking toward the evidence room and hid his flask in one of his back pockets, knowing it would probably not be a good idea to be caught drinking on duty … again.

He glanced toward the table where he had placed the evidence last night and was glad to see both the fan and the tantō were still present, despite his sleeping. The door opened and a dejected young patrolman entered, shooting up a quick salute. Kotaro heaved himself upright and returned the salute, briefly wondering what rule the patrolman had violated to be punished with evidence room duty. Kotaro could think of several ways, mostly because he'd done them.

Kotaro took the blade and the fan and walked past the patrolman out the door, down the hallway, and back to his desk, still burdened by its small mountain of incomplete paperwork. Just as he sat at his desk, he saw a very tired-looking Sugimoto enter from the front door. Sugimoto was thumbing a string of *juzu* prayer beads by his side while mumbling something Kotaro couldn't quite hear. When Kotaro trotted up to him, Sugimoto shoved the beads into his pocket.

"Lieutenant Sugimoto! Any news from the captain?"

Sugimoto frowned at the evidence in Kotaro's hands. "You shouldn't remove evidence without permission, patrolman. As for the captain…" He rubbed at the heavy bags under his eyes. "He was skeptical. He said he needed to see it in person to believe it."

"Then we'll show him when he gets back! When will he be in?"

"That might be a problem. Captain Fujita will be busy the entire day in the shipbuilding district. Security preparations for the *Hiei*."

"All day!?" Kotaro said. "But this can't wait! Every moment we hesitate, the man in black could claim more victims!"

"I suppose it would make sense to inform the captain as soon as possible, but the only way would be…"

"To bring the evidence to him!" Kotaro finished. "Of course! I'm a genius! I'll go right now!"

Before Sugimoto could stop him, Kotaro grabbed an empty linen evidence bag from his desk and slid the knife and fan into it. He put the bag into one of his jacket pockets and strode toward the door. Before he could get too far, Sugimoto grabbed his shoulder and yanked him back. "Where do you think you're going, Patrolman Yamada? You're not authorized to-"

"But sir, there's no time! I have to hurry before the man in black strikes again!" Kotaro yanked his shoulder away and ran out of the office, taking one of the side exits he usually used to sneak out for a quick drink, leaving the exhausted Sugimoto behind.

***

Makoto stood up from his futon and looked around the room frantically for any sign of his missing sword. He felt a chill of dread because he knew it would be impossible to replace it. Not seeing it, he rushed for the door and slid it open, startled to see Emiko standing as if she was about to pull open the door herself. She was not wearing her shrine maiden outfit. Instead, she wore a Western maid's uniform, a dark blue, ankle length dress covered with a white pinafore, which protected the front. The dress must have been for her job that Inzan mentioned last night. It suited her remarkably well.

"Oh! Master Mori. I'm sorry to intrude. I came to return this."

Makoto felt a rush of relief when he saw his sheathed sword in her hands. But relief turned to suspicion as he cautiously took it back. He looked it over and was surprised to see the handle he struggled with last night had been finished. It was woven with a glossy black silk in an intricate weave pattern. A thin red thread ran throughout the weave. He looked toward Emiko. "Did you?"

Emiko bowed. "I noticed it was incomplete last night, so I took it upon myself to finish it. I apologize if I imposed."

Makoto shook his head. "No. Thank you for completing it. I would never know how to make a weave like that." Makoto removed the sword from its sheath, held it upright, and stared at the handle, particularly the red thread which seemed to bind everything together. The weave felt perfect in his hand, and the sword somehow felt more alive and responsive than when he had used rawhide to wrap the handle.

Emiko noticed him staring. "The silk needed a separate thread to bind firmly to the handle. I took a length of thread from my *hakama*. Though ... please don't tell Master Inzan." Emiko blushed and looked down at the ground. Makoto nodded, returned the sword to its sheath, and slid it into his bag. His gaze turned to Emiko's uniform. The outfit showed off her form much better than the shapeless miko outfit.

She noticed his gaze and her blush deepened. "I-It's for my work at the Grand Hotel. I know I must look strange."

"I don't think so."

Emiko smiled at him. "I've prepared breakfast. Please help yourself."

Makoto felt the pang in his stomach. He hadn't eaten since yesterday morning and could use some food before heading back out into Yokohama. She led him to the low table where he had tea with Inzan the previous night. Already laid out was a traditional Japanese breakfast of rice, fish, miso, and pickled vegetables. As Makoto sat down, he noticed a pair of wooden chopsticks next to the food and picked them up, wracking his brain for the correct finger positions.

Emiko saw him struggling. "Do you know how to use chopsticks, Master Mori?"

"I used to."

Emiko chuckled and kneeled next to Makoto. "Here, let me help you." She adjusted the chopsticks into the correct position in Makoto's hand and smiled as he slowly clicked the two pieces of wood together. Satisfied, he started with the soup, drinking straight from the bowl, one thing that was the same for him both in Japan and in America. He never saw the purpose of spoons. After downing it in a couple of solid gulps he moved on to the fish, rice, and pickled vegetables and devoured them with similar voraciousness. He was even hungrier than he realized. After the dishes were empty, he nodded to Emiko. "Thank you for the food."

She giggled. "I'm glad you enjoy my cooking. Will you be staying with us again tonight?"

"No."

Emiko was a little startled at the blunt response. "Oh. I'm sorry our poor accommodations displeased you."

"It's not that. I'm searching for a certain group of people. And the old man is my only lead."

Emiko tilted her head in confusion. "Old man?"

Makoto stopped himself from saying more and shook his head, not wanting to drag her into his mess. "It's not important, but I don't think I'll be returning."

Emiko looked disappointed and stood up. Makoto averted his eyes, stood up as well, and returned to the room where he had slept. After picking up his boots and bag, he found his way to the entrance of the lodgings, which was much easier to see in the daylight. Emiko followed him. "Where will you search, Master Mori?"

"I'll try the bars around the docks and the warehouses first."

"But wouldn't it make more sense to first check the inn where you found the Shinsengumi, Master Mori?"

Makoto looked at her with surprise. "You know about the Shinsengumi?"

Emiko nodded. "I … overheard your conversation last night. The inn you spoke of is on the way to the Grand Hotel."

Makoto didn't recall mentioning too much about the inn, but in his haze of fatigue, he may have said enough for Emiko to recognize it.

Emiko looked down in embarrassment. "I know it is not my place, but would it be all right if I accompanied you there? It can be a little frightening to walk by myself, and I do not wish to disturb Master Inzan." She gave Makoto a warm smile.

"That's fine," Makoto replied. When they reached the entrance, Makoto put on his boots, coat, and hat, and slung his bag over his shoulder. Emiko slid on a pair of Western-style lace-up boots and pulled on a long, dark cloak that hid most of her uniform. Makoto started for the road which led back toward the inn, and Emiko followed several steps behind him. Makoto stopped and turned toward her. "What's wrong?"

"Nothing Master Mori. I am simply keeping my proper place."

Makoto frowned. "You can't lead me from behind."

Emiko looked down. "It would be shameful for a mere woman to lead you."

Makoto raised a confused eyebrow. He had forgotten more of the customs than he realized, or maybe the types of women he dealt with in the American West were a bit … different. "Then let's walk side-by-side."

Emiko blushed. "But that would be even more improper Master Mori! And I-"

"Please stop calling me 'Master.' Just call me Makoto. I'd rather you see me as a friend, Miss Hayashi."

Emiko looked at him in shock, but then let out a light chuckle. "Well, in that case, please just call me Emiko, Master- I mean, Makoto."

Makoto nodded. Smiling, Emiko walked up next to him and the two carefully made their way down the stone steps from the shrine to the town below.

Even though it took Makoto hours to navigate winding streets of the old town the previous night, Emiko knew the area well, and within half an hour they reached the familiar sights of the harbor. The *Abraham Lincoln* was still present, towering over the other ships, although the crowd that had gathered to gawk at it was significantly smaller than the day before. As they continued along the waterfront, Makoto caught sight of the bar from yesterday, Sakénomi's. Sweeping the street in front was the bartender. Jean noticed the two, smiled, and nodded in their direction. "*Bonjour* monsieur and mademoiselle."

Makoto touched the brim of his hat and nodded, while Emiko looked on with bewilderment. "He said hello," Makoto clarified for her.

"Oh, I see." Emiko stopped and made a polite bow toward Jean, which took the bartender by surprise.

"Lovely, and polite! A rare combination. You best be careful around these parts," Jean said in Japanese with a laugh.

"Careful?" Emiko asked.

"They say there's a killer on the loose. Just yesterday, poor ol' Watanabe was stabbed. The police say it was suicide, but you can't trust anything those guys say."

"Watanabe?" Makoto asked.

"Yes," Jean replied. "He was found in the Yasumi Inn. There are rumors that a foreigner killed him … Wait a minute…" Jean looked at Makoto, his face growing suspicious. "Weren't you heading that way?"

Makoto stiffened and tried to think up some way to change the conversation.

"Ah!"

Makoto, Jean, and Emiko turned toward the source of the sound and saw Kotaro standing in one of the alleys, pointing his finger toward Makoto. "Man in black! I've got you now!"

Chapter Ten

Kotaro pulled out his nightstick. "Halt! In the name of the Emperor!"

Makoto grabbed Emiko's hand. "Let's go." They started running.

Kotaro gave chase, dashing into the middle of the road. "Don't think you can escape the great and powerful- oof!"

There was a crash, and Makoto and Emiko stopped to look back. They saw a rickshaw man had crashed into Kotaro and both were sprawled out on the ground. Sitting in the tilted-forward rickshaw was the American woman Makoto saw yesterday, again wearing a purple dress.

She seemed a bit jostled from the crash, climbed down from the rickshaw, and stood over the two dazed men. "Are you both all right? For goodness sake, get up! You still have to take me to the shipbuilding district!" The rickshaw man did not stir. Helen sighed, looked around, and noticed Makoto. She quickly recognized him from his unique outfit. "Hey! You're that cowboy who pushed me at the harbor!"

Helen moved closer, but Makoto pulled at Emiko and the two walked away. They turned a corner.

Helen trotted behind them. "Hold on! I just have a couple of…" She turned the same corner and saw no one there. "Questions." She sighed and returned to the front of the bar. She approached the bartender.

"Bonjour madame, Jean Dubois at your service," Jean said with a gracious bow.

Helen frowned. "Madame? Do I really look that old?"

"Pardon me, madame. I saw your wedding ring, so I knew some fortunate man had captured your heart. It would be improper for me to refer to you as mademoiselle."

Helen chuckled at the compliment. "You're a quick thinker. But do you know who that man was with the young woman? Normally, men don't run away from me that fast ... unless I'm playing Lady Macbeth."

"I'm afraid I don't know him madame, but it seems your rickshaw man is returning to life." Jean nodded toward the sprawling man, who groaned and rubbed his head.

Helen turned to see her rickshaw man slowly stand back up with a stagger to his step. She climbed back into the rickshaw, sat down, and pointed down at the unconscious Kotaro with her umbrella. "What about him?"

Jean stepped beside Kotaro and looked down at him. "He'll probably wake up soon."

Helen frowned at Jean. "Are you actually going to leave him like that?"

Jean shrugged. "I don't see why not."

Helen gave Jean a pointed, matronly look. Jean shrank back a little. "I suppose I wouldn't want customers tripping over him. Just a moment." The bartender headed into the bar, came out with a box half-filled with saké, kneeled down, and placed the box near Kotaro's nose.

"Saké…" Kotaro muttered.

Suddenly, he sprang to life and reached for the box, but Jean yanked it away just in time. "You have to pay for that."

Kotaro groaned and rubbed his head. He looked toward the rickshaw man, to Helen, and finally to Jean. "Lousy foreigners," he grumbled.

"What was that?" Jean asked using a mocking tone, cupping his free hand to his ear. "Ah, yes, you're welcome that I didn't leave you to die on the street like a dog, even though you probably deserved it."

"What did you say, you filthy foreigner!?" Kotaro sprung upright and pointed his finger at the bartender.

Jean sneered at Kotaro, stood up, and addressed Helen in English with a friendly voice. "As you can see madame, the fat policeman is alive and well."

Helen nodded, and Jean made another over-the-top bow. Satisfied, Helen waved the rickshaw man to keep going, and he took off running, leaving Kotaro and Jean behind.

Kotaro rubbed his head once more. "What was I- ah!" Kotaro stood up and looked around. "Where did the man in black go? Have you seen him?"

Jean shrugged. "I make it a habit to not answer questions from the police, especially from ones who owe me for a broken table. Best of luck in your search." The bartender lifted the cloth at the entranceway of the bar and went inside.

Kotaro attempted to follow him for more information and maybe a quick drink, but as soon as Jean stepped in, the sumo-sized Tora stepped out, blocking the doorway. He crossed his arms. "Bar's closed. It'll open in a couple of hours."

"Bah! I don't have time for this." Kotaro walked away from the bar, muttering various curses for both the foreigners and the man in black. He doubted he could follow the man in black's trail on his own, but he could at least still show the evidence to Captain Fujita. Maybe once he finally saw the truth, the captain would assign an elite squad to hunt down the man in black, with Kotaro in charge, of course, pointing the way with a gleaming saber. Brushing the dust off his uniform, Kotaro headed once more toward the shipbuilding district.

***

Makoto and Emiko weaved their way through the alleys until they were across the street from the Yasumi Inn. Makoto looked the inn up and down, glanced toward Emiko, and noticed he was still holding her hand. She was blushing, and he let go. "Sorry."

"No. It's fine, really." She gave a warm smile that Makoto found himself getting lost in, but he forced himself to focus his attention on the inn. At the front was a single, very bored-looking policeman.

"You're good at navigating back-streets. Even I didn't remember some of those alleys," Emiko said.

"I always try to keep an eye out for a quick escape. It's a skill I picked up in America."

Emiko saw Makoto stare toward the inn. "Is that where you found him? The man from the Shinsengumi?"

Makoto nodded. He turned toward her. "You should go. I don't know what will happen next."

"But Master Mori! I mean, Makoto…" She breathed in, gathering her courage. "I want to help you any way I can. Your family was so kind to Master Inzan, and he's been so kind to me. I feel indebted to you and your family, and I would like the opportunity to show my gratitude. So please, let me help."

Makoto found himself staring into her eyes. She seemed to be genuine in her plea, and as much as he didn't like to admit it, he could really use the help. Plus, he found himself unable to say no to her when she looked at him like that. He reluctantly nodded. "All right." He pointed toward one of the second-story windows. "I need to get in there, without being seen."

Emiko looked at the window and down at the policeman. "Most inns have a back entrance for staff. I'll check to see if I can find it."

They quickly moved across the street. It was still early enough that only a few people were walking about. When they found the back entrance to the inn, Emiko slid the door open. All was quiet.

"I'll go first. I'm less likely to cause alarm."

Makoto nodded. Emiko quietly slid off her shoes and held them as she cautiously stepped inside. After an agonizingly long minute of waiting, Emiko returned and motioned Makoto to come in. He did so, following Emiko's lead by removing his boots. The two headed up the stairs. The inn was eerily quiet, and Makoto wondered if the police had forced everyone out.

When they reached the top of the stairs, Makoto pointed to the door on the left, and Emiko nodded. She slowly slid open the door and poked her head inside. The room was empty. As she stepped inside, Makoto heard the sound of a paper door sliding at the back of the hall. It seemed the inn wasn't abandoned after all. Not wanting to be seen, Makoto placed his hand on Emiko's back and urged her inside while he stepped in as well, sliding the door shut behind him.

"Makoto, what-" Emiko started before Makoto placed his hand over her mouth. The two stood in silence as footsteps walked past them. He heard the sound of sniffing and a light, "Poor Mr. Watanabe," from a young woman who Makoto suspected was the maid who had screamed at him the previous night.

The harsh voice of the innkeeper chimed in, "What happened to Mr. Watanabe was tragic, but keep your focus on the inn. Crying won't bring him back and we have a reputation to repair. Come along."

Makoto and Emiko stood motionless until the innkeeper and the maid were down the stairs and out of earshot. Makoto released Emiko and she took a couple of steps forward. He could tell she was flustered. "I'm sorry."

She let out a soft, nervous laugh and shook her head. "It's all right, though that did take me by surprise."

They turned their attention to the room. It was now brightly lit thanks to the sunlight streaming through the open window Makoto used to make his escape the night before. The room was completely empty, even the futons and low table had been removed, making the large, brown stain in the middle of the tatami mat all the more prominent. Makoto stepped closer, while Emiko stared. He kneeled down and studied the stain.

"Is that … blood?" Emiko asked.

Makoto glanced at her. She was fixated on the bloodstain. "Yes," Makoto replied. "Will you be all right?"

She gave a slow nod and a sad smile. "I've seen blood before … in Satsuma."

Makoto remembered Inzan mentioning her past and realized he was dragging her back into a world of death and suffering. He stood up and approached her. "You should go. I don't want to give you any more trouble."

"It's no trouble, really!" Emiko replied. "I want to help you, Makoto, I mean it. Please let me."

Makoto couldn't deny her and sighed. "Very well."

Her pleading look changed into a warm smile. "Thank you, Makoto."

Makoto both loved and hated it when she said his name. It sounded like the sighing of wind through the cherry blossoms to his ears, but he found himself unable to focus on anything except her. Through tremendous effort, he tore himself away from her gaze and began searching the room. He opened the large cabinet that was used to hold futons, but it was empty.

Emiko watched him. "What are you searching for?"

"Clues."

"What kind of clues?"

"I'll know it when I see it."

Emiko nodded and started looking around as well. Makoto's attention went back to the large patch of dried blood in the center of the room, and he remembered seeing the body. His emotions were mixed. He had sworn to kill the assassins who slaughtered his family, and the Shinsengumi were those assassins. He should be glad to see one dead, but thinking about the old man's body, sprawled on the floor gave him reservations. Would he be willing to kill a helpless old man in cold blood, even if he was Shinsengumi? Makoto supposed he should feel grateful to the old man for killing himself and saving Makoto the dilemma. But he couldn't shake a feeling in his gut that the old man may have actually been murdered.

"Oh! Makoto."

Makoto turned toward Emiko. She handed him a folded piece of paper. "I found this in the corner."

Makoto chastised himself for missing the paper when scanning the room. He took the paper and unfolded it. There was Japanese writing on it, and Makoto struggled a little bit with the rough handwriting but was able to make out the message. "Meet me at warehouse four in the shipbuilding district." Makoto reread the note once more. While it wasn't a strong lead, it seemed this warehouse was his next destination.

The sound of a young woman chatting outside the sliding door with a young man made Makoto and Emiko freeze. The woman was sniffing a bit and the young man's voice sounded exasperated. Makoto guessed it was the maid from last night and the policeman from outside.

"How are we going to get out?" Emiko whispered.

Makoto glanced at the open window. "Are you willing to trust me?"

She nodded. "Of course."

"Then put on your shoes."

"Inside? But that's hardly proper."

Makoto pointed to the bloodstain. "Neither is that."

"Very well." Emiko slid on her shoes and quickly tied the laces, while Makoto pulled on his boots. Makoto led her to the window, and Emiko gave a yelp when Makoto bent down, picked her up, and held her in front of him. "M-Makoto? What are we-" she whispered nervously.

"We're going out the window," Makoto interrupted. "Do you trust me?" he repeated.

She hesitated but nodded again. Makoto nodded in return and carefully climbed out the open window, to the now familiar ledge. With the advantage of daylight and dryness, he was able to easily make the jump to the roof of the nearby, now-occupied shop and slide his way down. He struggled to maintain his balance with Emiko in his arms and his bag on his shoulder.

He noticed the front side of the shop was filled with bins of vegetables and a couple of early morning customers picking through them. Makoto opted to slide down the other side of the roof. After reaching the edge, he jumped and landed in the narrow alley with ease, having pulled off similar stunts in America when escaping from a persistent band of horse thieves. He placed Emiko on her feet and saw one of the customers do a double take at their sudden presence but then quickly go back to searching for vegetables.

Emiko let out a sigh of relief after catching her breath and looked at Makoto with a flushed face and a timid smile. "That was exciting, wasn't it?" Her smile relaxed into a genuine one. "Thank you, Makoto. Even though I couldn't do much…" She gestured to the note in his hand. "I hope that 'clue' may be of some use to you. Will you be heading to the shipbuilding district?"

Makoto nodded. "Yes. I must find out more."

Emiko bowed. "Makoto, I'm sorry, but I must go to my job at the hotel But I hope ... I can see you again."

Makoto hesitated but returned her smile with a small one of his own. "I hope so, too."

Emiko bowed again and pointed toward the sea. "The shipbuilding district is that way. Please be careful, and please come back to us at the shrine."

At that moment, Makoto wanted nothing more than to return to the shrine and to her, rather than chase ghosts through Yokohama. But his mission came first. "Perhaps."

The two parted ways, and Makoto made his way to the warehouse district. The area was cluttered with many small ships in various stages of completion from naked keel and ribs to almost completed fishing boats. One partially constructed ship stood out from the others. It was much larger than the other half-completed boats; metal plates were fastened to the wooden ribs rather than the wood planking used on the smaller ships.

Makoto's eyes drifted from the ships to the many warehouses. Next to the ship under construction, he saw a warehouse with a large number four painted just above the freight door. It was flanked on one side by a standard-sized door for workers and a dark window on the other.

He looked over the warehouse, doing his best to keep to the shadows of the incomplete ships in order to avoid the stares of the workers. The last thing he needed was to have another run-in with the police just because someone found him suspicious. Just as he was about to reach the warehouse, he saw a Western foreigner walking by with a Japanese man. Makoto could tell by his clothing that the foreigner was an American. His suit would have been the height of fashion in Knob Hill, complete with a green waistcoat and a gold watch chain across his ample stomach.

The Japanese man wore a ludicrous parody of a British morning suit. The tails of his black coat hung almost to his ankles and his gray-stripped trousers hung baggy around his legs, reminding Makoto of the loose hakama Emiko wore as part of her miko outfit. His head was covered with an oversized silk top hat that wobbled dangerously at every step. Makoto stayed still to avoid being noticed, and he overheard part of their conversation.

"Suicide you say? It's all very vexing Tanaka," the foreigner said in an American accent.

"Y-Yes. Indeed, Mr. Arkwright," Tanaka replied in English with an accent implying heavy study but not mastery of the language.

"What does this mean for the contract?" Arkwright gave Tanaka an intense look. Tanaka sweated profusely under his gaze despite the cool morning air and patted his forehead with a handkerchief. "Not to worry, I will be taking over for Mr. Watanabe in overseeing your contract."

"That's what I'm worried about," Arkwright said. "First Ōkubo. Now Watanabe. Two suicides in one department is rarely a good sign. Let's get a status report, then finish up this blasted business." The two headed for the largest ship under construction.

Once they were out of earshot, Makoto made his way to the warehouse and tried opening the door, but it was locked. He looked up and saw an open window on the side of the warehouse. He leaped up, grabbed the ledge, and pulled himself into the warehouse with some difficulty since the window was small and his shoulders were broad.

Makoto clutched his duffle to his chest and quietly jumped to the floor, conveniently hidden by a large stack of wooden crates. He looked around for any sign that might lead him to the Shinsengumi. After hearing some rustling, he realized he wasn't alone in the warehouse. He kept close to the walls and noticed someone staring out one of the lower windows on the other side of the warehouse. Makoto couldn't make out his face, but he could see his coat, which was a familiar shade of bright blue with white trimmings, a Shinsengumi coat. Makoto laid his duffel down, drew his sword, and inched silently toward his adversary.

Chapter Eleven

Makoto crept toward the Shinsengumi, sword at the ready. He stepped silently around the seemingly random stacks of wooden crates and barrels in the room, ducking behind a tall stack whenever he saw the man in the blue coat stir. However, the Shinsengumi didn't seem to notice Makoto; his attention was focused on whatever was going on outside the dust-streaked window beside the freight door. Makoto inched closer and stepped behind another stack of boxes, but his sword was just a little too close to the wooden boxes and made a small *clack* when it's sheath brushed against one of them. The Shinsengumi glanced over his shoulder, and Makoto stayed as still as his body would allow.

After an agonizingly long minute, Makoto tilted his head forward enough to see the Shinsengumi had returned his focus to the window. At this distance, he could go for a lunge and run the Shinsengumi through before he could have time to react. Makoto took his sword with both hands and held it low, readying for the attack. He shifted one foot behind the other and bent his knees, preparing to spring forward. His focus honed in on the Shinsengumi's back, on the blue coat. Painful memories of the raid and seeing the lifeless bodies of his family flashed through his mind. But the memory of the dead old man also appeared, and he paused.

Makoto felt his hands trembling. During his time as a bounty hunter in America, he'd never stoop so low as to shoot or stab a man in the back. He faced his enemies head-on. If it was a gunfight, his opponent had always drawn or shot first. And even if he wanted to shoot the Shinsengumi, his gun wasn't anywhere near working order. He gritted his teeth and tightened the grip on his sword; he couldn't afford to lose this chance for retribution. However, before Makoto could launch his attack, the Shinsengumi spun around, drew his sword, and charged at Makoto. The

Shinsengumi's face was covered by a red-horned demon mask common in *Noh* theater.

Makoto cursed his scruples for letting his advantage slip by and raised his sword just as the Shinsengumi swung his. Their weapons clashed. The masked Shinsengumi was much stronger than anticipated, and Makoto was driven several steps back. As Makoto's back pressed against one of the warehouse walls, the masked man continued pushing, the intersected swords moving closer and closer toward Makoto's neck.

Recovering his composure from the attack, Makoto pressed with just as much force as the Shinsengumi. When the swords reached a standstill, Makoto slashed downward, slamming his blade into the small haft guard of his enemy's katana. The force of the blow nearly made the Shinsengumi drop his sword, and he jumped backward, giving Makoto the opening he needed to take the offensive. The Shinsengumi looked back and forth between his own blade and Makoto's gleaming steel. Makoto was not surprised the Shinsengumi was confused, since Makoto's sword, like him, was anything but ordinary.

Makoto swung back his sword and slashed, but the masked man recovered quickly enough to put up his sword in time to block the attack. It seemed the Shinsengumi was skilled in the use of his weapon, possibly more skilled than Makoto. The time for traditional tactics was over, and Makoto lunged forward, head-butting the masked man, who reeled back.

The mask cracked and came loose, but the Shinsengumi was able to grab it before it fell off. Holding the mask with one hand and his sword with the other, he crouched low and held his sword in a defensive position. Even through the mask, Makoto could sense his glare, which Makoto returned. They circled each other until Makoto's back was facing the door.

The masked man changed tactics and suddenly charged toward Makoto, swinging his katana back and forth with blinding speed, hitting whatever he could. Several stacks of wooden crates came tumbling down in the chaotic attack. Makoto knew he couldn't block the random, rapidly slashing strikes, and he jumped to the left just as the masked man brought down his sword with sudden deadly accuracy. With Makoto out of the way and a clear path to the worker's entrance, the Shinsengumi dashed to the door. Makoto followed.

***

Helen cooled her face with a purple silk fan that perfectly matched her dress, and with the other hand she held her trusty umbrella as the rickshaw man dashed through the shipbuilding district. The cool morning air quickly dissipated into broiling summer heat. As the rickshaw weaved its way around the half-built ships, Helen received plenty of stares from sailors, businessmen, and stevedores.

She noticed most of the ships under construction were relatively small and made out of wood, nothing her husband would associate with. He only dealt with the largest, gaudiest, and most expensive ships. She glanced around and her eye caught one ship that towered above the others, was plated with metal, and had exceptionally garish trim. "Wait! Take me to that one."

The rickshaw man stopped and looked at her with a confused expression. Helen snapped her fan shut and pointed it toward her desired destination. "That ship. Take me to it."

The rickshaw man cocked his head to the side, still not understanding. Helen frowned, grabbed her umbrella, leaned forward, and waved it at the ship in an over-exaggerated fashion, nearly tipping over the rickshaw. "There. Take me. There! Blast it!"

The rickshaw man ducked to avoid her swinging umbrella. He looked back and forth between her and the ship. Finally, something clicked and he slowly nodded. He picked up the shafts of the rickshaw and started running again, making certain to keep his head low to avoid the umbrella. Helen almost fell over as the rickshaw began moving, but she smiled when she saw they were heading for the correct ship. Helen let out a sigh of relief and slumped back in the cushions. She knew if her husband was anywhere in the shipyards, he would be there.

Helen started to feel sweat in the summer sun and pulled out her fan again with a sigh. "Sometime too hot the eye of heaven shines. Maybe John was right, staying at the hotel would have been much easier."

***

Kotaro panted as he jogged around the shipbuilding district. He passed by several bars and showed *heroic* restraint by not going in to search for criminals; though it did help that most of his favorites were still closed. As he wandered deeper into the shipbuilding district, he noticed the in-construction ships getting steadily larger. He stopped in front of a gigantic ship made of wood and plated with metal. He briefly wondered how the ship could float with so much metal, but quickly dismissed the thought when he saw a foreigner and a diplomat walking toward him.

He sucked in his stomach and stood at attention as the two walked by, recalling the many times he'd been scolded by the captain for not showing proper respect, but he resumed his slouching after they passed and ignored him, speaking in a language he couldn't understand. Kotaro glanced around, hoping to catch sight of the captain, but he didn't seem to be anywhere in the district.

Moaning in frustration, Kotaro wandered over to the nearest warehouse and leaned against the wall, pulling out his flask and taking a swig, but he was immensely disappointed when nothing came out. He gave the flask a shake and remembered he emptied it the previous night in "celebration." He sighed. As Kotaro lamented over his empty flask, the side door of the warehouse burst open. Kotaro recoiled at the sudden movement and turned just as a man in a mask and a bright blue Shinsengumi coat ran out. Kotaro gaped.

The Shinsengumi, who held his mask with one hand and a sword with the other, glanced at Kotaro and seemed to flinch at the sight of him. Kotaro shook off his shock and pulled out his baton. "Halt! You can't carry a sword in public! You're under arrest!" The Shinsengumi ignored his commands and fled. Kotaro was about to give chase, when the man in black suddenly ran out of the same door. "It's you!" Kotaro said, now aiming his baton at Makoto.

Makoto noticed Kotaro and gave a very heartfelt, "Damn." Makoto glanced around for the Shinsengumi and caught sight of the blue coat as the masked man turned the corner. Makoto was about to give chase when Kotaro bolted in front of him and aimed his nightstick at Makoto's chest. "Halt! Or I the great and-oof!"

With another resounding crash, the same rickshaw carrying Helen slammed into Kotaro, sprawling them out on the ground once more. Helen was nearly thrown out of the rickshaw and looked toward the mess in annoyance. "Honestly! I feel like I'm back in *The Comedy of Errors*!" She glanced toward Makoto and gasped. "It's you! The cowboy!"

Makoto gave a frustrated grunt and ran around the rickshaw, but by the time he was able to get past, the Shinsengumi was out of sight. He cursed to himself and ran at top speed, turned the same corner as the Shinsengumi, and tried to pick up his trail. Helen attempted to follow him but nearly tripped as the hem of her ankle-length skirt tangled with the wheel hub of the rickshaw. She had to grab onto the rim of the large wheel to avoid sprawling out on the ground with the policeman and the rickshaw man. By the time she regained her balance, the cowboy was gone.

She sighed, looked at the large ship, remembered her reason for coming, and started walking toward the ship, hoping to find her husband. However, before she could even take two steps, she felt a hand grab her arm. She looked in surprise to see an angry policeman, totally unlike the oafish one who lay gasping on the ground. He said something in Japanese she couldn't understand.

"Let go, you ruffian!" Helen grabbed her purple umbrella and waved it at the police officer. He let go of her and pulled out his sword to block the umbrella. In one swift motion, the sword sliced right through the silk canopy, metal ribs, and bamboo shaft, much to Helen's astonishment. She nervously glanced at the stump that was once her umbrella and backed away toward the rickshaw. The police officer kept his sword out and his glare deepened with each step she took back.

The rickshaw man struggled to get up, but when he caught sight of the police officer with a brandished sword, he nearly leaped out of his skin and skidded back to the rickshaw, just as Helen climbed back in her seat. "Take me back to the hotel! Now!" she said.

The rickshaw man didn't need to be told twice, not that he understood much more than "hotel." He bolted for the street. The police officer sheathed his sword and walked over to Kotaro.

"Blasted sickle weasels!" Kotaro grumbled as he lay on the ground.

"Get up, Yamada," the police officer said with an icy tone.

Kotaro looked up and saw Captain Fujita standing over him with an exceptionally sour expression on his face. "Ah! Captain!" Kotaro scrambled upright, nearly losing his balance in the maneuver, and gave a quick salute. "I was just looking for you, sir!"

"Why are you out of the evidence room?"

"Captain!" Kotaro and Fujita looked on to see Sugimoto running toward them. He was panting hard, having clearly just run a long way to get there. He also gave a quick salute. "I'm sorry, sir. I tried to stop him, but the patrolman is a surprisingly fast runner."

Fujita's brow furrowed further. "I expected better from you, Lieutenant."

Sugimoto stiffened and his hand twitched as it drifted toward the pocket hosting his juzu beads.

"But sir!" Kotaro said. "There's a good reason! The evidence!"

"What evidence?"

"Here sir!" Kotaro fumbled around in his jacket looking for the fan and blade, but as he patted around the right side of his jacket, he couldn't feel anything other than his flask. He patted the other side. Still nothing. As his hands rustled in his pockets he slowly grew more frantic. His stomach dropped when he realized that his evidence had disappeared.

Chapter Twelve

Makoto's eyes darted left and right as he rushed around the half-completed ships, searching for any sign of the masked Shinsengumi. After a few minutes of wandering and not finding a trace of the masked man, he spat out a curse, slowed his pace, and collected his thoughts. He had found a Shinsengumi, but lost his chance to finish him off. If there were others, they'd probably be warned about him and finding them would be even harder.

He cursed again and then paused when he saw the large metal-plated ship come into view. In his rush, he must have looped back around toward the warehouses. He remembered he left his duffel in the warehouse, and seeing as it contained all of his possessions, including the sack of coins and gold nuggets that represented his worldly wealth, Makoto hastened his pace in order to retrieve it before some stevedore helped himself. As he trotted back, he made sure to stay close to the wooden ship skeletons in case he needed to hide in the shadows from prying eyes.

He slowed his pace to a walk as he neared the entrance of warehouse four and saw three policemen, including the fat one who somehow kept managing to show up and cause him trouble. Makoto ducked out of sight under the keel of the large ship, completely hidden by barrels and stacks of coiled rope. He inched carefully forward to hear what the police were saying, hoping to get some useful information. Kotaro gesticulated wildly, while the other two were clearly unimpressed.

Makoto could hear the panic rising in Kotaro's voice as he patted one pocket, then another, and the first one again for good measure. "The knife! The fan! They're-"

"They're what?" The most senior officer gave Kotaro an icy glare, which caused him to shrink back. "Uh, well, you see … Captain Fujita … I- oh wait! I remember now! When that rickshaw man hit me the first time, they must've fallen out! I-I'll go fetch them!" Kotaro pivoted around, but before he could make his escape, Fujita clasped his shoulder and pulled him back.

"Don't think you can fool me, Yamada. I won't let you sneak away to indulge at a bar ... again."

"How did you- I mean no, sir! I mean, yes, sir! But- uh. You don't understand."

"I understand perfectly," Fujita interrupted. "We will be returning to the police station where you will be assigned to the evidence room ... permanently."

Kotaro swallowed a lump in his throat. "P-Permanently?"

"Yes, permanently. Starting right now. Consider yourself lucky that I don't send you to Abashiri."

Makoto had no idea what the captain meant, but Kotaro's reaction indicated that wherever it was, it wasn't good.

Fujita glared at the remaining officer. "And Sugimoto, I'm disappointed in you. I allowed you in the force despite your religious choices and until now, I was pleased with that decision."

Sugimoto lowered his head. "Please forgive me. I'll make sure it doesn't happen again."

Fujita eased his glare. "I still have high expectations for you, Lieutenant. Don't disappoint me again. Let's go."

Sugimoto gave a curt nod, his hand fidgeting with a set of beads half-stuffed in his pocket, and the three stalked away from the warehouse. Kotaro dragged the furthest behind with his head low.

After they were out of sight, Makoto crept back in the warehouse. He entered through the door and saw many of the boxes had been knocked over with their contents spilled out as a result of the Shinsengumi's wild attack. The boxes contained a variety of goods from ornate Western-style clothing to exotic spices. A few bottles of alcohol caught Makoto's eye, and he briefly wondered if they were destined for Sakénomi's or some other establishment.

Makoto had just about reached his bag when a different crate seized his attention; it had several rifles spilling out of it. He kneeled down and recognized the sleek design of the Sharps rifle. He often found himself at the unpleasant side of one during his bounty hunting days in America, but these rifles were pretty well worn and beat-up, probably used 1850s models from the Civil War.

Makoto was curious as to why a stockpile of American repeating rifles was hidden in a Yokohama warehouse but figured they were probably bound for the army. He briefly considered taking one for himself but dismissed the thought since finding cartridge ammunition for it would be exceptionally difficult. At least his revolver only needed gunpowder, metal balls, and percussion caps to work. Shaping lead pieces into bullets wouldn't be too difficult, and gunpowder was readily available in fireworks shops, but Makoto dreaded trying to find percussion caps. However, he needed to first assemble his gun before worrying about getting the materials to make it effective and deadly.

Makoto stood up and reclaimed his duffel from the corner where he had left it. As he surveyed the disorganized warehouse one last time for any clues that might tell him something about the Shinsengumi, he saw a folded piece of paper on the floor near the window where his assailant had crouched not too long ago. There was a slight smattering of blood on it. He hadn't noticed it before the Shinsengumi's attack, so Makoto snatched it up, hoping it might have fallen out of the masked man's coat. He unfolded it, and a small card fell out and fluttered to the floor. His eyes followed the card as it fell, but went back up to the paper. He was surprised to see it was a standard telegram form with the text written in English:

Mr. Watanabe,

The *Hiei* will soon be complete and will be heading to Yokohama. I will be joining the crew and we should arrive in two months' time. I will send telegrams to Tokyo with our expected arrival date from each stop. Telegraph me where you would like to meet.

Togo Heihachiro

Makoto vaguely recalled reading something about the *Hiei*, maybe in a newspaper, but it was the bloodstains on the paper that proved to be the most interesting part of the letter. Most of the stain was along one edge as if someone held it near a pool of blood. His mind trailed back to the dead old man in the inn and the large bloodstain on the floor. He didn't have any idea what it could all mean, but if this letter belonged to the Shinsengumi, it would probably be important. Perhaps this Togo Heihachiro was the very man he just fought.

He carefully folded the letter and slid it into his jacket. He readied to leave but recalled the card that had fallen out a few moments ago. He found it on the ground and picked it up. It was blank on one side and on the other was a single, red flower. Makoto thought it looked familiar and realized it was the same red flower on the tantō blade next to the dead man at the inn. Makoto could think of only one place where he might get information about the card with the red flower. He pocketed the telegram and the card, and after one last glance back, left the warehouse, unobserved.

***

Helen threw the door open to her room and tossed the remaining stump of her umbrella to the floor. "Really! The manners in this country are appalling! I've gotten better treatment when I played Katherina in *The Taming of the Shrew*!"

"Katherina? Ooh! Who's that?"

Helen nearly jumped out of her skin when she saw Aki standing in her room with another maid. Seeing it was only them in the room, Helen let out a relieved sigh. "Well, it's a role I played and … wait, what are you doing here, Aki?"

Aki held up a broom with a large grin on her face. "We're cleaning the room, ma'am! I thought you'd be coming back later. We're almost done. But we can leave now if you want."

"No. No. That's fine." Helen waved for the two to continue. "I need something to distract me from this horrid day."

Aki nodded and started sweeping again, though Helen noticed she seemed to be spreading dust around rather than actually sweeping it up. The other maid appeared to be more diligent, carefully polishing the wooden furniture. She and Aki wore matching long dresses, though she felt she'd seen the other maid before.

Helen stood up and took a few steps closer to the maid. "Wait a minute…" Helen studied the maid, looking her up and down. The maid paused and watched Helen quizzically.

"I've seen you before," Helen continued. "Earlier today … with that cowboy!" Helen took a few more steps forward, while the maid backed away.

Aki stopped her sweeping, stared at the two, and cocked her head. "You know Emiko, ma'am?"

"Emiko? Is that your name?" Helen asked. "What do you know about the cowboy? He was with you, right? You must tell me!"

Emiko stepped back as Helen moved forward until her back was against the wall. Both she and Helen looked toward Aki for assistance. However, by then Aki went to the front of the room, picked up Helen's umbrella stump, and was studying it. Emiko ducked down as Helen stepped closer, and the young woman scurried behind Aki. "Hey, wait a moment!" Helen called out.

When Aki continued to stare at the remains of the umbrella, Emiko gave her a light jab to the side. "Huh? Oh!" Aki turned her attention to Helen. "Sorry, ma'am. Emiko doesn't speak English."

"Then *you* ask her! What does she know about the cowboy?"

"What's a cowboy?"

"Well, it's, uh…" Helen didn't even want to try to explain since she knew Aki would have no idea what she was talking about. "Never mind! Ask her if she knows anything about the man she was with this morning!"

Aki cocked her head again, but turned and asked Emiko something in Japanese, which Helen couldn't understand. She couldn't understand Emiko's reply either.

"Sorry, ma'am," Aki said. "She doesn't know who you're talking about."

"Of course she does!" Helen said with a stomp of her foot, causing Emiko to duck back behind Aki. "That man in the black cowboy outfit! Ask her again!"

Aki did and again got the same response. "Sorry, ma'am."

"But … oh blast it, never mind!" Helen collapsed onto the couch near the fold-down desk and saw her book was perched there. She picked it up and started flipping through the pages. Aki and Emiko exchanged confused glances before continuing their work. Emiko cautiously approached and started wiping dust off of the desk. Helen held back a gasp when she saw Emiko cleaning the area near the scratched up lock she picked the previous night. "No! Stop cleaning!"

Emiko jumped back when Helen spoke, making Helen feel a little bad for frightening her. Aki paused her sweeping. "You don't want it cleaned, ma'am?"

"No, that is … uh…" Helen racked her mind for some sort of excuse. "M-My husband used the desk last night for business and he doesn't want anyone touching it until he's done."

"Oh … I see! No wiping the desk!" Aki replied, relaying the message to

Emiko, who bowed and moved on to cleaning a different part of the room.

Helen slumped back down in the couch and stared at her book cover, then placed it to the side with a sigh. "Speaking of John, has anyone at the hotel heard anything from my husband, Aki?"

"No ma'am!" Aki chirped.

"I see." Helen sighed again. "Blast it, where did he go?"

Aki, who was now more dancing with her broom rather than cleaning with it, stopped at Helen's rhetorical question. "The sir is missing, ma'am?"

Helen nodded. "He said something about 'business' and has been gone since last night! I can't be expected to just wait for him! It's so dull!"

Aki nodded. "Yes, ma'am!"

"Besides, where do men even go to do business in the middle of the night?" Helen grumbled.

"Hmmmm," Aki pondered, tapping on her broom. "Ooh! I know! I know! They go to the Miyazaki District! It's, uh, what do you call it in English? It's like Yoshiwara in Tokyo."

"Yoshiwara?" Helen vaguely recalled her husband mentioning the name, but she forgot the context. She racked her brain and recalled a mid-day rickshaw ride through Tokyo so John could meet some of his business associates, though his meeting was suddenly canceled when Home Minister Ōkubo was found dead.

On their way back to the hotel, John pointed out an area filled with red buildings and there were many women, their faces slathered in appalling amounts of white greasepaint makeup and bright red lips, waving from the balconies. John waved back at them but stopped when Helen jabbed him with her umbrella. The nature of the location dawned on Helen. "Yoshiwara!? But that's the red-light district!"

Helen sprang up from her lounge chair. Her frustration and fatigue were forgotten in her anger. "If he dared, I'd wring his neck! He ought to know better than to mess around with me. I've played Lady Macbeth *and* all three witches at the same time!"

"Ooh! Who's that?" Aki asked.

Helen was surprised to see Aki and Emiko still in the room. "It's ... never mind! Why are you still here?"

"To re-do your hair, ma'am! Aren't you preparing to go out?"

Helen took a quick glance in the mirror and saw her hairstyle was beginning to wilt from the heat and the day's activities. But she didn't want to waste another two hours just to get it fixed. "No, Aki I do not need you to re-do my hair, but I will be going out. I'm going to find my husband and give him a piece of my mind. Even if it means going to this Miyazaki District!" Helen stormed out of the room and slammed the door behind her, leaving Aki and Emiko looking at the door in confusion. Helen then opened the door a little and peeked in on the two. "Oh, and be dears and lock up when you're done, all right?"

Aki enthusiastically nodded and both she and Emiko bowed together.

"Good," Helen said as she slammed the door again. She stomped down the staircase, which led to the lobby and the rickshaws waiting outside. If John was engaging in a dalliance, he'd find out stepping out on his wife was a very bad idea. Medea, Tamora, and Lady Macbeth would be pale imitations of her fury.

Chapter Thirteen

Makoto lifted up the cloth entranceway to Sakénomi's and stepped inside. As he glanced around the bar, he noticed it was much emptier than the day before. Only a handful of foreign sailors were clustered around a couple of tables, speaking in languages Makoto didn't understand. The shambled remnants of the table Kotaro broke the previous day were piled in a corner on the floor. Tora was still standing in his usual place near the entrance and gave Makoto a suspicious look as he passed by.

Makoto ignored his gaze and went up to the bar. He noticed the large crack in the counter, also courtesy of Kotaro, was still there as well. Jean mindlessly spun one of the wooden masu boxes on its corner at the other end of the counter. It only managed one or two rotations before clattering down. When Jean saw Makoto, he stood upright and his bored expression shifted to a mix of curiosity and suspicion. "Not here to cause more trouble, right?" Jean looked around at the almost empty bar and rubbed his bare chin. "Then again, this place could use a bit of trouble. It'll be a couple of days before the next ship comes in. Ya here for a drink?"

"No. I need more information."

Jean shrugged and approached Makoto, though he made sure to keep a safe distance. "I already told you about the old innkeeper. She's more likely to know about the dirty dealings in town ... or is there some reason you can't ask her?" Jean raised an inquisitive eyebrow and crossed his arms, but Makoto remained silent. "And I suppose you don't know anything about poor ol' Watanabe showing up dead at her inn last night, do ya?" Jean asked in a more aggressive tone.

Makoto saw Tora slowly approaching from the corner of his eye. The last thing he needed right now was another fight. "I do."

"Huh?" Jean asked.

"I know something about this Watanabe person. I saw a body at the inn last night. That must've been him."

Jean blinked a few times and gave a puzzled look, clearly not expecting Makoto to be so blunt. "Oh, uh, I see. Did you kill him?"

"No."

"Got any proof you didn't?"

"No."

"So … any reason I should believe you?"

"No."

Jean snorted, then let out a full belly laugh. "Haha! When you're that blunt, it's hard not to believe you. So you're saying you had nothing to do with his death?"

"I only saw the aftermath."

Jean looked him in the eye for a few seconds, shook his head, and chuckled. "I have to say, if you're lying, you're very good at it. What's this information you're looking for?"

Makoto reached into his pocket and handed Jean the card with the red flower on it. "I want to know more about this symbol."

Jean held the card close and scrutinized the symbol. "This looks ... familiar. Hey! Tora!"

Jean motioned to the large sumo to come over. He walked to them at a brisk pace, his hands balled into fists and ready to attack. Just before he could pounce, Jean waved his hand. "No, no. You don't need to handle him, Tora. Not yet, anyway. I need you to look at this." Jean placed the card in Tora's massive hand. "You know this, right?"

Tora looked at the card and grew a bit pale. He took a couple of steps back and his eyes darted between Jean and Makoto, who were both staring at him with interest. He nervously shook his head. Jean crossed his arms and gave the sumo a stern stare. "Tora. You're a lousy liar. Where have you seen this?"

Tora's resolve to remain silent broke the moment Jean crossed his arms. He groaned a little as he stared at the card again. He spoke in a near-whisper that Makoto had to strain to hear, though Jean didn't seem to have any trouble understanding. "Yes. I've seen it. Back where I used to work."

"You mean that brothel in the Miyazaki District?"

Tora's face turned red with embarrassment, and he nodded. Jean chuckled a little and turned to Makoto, who was quietly waiting for some sort of explanation. Jean jerked his thumb toward the embarrassed Tora. "Miyazaki is Yokohama's red-light district. Tora here used to do sumo matches for the gamblers there. That is, 'till I bought out his contract." Jean gave Tora a jovial slap on the back. "Best decision I've made yet! Nobody makes trouble when Tora's here." Jean glanced down at the large crack in the counter and shrugged. "Well, at least most of the time."

Tora's humiliation from his previous place of work turned to a sheepish grin, and he rubbed the back of his neck. Jean took the card and handed it back to Makoto. "There you have it. Miyazaki is where you want to go. I remember the place now. The brothel you're looking for's got a green roof with a big warehouse in the back; I think this symbol is somewhere on the building. Oh, and I'd hang on to that card. If I recall the place is pretty exclusive, invitation only." Jean watched as Makoto pocketed the card. "But I can't help but wonder why you'd want to go to Miyazaki. I normally wouldn't ask, but that pretty girl you were walking with this morning seems like a much better choice than anyone you'd find in a brothel."

"I'm not interested in brothels. I'm searching for the Shinsengumi."

"Shinsengumi? Never heard of them."

Tora chipped in. "They were the shogun's elite guard. But they're all dead now."

"Oh?" Jean turned to Makoto. "Why'd you want to look for dead guys?"

Makoto's brow furrowed. Jean backed off and shrugged. "But if you don't want to say, I understand."

Makoto's glare eased. "They're not all dead."

"They're not?" Jean looked up at Tora. "That true?"

"I suppose there are a few left. Rumor has it Mr. Watanabe was found wearing one of their blue coats yesterday."

"That's right. Poor ol' Watanabe. I guess if he was one of these Shinsen-whatever guys, you're on the right track. But you'd better hurry to find them before even more end up like Watanabe."

Makoto nodded. He reached into his pocket, pulled out a couple of coins, and placed them on the counter. "Thanks for the information."

Jean smiled and scooped the coins into his hand. Makoto turned to leave and was almost at the exit when he heard Jean call out, "Oh! And feel free to raise hell there. Those dirty brothel bars are always trying to steal my customers!"

***

Kotaro frantically paced about the almost-dark evidence room, the single oil lamp desperately needing to be refilled. But he was far more worried about his own problems than the weakening flame. He knew with each moment that passed, the lower his chances of retrieving the fan and the tantō. And the higher the chance that Captain Fujita would send him to Abashiri, or run him through with his katana. He wasn't sure which was worse.

Every few seconds, Kotaro glanced toward the door and contemplated making a run for it to try and find the missing evidence. If he could just find it then everything would be cleared up and his duties would be restored to more than just guarding the evidence room. However, he dared not cross Captain Fujita in his current mood. For all Kotaro knew, even if he was successful in getting back the evidence, the captain might ship him to Hokkaido just for disobeying orders. But he knew he had to find that evidence before it was too late.

The hefty door to the evidence room opened, interrupting Kotaro's sulking, and Sugimoto stepped inside, letting the door slam shut behind him. Kotaro immediately perked up when he saw him. "Ah! Lieutenant Sugimoto! How's uh, the captain?"

Sugimoto sighed, pulled out his string of beads, and started fidgeting with them, clacking individual beads together. "He wasn't pleased to hear that some evidence has gone missing. Though when I told him the evidence was for an older case, he calmed down a bit." Sugimoto shifted his beads from one hand to the other. "For both of our sakes, I decided to be vague about which case the evidence was from."

"So, he doesn't know the fan is from the home minister case?"

"No. And it's best we keep it that way."

"But sir, what about the tantō? That was from yesterday!"

"That is a problem. But Captain Fujita will be busy with preparations for the arrival of the *Hiei* for the next couple of days, which should give you the time you need to find the missing evidence, especially with the emperor being scheduled to attend."

"Uh, me sir?" Kotaro asked. "But Captain Fujita said-"

"I know what he said, patrolman!" Sugimoto flinched and turned away, madly fidgeting with his beads. "However, unless you and I want one-way tickets to Abashiri, we have to get the evidence back. The captain will be expecting me to help with security for the *Hiei*, but he's expecting *you* to remain here."

Kotaro slowly nodded. "Yes. Yes, I understand sir! You can count on me to find the evidence. And then I'll find the man in black and bring him to justice!"

"Just focus on the evidence patrolman. That is your mission. Don't waste your time getting distracted by men in black … or bars. Understand?"

"Yes, sir! But what about the captain? If he finds out-"

"I'll make certain the captain doesn't know about your absence, but you had best hurry. Time is short." Sugimoto gestured toward the door.

Kotaro took a step forward but paused as he glanced at Sugimoto's beads. "Sir?"

"What is it? You're wasting time."

"Why do you carry around those beads? Doesn't it cause you trouble?"

Sugimoto jolted and shoved the beads into his pocket. "That is none of your concern, patrolman."

"But isn't being a Buddhist difficult nowadays?"

Sugimoto glared. "As I said before, that is none of your concern. You should focus on finding the evidence. Now."

Kotaro nervously nodded and headed for the door, but before he reached it, Sugimoto spoke. "Let me give you one final piece of advice patrolman, if you can't find the evidence, it would be in your best interest to not return, ever. Do you understand?"

Kotaro swallowed the lump in his throat and gave a solemn nod. Sugimoto nodded in return and opened the door. Kotaro bounded up the stairs, snuck around the lobby to avoid catching the attention of any other policemen, and crept out his favorite side door. Once outside and after shielding his eyes from the setting sun, he sprinted back to Sakénomi's bar, praying to every spirit he knew that his evidence was still there.

Chapter Fourteen

Even though the sun had not quite set, the Miyazaki District was teeming with life. Women in colorful, flashy kimonos with large, ornate hairstyles giggled and waved from balconies as men of various social statures wandered around. Most of the buildings were two to three stories tall, built in the traditional style, and adorned in bright red, paper lanterns which were supposed to be festive, but gave an almost ominous glow to the area. At least that's how it appeared to Helen as she marched through the dirt roads, earning the stares of both the patrons and courtesans. A rickshaw man had been willing to take her to the edge of the district but for some reason had refused to go inside. She didn't understand his ramblings, though she did hear him mutter the word *yakuza* many times, whatever that meant.

She glanced around the various buildings, searching for any sign of her husband, but these rows of buildings were so long and varied that she had no idea where to even start. She grumbled under her breath and cast an angry glare at a group of onlookers who were gawking at her. They looked away and scattered immediately. She supposed she was a bit of an odd sight in the area; especially since almost everyone was Japanese, save for the occasional European sailor. But even if she was the only American woman in the vicinity, that was no excuse to be rude or to stare. She shook her head and continued marching forward, steadily growing more frustrated at everyone around her, from the young courtesans that flaunted their charms about to the foolish men who made this industry possible.

However, no matter how far she walked, the district just seemed to go on endlessly with brothels and bars. If she had a rickshaw, at least the rickshaw man could do the running, but it seemed none were present in the area. Instinctively, she reached for her purse to check for her remaining coins but gasped when all she grabbed was air. She frantically looked around for any sign of her purse. For all she knew, the purse could have been missing for hours and she would have never noticed. Panic displaced her frustration and she began retracing her steps. She heard a squeaky-sounding man cry out, and she turned around to find the source of the sound. She had to silence a gasp at the sight.

In an alley, the cowboy she somehow kept running into was holding up a thin, balding man by the collar of his shirt, a straw hat on the ground next to him. And in the man's hand, Helen saw her purple purse. But the cowboy didn't seem to be interested in that and was exchanging words with the pickpocket in a language she didn't understand.

Makoto noticed that pesky American woman from the corner of his eye but kept his attention on the pickpocket he was interrogating, who through some strange coincidence of fate happened to be the very same one in the straw hat and geta sandals who tried to make off with his bag yesterday.

"You've got some nerve," Makoto hissed.

"I wasn't doin' nothin'!" the thief squeaked.

Makoto grabbed the man's hand and yanked out a card, the card with the red flower. He flicked the card so the thief could clearly see the symbol. "I don't take kindly to thieves. Or liars. You know which brothel this card is for, right?" Makoto tightened his grip on the man's collar and raised him high enough for the pickpocket's feet to dangle.

The pickpocket squeaked in shock and fear. "I don't know! Honest!"

Makoto raised him higher and the pickpocket started flailing wildly. Makoto showed him the card again. "I won't ask twice."

"Okay! Okay! It's for the tallest brothel! Just down the street. The one with the green roof!"

"What do you know about it? The brothel."

"J-Just that it's exclusive and you need one of 'dem cards to get in. And … uh, rumor has it, there's some dirty dealings going on there."

"What kind of dealings?"

"I-I don't know, I was just hoping to pinch somethin' valuable. That's all I know, I swear!"

Makoto frowned. It didn't seem like the thief knew anything of particular interest. He dropped him. The thief thudded onto the ground and scrambled upright. He was about to scurry off when Makoto grabbed the back of his coat. The pickpocket looked at him with fear in his eyes as Makoto held out his hand.

"The purse. Purple isn't your color. And I doubt it's yours."

The pickpocket chuckled nervously and handed the purse to Makoto, who let go of his collar. The thief dashed off into the shadows. Makoto stepped out of the alleyway, searching for the American woman. Just from the garish shade of purple, he knew it belonged to her. He caught sight of her ducking behind a cart and attempting to hide from him.

He shook his head and approached her. She backed away until she hit the wall of a nearby brothel and her expression grew more anxious as Makoto approached. "I-I wasn't spying on you! I was just … uh…" she stammered, trying to come up with an excuse.

Makoto shoved the purse into her hands. "This place is dangerous. You should leave," he said in English.

"So you do speak English! I knew it!" Helen said triumphantly. "Why didn't you stop when I asked you before- oh, never mind that. I can't leave until I find my no-good husband. I have reason to believe he may be around here. And-" However, before she could continue, Makoto turned around and started walking into the crowd, his attention focused on finding the brothel with the green roof.

"Hmmph! Rude man," Helen muttered as she caught sight of the back of Makoto's coat when he walked away. He hadn't even given her a chance to thank him. Deciding she had no other leads, she tightened the grip on her purse and trotted after Makoto.

***

Kotaro kicked a rock down the street with dejection. Despite his best efforts to search and interrogate, he couldn't find either the tantō or the fan near Sakénomi's. He retraced his steps over and over again until the sun began to set, but it was all for naught. Lieutenant Sugimoto's warning rang in his ears as he dragged through the street. If he couldn't return to the station, his career as a policeman was effectively over. At this rate, he would have to return to Osaka and face the wrath of his father and brothers, and for the first time, Abashiri sounded like the less worse option. Either way, there was no way he could go back to the station tonight. He stopped wandering aimlessly when he noticed a warm, red glow. He looked up and realized he had wandered just outside the Miyazaki District. Some exceptionally beautiful courtesans waved at him from one of the upper balconies. He gave a half-hearted chuckle. If he was to be sent to Abashiri, back to Osaka, or even if he was to be run through by Captain Fujita's katana, that could wait for tomorrow.

Granted, the pretty women and the free-flowing alcohol would not help alleviate any of his problems, but at least they could help him forget about them for the night. He gave his face a little slap, pulled out his recently filled flask, and downed the contents in a single gulp. Within moments, his face was just as red as the lanterns. "Watch out, ladies! The great and powerful Yamada Kotaro is here to have a good time!" He sauntered off further into the red-light district.

***

The summer sun set rapidly and soon the glow of paper lanterns, windows, and gas street lamps brightened the Miyazaki District in a various array of flashy colors, though red dominated all the others. Makoto found the green-roofed building, though it was difficult to know for certain since the lanterns gave everything a red tint. The brothel was wider than most of the others and had double the number of lanterns. He noticed a large, multi-story warehouse behind the brothel.

Makoto glanced along the exterior walls, hoping to catch sight of the red flower to make sure he was at the right place, but even with the extra lanterns, the dark wood hid any traces of the symbol. As he scanned the walls, Makoto noticed a middle-aged woman sitting at the main entrance. She was dressed in a black kimono covered with bright pink flowers, the kind that would be suitable for the wife of a crime lord. A group of men approached her and showed her a card. She looked it over, nodded, and pulled back the cloth covering the entrance, beckoning them inside.

Makoto approached her, keeping his hat low to avoid eye contact. She frowned at the sight of him. "Foreigners aren't allowed. Do you understand?"

Makoto did not reply, but pulled out the card with the red flower and showed it to the woman. Her eyes grew wide, and she gave it a second looking over. Eventually, she relented and pulled back the cloth, gesturing for Makoto to enter. "The meeting's in the back. You best hurry before you're late."

Makoto nodded, not having any clue what she meant, and stepped inside. The smoky scent of tobacco assailed Makoto's nostrils as he entered the room. Through the haze, he saw several women dressed in kimonos of various shades of red and black. The hair of the courtesans was pinned up in large, ornate styles with clips jutting out in all directions. Their faces were caked with white makeup, their lips were painted a brilliant red, and their eyebrows were invisible, but smoky blotches had been painted just above where the eyebrows should have been. Makoto felt a visceral dislike for the makeup; it made the women seem inhuman, more like porcelain dolls. He hadn't much cared for the garish face paint of the prostitutes and dance hall girls of the American West, but they had at least seemed to be people.

Several Japanese men of various ages leered lustfully at the women, making their selections. They clearly appreciated the aesthetic, even if Makoto did not. When the patrons made their decision, they approached one of the many heavily tattooed bouncers, each of whom looked like they could take on the sumo from Sakénomi's, and sauntered off with their choice to another part of the brothel. Makoto scanned the room for any sign of the Shinsengumi, or the meeting the woman at the entrance mentioned.

As he glanced about, one of the heavily made-up women approached him and smiled. "So ... What're you looking for, Mr. Black?" she asked seductively.

Makoto ignored her and continued searching for any trace of the Shinsengumi. The room was adorned with all manner of cushions, pottery, and erotic prints, which Makoto guessed were meant to teach just as much as to arouse. While some women wandered among the patrons, most were smiling from a distinct, "viewing area," which was blocked off with a short, wood railing.

Toward the back of the room, Makoto noticed a couple of doors guarded by two heavily muscled men dressed in dark robes, who directed any wanderers away. He walked toward them, leaving behind the prostitute, who scoffed and approached a different, much more enthusiastic man. As Makoto approached, the bouncers' eyes glanced toward Makoto, the wooden door between them, each other, and back to Makoto. They took a step together to block the door, which Makoto guessed was the way he should go to get to the meeting. Makoto pulled out the card and showed it to the men. They both leaned in at the same time and analyzed the card for an uncomfortably long time. Makoto kept his hat low and the two bouncers shifted their eyes up to him in sync. One asked, "You here for the trade?"

"Trade?"

"If you ain't here for the trade, you ain't allowed in the warehouse. Card or no card, we don't let foreigners in."

Makoto raised his head, the dim light revealing his Japanese features. "I am not a foreigner."

One of the men scoffed. "You'se dressed like one though. You some kind of foreign-lover?"

Makoto didn't respond, though his hand instinctively shifted to his duffel, which contained his sword.

"Hey! You were asked a question!" the other bouncer said, jabbing his finger at Makoto.

Makoto still didn't reply. The two bouncers sneered and cracked their knuckles in unison. "We don't take kindly to troublemakers," one bouncer started, "and we're going to show you how we deal with them," the other finished. They both lunged forward, fists poised, and ready to strike.

Chapter Fifteen

Helen had immense trouble keeping up with the cowboy through the bustling crowds of the red-light district. As dusk turned to night, the crowds steadily got thicker, putting even the crowd at the harbor in the morning to shame. She wished she had her umbrella to push away the obnoxious men who got in her way and also wished she had it to give a solid whack to the even more obnoxious men who stared in her direction. She shoved her way through a particularly slow group when she saw the cowboy enter a building with a green roof.

She looked over the building, and other than the excessive number of lanterns, it seemed to be just like any other. A woman in a black kimono sat next to the only entrance she could see along the street. The woman gave Helen a dark stare when she approached. She also barked something in Japanese that Helen couldn't understand.

"Do you speak English?" Helen asked.

The woman's frown deepened, which was enough of a "no" for Helen. The acrid stench of tobacco that wafted through the entrance and the upbeat chatter of drunk men signaled to Helen this was not the kind of place she wanted to be near, and it certainly was not the kind of low-class establishment her husband would associate with, even if he was somewhere in the district.

She sighed with annoyance and turned away from the building. It looked like following the cowboy was a dead end after all. However, after stepping a couple of hundred feet away, she heard a familiar boisterous voice: her husband's voice. She spun around just in time to see him standing next to a mousy Japanese man in a suit. The man was showing the woman at the front something. She nodded and pulled back the cloth at the entrance to let them inside.

Helen tried to call out to her husband, but the words just couldn't come out in her anger. She stomped back to the brothel, but before she could enter, the woman stood up and blocked the entrance, speaking rapidly in words Helen couldn't understand and in a tone of voice Helen did not find pleasant.

"Get out of my way! My husband went in there. To think I was actually worried about him. I'll drag him out here and kill him myself!"

The woman's expression shifted from stern anger to confusion for a moment; she clearly wasn't used to being shouted at, but her expression hardened again and she remained steadfast. Helen wished more than ever that lousy police officer hadn't destroyed her umbrella, since she could think of nothing better than whacking this woman and then smacking her husband senseless. Helen briefly considered hitting the woman with her purse but knew that probably wouldn't do her much good.

Before Helen had a chance to do anything, the woman's eyes grew wide, and she took a nervous step back. It was now Helen's turn to be confused. She turned around and was shocked to see the fat policeman her rickshaw man had run into earlier. The policeman was unsteadily wobbling around like a drunkard and his face was beet red.

Kotaro staggered forward, having had a few too many drinks and looked up at the green-roofed brothel with blurred vision. He remembered hearing warnings about the place from other police officers and to steer clear of it. However, in Kotaro's intoxicated mind, that was all the more reason to try and get inside.

Kotaro wobbled up to the woman in the dark kimono, who nervously took another step back as Kotaro neared, though she continued to block the entrance. The foreign woman in the purple dress also stepped back as Kotaro walked by. "Lemme in! I'm a member of the police!"

"This establishment is invitation only. And we don't give invitations to police," the woman said in a dark tone of voice.

"The ggggreat and p-p-powerful Yamada Kotaro doesn't need no invitation! I ought to arrest you and…"

Kotaro's slurs were interrupted by shouts and screams coming from inside the brothel. A small stampede of men and women streamed out the door, knocking the woman in the black kimono over and nearly trampling Kotaro. He was just able to lurch out of the way and land face first in the dirt, safe from the fleeing mob. As he stood up and brushed off the dirt, slightly more sober from the pain, he noticed the entrance was no longer guarded.

***

As the men charged toward Makoto, he braced himself and leaned low as they were about to strike. As the first one threw his punch, Makoto stepped to the side, grabbed the man's arm, redirected his charge, and slammed his face into one of the pillars, which cracked and splintered.

The other man froze at this sudden show of fighting prowess, but shook off his fear and continued to charge. Makoto, whose hand was still pushing the first one's head into the pillar, pulled him back and whipped the stunned man around like a rag doll so that he collided with his charging friend. The two collapsed in a heap on the floor, causing a hush to fall over the brothel.

Seven gangsters swarmed around Makoto, each with their own over-the-top, ornate tattoos. They all pulled out short swords in unison and glared at Makoto, who briefly wondered if these gangsters practiced in advance in order to get the timing right.

The sight of the blades caused panic and pandemonium from the prostitutes and the patrons, who all clamored for any exit they could find. In a few short moments, the brothel was completely empty save for Makoto and the gangsters.

Makoto swung his duffel from his back to the front, reached inside, and in a single motion, drew his now-complete sword from the bag. Its polished steel shone brightly in the dim room, the flickering lamplight further emphasizing how menacing his blade was compared to the short knives and swords of his attackers. Makoto dropped his duffel and readied the sword in an offensive position.

The gangsters exchanged nervous glances. They all turned to the leader of the group, a hefty man with large dragon tattoos all over his arms and chest. He also appeared hesitant to attack an armed opponent, but once he noticed the stares of his underlings, he gritted his teeth and readied his sword. Makoto pointed his katana toward the leader. "Where is the Shinsengumi?"

The leader's face shifted to one of confusion, as did the underlings. Makoto frowned. They genuinely didn't seem to know what he was talking about, which didn't bode well for him finding any Shinsengumi here. However, his thoughts were interrupted when he heard a female voice shout in English, "You! You accursed cowboy! I should have known you were colluding with him." Makoto glanced at the entrance and saw the American woman that somehow kept following him around and making his life difficult.

Helen Arkwright, who had just stepped into the brothel and waved away some of the tobacco smoke, pointed an accusatory finger at Makoto. "Where is my husband?"

Makoto could only reply with the blank, confused stare the gangsters had given him just a few moments ago. And on cue, to complete this three-ring circus, the red-faced patrolman, Yamada Kotaro, waddled into the brothel. He coughed at the sudden influx of smoke and looked around. His face dropped when all he saw was Makoto, the foreign woman, and the tattooed men with knives. "Where are the girls?"

The gangsters balked at the sight of Kotaro's dark blue police uniform. "It's a cop! Get 'em!" Half of the group split off and charged toward Kotaro and Helen while the other half focused their attention on Makoto.

However, these men were surprised to see Makoto was no longer standing in front of them. Instead, he dashed to the side and bounded forward, putting himself between the charging men and Helen and Kotaro, readying his sword in a defensive position. He may not have particularly liked the two he was protecting, but he couldn't allow a woman and an incapacitated policeman to get killed by thugs, even if they were an incessant bother.

Helen blinked in confusion at the sudden charge and at the cowboy stepping in front of her. When it finally hit that her life was in real peril, she staggered back. She glanced at the entrance to see if she could make a quick exit, but two burly men blocked any chance of escape.

Helen's eyes darted all over, looking for some sort of weapon to use. She reached down, grabbed a cushion, and swung it behind her shoulder to ready an attack, but in the process, accidentally knocked Kotaro upside the head, causing the inebriated policeman to stagger back and fall onto the floor. Helen flinched at her mistake and mouthed a silent apology, but her attention quickly returned to the menacing men at the door.

The first attacker who reached Makoto sported a large fish tattoo. He lunged forward with his short sword pointed directly at Makoto's chest, but Makoto brought down his sword on the man's blade, easily knocking it out of his hand. As the fish man looked up helplessly, Makoto used his free hand to punch him in the face.

The fish man teetered back and fell down, but two more took his place. They both attacked at once, but Makoto maneuvered himself to just dodge their attacks and cause them to collide into each other. The four remaining men at the front and the two in the back paused and stared in shock at Makoto's fighting skills. A gangster with tiger tattoos blocking the entrance decided to go the safer route and charged from behind, hoping to catch Makoto off guard.

"Behind you, cowboy!" Helen called out as she swung her pillow at the tiger man. It bounced off him harmlessly, but the warning gave Makoto enough time to spin around, grab the attacker's arm, and fling him downward. Caught off balance, the tiger man's head slammed into the reed mat floor, knocking him out instantly.

The dragon-tattooed leader cursed and directed the four remaining underlings toward Makoto. "Attack him all at once!"

The four gangsters obliged, three from the front and the one from the back. Makoto readied his sword. He slammed the handle of his sword into the face of the man attacking from the back. He heard the distinct *crack* of the man's nose break, and the gangster went down in a shriek, clutching his bloodied nose.

Reversing his momentum, Makoto plunged his sword forward, piercing one of the attacking men in the arm. Makoto twisted and pulled out his sword, and a splatter of blood burst from the man's arm. The gangster let out a wail of pain and clutched his wound, collapsing to his knees.

The last two led their attack with their short swords. Makoto held his sword in a horizontal defensive position and the three blades clashed. Not giving the men a chance to counterattack, Makoto stomped into one of the men's knees and slammed his fist into the other one's stomach. The first reeled back while the second collapsed. Makoto took advantage of the remaining man's discombobulation to get in a punch to the gut, causing the last underling to slump to the floor as well.

The dragon-tattooed leader, who had held back and hoped his underlings would take care of Makoto, let out a string of curses as he brandished his mid-sized *wakizashi* and rushed Makoto. Their blades clashed, and Makoto caught sight of a chip on the cutting edge of the short sword. The brittle blade was definitely much weaker than Makoto's steel sword. Makoto reared back his sword and swung at the leader, who held up his own weapon in defense. However, Makoto aimed for the chip in the edge, and with a strong swing, sliced through the blade, which snapped with a sharp *clang*, cutting the short sword in two.

Half of the thug's short sword fell harmlessly to the floor with a clatter. The leader gasped at the remaining stump. He took a few steps back, nearly stumbling over the cushions on the floor. Makoto readied his sword again, but instead of attacking, the leader fled toward the back, leaping over his unconscious underlings. When he reached the back wall, the dragon-tattooed leader heaved open the wooden door and bolted inside. Makoto gave chase, grabbing his duffel along the way.

Helen, realizing she was getting left behind again, ran after Makoto. "Wait! What about my no-good husband?"

Kotaro grumbled as he sat upright, slightly more sober from the pillow whack. However, sense returned to him far faster when he saw the string of gangsters lying all around the brothel. He stood up and caught sight of the man in black forcing open a door and running inside, with the foreign woman right behind him.

"What the … Wait! Man in black! Halt!" Kotaro lumbered after them. By the time he reached the back, the door slammed shut in his face. Kotaro strained to pull open the heavy door, but once he did, he saw it led into a dark series of hallways covered with wooden planks and were dimly lit by the occasional, hanging paper lantern. Swallowing the lump in his throat, Kotaro ran into the dark hallway and let the door slam behind him.

Chapter Sixteen

Makoto dashed behind the dragon-tattooed leader. The hallway was dark and the air was cool. Makoto guessed this passageway led to the warehouse behind the brothel. Thanks to the occasional paper lantern, the leader was in his sights, and despite being weighed down by his bag and sword, Makoto's longer stride gave him the advantage he needed to catch up. As he approached the retreating leader, Makoto made a surge forward, grabbed the leader's collar, yanked him back, and slammed him against the wall, hovering his sword near the leader's neck. "Where is the Shinsengumi?"

The leader, unconscious, slumped his head forward. Makoto cursed and lowered his sword. He must have hit him too hard against the wall. Makoto released the leader's collar, and he crumpled to the ground.

Makoto contemplated going back to the brothel, but the leader was trying to get somewhere. And that somewhere might give Makoto a lead in his hunt for the Shinsengumi, so he continued on. As he walked deeper into the hallway at a significantly slower pace, Makoto saw the hallways split off into several different directions. As he was deciding which hallway to take, he noticed a small passageway in one of the walls that was just large enough for him to crawl through. As he heard the sound of approaching footsteps, Makoto decided this would be his best route to avoid being caught, got on his knees, and crawled in.

The hidden corridor was completely dark and the rough wood tugged against Makoto's duster. Makoto kept his pace slow to give his eyes a chance to adjust to the darkness. His ears told him there were other people in the warehouse. And it wasn't just the sound of a few voices, but the murmurings of a mid-sized crowd. A dim light ahead told him the passage was nearing an end.

From the light streaming into the corridor, Makoto was able to discern the passage led to some sort of gathering area. The murmurs grew louder, but Makoto couldn't see anyone due to large stacks of wooden barrels at the end of the passage. Makoto dared not move and peered through a thin gap between the containers.

He couldn't see very much, but he could make out some of the crowd in the light of the dim paper lanterns. There were at least twenty men, possibly more toward the back. They all wore masks. A few wore old samurai masks without the helmet, while most wore masks representing various mythological creatures from Noh plays, from the white *kitsune* fox to the large-nosed, red *tengu.* Nobody in the crowd wore the blue Shinsengumi coat Makoto was hoping to see.

The sound of a man clapping his hands quieted the crowd and drew their attention to the front. Makoto was not able to get a clear view of the makeshift stage the audience was looking at. He leaned a little further out so that his head was nearly out of the corridor, but he was careful to not upset the precariously balanced barrels.

Fortunately for Makoto, the man clapping his hands stepped forward into view. Makoto could only see him from behind, but the bright blue Shinsengumi coat was all he needed to see. He never imagined he'd get a chance to redeem himself so soon. He secured the duffel on his back and readied his sword, waiting for the opportune moment to strike.

The Shinsengumi took a step back, while another man in a dark red coat and a fox mask stepped to the center and addressed the crowd in an icy voice. "I'll keep this short. You all have your orders. We will be ready when the *Hiei* arrives tomorrow. Those foreigners will rue the day they dared to encroach on our sacred land when we use their weapons against them! Am I understood?"

The crowd chimed in unison. "Yes, sir! Revere the Emperor; expel the barbarians!"

"That being said," the man with the fox mask turned to the Shinsengumi, "I've heard news that you let a foreigner see you. And worse, you let him escape with his life. Certain parties have called your loyalties into question."

"Who would dare!?" The Shinsengumi's hand clutched the sheathed katana by his side, causing the room to go silent. After a brief pause, the Shinsengumi let go of his sword, gave a dark chuckle, and tugged on his blue coat. "I may have only been here a short time, but *this* ought to prove my allegiance. My brothers-in-arms fell because those filthy foreigners turned the government against us. Now we will take our country back with the very weapons they used to strike us down!" The Shinsengumi gestured toward the wooden barrels which hid Makoto.

Makoto froze. He didn't even breathe for the short eternity the masked crowd stared at the barrels.

"It is only because you are Shinsengumi that your head remains on your shoulders," the man in the fox mask replied, returning the crowd's attention to the front. "However, I am in charge of the *Hiei* mission, and you will no longer be a part of it. You can return to the leaders in Kyoto and tell them that's my final decision."

"What!?" The Shinsengumi tightened his fists and looked ready to attack but backed down and made a bow. "Very well. It is your mission after all, and I am just here to assist. Though I cannot be blamed for the aftermath."

"I'll worry about my mission. You worry about yours." The man in the fox mask turned to the crowd and raised his fist. "Revere the Emperor; expel the barbarians!"

The crowd repeated the chant several times. Taking advantage of their distraction, Makoto took a moment to study the barrels. It didn't take long for him to recognize the crudely painted kanji symbols: gunpowder. Makoto shifted back a little from the barrels, now having another reason he didn't want to knock them over. He remained close enough to see through the gap between them.

Makoto's thoughts were interrupted when the gangster with the fish tattoo ran into the room. He panted and clutched the bloody wound on his face. "Outsiders! In the warehouse. There's a policeman!"

Murmurs of panic overwhelmed the crowd and several stood up, hands on their swords. Makoto cursed himself for not punching the fish man harder. Now everyone there would be on high alert and sneaking up on the Shinsengumi would be next to impossible. The mutterings grew silent as the group turned to the stage. Makoto guessed the man in the fox mask must have silenced them. "It seems the perfect opportunity has arisen for you to redeem your honor. You know what must be done."

The Shinsengumi hesitated for a moment before giving a deep bow. He drew his sword and headed for the large, open entrance to the room, which Makoto hadn't noticed in the darkness. Makoto resisted the urge to chase after him and kept still. The Shinsengumi paused at the entrance. All eyes were on him, but rather than leaving the room, he took a few steps to the side and held his sword at the ready. Makoto looked on, confused as to what he was doing. The crowd was silent.

The sound of running footsteps and ragged breath started faint but grew louder as the runner came closer. Makoto strained his eyes and caught a glimpse of the runner; it was the fat policeman, Kotaro, his blue uniform a dead giveaway even in the dim light. The Shinsengumi raised his sword over his head.

As much as Makoto hated losing the element of surprise, he couldn't let the Shinsengumi have his way. He surged forward and shoved one of the stacks of barrels in front of him, before ducking down to the floor behind the remaining casks. The stack of gunpowder containers wobbled for a moment before several barrels crashed to the floor, spilling gunpowder everywhere. This sudden sound got the attention of everyone in the room, who all whipped their heads in Makoto's direction. He lay against the floor, hoping to salvage whatever he could of the advantage he just squandered.

The distraction served its purpose, the Shinsengumi lowered his sword, and the sound caused Kotaro to slow his run to a trot. He walked into the room, huffing and puffing. But when he saw the small army of men in masks, he leaped back, yanked out his baton, and pointed it around wildly. "What's going on here? I demand you tell me, the great and powerful-oof!"

The Shinsengumi kicked one of Kotaro's legs before he could finish, causing him to topple over. He pointed his sword at Kotaro. "You fool." The Shinsengumi raised his sword over his head, ready to strike.

With no more tricks up his sleeve, Makoto clenched his teeth, readied his sword, and charged at the Shinsengumi, knowing full well it wasn't in his best interest. He dashed through the bewildered crowd of masked men who didn't have time to react. However, the Shinsengumi did.

The Shinsengumi raised his sword just in time to clash with Makoto's blade. The two swords interlocked. Now face-to-face, Makoto saw this Shinsengumi wore the same red demon *oni* mask as the man in the harbor, down to the same crack. After a brief stalemate, the Shinsengumi pushed back and forced Makoto away. The Shinsengumi readied into a fighting stance, and Makoto did the same. The other masked men drew their swords. Makoto slowed his breathing to avoid panicking, but he knew he couldn't defeat thirty men. Not all at once, and not without his gun.

"Wait." All eyes turned to the man standing in the front with the fox mask. Makoto gave him a quick glance. His red robes were simple, but his posture suggested he was a commander, a surprisingly young one. The man pointed to the Shinsengumi. "Let him prove himself worthy to be among us."

The other masked men backed away, giving Makoto and the Shinsengumi room to fight. Kotaro nervously crawled back as Makoto and the Shinsengumi circled each other. Makoto's heartbeat quickened. Even if it meant certain death, he finally had a chance to avenge his family.

Makoto made the first move. He lunged at the Shinsengumi, their swords connecting again, but the masked man was prepared and had no trouble leading Makoto's blade in a counterattack. The Shinsengumi swung his sword, but Makoto took a few steps back to avoid the strike.

The Shinsengumi took advantage of his retreat and went on the offensive, swinging strongly and powerfully. Makoto was able to block most of the attacks but had to dodge a few others, and he struggled to keep up. The crowd murmured in approval.

Makoto decided his best chance would be to take advantage of the superior steel in his sword and try to break the brittle steel of the Shinsengumi's katana, like he had done to the dragon-tattooed leader's short sword in the brothel. If he could hold out, he could cause the Shinsengumi's blade to nick and crack, making it more susceptible to breaking. However, the Shinsengumi was a much better swordsman than anyone in the brothel, possibly better than anyone Makoto had ever faced.

He attacked Makoto with a series of quick stabs, and Makoto couldn't find an opening to wear the Shinsengumi's blade down. When Makoto attempted to block the blows with his sword, the Shinsengumi quickly switched positions and went for a low attack, aiming straight for Makoto's leg. Makoto was able to shift away fast enough to avoid a serious wound, but the sharp edge sliced into his skin and left a nasty cut to his calf. The sudden pain from the wound distracted Makoto long enough for the Shinsengumi to go for an upward attack. Makoto's sword was knocked from his hand, and it clattered to the ground.

Makoto attempted to dive for his sword, but the Shinsengumi put his own sword in the way, the sharp edge aimed at Makoto's face. This forced Makoto to stop mid-charge, which threw him off balance. The

Shinsengumi kicked Makoto's chest, causing him to fall back and land on the ground.

The Shinsengumi pointed his sword toward Makoto to the enthusiastic cheers of the crowd. After a second of catching his breath, the Shinsengumi grabbed his sword with both hands and raised it above his head. "You lose."

Chapter Seventeen

Helen Arkwright would never admit it out loud, but she was thoroughly lost in the hallways. Charging in after the cowboy might not have been such a good idea after all. The corridors spread out in several different directions and were far more complex than she imagined. It also didn't help that the pathway was nearly pitch black, save for the occasional paper lantern.

Sliding her hand against the wooden wall, she stepped forward slowly and carefully. Her heeled shoes nearly caused her to trip a couple of times on the rough floors. As she pushed onward, the number of lanterns steadily decreased, forcing her to strain her eyes. She rubbed her eyes and looked to one of the few remaining paper lanterns hanging just above her head.

On tiptoe, she reached up and unhooked the lantern. Holding it in front of her, the lantern provided much better light, though not enough to give her a clear idea of where she was or where she should go, but that didn't deter her as she proceeded deeper into the warehouse.

After taking a few more steps, her foot caught on something which nearly caused her to fall over. After stumbling a few steps, she regained her balance and held the lantern down to see what tripped her. The light revealed the culprit to be an American-made rifle.

It looked like one of the slew of rifles her husband showed off to her during one of his self-aggrandizing speeches about how his donation of weapons was what *really* secured victory for the Union during the Civil War; though she doubted his weapons were as influential as he claimed. Her thoughts shifted to him in the arms of some pretty, young Japanese courtesan, and she boiled over with rage. She gave the rifle a solid kick and sent it skidding across the floor.

The sound of a gruff voice in Japanese startled her, causing her to drop the paper lantern, which bounced against the ground and rolled out of reach. She turned around and held back a gasp when she saw a brawny-looking Japanese man with several dragon tattoos covering his body. A couple of streams of blood ran down his face, and his deathly glare made Helen instinctively step back. "Um, I'm lost. Do you speak English?" Helen asked, slowly enunciating each word.

The tattooed man didn't reply, but his glare darkened, and he took a few menacing steps toward Helen. She took the same number of steps back and cursed herself for kicking away the rifle. Granted, she had no idea how to use it, but the sight of it may have deterred the man from approaching.

However, the tattooed man suddenly stopped, and his eyes grew wide. Helen tilted her head, and she glanced around for what he was staring at until the growing light behind her caught her eye. She turned around and leaped back when she saw the paper lantern she dropped was completely engulfed in flames. Bits of the flickering fire spread to a stack of nearby rifles and their straw packing, which burned quickly and spread the growing fire. In the better light, Helen croaked out a gasp when she saw the fire steadily approaching several wooden barrels that had "Gunpowder" stenciled on them in both English and Japanese.

Helen caught sight of the tattooed man running away. She did the same, going in the opposite direction and hoping to get as far away as possible from the blazing inferno that was about to be unleashed.

***

Just as the Shinsengumi's sword began its descent toward Makoto's head, an ear-shattering explosion shook the room. Large cracks developed in the pillars holding up the roof, and the ceiling began to crumble.

Panic gripped the crowd of masked men and they dispersed in all directions. Taking advantage of the confusion and the Shinsengumi's momentary distraction, Makoto dived for his sword, grabbed it, and stood upright. He winced from the pain from the fresh cut in his leg. However, the Shinsengumi had disappeared in the chaos. Makoto scanned for any sign of his foe or the man in the fox mask, but his searching was interrupted when a large pillar collapsed in front of him.

Makoto muttered a string of English curses while he yanked Kotaro upright by the front of his coat and dragged him out of the main entryway, snaking his way between the collapsing pillars and falling wooden beams.

The sound of another explosion rattled through the halls, forcing Makoto to pause as the building shook around him. Smoke and fire began to obscure the pathway.

***

Helen dashed through the hallways as fast as she could in her inappropriate running attire. The sound of an explosion made the entire corridor rumble, and the force of the blast knocked her forward. When the world stopped spinning, she looked around for any sort of indication that she was heading for the exit, but because of the explosion, all of the lanterns had been knocked out of place or extinguished, making the hallways completely dark and even harder to navigate.

As she stood up straight and squinted her eyes, the sound of another explosion boomed through the hallway. The sound was all the motivation Helen needed to hear to pick up her pace, even if she was running in complete darkness. She charged forward at full speed until she ran face-first into something she couldn't see. She fell back and landed on the ground. "Ouch! What in the-"

Helen looked up and froze. Through the dim light, she was able to make out that the thing she ran into was a man in dark robes. He wore a mask from one of those Japanese-style plays she had read about. The mask was white and was decorated with a large, over-the-top smile that made Helen uneasy. The man held a lantern and looked down at her. Helen shrank back from the blank gaze of the mask.

The masked man stared at Helen for a moment, not reacting to the noise and rumbling of the hallways. Helen flinched at the sounds and the bits of wood falling from the ceiling. The masked man extended his hand to her. Helen's eyes darted between the man's hand and his mask. She hesitated, but the sound of another explosion prompted her and she took the man's hand. He pulled her upright and began walking. When Helen didn't follow, he stopped and turned to her. He held up the lantern and swung it in front of him.

"Who are you? Do you want me to follow you?" Helen asked, not certain if she should trust this masked man.

The man didn't reply but simply turned back around and continued walking forward. As the dim light slowly grew weaker as the distance between them grew, Helen bit her lip and trotted up behind the man, hoping he knew how to navigate the hallways of this maze of a warehouse better than she did.

***

Makoto may have been good at finding hidden passageways and secret entrances, but usually his world wasn't collapsing around him, opening some paths and closing others at the same time. He yanked Kotaro along by the front of his uniform. Makoto heard Kotaro shouting at him, but couldn't discern his words because of the noise of the explosions. Makoto wasn't interested in listening to his bravado anyway. They reached a clearing where the hallway split off in three different directions. Makoto paused and let go of Kotaro's jacket.

Kotaro stumbled back at the sudden freedom and pointed an accusatory finger at Makoto. "So, man in black! You thought you could get the drop on…" Kotaro trailed off when he realized Makoto wasn't listening. He was holding the haft of his sword and looked ready to draw with a dark glare in his eye. Kotaro glanced in the direction Makoto was staring and flinched when he saw a man in dark robes wearing a smiling Noh mask. Kotaro reached for his baton but couldn't find it. It must have fallen out sometime during the skirmish back at the gathering.

Makoto stared at the man with the smiling Noh mask. He wasn't wearing a Shinsengumi coat and based on his stance, he seemed to be older than the Shinsengumi Makoto fought moments ago. That didn't mean he wasn't dangerous. He still wore one of the masks.

Makoto's grip tightened on the handle of his sword and he was just about to pull it out when the man in the Noh mask lifted his hand and pointed to the central corridor. Makoto glanced at the pathway and wondered if the masked man was trying to show him the way out or lead him into a trap.

His thoughts were interrupted when the persistent American woman peeked over the masked man's shoulder. Makoto blinked a couple of times. He knew his fair share of foolish American women, but gallivanting into the secret warehouse behind a brothel filled with armed men certainly put this woman in the top five. She gasped at the sight of Makoto, marched over to him, and jabbed her finger at his face. "What is wrong with you? No matter where you go, there's nothing but destruction and insanity!"

Makoto didn't reply.

"First there was this dreadful man with dragon tattoos, and then a lantern caught on fire, and well, never mind about that, but this masked gentleman here…" Helen turned around and winced when she saw the man in the smiling mask was gone. "What? But he was just..."

Makoto frowned. The man disappearing made his suggested corridor all the more questionable.

"You, man in black! Don't think you can play dumb. You're under arrest!"

Makoto and Helen turned toward Kotaro, who seemed to be insulted at being ignored. Makoto sighed in annoyance and briefly wondered if it had been worth the trouble of saving him.

"You best surrender now! For I am the great and powerful-"

Kotaro was interrupted when one of the overhead beams snapped and came crashing down, which would have hit Kotaro on the head, but Makoto pushed him violently out of the way. Kotaro fell backward, though he still managed to hit his head on the floor and slumped down unconscious.

Helen staggered back from the collapsing wooden beam. Makoto felt the sting of several wooden slivers hitting his face and scratching the open wound on his leg. He and Helen looked over at the unconscious Kotaro. She turned to Makoto. "We can't leave him here. Come on!"

Makoto thought about how much more convenient his life would be if he left both of them, but he bent down and put one of Kotaro's arms over his shoulders and lifted him upright. Makoto tried to drag him forward, but Kotaro was even heavier than anticipated and the wound in Makoto's leg didn't help matters either. Helen noticed Makoto struggling, bent down, and hoisted up Kotaro's other arm. With her help, the policeman's large frame became more manageable, much to Makoto's surprise. He stared at her for a moment.

"What?" she asked. "This is child's play for a proper actress. Especially compared to hauling sandbags on stage."

Makoto nodded, looked forward, and decided since he didn't have any better ideas, to proceed through the middle passageway. "This way."

They heaved Kotaro through the corridor as more explosions erupted in the hidden passageways of the brothel.

Chapter Eighteen

Luck was on Makoto's side since the path the masked man suggested proved to be the correct way out. Makoto, Helen, and Kotaro made it out of the warehouse just before the building collapsed in on itself. Helen gasped as she saw the flames spread to adjoining buildings, while Makoto pushed forward without looking back. He gritted through the pain in his leg and the frustration at his failure in killing the Shinsengumi. Even worse, he lost to the accursed devil in a sword fight. Makoto's jaw clenched tighter.

"What do we do with him?" Helen asked, wafting away smoke.

Makoto turned to Helen, who was struggling to hold up her half of the unconscious Kotaro. Makoto glanced at Kotaro and pointed toward a stack of hay in a street corner a few feet away. "Dump him there."

"We can't do that!"

"Why not?"

"The fire's still close, and we should at least take him to a doctor. Oh! Wait just a moment." Helen let go of Kotaro, forcing Makoto to hold him up on his own, and reached into her now tattered purse. She pulled out the card she received from the doctor back at the hotel. She looked over the card and smiled. "There's a doctor not too far from here … I think. We should at least take him there."

Makoto sighed. He placed Kotaro down and grabbed a small bit of cloth from the duffel on his back and made a makeshift bandage around his still-bleeding leg. He reached down and heaved Kotaro up again. "Fine. Lead the way."

Helen studied the card and looked around, but couldn't make heads or tails of where they were. She started walking in what she hoped was the right direction, but she couldn't be too sure.

Over an hour later, Helen exclaimed in relief and pointed to a hanging sign which read "Dr. Clement Halifax" in both English and Japanese. The doctor's office sat at the top of a short stairway and was in the best shape of the run-down buildings on the street. However, that wasn't saying much, since the building sagged and was in desperate need of a good cleaning. The office was the only building in the neighborhood with a swinging Western-style door in the front instead of a piece of cloth or a sliding door.

Even though it took Helen and Makoto an hour to find it, the office was actually quite close to the Miyazaki District. The scent of smoke was pungent in the air, the fire gave the night sky an orange glow, and the sound of the fire alarm bell rang through the neighborhood.

Helen trotted up the stairs and knocked on the doctor's door. After waiting a minute without an answer, Helen knocked again, significantly louder this time. She heard what sounded like grumbles from the other side, and the door opened up just a crack.

Through the sliver, Helen could see the man on the other side wore loose, dark blue robes, smoked a pipe, and had a sour expression. She gave a nervous chuckle and waved. The door opened wider, revealing the doctor, his expression shifting from annoyed to befuddlement. Based on his stare, Helen realized at that moment she must look pretty frightful since her face was covered with scratches and her clothes were caked with dirt and grime.

"I had a feeling you'd get yourself hurt, but I didn't think it would be this soon," Halifax said.

"Huh? Oh! No. It's not me. The patient is over there." Helen pointed behind her.

Halifax opened the door fully to see Kotaro hanging off of Makoto's shoulder. "Well, that's not a sight you see every day."

"Can you help him?"

"It's late, but I'll see what I can do. Go ahead and bring him in. I'll get my instruments."

Helen nodded and returned to help Makoto drag Kotaro up the steps and into the doctor's office. Halifax directed them to put Kotaro down on a table wide enough to hold the corpulent policeman. The doctor washed his hands with soap and water poured from an ewer into a basin. He grabbed some sharp-looking instruments, laid them on a small nearby table, and looked over Kotaro. However, what started off as intense interest, quickly turned to boredom. "Hmm. How dull. Just a minor concussion."

"Is he going to be all right?" Helen asked.

"Yes. Hardly worth any concern. Though I should also take a look at that." Halifax pointed toward Makoto's leg. The makeshift bandage was soaked with blood and sagged on his leg.

Makoto instinctively shifted his injured leg back. "It's fine."

"I'll be the judge of that. Sit down over here."

Makoto didn't argue. He sat down in a wooden chair and removed the cloth bandage, which was now saturated with blood. Halifax pushed up the bloody and cut pant leg and took a look at the wound, which still oozed blood. "Looks like you've aggravated it by carrying around the big blue whale over there." Halifax jerked his thumb toward Kotaro, who was still lying on the table.

"If you're not careful, it'll get gangrene and then need to be amputated. But I've got something that should help."

Halifax went into one of the adjoining rooms and came back with a bottle of tan-colored liquid labeled, "5% Carbolic Acid." He splashed some onto a clean piece of cloth.

Helen looked at the bottle as Halifax worked. "What is it?"

"Antiseptic. It's becoming quite popular in Europe." Halifax turned to Makoto. "Now hold still. This will sting … a lot."

He placed the wet cloth on the wound. The doctor hadn't lied. Makoto breathed in sharply and gripped the armrests so tightly they creaked as if they were about to break. He suppressed the urge to pull his leg away from this unpleasant doctor. After a few seconds, which felt like hours to Makoto, Halifax removed the cloth and dressed the wound with proper bandages.

"We've got ourselves quite the trooper here. But then again, most actual troopers I put carbolic acid on start screaming like there's no tomorrow, so that may not be the best metaphor."

Makoto relaxed a bit as the pain finally wore off. "With your bedside manner, I'm surprised you ever get repeat business."

Halifax blinked. "So you can speak after all. Your English is quite good for a native. Based on your clothes, I suppose you've lived abroad." Halifax stood up and began putting away his instruments. "You're right, though. I don't get much repeat business. But that's due to most of my patients being visitors who return home or locals who fear I'll put a curse on them.

Have you been treated for wounds like this before?"

Makoto nodded. "In America. The doctor lets you have a swig of whiskey before he pours it on the wound."

Halifax chuckled. "Trust me, you don't want a swig of carbolic acid. The Yankees use whiskey you say? What a terrible waste of good alcohol."

After putting away the disinfectant and his tools, Halifax went back to look over Kotaro, who was beginning to stir.

"Saké … Saké…" Kotaro mumbled.

Halifax rolled his eyes. "Typical policeman, valuing his liquor over his life." Halifax reached over and grabbed a large, menacing saw from his tool set and plastered on a fake smile. He spoke loudly in Japanese, "He seems to have taken a few minor hits. But I fear the entire head is faulty. Clearly, we must amputate." He loomed over Kotaro.

Helen slowly backed away, while Makoto's attention was diverted to a large chemistry set in one of the adjoining rooms. Kotaro's eyes opened just in time to see Halifax's silhouette with the large saw in hand. His eyes bulged as wide as they could go and he nearly leaped off the table. "Aah! A Western devil doctor!"

Halifax's expression shifted from a fake smile to a smug sneer as he put away the saw. "He lives! Now that all of you have been treated, get out of my sight. And those little checkups will be one yen."

"One yen? How much is that again?" Helen asked glancing into her purse.

Halifax repeated the fee to Kotaro in Japanese, who jolted upright. "One yen! That's robbery!" Kotaro said.

Halifax shrugged. "Doctors have to eat, too. And food is expensive."

Kotaro's eyes shifted from the doctor to the door, internally debating whether or not to make a run for it. But his eyes landed on the array of saws and scalpels on Halifax's side table, and he shrank back.

Helen pulled up her purse and rummaged through it. "That fustilarian pickpocket! He must have stolen all my money!"

Halifax leaned on the wall, clearly enjoying himself. "That's what they all say. Well, except the fustilarian part."

"But! But I-" Helen stammered. "Wait a minute, where's the cowboy?"

Halifax and Helen noticed Makoto looking over Halifax's large chemistry set. "Why does everyone want to touch that?" Halifax started to walk toward Makoto but also looked back at the nervous Helen and

Kotaro. "Now don't go anywhere, I'll be right back to collect my fee." He repeated the statement to Kotaro in Japanese and walked away. Helen and Kotaro looked nervously at each other.

Makoto noticed Halifax come into the room and took a step back from the chemistry set.

"If you break it, you'll be responsible for paying for another one, and I assure you, this set was very expensive to import," Halifax said.

"I see."

"You don't seem like the chemistry type."

"I'm not."

"Then why the interest?"

"Percussion caps."

"Percussion caps? For a gun?"

Makoto nodded.

Halifax grew suspicious. "Then I suppose your interest makes sense. Percussion caps need mercury fulminate, which can be very difficult to create without a set like this. But just who are you hoping to shoot?"

Makoto didn't respond. He turned away from the set and walked back toward the waiting area, Halifax following. In the waiting area, they noticed Kotaro and Helen were gone. Halifax shook his head but didn't seem too angry. "Typical. I should've sawed off that policeman's head."

Makoto reached into his pocket and handed Halifax a small lump of gold. Halifax looked at him in confusion. "What's this?"

"About three yen's worth of gold." Makoto tipped his hat. "Thanks for your help."

Makoto walked out of Halifax's office, leaving him staring down at the small lump of gold in his hand.

Makoto stepped out of the doctor's office and quietly shut the door behind him. He glanced around for any signs of the troublesome policeman or the American woman. The American was partially hidden behind a neighboring building, and the policeman was barely obscured by a nearby bush. Makoto shook his head and made his way down the steps, preparing for the onslaught of annoyance.

Right on cue, Kotaro leaped from behind his bush and pointed an accusatory finger at Makoto when he reached the bottom step. "Aha! I have you now, man in black! You're under arrest."

Makoto glanced in Kotaro's direction, let out a half-snort, and turned away. He walked down the street and heard Kotaro stammer a few words before trotting up behind him. "Didn't you hear me? You're under arrest for the murder of poor ol'- I mean, Mr. Watanabe!"

Makoto didn't slow his pace, even though he didn't really know where he was going. He just wanted to get away from the pestering policeman. "I didn't kill him."

"Ha! You expect me to believe that?"

"Believe what you want."

Kotaro bristled at Makoto's impertinence and struggled to keep up with his longer stride. After a minute of trotting after Makoto, Kotaro began huffing and puffing. "So, you think you can escape the great and powerful Yamada Kotaro?"

Makoto didn't bother replying. Irritated at being ignored, Kotaro sprinted ahead of Makoto, rounded to face him, stopped, and put out his arms. "Didn't you hear me? You're under arrest!"

Makoto stopped and glared. Kotaro felt his muscles tighten under the dark gaze, but he held his ground. Makoto attempted to walk around, but with any step he took, the policeman jumped clumsily to stand in his way.

"Move. Now," Makoto said through gritted teeth.

"I will not! The great and power…" Kotaro trailed off as Makoto drew his sword.

Makoto leveled his blade so the tip was only a few inches away from Kotaro's belly. "I won't ask again. Move."

Kotaro felt his knees begin to wobble, but he sucked in his breath and pointed his finger at Makoto again. "So that's how it is! You draw your sword to attack. Just like in the Miyazaki District and against Mr. Watanabe!"

Makoto's glare shifted to confusion but hardened again. "Even your memory is incompetent. I wasn't the one who drew my sword on you in the warehouse."

"Ha! You expect me to…" Kotaro trailed off and rubbed his chin. "Wait a minute…"

Hazy memories started to become clear to Kotaro as he remembered fragments of what happened earlier that evening, especially the sight of the man in the Shinsengumi coat holding his sword above Kotaro's head. And the man in black … rescuing him.

Kotaro snapped out of his thoughts and glanced around for any sign of the man in black, but he was gone, and so was his only lead in the case. Then he remembered the foreign woman. He may not have been able to communicate with her, but she may know something about what happened in the Miyazaki District.

Kotaro trotted back to the doctor's office but was dismayed to see the woman was gone, and the frightening doctor was looking out from his open door with an amused expression. "Why are you still loitering around here?"

Kotaro took a few nervous steps back, making certain the doctor wasn't still carrying his saw.

Halifax chuckled. "Relax. That friend of yours in black already paid for your treatments." He flashed the small bit of gold in his hand before sliding it into his pocket. "You owe your friend a great deal."

"He's not my friend! He's a suspect for murder," Kotaro said with bravado before deflating. "But I don't understand. Why would he help me?"

Halifax shrugged. "Why anyone would help you is beyond me."

Kotaro shook his head, choosing to ignore the doctor's insult. "No. I can't get distracted. I have to get back the lost evidence or the captain will have my head!"

Halifax chuckled. "I have a saw if he needs to borrow it."

Kotaro gave the doctor a wary look, which only made Halifax sneer.

"Well, Mr. Policeman, whatever your problem is, you'll have to deal with it on your own time. Have a nice evening." Halifax stepped back inside and slammed his door, making Kotaro flinch.

Kotaro sighed, glanced up at the pillar of smoke and burning embers rising from the Miyazaki District, and shuffled away in no particular direction.

***

After a few minutes of walking nowhere in particular, Makoto returned his sword to its sheath, slowed his pace, and stopped. He was slightly surprised the policeman hadn't noticed him walk around him, but dismissed the thought.

He stared at the pillar of smoke and wondered how far the fire would spread. Fires were always bad news, but in a town where most of the buildings were made from wood and paper, even a small fire could be disastrous. And the fire in the red-light district was anything but small.

He noticed some clouds forming for another summer storm, but he didn't know how long it would be before it started raining again. While a sudden downpour would help quench the fire, he remembered being caught in a storm the previous night and did not want to repeat the experience. His thoughts drifted to the temple, Inzan, and Emiko.

The memory of that evening's debacle was sharp in his mind as well. Makoto drummed his fingers on the handle of his sword, growing more frustrated with himself. Despite his skills, he was no match for the Shinsengumi. He stared down at his sword, swung around his duffel, opened it up, and slid the sword inside. As he positioned the blade into its hidden sleeve, his eyes landed on the frame of his gun.

Makoto knew if he ever hoped to avenge his family, he would need to use all of the tools available to him, including his gun. He would need somewhere safe to reassemble it away from both rain and prying eyes. A crack of thunder echoed across the sky, and Makoto decided to head for the hill which housed the temple, hoping Inzan would let him impose for one more night.

He eventually reached the stone steps under the torii gate. It would have taken him even less time if he hadn't intentionally slowed his pace to avoid putting excessive pressure on his wounded leg. He limped his way up the steep, stone steps, his leg still throbbing even with the doctor's treatment. But the further up he went, the more doubts began creeping into his mind. He didn't want to involve Inzan and Emiko with his problems. And assembling weapons under their roof was likely to invite trouble; trouble he wasn't strong enough to defeat. 'You lose,' rang through Makoto's mind over and over again.

Makoto's grip on his duffel tightened, and he hesitated. He knew if he faced the Shinsengumi again in his current state, he wouldn't be able to protect Inzan or Emiko from him. He couldn't even protect himself. He considered turning around and finding somewhere else to stay, but a bolt of lightning flashed through the sky, a crack of thunder rang through the air, and the first heavy drops of rain began to fall, promising a heavy downpour. Makoto glanced at the weakening plume of smoke rising from the Miyazaki District and guessed the rain was helping to quell the fire.

At the moment, the rain was more a hindrance than a help to him. He continued up the stone steps, careful not to slip on the slick surfaces. He staggered over to the temple entrance as quickly as his injured leg would allow and went up the steps to the protection of the overhanging wooden roof. He weaved his way around the holes in the roof where the water poured down with extra ferocity. When he reached the living quarters, he was about to call out when the door slid open, and Inzan stood there with a lantern in his hand.

His expression shifted from suspicion to delight when he saw Makoto. "Ah, Master Mori! You've returned." Inzan slid the door open further, and beckoned Makoto inside. "Come in, come in. This weather is far too miserable to be outside."

Makoto paused and gave a slight bow. "Thank you."

Inzan beamed as he stepped away to let Makoto inside. Makoto took a step forward but stopped and turned abruptly when he heard a sneeze. Inzan stuck his head out at the sound as well and stepped in front of Makoto. They both glanced around for the source of the sneeze. Inzan was about to round the corner of the living quarters when Makoto put his hand on his shoulder.

Remembering the men in the masks and the potential danger, Makoto stepped ahead of Inzan and headed for the corner first. Inzan gave a concerned look but followed Makoto's lead. Makoto reached into his duffel and drew his sword as he stepped around to the side of the building.

However, when he saw the source of the sneeze, he stopped and stared. Inzan, growing impatient, stepped up behind Makoto, and his face twisted in fury. "W-What's a Jesuit doing here?"

Makoto lowered his sword and returned it to the duffel. Sitting there, shivering under the overhanging roof of the living quarters in a soaking wet and completely tattered dress was that frustrating American woman, Helen Arkwright.

She gave Makoto an embarrassed smile. "Heh. Fancy meeting you here, Mr. Cowboy."

Chapter Nineteen

Helen sneezed again and tried to organize her hair, which had fallen into disarray.

Makoto felt Inzan tug at the side of his coat and whisper harshly. "A Jesuit pollutes these hallowed grounds, Master Mori."

Makoto gave Inzan a slightly annoyed glance. "I doubt she's a Jesuit."

"Don't be ridiculous. All foreigners are Jesuits!"

Makoto wondered where Inzan had heard such a ridiculous claim but decided not to argue with him. He turned his attention back to the American woman and wondered how she managed to follow without him noticing, considering she was hardly a master of stealth.

"It's rude to talk about a lady in her presence," Helen said, crossing her arms. "Granted, I don't know what you're saying, but I can tell it's about me."

"What are you doing here?" Makoto asked in English.

"Isn't it obvious?"

"No."

Helen frowned at Makoto's bluntness. "I'm looking for my husband of course."

"And you think he's here?"

Helen glanced around the temple. "I'm not sure. But one thing I know for certain is that I wasn't able to find him until I saw you. Tonight, in that dreadful building this evening. I didn't see John until after I ran into you. You must know something!"

"I assure you I don't."

Helen frowned. "Well, even if he's not here now, I'm sure he'll show up eventually. Like you, he has an impressive tendency to get into trouble."

"As opposed to you?"

Helen let out a half chuckle. "I'll have you know I was doing just fine keeping out of trouble until I started following you."

"Is that supposed to be my fault?"

"No." Helen's smile disappeared. She sighed and rested her head on her knees. "Looks like John was right. I shouldn't have obsessed over these flights of fancy after all."

Makoto felt a tinge of pity for the American woman, but that shifted to internally chastising himself for getting so distracted he hadn't noticed her following him since he left the doctor's office. His thoughts were interrupted when Helen sneezed again.

She looked up at him. "Well? Aren't you going to let me in?"

Makoto glanced at Inzan, who had been staring his way the entire time. "What does she want?" Inzan asked.

"She wants to stay the night."

Inzan balked. "What!? Absolutely not! I could not let a Jesuit defile the temple. What would the spirits of your family think?"

Makoto nodded. "I understand."

Inzan let out a sigh of relief, but Makoto continued, "In that case, I'll find her somewhere else to stay the night. Thank you for your kindness."

Inzan stammered, "Y-You're leaving? Because of this Jesuit woman?"

Makoto nodded again. He may not have particularly liked the American woman, but he couldn't just leave her to fend for herself. He remembered all too well what it was like to be left on his own in an unfamiliar land. He approached Helen, but before he had a chance to inform her of the situation, he felt Inzan tug on his arm.

"No. No. She is..." Inzan sucked in a frustrated breath and spoke through gritted teeth. "Welcome here ... I suppose. So long as you are here, Master Mori."

"Are you sure?"

Inzan gestured to the pouring rain. "It is far too miserable to go out now. So please stay."

Makoto nodded and turned back to Helen. "He said it's all right for you to stay."

Helen smiled and stood up. "Something tells me that I have you to thank for convincing him."

Makoto blinked in surprise. "You understood what he said?"

Helen shook her head. "Not a word. But reading body language and tone of voice is child's play for a proper actress."

Makoto shrugged. "Well, you're not wrong. But it's better than sitting out in the rain."

"Agreed. Thank you." She brushed off some of the dust from her dress. Makoto slid open the door, yanked off his boots, and placed them by the entrance. Helen looked back and forth between Makoto and his boots.

Makoto glanced back at her. "Be sure to take off your shoes. It's considered disrespectful to wear them inside."

Helen frowned and sighed. "Oh, all right." She unlaced her shoes and pulled them off with a bit more difficulty than Makoto. She wondered what other strange customs were common in this country which she wasn't aware of. After finally yanking them off with a solid tug, she placed her shoes near Makoto's. From the corner of her eye, she noticed Inzan glaring in her direction. She was tempted to return the glare but decided it wasn't in her best interest to further agitate her host and went inside.

She wasn't used to seeing so many Japanese fixtures since she had spent most of her time at the Western-style Grand Hotel. As she took in the sights of the room, she wondered why the table was so low and why there weren't any gas lamps. She was distinctly unimpressed with the leaky roof that dripped water on the reed mat floor, which felt rough to her feet. Makoto sat down on one of the cushions and motioned Helen to do the same.

"Y-You sit on the floor?" Helen recoiled a little.

Makoto nodded. "No one wears shoes, so the floor isn't dirty." He glanced at one of the wet patches on the floor courtesy of the leaky roof. "More or less."

"Oh, I see," Helen said in an unconvinced tone of voice. She sat down on one of the cushions, pressing her dress down as she sat cross-legged underneath.

Inzan stepped inside and glared in Helen's direction, but after staring for a moment, he started snickering, prompting a curious look from Makoto. "Heh. The Jesuit woman sits like a sumo. I'll get some tea." He left the room.

Helen frowned in the priest's direction as he left. "What did he say?"

"He said you sit like a man."

"What!? Why I ought to…" Helen stood up to go after him, but Makoto stood and stepped in front of her.

"Get out of my way. I'm going to teach that louse a thing or two about manners."

"How?"

"First I'll give him a piece of my mind and then…" Helen trailed off, gave a sigh, and sat back down. "Then I'll get kicked out into the rain. I can tell where this script is going. I suppose I shouldn't push my luck."

Makoto also sat down. Inzan returned with a pot of tea and cups and placed them on the low table.

"Inzan, is Emiko around?" Makoto asked.

Inzan seemed to grow irritated. "I haven't seen her all night. My guess is she was held up at that accursed hotel she works at and may have been delayed by the fire in town."

Makoto stiffened at the mention of the fire, but his worries were eased when one of the sliding doors in the back opened and he heard Emiko call out, "I'm back." A rustling sound suggested she was hanging up her cloth cloak.

"Welcome back," Inzan said, "Master Mori has chosen to join us again tonight, plus a … guest." Inzan gave Helen a dirty look.

"Oh!" Emiko stepped inside. She was still wearing the well-fitting dress from earlier. She made a deep bow. "Thank you for taking care of the tea, Master Inzan, and I'm glad to see you return, Master Mori." She raised her head and gave Helen a quizzical look, her eyes grew wide, and she suddenly looked back down.

Helen squinted and studied Emiko. She snapped her fingers. "Ah ha! I knew I recognized you! You're the girl from the hotel."

Makoto looked toward Helen. "What do you mean?"

"This girl works at the hotel I'm staying at." She jabbed her finger in Makoto's direction and spoke in a triumphant tone of voice. "And I saw her with you this morning at the harbor."

"So?"

Helen's tone shifted to one of annoyance. "Because I asked if she had seen you before and she denied it. She lied to me!"

Makoto found the claim odd but decided to translate Helen's words. Emiko's face shifted to one of embarrassment and horror. She made a deep bow toward Helen, which surprised everyone, especially Helen. "Please forgive me, madam. I didn't understand what Miss Aki was saying, and I didn't mean to deceive you. I am truly sorry!"

Inzan grumbled something under his breath about 'accursed Jesuits.' Helen, not having a clue what Emiko just said, looked back and forth between her and Makoto.

"She said she's sorry. Whatever she did, it was a mistake."

Helen sighed and adjusted her tattered dress. "Oh well. So long as it was an honest mistake. No harm done, I suppose."

"She accepts your apology," Makoto said.

Emiko raised her head and gave an embarrassed smile that Helen returned. Emiko looked over Helen's tattered clothes. "Please wait just a moment. I have something that could be helpful." Emiko headed to a back room of the living quarters.

Makoto found himself staring after her as she left. His eyes drifted back into the room, and he grew irritated when he saw Helen giving him a smug look.

"You know, as an actress, I'm a bit of an expert in seeing behind people's masks. And you may try to hide it, but I can tell. You're quite fond of that girl, correct?"

Makoto didn't respond. Helen kept her smug smile and leaned back, though her smile dropped when she caught sight of Inzan's glare as he loudly took a sip of tea. She instead focused her attention on the room, and her eyes fell on a strange weapon hanging on the wall. It consisted of a long, black pole with a curved blade at the end. "What's that?"

Makoto glanced up. "That's a *naginata*. A weapon."

"I know it's a weapon. But what's it doing here, in a temple?"

Makoto wondered the same thing. He didn't notice it the last time he was at the temple, but he didn't even realize it was there until the American woman pointed it out. He turned to Inzan. "Why is there a naginata here?"

Inzan blinked in confusion at the question, then glanced over to the weapon and nodded. "It is one of the few surviving heirlooms of the Hayashi family. It belonged to Emiko's mother."

"I see." Makoto relayed the information to Helen, which only piqued her curiosity even more.

"Women used that weapon? How … unorthodox."

"Samurai class women did. As did warriors on the battlefield, but the naginata for men tended to be larger."

"How does one use that?" Helen asked.

"I've never used one," Makoto curtly replied.

Helen wanted to ask more, but Makoto turned away and reached into his bag. Helen could feel Inzan's eyes burning into the back of her head, so she decided to drop it.

Makoto fished around his duffel for his gun. As his hand tapped against his sword, he had the urge to sharpen it after a long day, but he suppressed the feeling to focus on the gun instead. He pulled the frame out, which made Helen gasp. "Is that a Navy Colt?"

Makoto nodded. "A model 1851. You know about revolvers?"

"No. Not really. Though my husband wouldn't stop going on and on about those silly firearms. They're the only thing he obsesses about as much as ships. But how did you sneak it into the country? I heard weapons like that are forbidden."

"With great difficulty."

Inzan interrupted. "Master Mori, what are you doing with such a disgraceful Jesuit weapon?"

Makoto glared at Inzan. "This 'disgraceful' weapon will avenge my family."

Inzan didn't reply but took another long sip of tea. Makoto returned to pulling out the weapon's cylinder and ramrod and began assembling the gun. There was an awkward silence between the three until Emiko returned with some robes in her hands. She glanced down at Makoto and didn't give any visible reaction to the gun. "Master Mori, could you please tell the madam I have some fresh clothes so she doesn't have to remain in her dirty ones."

Makoto nodded and relayed the information to Helen, who stood up with a large smile on her face. "Oh, thank goodness. This dress is in terrible shape and is practically scandalous to wear."

"She said, all right," Makoto said to Emiko.

Emiko smiled. "Then please instruct her to follow me and allow me to help her get dressed."

Makoto translated, and Helen followed Emiko out of the room. After the women left, Inzan looked like he wanted to say something but was choosing not to. Makoto continued constructing his gun but found Inzan's gaze to be overbearing. "If you have something to say, just say it."

"Forgive, me Master Mori, but it just seems wrong to use a Jesuit weapon like that in a matter of family honor."

"Foreign guns were good enough for Tokugawa at the Battle of Sekigahara."

Inzan bristled and opened his mouth to retort, but closed it just as quickly. He took another sip of tea. Makoto brushed it off and continued working. They heard the sounds of Helen rambling to Emiko in English, but between the pounding rain and the wooden walls, Makoto couldn't make out what she was saying. After a few more minutes of work, Makoto finished assembling his gun. He put the completed revolver to one side and pulled out his sword. He unsheathed it and looked down at the blade with disdain. Inzan looked at the sword and then at Makoto's dark expression. "Is something troubling you, Master Mori?"

Makoto glared darkly toward Inzan, but his gaze softened when he saw the look of concern on Inzan's face. "Today … I found a Shinsengumi."

Inzan nearly choked on his tea. "Shinsengumi!? In Yokohama? You found one?"

Makoto nodded. "He wore a mask so I couldn't see his face. I saw him this morning in the shipbuilding district and again in the Miyazaki District."

Inzan's expression grew grave. "And you fought him?"

"Yes … But…" Makoto stared down at his sword. "I was no match for him. He defeated me. If it wasn't for those explosions…" Makoto let out a grim sigh and returned the sword to its sheath. "I can't rely on my sword alone to avenge my family."

Inzan's eyes shifted to the gun on the table. "So … you believe you have to rely on that?"

Makoto placed the sheathed sword back into his duffel and picked up the revolver. He snapped it open and checked the barrel. "Not yet. I still need blasting caps and gunpowder." He snapped the gun's cylinder into its frame, reached into his bag, and pulled out his chess set. "As for ammunition…"

Makoto opened the box, revealing a regular chess set, with lead pieces. He picked up one of the pawns and held the body in one hand while holding the circular head of the piece with the thumb and index finger of the other. He twisted the head one way and the body the opposite, which caused the ball to snap off. He silently thanked the San Francisco pewter smith who had crafted the set as Makoto specified, sawing almost completely through the necks of the pawns to make the balls break away, leaving Makoto with sixteen .36 caliber bullets.

Chapter Twenty

Kotaro wandered around the harbor. He sighed in exasperation as his uniform became sodden from the downpour. The rain pounded his face, and he nearly slipped on the muddy roads several times as he sulked. He knew he couldn't go back to the police station without the evidence, and to top things off, he lost track of the man in black. As he passed by the boats near the harbor, a large wave crashed into the stone breakwater, giving Kotaro an extra splash of salt water.

"Bah! It's as if the gods are laughing at my misfortunes," Kotaro whined as he walked further inland, getting away from the docks. He glanced around for some sort of shelter and was surprised to see the lanterns still lit at Sakénomi's bar. Having nothing to lose, he hurried inside.

Inside the bar was completely empty, save for the bartender behind the counter and the sumo at the entrance. They both gave him dirty looks as he entered, but didn't say anything. Kotaro shuffled his way to the counter and waited, dripping wet, as the bartender begrudgingly went up to him.

"What do you want? Shouldn't you policemen be helping with the fire down in Miyazaki?"

Kotaro ignored the bartender's taunts and put a coin on the counter. "Saké."

The bartender stared and crossed his arms.

Kotaro glanced down. "Please."

Jean sighed, took the coin, filled a box of saké, and placed it on the counter. "You still owe me for a broken table, monsieur."

Kotaro groaned and took a sip of his saké. "How am I supposed to do that? At this rate, I'll be kicked out of the police department."

"You mean they think they can get by without your brilliance, agility, and modesty? Who would have guessed?" Jean replied with a sneer.

Kotaro looked up. "I know! I'm trying to find the identity of the real killer and no one is taking it seriously! I first thought the man in black was responsible for everything, but now … I'm not so sure."

"Man in black?" Jean asked.

"The man with the sword. He was here yesterday, when I, uh, broke the table."

"Oh yes, him. I saw him this morning with a pretty young lady."

"That's not important!" Kotaro said. "What's important is who killed Watanabe."

"Right, poor ol' Watanabe."

Kotaro suppressed the urge to make another checkmark on the sheet of paper in his pocket with all the others. "You knew him?"

"He was one of my better customers. Though according to that 'man in black' he may have been a Shinsen-something or another, which is weird since Watanabe had a tendency to brag about everything: the class of his family, his cousin's connections, working for the home minister. He was a bit of a braggart."

"Kind of like someone we know," chimed in the bouncer from the doorway.

Jean chuckled. "That's right, Tora. Like some *policemen* we know."

Kotaro remembered seeing Watanabe in his Shinsengumi coat, but he looked up in confusion. "Watanabe worked for the home minister?"

Jean seemed a little disappointed Kotaro hadn't reacted to his jab but shrugged. "At least he claimed he did. But it was for the previous minister, Ōkubo, I think? Watanabe was pretty jittery when that guy killed himself a few weeks ago."

Kotaro's eyes widened, and he took another swig of saké. "Wait a moment. Are you sure? But if they both died in the same way … And if Watanabe was Shinsengumi…" Kotaro mumbled to himself, and when the realization hit him, he slammed his fist on the table and accidentally knocked over his almost empty masu box.

"Hey, watch the counter! It's cracked enough as is," Jean said.

"That's it! That's the connection!"

The bartender tilted his head. "Huh?"

"The man in the mask and Shinsengumi coat. He must be the killer. He got to Home Minister Ōkubo through his connection with his old Shinsengumi comrade, Watanabe. Or maybe even Watanabe killed the home minister. Either way, once the deed was done, and the home minister's death was made to look like a suicide, Watanabe was silenced. The killer even used the same trick to cover his tracks. Of course! It even matches the evi-"

Kotaro stopped mid-sentence and leaned forward to lay his head dejectedly against the counter. "At least it would have if I hadn't lost the evidence."

"Tora, I think our dear policeman has lost his senses." The bartender continued speaking to the sumo, but Kotaro didn't hear as his fatigue finally caught up with him, and he fell asleep with his head on the counter.

After what seemed like an instant, he was shaken awake by the bartender. Kotaro blinked. "Huh, what?"

"You've been asleep for a couple of hours, it's closing time. Unless you're willing to pay for one of the rooms upstairs, I'm going to have to ask you to leave."

Kotaro grumbled and rubbed his eyes. He glanced up and saw Tora standing over him, ready to throw him out if necessary. Kotaro decided not to object and slunk away. When he opened the cloth, he groaned when he saw the rain pouring down as hard as ever. With a frustrated sigh, Kotaro sauntered off into the rain, hoping to find some other form of shelter.

***

The downpour continued, rain pounding on the roof of the temple. Helen stomped back into the room where Makoto and Inzan were sitting. She tugged at the purple yukata she was haphazardly wearing. "What's with this ridiculous dressing gown? Is this what people actually wear in this country? The color is all right, but it's practically indecent. Even worse, it looks like my husband's ridiculous smoking jacket!"

Emiko followed closely behind, clearly frazzled from dealing with the American. "My apologies, Mako-" She stopped herself when she saw Inzan. "I mean, Master Mori. Unfortunately, I wasn't able to explain to the madam about how to wear the yukata correctly and…"

Makoto glanced over Helen and noticed the yukata was folded wrong, and parts of her chemise were visible. He guessed Emiko hadn't been able to persuade her to remove more than the bare minimum of clothing. He considered informing Helen of her mistakes but decided against it. Inzan snorted.

Helen frowned at the priest, sat down with as much dignity as she could muster, and stared at Makoto's open chess set. "Those are some strange pieces you have there. It looks like your pawns have lost their heads."

Makoto closed the chess set and placed it on the table next to his gun. "I sacrificed them in an opening gambit."

Helen frowned when Makoto didn't elaborate further. Emiko stared on with a worried look, while Inzan glared.

Helen stuck up her nose and attempted to ignore Inzan's glare. "Well then, can you ask the girl about that nagi-something on the wall? I'm quite curious about it. Women actually use that weapon? Can she?"

Makoto would have been lying to himself if he wasn't curious about the weapon as well. He looked at Emiko, who glanced between Inzan and Helen with a worried look. "I heard from Inzan the naginata on the wall is a family heirloom of yours."

"Hmm?" Emiko glanced at the weapon. "Oh, you mean that. Yes. Sadly, it was one of the few things I was able to save before the soldiers came."

Inzan's frown deepened. "Emiko. If you don't want to talk about it, you don't have to."

"No. I do," Emiko said with a soft look in her eyes. "My family was on the wrong side of the rebellion last year. They were stripped of their title, land, and even their lives. It's my last memento of them, though I've never used it. That's why it always stays on the wall."

Makoto didn't recall seeing the weapon when he first arrived at the temple, but he also hadn't noticed it until Helen pointed it out just that night, and there were more lanterns set out now than before. Makoto gave a solemn nod. "I'm sorry. I … know how that feels." Makoto pulled out a sheet of paper with the crest of his family on it. "This is my last memento of my family."

Emiko stared at the paper and looked up with a sad smile, her eyes glistening from blinked back tears. "That's why you're hunting the Shinsengumi, right?"

Makoto nodded and returned the paper to his coat. Helen looked over at them impatiently but after seeing Emiko's sad look, decided to bite back her curiosity about what they were saying. However, Inzan was even less patient and coughed loudly, which broke the two's stare.

"What did she say?" Helen asked, taking advantage of the silence being broken by someone else.

"Nothing of concern to you," Makoto replied.

Helen frowned but decided not to push it further. "So … what are you going to do now?"

"What does it matter to you?"

Helen's frown deepened at Makoto's reply, and she tapped her fingers on the table. "Because I'm searching for my husband, remember?"

Makoto sighed; he didn't really know what to do next either. He had focused on putting his gun back together and was less concerned about what to do tomorrow. But then a thought hit him and he searched in his pocket. He pulled out the card with the red flower. He showed the card to Emiko and Inzan. "Does this symbol mean anything to either of you?"

Emiko kneeled down on the ground and stared at the card, but shook her head. Inzan stiffened a bit, which wasn't lost on Makoto, but eventually shook his head as well. "I-I don't think so."

"I see."

Helen peeked her head over Makoto's shoulder to try and get a look at the card. "What's that?"

Makoto hesitated but showed her the card. She stared at it. "That flower looks … familiar. I could have sworn I've seen it before." She racked her mind, then snapped her fingers. "Of course! Now I remember, it was on a letter addressed to my husband which … got lost. But I saw it yesterday."

Makoto stared at her. "Addressed to your husband?"

"Yes. And it was from someone named, oh blast, what was his name again? Warabe? Watabe? Uh…"

"Watanabe?" Makoto said.

Helen nodded. "That's it, Watanabe! Why? Do you know him?"

"I saw him once … dead at an inn last night."

Helen balked. "Dead!? At an inn? But my husband was supposed to meet up with him. D-Do you think my husband's in some kind of trouble?"

Makoto shrugged. "Or maybe your husband killed him."

"What!?" Helen pounded her fist on the low table. "My husband may engage in some sharp dealings, but he's no killer!"

"Did he ever mention the Shinsengumi?"

Helen was thrown off by the sudden question and shook her head. "No. I don't think so. Though I do tend to let my mind wander when he starts rambling. Oh, curse it all. What kind of trouble has he gotten himself in now?"

"I don't know," Makoto replied. "But this card was needed to enter the brothel."

Helen grumbled and crossed her arms. "The one you entered? My husband went into that wretched place as well. You men are all the same."

Makoto ignored her jab and focused on the card, remembering the strange gathering before the fight, and their cryptic plans. He addressed Inzan and Emiko. "Have either of you heard of the *Hiei*?"

Inzan and Emiko exchanged worried glances. It was Emiko who spoke, "I believe I heard of it. It's a battleship coming in tomorrow. I think. Why?"

Makoto stopped himself from bringing up the evening's affairs. He didn't want to involve Emiko. "It's not important. Better that you don't get involved."

Emiko's expression shifted from curious to hurt, but she made a respectful bow. "I understand Master Mori." She stood up. "I'll trouble you no longer."

Makoto stood up as well. "That's not…"

Emiko made another bow and walked out of the room. Makoto stared, not certain what to do. Inzan looked on with worry in his eyes, while Helen coughed to get Makoto's attention. "I'm not sure what foolish thing you said young man, but you best hurry and apologize to that young lady right now."

"I didn't-"

"It doesn't matter if you didn't do anything wrong. Matters of the heart are child's play for a proper actress. Go and apologize!"

Makoto nodded and followed after Emiko. He caught up with her down the hall and grabbed her hand. "Wait, Emiko."

She stopped and turned to him, though kept her head down. "I'm sorry Master…" Emiko glanced up and saw Inzan was out of earshot. "I'm sorry, Makoto. I want to help, but if you don't want me to be involved…"

"It's not that."

Emiko looked up at him in confusion.

"These men I'm up against, they're stronger than I am. I don't think I can protect you from them."

She tightened her squeeze on Makoto's hand and placed her other hand on top so that she held his hand in both of hers. For a moment, that was all Makoto could focus on. What they were talking about didn't seem important anymore. But her voice brought him back to reality. "Makoto, there's something I need to tell you … about the Shinsengumi and the *Hiei*."

Makoto's eyes widened. "What about them?"

"Well…"

"Emiko." Makoto and Emiko jolted at the sound of Inzan's voice. Emiko let go of Makoto's hand and made a bow. Makoto noticed a small piece of folded paper was left in his hand.

Inzan frowned. "Emiko, what are you doing? The futons need to be made."

Emiko made another bow. "Forgive me Master Inzan."

Makoto opened his mouth to object, but stopped when Emiko gave him a pointed look. Her eyes shifted to his hand, and he tightened his grip on the note. She gave a sad smile and left the hallway.

Inzan turned to Makoto. "Please, Master Mori. Stay away from Emiko … and the *Hiei*."

Makoto glared. "What do you know, Inzan?"

Inzan only looked down and walked away. The thought of forcing Inzan to talk flashed through Makoto's mind, but he knew he couldn't bring himself to do something like that.

He tried to speak with Emiko again as she laid out the futons, but whenever he approached, she looked away, and Inzan loomed near. Eventually, Makoto returned to the room with the low table, where Helen was smiling smugly, a look which disappeared when Makoto sat down with a grim expression.

"I take it didn't go so well. Did you properly apologize?" Helen asked.

Makoto didn't reply. Instead, he looked down at the paper in his hand. He opened it up. Inside was a small, wooden shogi piece with Japanese symbols on both sides. He focused his attention back on the note, which read: "The Shinsengumi plan to infiltrate the *Hiei*. Meet me at the harbor tomorrow."

Chapter Twenty-One

Helen glanced over at Makoto's note. "What's that say?"

Makoto shoved the paper and wooden piece into his coat. "It's not important." He slid his chess set back into his duffel and placed it by his side.

Not happy at being ignored, Helen continued talking. "What do you suppose those dreadful men were up to this evening? Do you think that policeman's all right? And what do think of that doctor? He was so greedy."

Makoto didn't reply. Before Helen could ask any further questions, Emiko appeared back into the room and bowed. She and Makoto exchanged brief glances, and she gave a small nod. "I've prepared a futon in the spare room, but…"

Makoto turned to Helen. "A futon is ready for you to sleep in the spare room."

Helen cocked her head. "Futon? What's that?"

"You sleep in it. On the floor."

Helen frowned. "On the floor again? Why are you people so obsessed with being on the floor?"

Makoto turned to Emiko. "Give the futon to her. I'll sleep here."

Emiko gave a concerned look but bowed again. "Of course."

Helen looked back and forth between the two, wondering what they were saying. She frowned. "If you haven't apologized yet, now's a good opportunity."

"Follow Emiko to the room, she'll show you where you can sleep."

Helen let out an annoyed sigh and stood up. She was about to follow Emiko but stopped. "Oh, before I forget!" Helen reached into her purse and handed Makoto a hatpin.

He looked at it in confusion. "What's this for?"

Helen smiled. "You never know when there's a lock which needs to be picked." She followed Emiko out of the room. Makoto stuck the long, sharp pin in the canvas of his duffel and leaned his back against one of the sturdier walls. He waited to see if Emiko would return, but when she didn't, he lowered his hat and drifted into a rough sleep.

The next morning, Makoto awoke with the sunrise. He had woken at dawn so many times it was natural to him now, even if he didn't get enough sleep. He stood up and cracked out a few kinks from sleeping in a sitting position.

He remembered Emiko's note and searched the temple to see if she was there. He couldn't find any sign of her, and no sign of Inzan either. He returned to the room and placed his gun in his coat pocket. Even if it couldn't fire, it could still be useful. However, his sword drew too much attention so he left it in the duffel, which he grabbed and headed for the exit.

"Wait just a moment! You're not leaving without me, are you?"

Makoto turned around to see Helen trotting up to him. She was still wearing the purple yukata, but at least it was worn correctly.

"Still wearing that?" he asked.

"It's not like I can change into my old dress. It fell apart for goodness sake. You know dresses aren't made to handle fires, tunnels, and explosions!"

Makoto shrugged. "I'm just impressed you're willing to adapt."

Helen looked down at her yukata and tugged at it. "You really think so? I'm sure John would find it appalling. Speaking of that, I need to get back to the hotel to change into something more decent."

"You're welcome to go there, but I'm going to the *Hiei* to meet Emiko."

"What? But I'm coming too! I have to find my husband."

"Then you'll have to skip the hotel until later."

Helen groaned but straightened upright. "Fine then. Let's just get this over with as quickly as possible."

Makoto nodded, opened the sliding door, forced on his shoes, and started walking. Helen struggled to lace up her smoke and water damaged boots, but after tying up the laces, she trotted after him. She made a strange sight with the Japanese yukata and western-style shoes, rather than the traditional geta. "Wait up, cowboy."

Makoto didn't reply but slightly slowed down his pace, allowing her to catch up, and they headed for the harbor, just as the sun began to rise above the horizon.

After they made it to the docks, they saw a large crowd gathered, even larger than the one that had assembled for the *Abraham Lincoln*. The crowd was staring at a battleship. Its three masts reached high into the skies, taller than any other ship in the harbor, and it had a long bowsprit which pointed forward like a lance. In the middle of the ship, there were two small smokestacks, which billowed dark smoke.

From stem to stern, the ship was 220 feet long, and the visible part of the hull was painted black. Two large artillery pieces pointed forward, and one pointed at the stern. The barrels of three larger caliber cannons emerged over the starboard side of the ship, and the same number protected the port side. Doubtless, there were more guns, which were not visible.

Makoto's height advantage made it easy for him to see the proceedings, while Helen rocked up and down on her toes to see. On the deck of the ship, there were several men in uniforms saluting each other. Makoto didn't understand what it meant. However, Helen recognized what they were doing. "Oh, it's a changing of the crew."

A Japanese military band prepared their instruments on the dock next to the looming warship. A red-faced Englishman stood in a formal suit with a long black jacket, gray slacks and vest, and a four in hand tie. His head was topped with a silk hat similar in shape to the one favored by former President Lincoln.

Helen recognized him as the British ambassador from a reception she attended with her husband when they arrived in Japan. A group of similarly dressed flunkies stood behind him and were clearly members of the embassy staff. Facing them was a group of Japanese men also in formal morning suits.

Roughly two hundred English sailors and officers stood in neat ranks on the port side of the ship, facing a smaller group of sailors and officers of the Imperial Japanese Navy. The British civil ensign flag fluttered from the stern flagpole.

The band began playing "God Save the Queen." A British honor guard consisting of a boatswain's mate and four sailors marched to the flagpole and began to lower the red flag with a Union Jack in the upper corner. The Japanese sailors stiffened to attention and saluted, while the British sailors sang their national anthem.

The British sailors went quiet when the music stopped; the honor guard carefully folded the flag and presented it to the British ambassador. He stepped forward and handed over the bundle of papers that transferred ownership of the *Hiei* to the Japanese minister.

The band then played "Kimigayo" as a Japanese color guard raised the Imperial Rising Sun flag. The British sailors stood to attention and saluted, while the Japanese sailors sang and hundreds of spectators on the dock added their voices to the recently adopted Japanese national anthem.

The crowd cheered loudly as the flag fluttered in the breeze. After the salutes were complete, the British sailors gathered their duffel bags and departed the ship via the gangway. Makoto noticed the crew leaving was significantly larger than the one which was left behind.

He was also surprised to see one of the men leaving the ship with the British crew was a Japanese naval officer. He was conversing with the British officers in English and wore the same uniform as them. The officer split from the crowd and appeared to head in a different direction, but was stopped by a police officer.

Trusting his instinct, Makoto maneuvered himself through the crowd to get within listening range. Helen followed him. He heard the police officer speak first. "Lieutenant Togo Heihachiro?"

The sailor nodded, and the police officer continued. "I'm Police Lieutenant Sugimoto. I have instructions from the home minister requesting you remain on board the *Hiei* until the ceremony tomorrow."

Makoto thought Togo's name sounded familiar; he'd seen it somewhere before, but couldn't quite place it.

Togo gave the police lieutenant a suspicious look. "Why would the home minister send a police officer to relay instructions? The military doesn't take orders from police." He glanced down at the beads in Sugimoto's hand and frowned. "Especially not from Buddhist ones."

Sugimoto bristled at Togo's words and spoke through gritted teeth. "My orders are clear and you have to remain on the ship, *sir*."

"Very well. But first, I promised to meet up with an old friend when I arrived. I'll return in a couple of hours."

Sugimoto frowned. "I'll have to check with my superiors to see if that's allowed."

"Surely you can spare a couple of hours? The ship is tied to the dock; it's not going anywhere."

"Even so, Lieutenant Togo, I must insist. Even if it's not approved, I'm certain your friend can wait a day."

Togo let out a sigh. "Very well, I'm sure Watanabe won't mind. Besides, he works for the home minister, so he'll probably understand."

Makoto's ears picked up at the name of the dead man from the hotel. He dug through his pockets and retrieved the telegram he found the day before. Sure enough, both the names Togo and Watanabe were on it.

Sugimoto also seemed astonished at the name. "Watanabe?"

"Oh, do you know him?" Togo asked. "Since he works for the government, you may have run into each other."

Sugimoto shook his head. "No. I must be thinking of someone else. Please wait here a moment while I speak to my superiors." Sugimoto left Togo on his own. After glancing around, Togo pulled out a sheet of paper, paced around for a bit, and finally snuck away from the crowd, walking into the street.

Makoto decided to follow this new lead instead of waiting for Emiko. He turned to Helen. "I have a favor to ask you."

"Huh?"

"If you see Emiko, could you tell her to wait here? I'll be right back, there's something I need to check."

"How am I supposed to do that? I don't speak a word of Japanese and she doesn't know any English!"

"Improvise."

"Oh, so you think you can just wander off and leave me behind again?" Helen said, crossing her arms.

Noticing the Japanese sailor was nearly out of sight, Makoto trotted behind him without answering Helen's question.

"Hey, wait a moment!" Helen tried to trot behind him, but tripped over her yukata and fell to the ground. She lifted her head and snarled. "Get back here you starveling, you elf-skin, you dried neat's tongue, bull's pizzle, you stock fish!"

"Helen?"

Helen was shocked to hear the familiar voice, sat up, and turned around to see her husband with the Japanese man he was with before, standing above her.

"What are you doing here? And why are you in that ridiculous getup?"

Chapter Twenty-Two

The sound of loud cheering woke Kotaro with a start. He rubbed his eyes and stared out from his shelter on the porch of a shuttered marine carpenter shop. Wondering what was going on, Kotaro stood up and approached the source of the cheers. He was surprised when he came upon a large crowd admiring a battleship. Kotaro noticed the name "*Hiei*" painted along the front.

Kotaro approached the crowd but kept to the back. He noticed Sugimoto talking with a naval officer. He knew he couldn't return to the station now, but maybe he could speak with Sugimoto and come up with a plan. He made his way through the crowd, but when he neared the other side, he lost track of Sugimoto. Kotaro flinched when a cold, familiar hand firmly clasped on his shoulder.

"Well, well, well. The patrolman has finally graced us with his presence."

Kotaro winced at the acidity of the familiar voice. He nervously turned around to see the dark gaze of Captain Fujita staring down at him. "A-Ah, Captain Fujita. I … uh…"

"It seems you're talented at disobeying orders. And I've heard a certain patrolman was seen in the red-light district ... setting off explosions."

"T-There's an explanation for that," Kotaro stammered.

"I don't want to hear it. You're not qualified to handle the responsibilities of a patrolman. Perhaps you can manage the less demanding job of a prison guard. You're heading to Abashiri prison first thing tomorrow."

Kotaro grimaced at the name, being stationed in the frozen prison in Hokkaido was almost as bad as being a prisoner there. "But sir! I have a new lead on the home minister killing, and Watanabe's death as well."

Fujita's voice started calm but steadily became angrier and louder. "We are in the middle of an important inspection to make sure the *Hiei* is ready for the emperor's visit tomorrow, and you're wasting time with cases that are no longer relevant?!"

Kotaro shrank back with each word Fujita said, but before he could scurry away, Fujita grabbed his collar. "We're going back to the station. Now. And I will not have you running off again and tarnishing the name of the Yokohama police department." Fujita yanked Kotaro by his collar and dragged him back toward the police station.

***

Helen and John entered their hotel room. John shut the door behind them, snickering to himself. Helen turned to him angrily. "It's not funny!"

John cleared his throat and attempted to be serious, but soon began chuckling again. "I'm sorry dear, but really? Sword-wielding Japanese cowboys? Mysterious temples? Explosions? And you're actually wearing one of their outfits? The water must have gotten to you."

"It's no more farfetched than your story! You really expect me to believe you just spent this entire time 'on business.' I was worried sick! Tell me what's really going on!" Helen retorted.

"It's as I said before. Business ran a little late and then Tanaka took me out to see some of the sights."

"One of those sights wouldn't happen to be the red-light district, would it?" Helen asked with an annoyed snarl.

John was flabbergasted by the accusation. "What!? What are you talking about?"

"I saw you with that Tanaka fellow. You can't deny it!"

"You're getting delusional, Helen. I knew there was something strange about the food here. Well, the good news is we won't have to be worrying about that from now on."

Helen gave John a confused look. "What do you mean?"

"We're leaving. A couple of days after the arrival ceremony, the *Abraham Lincoln* will be setting sail, and we'll be on it. We can finally get out of this blasted country."

"Leave? But I..." As much as Helen hated admitting it to herself, there really was no reason for her to stay. Everything she'd got involved in had been of her own accord, but she hated the idea of just leaving without seeing the resolution of the mysteries she'd found.

John, a little surprised when his wife suddenly went quiet, shrugged and went to the desk. "I have one last meeting to handle tonight, then things will be taken care of."

John took the key out and went to unlock the broken drawer. Helen flinched and followed her husband to the desk. "Ah, wait John, I…"

She trailed off again and her eyes grew wide as she stared down at the papers John was holding. At the top of the stack, was a paper which had a very familiar red flower at the top.

"What in the world happened to this drawer?" John asked, mostly to himself. "Was one of those blasted maids trying to break into the desk?"

"That's-!" Helen grabbed the paper out of his hands and looked it over. She then showed it to her husband. "This flower! What is it?!"

John leaned forward and squinted at the flower. "A chrysanthemum, I believe."

"Not that! Who's flower is it?"

John looked at her like she was crazy. "They're my business associates. Nothing important."

Helen loomed over John and gave him a stern look. "Tell me! Otherwise, thou wilt be condemned into everlasting damnation!"

John threw up his hands in mock surrender. "It's not that I don't want to tell you, they actually never gave me their name. I asked Tanaka but he just said they preferred to be nameless, though they do have close contacts with the government."

"Why are they so secretive?"

John hesitated but relented and shrugged. "This transaction was a bit 'under the table.' But the next shipbuilding contract is guaranteed to be through Arkwright Shipyards!"

Helen didn't care about the shipping contract. "What did you sell them?"

John frowned at the question. "Sorry, Helen, but *that* I was specifically told not to say."

Helen gave him an angry look, but she saw in his eyes that he wasn't going to budge on this. She thought back to the red-light district and her mind drifted to the guns in the warehouse, the American guns. "Did you sell ... weapons?"

John gave her a shocked look.

Helen realized she was on the right track. "American rifles? And ammunition?"

"Wha-? How did?"

"Mere child's play for a proper actress. Besides, I'm your wife, I can tell when you're hiding something."

John shook his head in amazement and disbelief. "I guess I dismissed those silly detective stories a little too soon. There were a few firearm transactions."

"How many?"

"Just a few, about five thousand."

Helen's glare deepened.

John noticed her angry expression. "But they'll go to the military! The Japanese government wanted to import more weapons, but the current trade restrictions make that ... difficult. So I gave them a little help in exchange for an exclusive contract to build their next battleship."

"How did you know you sold it to the government and not some crazy mask-wearing secret society?" Helen asked.

"My point of contact works for the government! So unless he's part of this cult of yours, I don't see how it's possible."

"And your contact person? He's Watanabe, right?"

"Yes. Though it's Tanaka now, and we were conducting business all of last night. No crazy masked men."

"He just thought meeting in some dangerous brothel in the red-light district was a good idea?"

"Tanaka told me the brothel was a stratagem to disguise the real business from government enemies. No masked men assailed us, and no pretty ladies either. After showing the woman in front a card, we went straight to a corridor, which led into a warehouse to fill out paperwork for the transfer. Then some damn fool set off the gunpowder, and we had to leave."

Helen nervously shifted around. "O-Oh. I see."

"After that, I stayed at the Home Ministry for the night to make sure the transfer went through. The accursed telegram took all night, and I slept on an uncomfortable couch in Tanaka's office. That's all that happened. And speaking of Tanaka…" John threw some of the papers into a briefcase and put on his hat. "He's insisting this final meeting happen at some strange temple and is waiting for me out front."

Arkwright opened the door, tipped his hat toward his wife, and shut the door behind him. Helen frowned and opened the door to look down the corridor, just enough to see her husband meet up with Tanaka and head down the stairs. She stepped out and nearly tripped over the yukata again. She would have to change if she hoped to follow her husband. But he was already on his way out the door. She glanced around for some solution and was surprised to see Aki leaning on the wooden railing, staring at the chandelier.

"Aki! What … what are you doing?"

Aki looked toward Helen and smiled. "Oh! Ma'am. I was counting the lights. Did you know there are one hundred and seventy-two lights on the chandelier?"

Helen glanced at the chandelier, not certain why the number of lights was significant. "That's … nice. Aki, I need you to do me a huge favor."

"Ooh? What?"

Helen pointed toward her husband and Tanaka. "I need you to follow them and tell me where they go."

Aki cocked her head to the side. "Follow them? Why?"

"Well, er…" Helen racked her mind for a reasonable excuse. "It's because … uh…" She went with the first thing that popped into her head. "Because … I'm worried he may be meeting another woman."

Aki tapped her lip with her finger. "But isn't that normal for rich businessmen?"

Helen frowned. "No. It's not. You have to hurry, they're leaving."

"Oh … all right! *Wakarimashita*!" Aki bounded down the stairs, making Helen worry if she would be noticed by her husband and Tanaka, but her fears were put at ease when Aki slowed down to a more natural pace. Helen was a little surprised Aki was so willing to gallivant off on what must have sounded like a crazy request, but after thinking about it, she decided it wasn't so surprising for that scatterbrained girl after all.

***

Makoto followed Togo as he made his way from the harbor into town. The streets were now very familiar to Makoto, but the lieutenant seemed to struggle a bit with the layout, frequently looking down at a sheet of paper in his hand. Eventually, he stopped and nodded when he reached his destination, the Yasumi Inn.

Makoto kept his distance when he saw the woman sweeping in the front was the very same one who shouted "Murderer" at him a couple of nights ago. He saw Togo approach the woman and say something to her. Makoto was too far away to hear what he said, but the woman started crying and wailed, "Poor, Mr. Watanabe," loudly enough that even Makoto could hear. The woman then opened the sliding door and ran inside the inn, slamming the door behind her, leaving the confused lieutenant at the front.

Makoto took out his sword and slid it through his belt for easy access. He slowly approached Togo, who turned around to look at him. Makoto saw his eyes dart to Makoto's sword, and Togo's hand went to the saber by his side. "Can I help you?" Togo asked.

"I heard you mention at the harbor someone named Watanabe," Makoto said in Japanese.

"You know Mr. Watanabe?" Togo asked, his grip tightening on his saber.

Makoto nodded, but before he could say any more, something caught the corner of his eye. Five men approached, crawling from various corners and crevices. Makoto frowned when he saw they all wore masks.

Togo took a step away from Makoto and drew his saber. "Oh, so six against one? Hardly honorable."

Makoto didn't reply. He drew his sword and faced away from Togo as the five men all drew knives and dashed toward them.

Chapter Twenty-Three

The five men charged straight for Makoto and Togo. None wore the bright blue Shinsengumi coat, but their swords and knives were of greater concern. As Makoto glanced at his blade, he realized he could not defeat all of the charging men. He decided to try a bluff. He lowered his sword, reached into his coat pocket, and pulled out his gun.

He pointed it toward the attackers, and the five men skidded to a halt at the sight of the weapon. They exchanged wary glances. While the gun wasn't able to fire, it was still a very large, intimidating weapon. Makoto darkened his glare and pulled back the hammer.

The clicking sound was enough to cause the attackers to back away, and after a few seconds of indecision, they turned and fled. Makoto let out a relieved sigh and let his hand relax, though he kept his gun at the ready. Makoto glanced over at Togo, who still held onto his saber.

"Who were those men? Don't you know guns are illegal? Who are you?" Togo pointed his saber at Makoto, who responded by pointing his gun at him. Togo flinched and took a couple of steps back, but he kept his sword at the ready.

"Who I am is none of your concern. Tell me what you know about the Shinsengumi," Makoto demanded.

"What are you talking about? The Shinsengumi disbanded years ago."

"Not all of them. That man, Watanabe, was one of them."

Togo looked startled to hear Makoto say the name. "You knew Mr. Watanabe? How?"

"I saw him at this inn." Makoto pointed at the second story window. "He was dead. And he wore one of the blue coats of the Shinsengumi."

Togo's eyes grew wide, and he looked toward the inn. Makoto realized Togo didn't know about Watanabe's death or his connection to the Shinsengumi.

After putting the hammer back to the safe position, Makoto holstered his gun.

Togo stared aimlessly at the inn as he returned his saber to its sheath. "He sent me a telegraph saying to meet him here. He said he had something important to say."

Makoto remembered the telegraph he found at the harbor. He reached into his coat, pulled it out, and showed it to Togo. "Was this what you sent?"

Togo looked at the telegraph and somberly nodded. Then he glanced at the spatters of blood on the telegram and his expression hardened. "Where did you get that? Did you kill him?" He grasped the hilt of his sword ready to draw it again.

Makoto shook his head. "No. He was dead when I got there." Makoto looked down at the telegraph. "I found this in the harbor after I fought a different man in a Shinsengumi coat and an oni mask."

"Are you saying this masked Shinsengumi killed Mr. Watanabe?"

"I think so." Makoto dug into his jacket and pulled out the card with the red flower symbol. He showed it to Togo. "The Shinsengumi also had this card. Have you seen this symbol before?"

Togo studied the card but shook his head. "I've never seen it before in my life. But I don't understand. Why would anyone kill Mr. Watanabe?"

Makoto shrugged. "I've never met him before, so I don't know. What do you know about him?"

Togo gave Makoto a wary glare. "Why should I tell you?"

"Because I'm looking for his killer." Makoto didn't know why he blurted that out. Granted it wasn't a lie, he was looking for the man in the Shinsengumi mask who *may* have killed Watanabe, but he didn't know for sure. He wasn't a detective, but if he could find the killer, he could clear his name, and if the police weren't hunting for him, his quest would be easier.

The half-truth worked, and Togo's face softened slightly. "Mr. Watanabe was the father of one of my good friends growing up. He always looked out for me in my youth. He was a clerk serving the current home minister, Ōkubo Toshimichi."

"Ōkubo is dead too."

"What!? When did that happen?"

"A couple of weeks ago, according to the newspapers."

"I was out at sea then. But how is this possible? Who is the acting home minister?"

"I don't know. But what was Watanabe's connection to the Shinsengumi?"

Togo shook his head. "There couldn't be any connection. Watanabe never learned to fight. He may have had some bravado when speaking about his family connections, but he was timid and couldn't have been a part of the Shinsengumi. A field mouse would have been more suitable. Also, his superior, Minister Ōkubo, was actively against the Shinsengumi. Watanabe looked up to the home minister and would never betray him. The very idea is absurd."

"Your 'timid' friend had a Shinsengumi coat and was stabbed to death. And this former home minister is dead too. I've heard the Shinsengumi have even infiltrated the *Hiei*." Makoto refrained from telling him his source was just a cryptic note from Emiko.

Togo staggered back. "That's insane! The *Hiei* just arrived this morning. How in the world could they infiltrate it with the police right there?"

Makoto did not reply since he didn't know the answer, but Togo seemed to come up with an explanation of his own. "Wait ... the crew. They seemed rather ... unprofessional, more like pirates than proper sailors, especially for a skeleton crew. And all of those extra weapons..." Togo stood up straight. "I'm going back there to question the captain. Do you think you'd recognize any of the men if you saw them?"

Makoto remembered the extensive tattoos which decorated the arms and chests of some of the men in the brothel. "Possibly."

"That's better than nothing. Come on."

When they arrived at the *Hiei*, there was still a small crowd gathered around, gawking at the ship.

Togo whispered to Makoto. "Stay here. If anything is amiss, it's best if they don't see you." Togo forced his way through the crowd.

Makoto went over to a watchman's shack on the pier and leaned casually against the wall, trying to look like an aimless idler while keeping an eye on the ship and the harbor. The sailor at the bottom of the gangway stopped Togo from going onboard. "Sorry, sir. Nobody's allowed on until tomorrow."

"I just came from the ship. I must speak with the captain."

"I don't think-"

"Now!" His commanding voice made the sailor nervous. He nodded and went partway up the gangway and called out. The captain, a Japanese man with gray hair and a polished uniform, came down. "Lieutenant. I wasn't aware you left the ship."

"There's been a change in plans. We have to inspect this vessel again. Some members of the new crew are questionable."

The captain's eyes grew wide and had almost a panicked look to them, but he calmed down and gave a smile. "Of course, Lieutenant. Right this way."

Togo looked back at Makoto, nodded, and began following the captain up the gangway. They reached the top, Makoto observing from the pier.

Makoto planned to wait for Togo to return and question him further but remembered he was supposed to meet Emiko. He wandered around the area, weaving his way between the sightseers while searching for Emiko or the American woman.

The cool morning air quickly heated into a humid, summer day, prompting the crowd to disperse. With the crowd mostly gone, it was easier to search, but there was no sign of them. Togo had not returned from the ship either, and Makoto was quickly running out of leads.

He couldn't count on Inzan to cooperate with him after last night, and based on his current string of bad luck, Makoto half-expected the bungling policeman to show up and try to arrest him again. After circling the area several times, Makoto leaned against one of the walls and waited. Even if he had missed Emiko, he might find out information from Togo when he disembarked the ship.

However, after an hour of waiting, there was no sign of him leaving the ship. Makoto knew Togo hadn't left while he was searching for Emiko because he kept an eye on the gangway while he wandered around. Makoto found himself growing restless under the heat of the early afternoon sun.

As Makoto glanced around, he noticed the crowd had all but dispersed save for a few individual gawkers who lingered briefly to stare at the ship before hurrying off to find shade. Shifting away from the wall, he stalked near the gangway which led to the *Hiei.* The single guard who was there had now been joined by four more. This piqued Makoto's curiosity, and he wondered why more guards would be stationed when the crowd was already gone. Was it to keep outsiders off the ship or to keep anyone from leaving?

Makoto kept his distance to avoid being spotted by the bored guards, but inched his way closer, keeping behind several crates being loaded onto neighboring ships. Makoto strained his ears to try and pick up what the guards were saying, but they mostly kept quiet, save for a few low whispers. Makoto could only pick up a few fragments. "… Thrown in the brig … Changes in the plan … Tonight's delivery."

Makoto remembered almost being thrown in the brig himself on his journey to Japan from America and wondered if they had placed Togo in there and hadn't allowed him to leave. Emiko's note flashed through his memory and his fists tightened. He resolved to get onboard the ship and root the Shinsengumi out of hiding. But before he could sneak aboard, he decided to head where he could get more information.

***

Makoto lifted the cloth at the entrance to Sakénomi's and found the bar teeming with life. British sailors were sitting around most of the tables and laughing merrily, all while slaking their thirst for alcohol after the long journey. Jean was handing out box after box of saké.

As Makoto approached the counter, he saw several empty saké barrels on their sides. He also noticed a couple of British sailors look longingly at the expensive bottles lined along the back, but they began muttering angrily about the price, while others ogled the obscene prints along the walls. None of them seemed to pay Makoto any heed as he patiently waited for the bartender to fill up another batch of saké boxes.

During a brief lull in the chaos, Jean strode over to Makoto. The bartender was clearly flustered by the crowd of men who demanded service but made an effort to appear polished and poised. "It's you, monsieur! Here for another round? Business is actually booming for once. *Dieu merci* for fresh ships and the low standards of their sailors."

Makoto shook his head. "I don't need a drink. I'm looking for more information."

"Is that so? I suppose I could always use a few more coins, but you're not going to take me literally again are you, monsieur?"

"What do you mean?"

"The Miyazaki District of course! When I said to give them hell, I didn't mean actually setting the place on fire. You know those brutes from the fire department had to tear down half the place to keep the fire contained?"

"I see. Then you won't help me?"

"I never said that, monsieur. Just don't burn anything else down … if possible."

"I didn't burn anything."

"But you were involved with the warehouse fire, weren't you?"

Makoto was surprised by Jean's astuteness and didn't reply.

Jean lowered his voice. "I heard some strange things in the rumor mill. Men in masks, a man in a black outfit fighting them all, explosives, weaponry. Quite the story. But something tells me if you were involved, you didn't pick the fight, right?"

Makoto thought about his fight against the Shinsengumi and still didn't reply.

Jean shrugged. "I understand if you don't want to go into details. Information is valuable. I'll find out on my own anyway. So what is it you want to know?"

Makoto was confused by Jean's willingness to answer his questions but decided not to give it much thought. "Do you remember the woman I was walking with before?"

"A vision. How could one forget a lady so fair?"

Makoto felt himself grow irritated at the bartender. "Have you seen her around here?"

Jean shook his head. "I would have remembered seeing a mademoiselle like that. Besides, women of her quality tend not to come around here. It's more the ones who are less … refined." Jean made a quick gesture at the sailors guzzling down their saké.

"I see. Then have you seen an American woman around here? She's middle-aged and wears purple."

Jean chuckled. "Ah, I remember the madame. And while I agree she is a bit less refined than the mademoiselle, I haven't seen her either."

"I see." Makoto reached into his pocket and handed Jean a coin.

"You know, monsieur, I'm growing to like you quite a bit, especially your spending habits. Is there anything else you want to know?"

"Yes, the *Hiei*. That ship which came in this morning."

"Ah, now that's valuable information. But I suppose I can be generous. From what I've heard, the ship's more a status symbol than anything else. The government wanted to commission a battleship all their own rather than take seconds from the Americans or the English." Jean chuckled. "Although since they had the ship built in England, is it really that much different?"

Makoto glanced at the merry sailors and switched his language from English to Japanese. "Have you heard of the ship being infiltrated?"

Jean blinked and paused for a moment but responded in Japanese. "Infiltrated? By who?"

"The Shinsengumi."

"Them again? It seems you have a one-track mind, monsieur."

Makoto didn't reply, while Jean seemed to ponder for a moment. "I have been hearing rumors that the crew onboard aren't actually sailors."

"Not sailors? Why?"

"I've heard some government paper pushers threw their weight around to get certain people onboard, but I don't know why. Though it hardly matters, the ship won't be leaving the harbor for at least a week because of the upcoming celebrations. So even if the men don't know how to sail, it won't change anything."

"Could those men be Shinsengumi?"

"I don't know. Anything's possible I suppose. But it sounds foolish to me, monsieur. Though I did hear another interesting bit of information from these thirsty sailors. Apparently, the English engineers who brought the *Hiei* here aren't allowed to leave until the celebration tomorrow is over."

Makoto remembered what Togo said about the crew being inexperienced and unprofessional. "Do you think they're holding the English sailors against their will?"

Jean raised his eyebrows but shook his head. "I doubt it. There haven't been any rumors of escape attempts. But with all of the fuss from the changing of the crew this morning, I suppose one or two may have been thrown in the brig without anyone noticing."

Makoto's face hardened. That possibility made sense and seemed all the more likely the more he thought about it. This meant most of the men on the ship were either Shinsengumi or working with that group of masked men from the warehouse. His resolve to sneak aboard the ship only strengthened, and he intended to make an attempt that very night.

Makoto handed Jean another coin. "Thanks. Would it be all right if I stayed here until dark?"

"Stay as long as you need, monsieur. We've even got rooms upstairs for rent if you wish to stay the night."

"That won't be necessary."

Jean shrugged. "Very well. But if you change your mind, the offer still stands."

***

As the street lanterns were lit with the setting sun, Makoto made his way back to the harbor. The night air was cooling to a more pleasant temperature, but a quick glance up to the dark, gray clouds above let Makoto know another summer storm was coming. As Makoto approached the *Hiei*, he saw the five guards from the afternoon were still there, though the way they slouched and muttered to each other implied they were tired and bored.

Makoto made sure to keep hidden since he knew it wouldn't be wise to engage all of them in a fight. The noise would alert all of the other sailors onboard. He would need to find another way in. As he contemplated what to do next, he stiffened as he heard the sound of three stevedores heaving heavy crates toward the gangway to the *Hiei*.

Makoto hid further back and noticed they weren't stevedores at all, but patrolmen being directed by Lieutenant Sugimoto, the one who ordered Togo to stay on the ship. The guards at the front rose to attention and cleared a path for the police officers. Sugimoto ordered the gangway guards to help the police move the heavy boxes. They obeyed, leaving the gangway unguarded for at least a few seconds.

Makoto saw an opportunity to cause a distraction, but he knew he would have to work fast. He reached into his duffel and quietly pulled out his chess set, opened it and grabbed a couple of the lead rooks.

He held one in his hand and breathed in and out deeply, a technique he learned to improve his aim in America. After another deep breath, he hurled one of the rooks at the head of the middle police sergeant. He hit his mark. The sergeant let out a yelp of pain and dropped his heavy crate, scattering its contents. Makoto couldn't see what it was in the dark, but it did result in a curse from Sugimoto and the guards bent down to scoop up the contents of the crate with the policemen.

Seeing another opportunity, Makoto aimed his other rook at the most irritable-looking guard. He repeated the process, and the second rook hit its mark as well.

"Ow! Why I ought to-!" The angry guard swung his fist and punched the face of the policeman closest to him. A brawl quickly broke out between the two; they exchanged a flurry of blows. Soon the police officers and the other guards got roped into the fight as well, which was better than Makoto could have hoped. Tensions must have been running high.

Half of the men were exchanging blows, and the other half were trying to break them up. Leaving his duffel hidden behind a shed on the dock, Makoto made a dash for the gangway, careful to avoid getting close enough to be caught up in the fight as well. With another sprint, Makoto was up the gangway before the men had a chance to notice him.

As soon as Makoto was up on the deck, he ducked low and took cover behind a few stacked crates. He scanned the area for any signs of other men onboard. For the moment, the deck was clear.

Makoto hid in the dark shadow cast by the wheelhouse and took a moment to study the deck to see if anything there could be used to his advantage. The large mast in the center of the ship towered like one of the giant Sequoia trees he remembered from California, but nothing else caught Makoto's eye save for a hatch. He opened it, revealing a set of stairs heading down into the depths of the ship. Hoping the stairs may lead him to the brig, Makoto entered, closing the hatch above him.

As Makoto felt his way through the dark corridor inside the ship, he noticed a dim light, which he decided to follow. It was coming from underneath a thin gap to a large, metal door. Makoto quietly reached it and tried the handle. Locked. Searching his pockets, Makoto found the hatpin the American woman had given him back at the temple. He remembered her mentioning something about it being useful for picking locks.

He felt foolish following the strange woman's advice, but having nothing to lose, stuck the pin into the lock and began poking around. The sharp pin quickly bent out of shape as it scratched and prodded against the heavy lock. Makoto pulled it back out and tried to straighten the pin before sticking it in again. He pushed it up and down within the lock, trying to force it open. He was startled when the lock gave way with a *click* and the door opened.

Makoto pulled out the mangled hatpin and stuck it back in his pocket, both surprised and pleased it actually worked. He pushed open the door the rest of the way and had to blink a few times to adjust to the light coming from several lanterns inside the room.

However, the room was not the brig; it was an armory. The room was chock full of weapons, but it was a stack of rifles that caught his eye. They were the exact same type of rifles he saw in the warehouse on the harbor where he first fought the Shinsengumi. Makoto kneeled down to get a closer look at the rifles when a voice interrupted him.

"Hey! You! What are you doing here?"

Makoto turned back and saw the three police officers from the dock, each hauling a crate.

Chapter Twenty-Four

Inside the police station, a still infuriated Fujita stared down Kotaro, who wished the masked Shinsengumi had just cut him down back at the warehouse. He tried explaining his case once more, "But sir! You don't understand. Those men in the masks killed both the home minister and Watanabe."

"I don't need to understand your ridiculous claims. All I need to know is that you pursued pointless cases, ignored your duties, abandoned your post, destroyed evidence, drank on the job, and disobeyed direct orders!" Fujita replied.

"W-When you put it that way it sounds pretty bad, but I didn't destroy the evidence! It ... disappeared. And the cases are important."

Fujita breathed in and out. His hand tapped the hilt of the sword by his side. "Considering we have the arrival ceremony for the *Hiei* tomorrow and the emperor himself will be attending, any and all cases are not important until the day after tomorrow."

"But-"

"There are things going on beyond your rank and beyond your comprehension patrolman. Best you remember that." Fujita rose to his full height and loomed over Kotaro with a dark glare. "I will not tolerate further insubordination." Fujita stepped forward, grabbed Kotaro's collar, and dragged him down one of the hallways.

In the dark, back area of the police station, there were a couple of holding cells. Fujita opened one up and pushed Kotaro inside. "At least from here, you won't cause any further trouble. After the arrival ceremony, you will be sent straight to Abashiri. And if you even *think* about trying to escape, I'll personally make certain a far worse fate awaits you."

Fujita slammed the cell door, locked it, and walked away, hanging the key on a peg far out of the reach of any inmate. Kotaro stared at the dark cell in complete shock. Him? Being treated like a criminal? He'd always gotten away with more than he should, thanks to his family's police connections, but what would his family think of him now as a lowly criminal? He slumped onto the bench and drooped his head. Maybe he wasn't so great and powerful after all.

***

Makoto's hand drifted to his sword. However, the room was so crowded with racks of weapons that there wasn't room for him to draw it. The police officers dropped their crates and approached him. Unable to use his sword, Makoto reached for the closest weapon. He grabbed one of the rifles from the stack and aimed it at the three men, who all froze.

"What's taking so long?" The senior officer, Sugimoto, stepped into the room, his eyes grew wide, and his face hardened for a moment. "But then it lightened, and he snorted. "That rifle isn't loaded."

Makoto glanced down at the rifle in his hand and saw the chamber was open and empty. The other police officers breathed sighs of relief and chuckled. "Good catch, sir."

Before they had the chance to reorganize and attack, Makoto dropped the rifle and pulled out his revolver.

"This one's loaded." Makoto was lying, but they didn't know that. The police officers looked to Sugimoto for guidance, who's face hardened again as he shoved his hand into his pocket. Makoto pulled back the hammer, and the click made the men take a step back. "Move."

The men obliged, the last one being Sugimoto, who pulled out a string of prayer beads from his pocket and held them by his side.

Once the path was clear, Makoto bolted through the door, kicking one of the police officers so that he fell in the doorway and blocked the others. They scrambled to follow him as Makoto ran through the dark corridor back to the deck. As much as he would rather search the ship for the brig and for the Shinsengumi, he was found too soon and knew he had to get off as soon as possible.

As he neared the stairs to the deck, he heard the police officers calling for help. "There's some crazy foreign-lover on the ship. Stop him!"

Makoto slammed open the hatch and cursed his luck when he saw a small group of sailors on the deck. Whether they had heard the policemen's shouting or not, they seemed to know Makoto wasn't supposed to be there.

Makoto aimed his empty revolver at the men. "Out of my way!"

The sailors exchanged nervous glances, but after a few more showed up, they regained their courage and called his bluff. They circled around him, cutting off his escape route to the pier. The guards from the foot of the gangway gathered on the deck as well, making that escape route all the more impossible.

Since the gun didn't deter them, Makoto holstered it and drew his sword. The men closest to him took a few steps back, but most of them sneered at his weapon. Before Makoto had the chance to show the sailors just how deadly his blade could be, the police officers from below came up, Sugimoto leading them. He was carrying a rifle. The chamber was closed, so Makoto guessed it was now loaded.

Sugimoto aimed the rifle straight at Makoto. "Surrender. Now."

Makoto gritted his teeth. He couldn't afford to get arrested now. Between the real and the trumped-up charges they could come up with, Makoto wouldn't be surprised if they locked him up indefinitely. However, getting shot wasn't a much better alternative.

He lowered his sword from his fighting stance. This lulled the sailors into a false sense of security and gave Makoto a few precious moments to come up with a plan. His eyes darted around for an escape route. The only option seemed to be diving over the rail and into the water. It was a risky plan since his back would be exposed, and he was sure Sugimoto would just love to use the symbol on his back for target practice. But, he'd have to risk it. His swimming skills were rusty but good enough.

Once Sugimoto relaxed his grip on the rifle, Makoto bolted for the rail, prompting shouts from the sailors. Two stood in his way, but a few quick swings of his sword were enough to make them flee. There was a clear path to the rail, and Makoto ran as fast as he could.

Just as he made it to the rail, there was the sound of a gunshot. Makoto felt a searing pain in his upper right arm as the bullet grazed him. The bullet ripped through the cloth and tore off some skin, which caused Makoto to drop his sword. It clattered on the deck.

The force of the shot nearly knocked Makoto to his side, but he grabbed the rail to keep from falling. He hoisted himself over the rail in one movement, gritting his teeth through the pain. He looked back and reached down for his sword, but another bullet whizzed by his face, causing him to lose his balance and fall into the sea.

The salt water made Makoto's wound sting, but he kept below water for a few extra seconds to avoid being spotted by the men above. He swam to the underbelly of the ship and stuck his head just above water, keeping close to the ship and out of sight. He saw his hat, which had fallen off in his dive, bobbing in the water and quickly grabbed it to keep it from floating away.

Makoto heard the clamoring of feet as several of the sailors peered over the side, some of them now armed with rifles. As he glanced up, he saw Sugimoto, still holding his smoking rifle. So he was the one he had to thank for his new wound. Makoto promised himself to repay the favor tenfold. After about a minute, Makoto heard Sugimoto curse the dark waters and turn back toward the deck.

"That was an excellent shot, sir," one of the sailors said.

Sugimoto scoffed, and Makoto heard a clacking noise, which he guessed was those prayer beads. "Not good enough. "

Everything was quiet on the deck for a few moments. Makoto stilled his breathing, both to avoid being spotted and to overhear any useful conversations.

"This is a strange sword," Sugimoto said. "Put it with the other weapons."

Makoto felt his stomach drop when he heard the rasp of his sword being lifted off the deck and handed to the sailors to be taken away. After everything he and that sword had been through, he lost it so easily. He silently cursed himself. Without his sword, and with his gun out of commission he wouldn't stand a chance in another fight on the ship.

The agonizing sting of the salt water on his open wound tore Makoto from his thoughts and he planned on swimming to shore until he heard the men above speak again. "Who was that, sir?"

"I don't know. I saw him at the warehouse, but I thought he died in the explosion. He must have a devil's luck. Clearly a foreign-lover with that ridiculous outfit. And it was all black … wait a moment." Makoto noticed Sugimoto's tone grow dark. "I think I know someone who may know something about our foreign-loving intruder, someone who *should* have also died in the warehouse."

"Does this change the plan, sir?"

"Absolutely not. Have the loose ends at the temple been taken care of?"

"Yes, sir."

"Good. It's high time they pay for their treachery against me. Maybe they'll be more loyal in the next life." Sugimoto let out an acidic chuckle.

Makoto wasn't sure what Sugimoto meant but felt ill at ease. He thought about the temple which stood on his family's land under the care of Inzan and Emiko, and he briefly wondered if they were in danger from Sugimoto's threat. He dismissed the thought. There would be no reason for Inzan and Emiko to be involved, and there were dozens of temples in Yokohama. Still, he decided once he got back to shore, he would check on the temple, just in case.

He wanted to swim back to shore then and there but dared not move as he saw Sugimoto gaze over the sea once more. "Take care of things here. Make sure no one escapes, and if anyone else tries to sneak aboard, shoot them on sight."

"Yes, sir."

Sugimoto's footsteps quieted as he left the deck. After waiting a few more moments that felt like an eternity, Makoto swam back to the shore. He reached the wooden pier and placed his hat back on his head and his hands on the edge. With a great effort, he heaved himself up, which was difficult without the use of his right arm and the extra weight from his soaking wet clothes.

His wound pulsed and continued to bleed. He dragged himself back to his previous hiding place and stiffened when he saw someone rummaging through his duffel bag and muttering in low tones. Makoto went up behind him, grabbed the thief by his collar, and threw him away from his bag. The man let out a familiar yelp as he fell to the ground.

Makoto let out an annoyed groan as he recognized him as the same thief he managed to keep running into over the past few days. The man rubbed his head and adjusted his straw hat. As he looked up at Makoto, he flinched and shuffled back. "I-I didn't do nothing! I was just … looking at it."

Makoto gave a glare which made the man let out a squeak of fear, and he scurried to get away, but Makoto was too quick. He grabbed the thief heaving him up by the collar.

"I was framed! I'm innocent!" the thief squeaked.

"Why are you here?"

"Who? Me? I, uh, it's nothing."

Makoto's grip tightened around the man's collar.

"Okay. I heard there were some good things in those crates over there!

F-Foreign weapons go for a pretty penny on the black market."

"The black market?"

"Y-Yes. The black market. They sell anything you need there."

Makoto loosened his grip. "Even swords?"

"Uh, maybe? I heard someone tried to sell stolen police sabers, but it didn't go well for him."

"Where is this black market?"

"What do you mean, where? It's just the regular market. You just got to know what to ask for. Now put me down! Come on!"

Makoto dropped the man, who scurried away as fast as his legs could carry him. Even if Makoto couldn't recover his sword, maybe he could find one to fight with. However, that would have to wait until after he checked on Inzan and Emiko.

Makoto pulled out an extra bandanna and used it as a quick wrap to slow the bleeding from his wound. Since the injury was to his dominant arm, the wrapping was haphazard and not quite tight enough. Still, it was better than nothing. He could go to the doctor after he checked up on Inzan and Emiko.

It was awkward carrying the duffel with his left hand, but he dared not put any pressure on his injured right arm. He made his way through the winding streets of the old town and found himself back in the familiar neighborhoods that led to the temple.

Makoto briefly wondered what he would do without a sword if the temple was under attack. While his gun was fully assembled, it couldn't fire without gunpowder and percussion caps. He pushed those thoughts away.

He'd improvise as necessary. He had done so in the past to get out of situations without his weapons back in America, and he didn't see how this would be any different. At least he hoped it wouldn't. Makoto's clothes were slow to dry in the humid weather, but his quick pace made his movements freer, even with the extra weight of his wet clothes and his duffel.

Makoto glanced up and saw the clouds were not only growing thicker, but they were black as well, far darker than any storm clouds he had seen before. He felt panic start to rise when the familiar, suffocating smell of smoke filled the air as he reached the foot of the hill. Picking up his pace, he ran up the steps, two at a time, to reach the temple. As he went higher, the smell became stronger, the smoke became thicker, and an ominous, orange glow came into view.

When Makoto reached the top of the hill, he coughed as smoke irritated his lungs. He waved it away, his eyes stinging and out of focus. As he rubbed them and looked back up, his heart sank. The temple was enveloped in flames.

Chapter Twenty-Five

Helen paced her room, having recently changed from the "scandalous" yukata into one of her many purple dresses. Her shoes from the day before were ruined beyond repair, and she tossed them away. She replaced them with a different pair, which was not as well broken in. As she fretted impatiently, Helen wondered if sending Aki to follow her husband was such a good idea; for all she knew, she was sending the poor girl into danger.

Helen bit her lip. Even if she went out looking for her husband, or Aki, there was no way she would be able to find them on her own. She hadn't even the faintest idea of where they might be. She remembered the temple from the previous night, but it was ridiculous to think her husband went there. She doubted he and that obnoxious priest could stand each other's company for more than two minutes.

Trying to distract herself, Helen returned to her book and paged to the end where the detective had all of the suspects gathered in a room and pointed out the real culprit with ease. Helen frowned. The detective was able to arrange everything neatly and in an organized fashion, while everything happening around her felt more akin to a confusing jumble. She had a feeling her husband was getting into serious trouble, even if he didn't believe it himself.

As she pondered to herself, there was a knock on the door of the suite. Helen tossed her book aside and quickly opened the door. To Helen's delight, Aki was standing there with a big smile on her face.

"Were you able to follow them?"

Aki nodded enthusiastically. "They went to a temple not too far away. Do you want to go there?"

"Of course. Just a moment." Helen grabbed her purse and handed Aki some large coins for a job well done. She didn't know how much they were worth but figured John wouldn't miss them much. "Lead the way."

Aki's eyes grew wide at the sight of the coins, and she nodded even harder. "Yes, ma'am. This way." Aki hurried down the steps at a pace Helen had trouble keeping up with. The man at the front desk wearily eyed Helen and Aki as they headed out the door.

Helen noticed the sun was already nearing the Western horizon. More time had passed than she realized. Aki kept up her quick pace but slowed down when she saw Helen struggling to keep up. "Come on, ma'am!"

"Just a moment, Aki," Helen said between huffs. "I can't bound across the stage at your speed anymore. And we're in no rush."

"But I am, ma'am! I still have rooms I'm supposed to be cleaning."

Helen felt a bit guilty for dragging Aki away from her duties and hurried her pace to try and catch up. "All right, all right. I'm on my way."

However, as they continued making their way through the streets and as the sun began to set, Helen felt her pace continue to slow down. She had definitely been this way before when she followed that cowboy the previous night. While she might not know her way around this area, she recognized several of the strange-looking buildings as they approached a hill. She stopped when they reached the stone gate, which marked the base of a series of steps that were covered with an overgrowth of moss and weeds.

"The temple's just up there, ma'am!" Aki said, pointing to the top.

"John went here? Are you sure?"

Aki nodded. "Yes. I saw him huff and puff as he climbed the stairs."

That certainly sounded like John to Helen. He never did like stairs. She scrunched her nose when an unpleasant smell wafted its way down. "Is that … smoke?"

Aki looked up and pointed to a plume of smoke slowly rising from the top of the hill. "It's probably a ceremony of some sort."

Helen began climbing the stairs, with Aki following. Helen nearly tripped a couple of times with her new shoes and dress. She most certainly would have fallen if she had tried this while wearing the yukata.

When she made it to the top of the hill, Helen let out a gasp. The entire temple was on fire. Helen dashed toward it. "Oh God! John! Are you there? John!"

Aki ran up behind Helen and tried to hold her back. "The fire's out of control, ma'am. We have to get to the fire bell."

Helen broke free and ran closer to the temple. "John! Answer me you fool! Where are you?" As she approached, she stiffened when she saw the outlines of two bodies through the smoke and flames. One was a man in a Western-style suit who looked like John.

She tried to approach them, but the roof collapsed in. If there was anyone alive in there, they were certainly dead now. Helen froze, her mind spinning with shock. Aki ran up and tried to drag her away from the fire. "It's dangerous here, ma'am! We have to go back."

Helen felt tears flooding her eyes as she stood up and let herself be led back down the stairs by Aki. She heard Aki tell her to wait while she went to the fire bell. After she ran off, Helen stared at the steadily growing plume of smoke. Moving rather than thinking, she wandered off into the streets.

***

Makoto couldn't help but stare at the flames for a moment. A flood of painful memories entered his mind as he recalled the aftermath of the raid on his family home fifteen years ago. He remembered the flames consuming all and how he could do nothing to stop it. But this time would be different.

Makoto yanked out the last bandana from his duffel and tied it around his face to avoid inhaling too much smoke and placed the duffel a safe distance away. His clothes were still wet from his dive off the ship, but they were drying fast under the intense heat. If anyone was inside and alive, he only had a few minutes to rescue them.

Makoto kept low and ran to the living quarters near the temple, hoping for any sign of Inzan or Emiko. The flames were hot and intense. He ran up the steps and slammed open the door. "Emiko! Inzan! Are you here?"

There was no response, but Makoto pushed inside and looked around wildly for any sign of them. The fire was eating away at the structure and the building looked ready to collapse at any moment. Makoto began coughing and kept his head low to avoid the smoke.

A beam collapsed behind him, preventing him from leaving the door he entered. He pushed further inside, surprised and relieved to see a back door. The flimsy door was mostly consumed by the flames, and he kicked it down.

After staggering out to the slightly cooler air, Makoto hesitated as he looked at the raging fire consuming the temple, for as hot and smoky as it was forcing his way through the lodging area, the temple would be far worse. He also had never been inside the temple and didn't know what to expect.

He had to risk it. His clothes were mostly dry from the heat, and he rushed up to the temple and kicked down the door, forcing his way inside. The room was almost entirely bare, save for some stacks of wood by the walls that were fueling the massive fire.

As Makoto squinted his eyes to get a better look at the wood, he was shocked to see it wasn't stacks of firewood, but rifles. Lots of them. A large plume of smoke obscured Makoto's vision and he had to keep going, he didn't have time to focus on anything but the need to find Inzan and Emiko.

He kept low, but the fire spread along the rafters and beams, making it almost unbearably hot. Despite the heat, Makoto felt his blood freeze when he saw two figures lying face down on the floor. He moved in for a closer look, but the smoke obscured the bodies. He kneeled next to them and felt a surge of relief; neither of the two were Inzan or Emiko. Through the smoke, he could see large pools of blood staining the tatami where the two bodies lay. Makoto tried to feel around for their necks to get a pulse, but he felt his senses were beginning to dull.

After a few moments, Makoto gave up trying to find a pulse and resumed his search for Emiko and Inzan. He coughed a few times in the smoke before being able to call out, "Inzan? Are you here? Emiko?"

The sound of a weak groan alerted Makoto there was at least one survivor, and he looked around for the source. "Inzan? Answer me!"

"H-Here."

Makoto's spirits rose when he heard Inzan's voice, but it was faint and pained. Makoto pushed toward the sound, trusting his ears over his eyes, until he finally saw the priest through the smoke. He was lying on the ground, near some collapsed support beams.

Dread filled Makoto again when he saw Inzan's white robes were stained with a dark, red blood splotch, and the way Inzan held his side indicated that he was badly wounded. He would need to be treated quickly. Makoto kneeled down and heaved Inzan up onto his back. He bolted for the door, but as he approached, more beams collapsed and part of the roof caved in, covering the door and the bodies of the other two men. Makoto cursed as he looked for another way out.

Makoto's eyes darted around. The temperature was already unbearable, but it wouldn't be long before it became deadly. He ran to the back of the large room and along the way, caught sight of the remnants of even more rifles. Makoto ignored them and focused on his escape.

Much to his relief, a back entrance was half-open, but large beams, which had collapsed when the roof caved in, blocked the way. Makoto didn't want to lay Inzan down to try and move the beams, so he had to maneuver around them.

However, one of the pieces caught against his injured leg, and Makoto toppled over. He heard Inzan groan as they hit the floor, but Makoto forced himself up and pulled Inzan onto his back again. However, now both his arm and his leg pulsed with pain. He could barely even see the door anymore and had to rely on his instincts more and more to find the way out.

Gasping for breath in the heat and blinded by soot and smoke, Makoto's instincts still didn't fail him. He felt the air growing cooler and clearer as he avoided the beams and finally found himself outside the temple. He couldn't move quickly with his burden but was at least able to breathe again. He made his way up to his duffel but his legs gave way, and he fell to his knees. He took several deep breaths of the partially clear air and lowered Inzan off his back and onto the ground.

"Makoto!"

Makoto glanced up at the familiar voice to see Emiko running up to him from the side of the hill. She seemed unharmed, but there was a look of concern in her eyes that made Makoto happy to see she was worried about him and irritated at his own weakness.

She was wearing her maid outfit, kneeled down, and breathed hard. "The temple! Is Master Inzan…"

"He's alive," Makoto replied. "But he's hurt. He needs a doctor."

"A doctor? But most will be closed at this hour."

A booming thunderclap filled their ears and some large raindrops began falling. Makoto looked up at the sky and grew annoyed the rain decided to start *after* he had escaped the raging fire. He turned back to Emiko. "I know a doctor who should be open. Let's hurry."

Makoto staggered to his feet, carefully lifted Inzan, and positioned the unconscious priest on his back. Makoto glanced at his duffel, wondering if he could carry it as well, or if he should risk leaving it behind. However, before he had a chance to make a decision, Emiko picked up the duffel with both hands. "You need this, right?"

"Is it too heavy?" Makoto asked.

"I'm fine. But we should go. The rain's picking up."

Makoto nodded, more relieved than ever to have Emiko by his side as they headed to Halifax's office.

***

Makoto banged on Halifax's door. After a second set of rapid bangs, the door opened a crack, and Makoto saw Halifax's wary face.

After looking them over, Halifax opened the door fully; his eyes immediately went to Inzan who was hunched over on Makoto's back. "What? Another one? Do you plan on bringing me an injured person on a daily basis? Are you sure you're not the one hurting them?"

Makoto replied with a glare. His shoulders were tired from the trek and his wounded arm and leg were pulsing.

Emiko stepped forward, and made a bow, still looking dignified and poised despite the rain. "Please let us in, good sir. Master Inzan desperately needs your help."

Halifax's irritated expression shifted to a softer one. He sighed and motioned for them to enter. "Very well. Come in."

Makoto staggered into the office, and Emiko followed. After they entered, Halifax shut the door. "Set him on the table."

Makoto did as he was told and gently laid Inzan on the hard examination table. Within moments of doing so, Halifax was there with his set of surgical instruments. "Now, what do we have here?"

The doctor checked Inzan's vitals and injuries, paying special attention to the wound on the priest's side. He used a hook-shaped knife to cut away at the robes. It was a deep, bloody cut to the side, and the full sight of it made Makoto stiffen. He glanced at Emiko and saw she was looking down at the floor. He guessed she couldn't bear to look at something so grotesque.

Halifax on the other hand, seemed more impressed at the wound than anything else. "I'm surprised he didn't lose more blood. Oh, I see. His *sarashi* compressed the wound."

The doctor cleaned the wound, dabbing it with chemicals that Makoto didn't recognize. He also took an extra-long, flat-bladed scalpel and placed it in a special tray hovering above the fireplace. He then pulled out surgical thread and a curved needle and began stitching the wound like some sort of macabre tailor. But despite the doctor's impeccable handiwork, the wound still bled.

Even though that worried Makoto, the doctor didn't seem concerned and went back to the fireplace, retrieving the now red-hot scalpel with a gloved hand. After further cleaning the wound, Halifax pressed the hot scalpel to the skin. The harsh sound of skin scorching and blood flashing into steam made both Makoto and Emiko blanch.

The grim odor of burnt flesh wafted through the room, and Makoto wanted to step outside into the rain to avoid it. But he didn't want to leave Inzan's side at this critical moment. And while the sight was gruesome, the doctor's technique worked. The area that Halifax cauterized was no longer bleeding. He reheated the scalpel and pressed it to Inzan's wound a few more times to complete the seal. Each time the sizzle made Makoto's skin crawl, and the smell got stronger.

Emiko tugged at Makoto's sleeve, and he glanced her way. "I don't know about foreign medicine Makoto, but are you sure this man is helping Master Inzan? This is like nothing I've ever seen. It seems like he's trying to torture Master Inzan and hurry his death."

Makoto stared into her eyes and wasn't sure how to respond.

"Just because I'm working doesn't mean I'm deaf, young lady," Halifax said as he wrapped the wound in bandages. "And I assure you I am not trying to hurt him. He's done a fine enough job of that on his own."

Emiko gasped and stepped behind Makoto, lowering her head.

"Will he survive?" Makoto asked, partially changing the subject.

Halifax finished his bandaging and stepped back from Inzan before turning to Makoto with a grim expression. "Doubtful. Unfortunately, his wound is much more severe than your thick-headed police friend from yesterday." Halifax pointed toward Inzan's chest. "The only reason he's still alive is because his rib partially deflected the blow and his sarashi, that under-wrapping you folks seem to like to wear, reduced the amount of blood he lost."

Halifax started collecting his tools to clean them. "It took me fifty-seven stitches and cauterization to stop the bleeding. Good thing he was unconscious. The shock of hot metal against the skin would have killed him for sure if he was awake. Then again, he's a tough old bird to have survived this long. I'll do what I can, but you had best prepare for the worst." Halifax pointed toward a back room. "There are some extra cots in there where he can lay while we wait. Better than this hard table anyway."

Makoto gave a solemn nod and a respectful bow. "Thank you for doing what you can." Emiko glanced Makoto's way and also bowed to the doctor.

Halifax shrugged. "Save your thanks for if he survives. You can go ahead and move him to the cot."

Makoto nodded, picked up Inzan, and carried him to the back room. Emiko followed. As Makoto laid Inzan down on one of the cots, Emiko looked on with her usual poised and calm demeanor which made Makoto's words get lost in his throat. However, there was something he had to ask her and get his mind off of Inzan's condition. "Emiko, I saw weapons in the temple, rifles. Do you know anything about them?"

"Rifles?"

Before she could answer further, Halifax walked in, carrying something in his hands. "Sorry to interrupt, but I was sorting the old man's clothes that I had to cut away to treat his wounds. I found this there. Ever seen it before?"

Makoto's eyes grew wide. The doctor held a mask, a smiling mask. The same smiling mask Makoto saw the previous night being worn by the man who had led him out of the warehouse in the Miyazaki District.

Chapter Twenty-Six

Helen found herself wandering the streets near the harbor, doing her best to sniff back tears. She thought about going to the police for help but knew she had no way to get past the language barrier. Not that her experiences with the police so far have been helpful or pleasant. Plus, she didn't know where to look for them; she couldn't even find her way back to the hotel.

She glanced up and saw dark storm clouds gathering for yet another nightly storm. She mumbled a series of curses under her breath. She cursed the weather for being too wet, cursed Yokohama for its strange customs and stranger people, and cursed the whole of Japan for killing her husband. He may have been a pompous bore at times with a poor attitude, but he was still her husband. And if Helen was totally honest with herself, she was a bit of a pompous bore with a poor attitude at times too.

A crack of thunder made her jump. She felt raindrops plop against her head, and she rushed forward. As she tried to get out of the rain, she bumped into a man wearing a dark blue police uniform. She felt her spirits rise. "Ah! Excuse me. I need your help! You see-"

The officer shouted something at her that she was glad she couldn't understand, and he hurried away. She saw him nervously fingering a string of beads like a rosary in his hand.

As she wandered, she found herself back near the *Hiei*, where she last saw the cowboy. The crowd from the morning had completely vanished; now there were just a few sailors stuck at their posts who were armed with rifles.

Helen thought about John lecturing her about the different gun models, and she had to stifle a sad chuckle. As expected, there was no sign of the cowboy, not that she really wanted to see him anyway. It wasn't as if he could resurrect her husband.

Helen shivered and pulled her dress in tighter, even if it didn't warm the chill in her heart. As the rain picked up, she had to strain her eyes to see ahead and her pace slowed, causing her to get even wetter as she walked. She groaned. "Some detective I turned out to be. I couldn't even help John."

"Madame?"

Helen turned to the sound of the voice, surprised to hear someone speaking in French. Someone dressed in Western-style clothes was calling out to her from an entrance, beckoning her to come inside. She gave a quick glance and saw a sign that labeled the location as a bar. But any shelter was better than none, and she hurried inside.

***

The Yokohama police station was nearly empty due to everyone preparing for tomorrow's ceremony. Kotaro paced about his holding cell, trying to figure out what to do next. He tapped his head against the jail cell door, hoping the blows to his brain would stir up some new ideas. Unless he found a way to prove himself before he was sent up north, he would be stuck at the freezing Abashiri prison in Hokkaido for the rest of his life.

The cold was bad enough, but it was the thought of the smug sneers of his little brothers, the chastising of his older brother, and the dark, disappointed glare of his elderly father that made Kotaro's blood freeze more than the thought of the icy dungeon. He had to find some way out of his cell and show the captain that he was useful, or die trying. Well, maybe not die, but at least be highly inconvenienced.

As he was contemplating what to do, the door swung open, and he looked up to see a couple of policemen dragging in a shady-looking man wearing a straw hat. The man in the straw hat was protesting, "I was framed I tell you! Framed! I didn't steal nothing. That weird man in black wouldn't let me! I mean … I'm innocent."

The policemen ignored his protests and tossed him into one of the holding cells. After they slammed the door, they walked past Kotaro's cell and gave him condescending glares. Kotaro looked away. Under normal circumstances, he would have brushed them off with some false bravado about his own greatness, but this time it was different. He was in serious trouble now, and it looked like there was no way out.

When the prison guards left, Kotaro put his hands around the bars of the prison cell. He tried rattling the door with all his strength, wondering if there was some sort of weak spot. It barely budged.

Kotaro's escape attempts were interrupted when Sugimoto slammed open the door and stomped inside, dripping wet. Kotaro flinched at the sound and gave a quick salute, though dropped his hand when he wondered about the protocol of saluting from a jail cell. "Ah, Lieutenant Sugimoto. I didn't expect to see you … here."

Rather than immediately respond, Sugimoto looked at him with a guarded and calculating scowl. Kotaro felt himself shrinking down under Sugimoto's harsh gaze, which could rival even Captain Fujita's.

"You never cease to amaze me, patrolman," Sugimoto said.

"Well, the great and powerful Yamada Kotaro always strives to be amazing." Kotaro chuckled weakly.

"That wasn't a compliment."

"Oh."

"Why didn't you heed my warning patrolman? Why did you come back?"

"I … didn't mean to. Captain Fujita sort of found me."

Sugimoto shook his head. "Hardly surprising. But that doesn't matter at the moment, and it's better that you're here. I need your help patrolman."

Now it was Kotaro's turn to stare, but more in confusion than anything else. "My help?"

"Yes. As much as it pains me to say it, you were right. I saw the man in black you kept going on about. He tried to sneak aboard the *Hiei* just now. I think he may try to jeopardize the ceremony tomorrow. Tell me everything you know about him."

Kotaro cocked his head. "The man in black? Are you sure?"

Sugimoto nodded. "He was dressed in black and had a sword and a gun."

"He had a gun!?" Kotaro balked. "How did he get one of those?"

Sugimoto motioned for Kotaro to be quiet as he stared over into the holding cell where the man in the straw hat was staying. Kotaro also glanced that way. The other prisoner had his ear pressed to the bars and seemed to be trying to take in what information he could, hoping to use it to his advantage. Sugimoto took the keys off the wall and unlocked Kotaro's cell door. "Let's talk somewhere else."

Kotaro looked on in surprise at Sugimoto. "Uh, where?"

"The evidence room. Because of the ceremony preparations, it's currently unguarded, and nobody should be going there anytime soon. Follow me." They slowly made their way down the corridors lit by oil lamps. The hallways felt much more sinister in Kotaro's eyes now that he was seeing them from a prisoner's point of view.

They passed another policeman and Kotaro felt himself tense up, but Sugimoto simply nodded as if nothing was wrong. The other officer returned the nod and continued on. Kotaro relaxed a little and was impressed Sugimoto was so good at hiding his emotions from his fellow officers, but Kotaro could hear the sound of beads clacking together and saw one of Sugimoto's hands was in his pocket.

As they made their way down the dim hallway, Kotaro thought about the beads. He knew many Buddhists carried juzu counting beads, but he had never seen anyone constantly fret with them like the lieutenant. His thoughts were interrupted when Sugimoto put out his hand, signaling Kotaro to stop.

Kotaro saw they had stopped right in front of the large, metal door which led to the evidence room. Sugimoto looked around to make sure no one was watching and yanked the door open. Kotaro followed Sugimoto and caught the heavy door, stopping it from slamming shut. He entered the room and carefully closed the door to avoid attracting attention.

Sure enough, as Sugimoto said, the evidence room was empty. Sugimoto lit the oil lamp on the small table. In the dim light, the room seemed darker and grimmer than ever before. Kotaro had snuck out of the evidence room so many times; it felt strange to break in. Sugimoto pulled up a chair to the small table and motioned for Kotaro to take the other seat.

"Tell me what you've found out about this man in black."

"I saw him at the bar, the harbor, and in the Miyazaki District."

Sugimoto frowned. "The Miyazaki District? What were you doing there?"

"Uh, looking for the, uh missing evidence?"

Sugimoto's frown deepened. "In a brothel?"

"No! I was just, uh looking there for … Anyway! The past couple of times I saw him, he was fighting some strange man in a Shinsengumi coat and oni mask. I think that man may be of interest to the case."

"What case?"

"The home minister's death, of course! And Watanabe's as well."

"That can wait for the day after tomorrow, patrolman. Right now, the *Hiei* ceremony is all that's important."

"But the man in the mask is very suspicious. I think-"

"What you think is irrelevant, patrolman. Tell me what you know about the man in black. Now."

Kotaro didn't want to push his luck; he knew Sugimoto could easily throw him back in the cell. "Well, he is skilled with a sword. I also saw him with a pretty lady near the bar."

"What else? What's his name? What does he want?"

"Well, er…" Now that he mentioned it, Kotaro realized he never found out the man in black's name.

Sugimoto sighed, pulled out his beads, and started shifting them around on their string. "So, as usual patrolman, your information is useless."

Kotaro winced at the accusation. "But sir, I think the man in black is innocent. He helped me in the Miyazaki District by fighting the man in the mask."

Sugimoto gave Kotaro an annoyed glare. "Your 'thoughts' don't change what I saw on the *Hiei*. Or what that woman saw back at the Yasumi Inn."

"True, but-"

"Enough. Do you have any other useful information about the man in black or not?"

Kotaro tensed up and shook his head.

Sugimoto sighed and stood up. "Typical. I have to do everything myself. I have no further use for you." He turned to leave, but stopped and turned back to Kotaro. "By the way, I have something of yours."

Kotaro looked up, not certain what Sugimoto was talking about, but his eyes grew wide as Sugimoto tossed a fan and a blade down on the small table. Kotaro scrambled forward over the table. It couldn't be, could it? As Kotaro grabbed the two pieces his jaw dropped. Sure enough, they were the tantō blade and the blood-soaked fan he lost back at the harbor. "What? How did you find them?"

"You never lost them. I relieved you of them back at the station before you went running after the captain."

"Huh? B-but why?"

Sugimoto grabbed the tantō and the fan from Kotaro's hand and dropped them on the floor. Kotaro dove off his seat, but Sugimoto stomped on the fan before Kotaro had a chance to grab it.

"Why? Why not? It's not like the captain will hear of it. He'll hear you stole them, patrolman. Stole them for your foolhardy investigation. And after you ruined them, you decided to do the honorable thing and commit seppuku to atone for your sins."

Kotaro froze as he heard the rasp of Sugimoto's saber as he drew it from its sheath. Sugimoto pulled his blade back, aiming the point at Kotaro's gut. "It would have been so much simpler if you had just died at the warehouse. Useless to the end, patrolman. Try to do better in your next life." Sugimoto lunged his sword straight at Kotaro.

Chapter Twenty-Seven

As Sugimoto attacked, Kotaro's instincts took over, and he dived to the side, narrowly avoiding the saber. Sugimoto rounded and tried to strike again, but Kotaro knocked over the small table, causing the oil lamp to crash to the ground and plunge the room into darkness. Kotaro put his hand on the nearest wall and felt along it for the door.

Because he'd accidentally extinguished the oil lamp several times in the past, Kotaro knew the layout of the room, even in the dark. He could hear Sugimoto swinging his sword wildly, muttering curses. Kotaro continued sliding along the wall till his hand touched the latch of the metal door. Kotaro threw open the door as fast as he could with his eyes shut, hoping the sudden brightness from the station hallway would blind Sugimoto.

Kotaro's fear lent speed to his feet, and he was out the door in record time. He glanced back once to see Sugimoto rubbing his eyes and charging for the door. Kotaro bolted toward one of the side exits as fast as his legs could carry him. He rushed past two policemen and nearly tripped over his own feet as he rounded back to see if he could ask for their help. But before he had a chance to speak, he heard Sugimoto's voice. "Stop the patrolman! He's a threat to the plan!"

The two policemen lunged after Kotaro. Relying on his feet, Kotaro dashed off again, keeping his focus on his escape route. At this rate, all the remaining policemen in the station would be alerted to his presence before he had the chance to escape. He knew if he was caught, he'd never even make it to Abashiri alive.

Catching sight of one of the unguarded side-doors, Kotaro grabbed the knob and slammed his weight against the door, forcing it open. The sun had set and rain was pouring down hard, but Kotaro did not even slow down and ran into the night to put as much distance between him and the station as humanly possible.

After a few falls in the mud, Kotaro found himself near the harbor. He took shelter under one of the empty, open-air stalls which belonged to the fishmongers. His blue uniform was soaked and stained brown from the mud, and he smelled like a drowned dog.

Kotaro knew he couldn't go back to the station. Sugimoto had shown his hand and would not stop until Kotaro was silenced or dead, probably both. He had to hide somewhere, at least for the night. As he glanced around, only one place came to mind, and he trudged his way back through the rain to get to Sakénomi's.

By the time he reached the bar, the heavy rain had eased into a light drizzle. Kotaro pulled back the cloth and stepped inside, treading mud and water with him. There were few patrons inside; Kotaro guessed the foul weather kept most drinkers at home.

As Kotaro glanced around, he balked when he saw that crazy foreign woman in a purple dress sitting at one of the small tables. She was the one who had run him down with her rickshaw yesterday. He briefly considered going back out into the rain, but after realizing there wasn't a rickshaw in sight, decided to stay. Besides, even if she did crash a rickshaw over his head, it was probably still safer than facing Sugimoto's sword.

Kotaro went up to the counter and waved down the bartender. He appeared rather quickly, but winced at the sight of Kotaro and wafted the air around him. "Monsieur, you smell like a drowned rat, even worse than our usual clientele."

"Just give me saké." Kotaro put one of his last remaining coins on the table. Of course, this had to happen just before payday.

Jean shrugged and picked the coin up without complaint. As he headed to the back to get a box of saké, Kotaro glanced at the foreign woman. She was staring down at a cup of tea, barely moving. Her eyes were red and her clothes were wet. She had clearly been out in the rain as well, but Kotaro dismissed the thought and turned to face the bartender when he returned with the box of saké.

"I must say, monsieur, between you and the melancholic madame over there, my bar has been getting drearier by the minute. Dare I ask what happened?"

Kotaro took a swig of the saké and glanced down. "My superior officer just tried to kill me."

Jean chuckled awkwardly. "Perfectly understandable, if a bit hasty. I always thought you'd get kicked out or transferred away sooner than getting your head chopped off. Then again, I've been wrong before. What did you do?"

Kotaro gave Jean an angry look. "I didn't do anything!"

"Is that so? Because I've heard some rumors a certain, fat policeman was responsible for half of the Miyazaki District burning down last night."

Kotaro winced at the accusation. "T-That wasn't me! I may have been there, but I didn't start the fire."

Jean chuckled. "Calm down, monsieur. I just said they were rumors. And to be fair, it was the fire brigades tearing down the buildings to contain the fire which caused most of the destruction. Those men are a bit too enthusiastic, but they are good customers."

Kotaro stared down at his box of saké and replayed the events from the previous night in his head. The brothel, the warehouse, the man in the mask. His mind shifted to Sugimoto's words; it was as if he knew what happened there. Kotaro gasped. "Ah! I got it!"

"Huh?" Jean cocked his head to the side.

"The man who wore the Shinsengumi coat. That man, he must've been Sugimoto! It makes perfect sense."

"I have no idea what you're talking about monsieur. Do you understand his ramblings Tora?"

The bouncer shook his head. "I've never heard of Shinsengumi wearing masks."

Jean scratched his head. "Well, it's official. You're weak in the head, Monsieur Policeman."

"My head is fine," Kotaro retorted. "But it all makes sense now. The mastermind behind all my problems has to be Sugimoto! Hah! The great and powerful Yamada Kotaro strikes again!"

Kotaro stood up triumphantly, but then slumped back down on the seat and drooped his head. "But he's a well-connected lieutenant, and I'm just a lowly patrolman. Who would believe me?"

Jean shrugged. "I don't know this Sugimoto, but I think the mastermind behind most of your problems is *you*, monsieur."

Kotaro put his head in his hands. "What am I going to do? I can't show my face at the station. The captain would throw me in jail, Sugimoto would kill me, and nobody would believe me."

"Sounds rough." Jean left Kotaro to sulk and approached his other customer.

Helen stared down at her tea, ignoring everyone else since she couldn't understand what they were saying. She didn't even notice the bartender approach her.

"Are you doing all right, madame? Do you want more tea?"

Helen looked up and shook her head. "No, I'm fine. I suppose. But thanks."

"Don't you have a hotel you're staying at? Once the rain stops, Tora can take you there if you like."

Helen looked back down at her tea. "Thank you, but I don't want to go there for a while. Being there without my husband would be too painful."

Jean gave a sympathetic nod. "I understand, madame. Sometimes being away from loved ones can be helpful in a relationship. I should know. I try to stay as far away as possible from all of them."

Helen's head dropped lower. "I don't think … he's coming back this time."

"Oh. Well … if any man is foolish enough to leave you, madame, he must be blind."

Helen let out a sad groan, which made Jean wince.

"Er, well, if you need a place to stay the night, how about here, madame?"

Helen looked up in confusion, doing her best to blink back tears. "Huh? What do you mean?"

Jean gestured toward the stairs. "We have a couple of spare rooms upstairs we rent out. Originally they were for … well, the Miyazaki District wasn't the only place to find female companionship."

Jean forced a laugh as Helen stared at the stairs. She turned back to the bartender and nodded. "Yes, thank you, I'd like that." She pulled out her purse. There wasn't much left. "How much?"

"No, no. No charge for such a lovely madame." The bartender made an over-the-top bow. "Those rooms are never used anyway. There are three at the end of the hall. Choose whichever one you like. Though not the locked one. That's mine."

Helen gave Jean a surprised look. "You live here?"

The bartender smiled. "How else am I supposed to keep an eye on this place? Go ahead."

"All right. Thank you." Helen paused, staring at the man who came in earlier. He looked familiar, but was so ragged she couldn't recognize him. "Will he be all right?"

"I doubt he was ever 'all right' madame. The poor man thinks people are trying to kill him."

Helen raised her eyebrows and took a closer look at the policeman. "Ah! It's you! From the brothel and the doctor."

Seeing the foreign woman point at him, Kotaro jerked his head up and looked between her and the bartender. "Why is that foreign woman pointing at me? What is she saying?"

Jean gave Kotaro a curious look. "She says she saw you at a brothel."

Kotaro straightened himself up and attempted to look poised. "Well, the great and powerful Yamada Kotaro gets around. Everyone sees me."

Jean raised an eyebrow. "So it would seem."

The bartender turned to Helen, who was attempting to follow their conversation to no avail. "The monsieur says he was at the brothel. But I don't understand why you'd want to speak with him. I suggest you get some rest instead."

"No! I can't. He's a policeman, isn't he? I have to report a murder!"

The bartender's eyebrows flew up. "A murder?"

"Yes. The victim is … my husband. I think he was killed at a temple not too far from here."

"Really? Are you sure? Is that what you meant before?"

"I'm not completely sure. There was a fire there. Ah! Oh no, I lost track of Aki back there."

"Who?"

"N-Never mind. I did see two bodies at the temple, and my husband was traveling with someone."

"I see. I'm very sorry for your loss, madame. I'll let him know."

Jean turned back to Kotaro, who was staring at the two in confusion. "The lady here wants to report a murder."

Kotaro straightened up. "A murder!? Where?"

"At some temple which isn't far away, according to the madame. Think you can help?"

"Of course! The great and powerful Yamada Kotaro is on the case!"

Jean raised an eyebrow. "But what about your murderous superiors?"

Kotaro flinched at the mention of Sugimoto. "Well, that's true I suppose … but no matter! A true policeman solves all the crimes that come his way.

Even the ones reported by obnoxious foreigners."

Jean snorted and gave a smile. "You're not as bad as I initially thought, Monsieur Policeman."

Jean turned back to Helen and spoke to her in English. "He says he'll help. Where is this temple?"

Helen was surprised; she honestly expected the policeman to say no. "I can take him there."

"No, madame. You should rest. You've been through enough. I don't think you should go back to the temple."

If Helen was honest with herself, she really didn't want to go back and confirm her fears about her husband. However, she pushed back those doubts and stood up straight. "You cannot stop me. I will be going, and I will see justice for my husband's death."

The bartender was startled, but smiled and summoned the large sumo. "Tora, I want you to watch the shop until closing time. All right?"

Tora furrowed his eyebrows but nodded. "Where will you go?"

Jean smiled and declared in Japanese for both Tora and Kotaro. "I will be accompanying the madame and the fat policeman to the temple."

As Jean repeated the phrase in English for Helen, Kotaro gave Jean an annoyed look. "You are not! I don't need help from foreigners."

"Oh? So you know the way to the temple?" Jean sneered at Kotaro.

Kotaro muttered a curse. "I suppose not. But you two are only allowed to be my assistants, nothing more."

"What an honor," Jean said with a heavy dose of sarcasm. The bartender turned back to Helen and made another deep bow. "Lead the way madame." Jean held open the cloth hanging over the entrance to let Helen and Kotaro pass. By the time they stepped outside, the rain had completely stopped. The three made their way through the muddy streets toward the temple.

Chapter Twenty-Eight

Makoto took the mask from Halifax and looked it over. It was definitely the same mask he had seen the previous night. He glanced toward Emiko, who was also staring at the mask. "Have you seen this before?"

Emiko studied it for a moment before shaking her head. "It looks like a mask for a Noh play. But Master Inzan doesn't act. Not to my knowledge. Why would he have something like this?"

"I can think of a reason."

"What? Why?"

"I've seen this mask before. In the Miyazaki District."

Emiko gasped. "You can't be implying Master Inzan would go to a place like that!"

Halifax let out a hoarse chuckle. "My dear, every man goes to 'a place like that,' even priests. I should know, I've treated plenty of people from all classes and creeds that got in trouble there."

Emiko looked down, and Makoto changed the subject. "I saw a man wearing this mask in a warehouse in Miyazaki. Other men were wearing the masks too, including a Shinsengumi." Makoto tightened his fists as he remembered his defeat.

Emiko gave him a worried look. "Are you sure? But does that mean Master Inzan is a Shinsengumi?"

"I don't know."

Halifax gave the two curious looks. "Shinsengumi? Never heard of them. Are they supposed to be important?"

"We think they may have taken over the *Hiei*," Makoto said.

"Oh, the *Hiei*? That is…" Halifax scratched his chin. "I have no idea. What is that?"

Emiko gave Halifax a confused look. "You don't read the newspapers?"

Halifax shrugged. "Not recently. It's all just drivel and yellow journalism anyway."

"The *Hiei* is a battleship which arrived this morning. There will be a grand ceremony for it tomorrow," Emiko said.

Halifax snorted. "All this fuss for a boat?"

Emiko frowned at the doctor. "Many see it as a symbol of strength and stability. Two things the country seems to be lacking right now. And if they attack at the ceremony tomorrow, the Shinsengumi could hurt a lot of people."

Halifax raised an eyebrow. "That's a lot to believe, young lady."

"I believe her," Makoto said, putting his hand on her shoulder.

Halifax glanced at Makoto. "And why is that?"

"I've found her information to be accurate. And I trust her."

Emiko smiled at him.

"Trust is fine and dandy, but do you have any proof? You won't be able to convince anyone with good feelings and words."

Makoto nodded. "There is proof, but it's on the ship. There were several rifles onboard that I've seen before in the warehouses near the harbor and at Inzan's temple."

"There were rifles there?" Emiko asked. "Master Inzan requested I not go inside the main temple for a couple of days, but I thought it was because he was strengthening the support beams."

"It seems Inzan deceived both of us." Makoto was relieved to hear Emiko hadn't known about the rifles, but he didn't want to fully cast his suspicion onto Inzan either.

Halifax rubbed his chin. "But all the proof you have is her word and some rifles. And aren't battleships supposed to be armed?"

Makoto nodded. "True, but all of those rifles were the same American model. And that's not all. People have been disappearing on that ship."

Emiko's eyes widened. "Disappear? What do you mean?"

"Someone I met today went on the ship, but never got off. I investigated, but was attacked." Makoto remembered losing his sword and tightened his fists.

Emiko gasped. "Is the ship haunted?"

Halifax snorted. "Don't be ridiculous. Ghost ships are not known to pull into harbors. Your friend probably got lost. Was it that fat policeman?"

Makoto shook his head. "No, this man seemed competent. I'm going back there to see if I can find him and my sword." Makoto dug into one of his pockets and handed Halifax another small, gold nugget. "Thank you for helping him." He turned to Emiko, putting his hands on her shoulders. "I'm going to go back to the *Hiei*. I want you to stay here."

Emiko shook her head. "But Makoto, you can't leave now. If you go back on that ship unarmed, you'll never come back off. And Master Inzan may die soon. He needs you here. And … I do too."

Makoto stared at her, getting lost in her pleading eyes once more.

Halifax walked up between the two. "Also…" Halifax grabbed Makoto's injured arm, causing him to flinch. "I know an injury when I see one. You managed to hurt yourself again?"

Makoto looked away. "It's nothing. Just a graze. Inzan is the one you should be treating."

Halifax frowned. "You've already paid enough for the priest, yourself, and a small battalion. Let me treat you. Then you can go gallivanting around town if you want."

Makoto hesitated, but he felt Emiko place her hand on his good arm. "Please do as he says, Makoto. You need your strength."

Makoto relented, sighed, and nodded. He removed his duster, sat down, and rolled up his sleeve, revealing his makeshift bandage.

Halifax untied the bandanna and glanced over the wound. "Not terrible. But not good either. What happened here?"

"It was from a policeman on the *Hiei*."

Halifax gave a concerned look. "Was it the fat one?"

"No. A different one."

"And you want to go back there? Can't say I'd want to do the same." Halifax chuckled as he began cleaning the wound and bandaging it properly. Emiko watched Halifax work.

After a couple of minutes, the doctor was finished. "There. And here I thought business would slow down when the Miyazaki District went up in smoke."

Halifax stood up straight, and Makoto did as well, rolling down his sleeve.

"So you still intend to go? Injured and without your sword?" Halifax asked.

Makoto rubbed his arm. "I'll manage."

Makoto headed for the door, but before he could leave, Emiko stepped in front of him. "Please Makoto, you should rest for the night. You're in no condition to go back and fight."

Makoto found himself hesitating again. He didn't want to go against Emiko's wishes, but he couldn't just stand there either. From the corner of his eye, he saw Halifax rubbing his chin.

"Didn't you want percussion caps before? Does that mean you have a gun?"

Makoto was surprised by Halifax's question but nodded. "I have one, but without the caps, it can't fire."

Halifax stuck out his hand. "Give it to me."

Makoto gave him a suspicious look. "Why?"

"So I can make your percussion caps. I'll need the gun to make sure they're the right size. I don't want to get too involved in whatever situation you've gotten yourself into, but I can at least help out in this way."

Makoto still wasn't completely convinced. "You said no before. Why did you change your mind?"

Halifax shrugged. "It's not entirely out of charity. If you're right and there's some plot against this battleship, that'll spread panic among the populace. And panic is never good for foreigners like me. Just think of it as a bonus for actually paying me."

Makoto considered, nodded, and handed Halifax the gun.

"It'll take a few hours to get this done," Halifax said. "So you and the young lady best stay the night."

Halifax pointed to a small staircase. "There's a spare bedroom upstairs if the young lady would like to use it."

Makoto nodded and turned to Emiko. "You should rest."

Emiko smiled but shook her head. "I can't rest. Not with Master Inzan in this state. And I would like to help the doctor if possible."

"That won't be necessary," Halifax interjected. "Besides, making mercury fulminate is a delicate process which can be rather dangerous. It's best you don't stand too close."

"But-"

"No buts. Instead," Halifax pointed to Makoto, "you should worry about getting bullets and gunpowder."

"I already have the bullets. But the gunpowder may be a problem…" Makoto remembered the thief mentioning the black market and turned to Emiko. "Have you heard of the black market?"

Emiko blinked, then looked down with an embarrassed smile. "Well, in passing. Master Inzan needed to buy a few things from there for the temple. Nothing illegal, mind you. I accompanied him, but didn't buy anything myself."

"Do you know if they sell gunpowder?"

Emiko stared at Makoto for a moment and nodded. "I remember a man was selling fireworks from his shop, and the gunpowder from the back. I can take you to the shop."

Makoto nodded and grabbed his duffel. "Then let's go."

***

Most shops had closed for the night during the rainstorm, but once the rain let up a few evening vendors reopened their stalls for the night market. One of them was the fireworks seller Emiko had mentioned. With the multitude of summer festivals coming up, there was strong demand. Makoto and Emiko walked up to him, and he grinned. "Would you like some fireworks for the summer festival next week?"

Makoto shook his head. "No. I need gunpowder."

The seller balked at Makoto's bluntness and gave him a suspicious look. "I don't sell gunpowder. That wouldn't be allowed by the authorities, you know?"

Emiko chimed in. "Oh, we would never assume you're selling gunpowder, good sir. It's just we are associated with the local theater. There is a theatrical performance coming up soon which requires special effects and we were hoping you may have some extra just … lying around."

The seller leaned down and studied Emiko, then Makoto. He laughed. "Oh, right! I heard about that show. It's the one with the ninjas, right? That explains his weird costume." The seller laughed again and gestured at Makoto's clothes. "Sure, I think I may have some extra gunpowder I can sell, though not officially of course."

"Of course," Emiko replied with a smile.

Makoto gave an impressed glance to Emiko, who returned his look with a smile. The seller carefully poured some gunpowder into a bamboo container. Makoto handed him some of his last remaining coins, took the canister, and slid it into his duffel. "Do you know if anyone is selling swords? For our … play."

The seller shook his head. "Sorry. That's not something on sale today. Maybe next week."

"I see." Makoto tipped his hat and turned to Emiko. "We should head back to the doctor."

Emiko nodded and the two left the smiling seller. As they made their way back to Halifax's office, Makoto noticed Emiko staring out into the distance. Remembering her note from last night, he reached into his coat and pulled out the pentagonal wood tile with the Japanese symbols on each side. "How did you know about the Shinsengumi on the *Hiei*?"

Emiko lowered her eyes. "To be honest … I heard it from Master Inzan."

"Inzan?"

"He didn't tell me, mind you, but I overhead some men who came to visit the temple. I couldn't see their faces since I was behind the sliding door, but I could hear their conversation … not that I meant to eavesdrop."

"Then Inzan must be involved, but how?"

"I wish I knew, Makoto."

Seeing Emiko's worried expression, Makoto changed the subject and showed her the tile. "I found this with your note. What is it?"

Emiko smiled. "Have you played shogi, Makoto?"

Makoto glanced at the tile. "I remember my father playing the game. But I never learned."

Emiko gave a light laugh. "That's the flying chariot. A powerful piece which can span the board in a single move. Kind of like how you traverse the world. And once you reach your destination…" Emiko took the piece, flipped it over, and pointed to the more ornate symbol on the other side. "You will become the dragon king, one of the most powerful pieces in the game. I wanted you to have this piece."

"But won't your set be incomplete?" Makoto asked.

Emiko gave a sad smile. "The set is gone with everything else in the fire. But several pieces have been missing since the Satsuma rebellion last year. I was hoping the tile might bring you luck in your quest."

She handed the piece back to Makoto, but he hesitated to take it. "I don't deserve that."

"What do you mean?"

"My goals are not worthy of a dragon king, a flying chariot, or even a pawn. The men I'm fighting against are stronger than me. I probably won't succeed."

Emiko gave him a concerned look. "You speak as if your cause isn't honorable. There is no greater honor than avenging your fallen family. I only wish I could do that as well."

She put the tile in his hand. "And I have confidence in your strength Makoto. You will overcome any enemies who stand in the way of your revenge."

Makoto stared down at the tile, not certain whether to take it back or not. He finally slid it into his pocket, evoking a smile from Emiko. He reached into his duffel and pulled out his chess set. "In that case, I have something for you as well."

"Oh?"

Makoto opened up the set and handed her a tall piece with a crown at the top. "This is the queen. The most powerful piece in the game. It doesn't promote like the flying chariot, but even a pawn can become a queen when it reaches the other side of the board."

Emiko looked up demurely and took the piece. "Thank you, I will treasure it."

That wasn't all Makoto wanted to say to her, but before he could speak further, they were interrupted by a voice calling out to them. "Emiko! You're here! I've been looking for you!"

Makoto and Emiko turned to see a woman dressed in the same hotel uniform Emiko wore, running in their direction. She stopped in front of them, panting and out of breath.

"Miss Aki! What are you doing here?" Emiko asked.

Aki looked up, her eyes darting wildly around. "What am I doing? What are you doing? I saw *your* temple on fire! Don't you know?"

Emiko's expression fell. "Yes, I know. I was there."

"I didn't realize it was your temple until, well I'm getting ahead of myself, I saw some strange men enter. Then I brought Mrs. Arkwright; she's the one in the purple dress. But it was already burning!" Aki said at a rapid pace.

Emiko balked. "Why did you bring foreigners to the temple!?"

"Because she asked me to. But that's not important anymore. I lost her at the temple! I'm not sure where she is. Can you help me find her?"

Makoto stepped forward. "You said she wore purple?"

Aki jolted, not seeming to realize Makoto was standing there and nodded. "Yes, she was searching for her husband. And, uh, who are you?"

Emiko motioned toward Makoto. "This is Mori Makoto, his family owned the land where the temple … used to stand. And Makoto, this is

Nakamura Aki, she is my associate at the Grand Hotel. She's … unique."

Makoto didn't need Emiko to tell him that based on the way Aki impatiently bounced up and down, eager to get in another word.

"Yes, yes, nice to meet you. Now, do you know Mrs. Arkwright?" Aki asked.

Makoto gave a slow nod with a sigh. "Yes. We seem to have a tendency to run into each other. Knowing her, she's gotten herself into some sort of trouble. Take me where you last saw her."

Aki nodded eagerly. "Thank you, sir! This way." Aki motioned for Makoto to follow, as she trotted ahead.

He glanced back at Emiko, who seemed to hesitate. "Do you want to go back to the doctor's office?"

Makoto's words seemed to snap her out of her thoughts, and she shook her head. "No. I'm coming too. Where you go, I follow."

Makoto nodded, and he and Emiko followed Aki toward the temple.

Chapter Twenty-Nine

The hour was growing late when Jean, Helen, and Kotaro arrived at the stone steps of the temple. Helen pointed up the hill. "It's this way."

Jean nodded and took a few steps forward, but stopped and glanced back at Kotaro. Kotaro stared up at the pathway, worry growing in his eyes. "W-We're going here? We can't!"

Jean raised an eyebrow. "Why? What's wrong?"

"This temple is haunted! I've heard angry spirits reside here that curse any who enter!"

Jean snorted. Helen looked on at the two, unable to discern their conversation. "What did he say?"

"Apparently, this temple is haunted," Jean said with a chuckle.

"Really? By the prickling of my thumbs." Helen looked up the steps. "But I don't remember there being any witches, ghosts, or any sort of spirits when I was there last night." Memories of the blazing fire flashed through Helen's mind. "Though I suppose the place could be unlucky."

Jean made an over-the-top bow. "No need to fear madame, I will gladly slay any ghosts that dare show themselves."

Helen gave a forced laugh. "I highly doubt we'll run into any."

Jean smiled. "Well, that's good, especially since I don't know how to fight ghosts. Let's continue." Jean started up the steps, and Helen followed.

Kotaro hesitated and glanced around with a nervousness in his step. "You're going? What about the spirits?"

Jean shrugged. "I thought you were 'great and powerful.' And you're scared of a few measly ghosts?"

Kotaro groaned. "Blasted sickle weasels." He started up the steps behind the bartender and the American woman. They made it to the top and saw the charred remains of the temple. Jean let out a whistle, while Helen averted her eyes from the sight.

Kotaro swallowed a lump in his throat. "Evil spirits I tell you. We should go before they possess our shoes!"

Jean chuckled and nonchalantly approached the temple. Kotaro groaned again but trotted behind. Helen held back for a few moments, but after a deep breath, followed after them. She didn't want to be back there so soon, but if she could find any leads about her husband's death, she felt she owed it to him to find those responsible as soon as possible.

As the group approached the charred remains of the temple, the bartender waved away some smoke. "Smells worse than closing time after a new ship comes in."

Kotaro kept a safe distance, and Helen remained a few steps behind the bartender. Jean stepped into the incinerated remains of the temple, careful to avoid the still hot embers which remained after the downpour. Helen flinched when she saw two bodies on the other side of the temple. She pointed to them. "I … I think my husband may be over there."

Jean visibly paled when the bodies came into view and slowly moved toward them. Helen came around on the other side with Kotaro, who seemed to follow the others to avoid being left alone. As they approached the bodies, Helen averted her eyes to the sight while Jean and Kotaro went in for a closer look.

"Mon Dieu. Poor souls," Jean muttered.

Kotaro looked around nervously for *yokai* spirits until he saw Jean approach the bodies. He remembered his duty, straightened himself, and followed the bartender. Both bodies were face down and partially covered with debris; he began pushing some of it away, and Jean assisted. Once enough was cleared away, Kotaro turned the bodies so they were on their backs, and he looked them over. He noticed the burn marks on their faces were minimal and the bodies were in surprisingly good condition.

"These men didn't die from the fire," Kotaro said.

Jean raised an eyebrow. "Oh? Then how?"

Kotaro pointed to the abdomen area of the two men, which were heavily stained with blood.

Jean winced. "Maybe the debris caused that?"

Kotaro shook his head. "No. I've seen this type of wound recently. Watanabe had a similar wound."

Kotaro pulled up the shirt from one of the bodies to get a closer look at the wound. Jean couldn't help but look away at the savage gash. Kotaro studied the wound and nodded. "The cut looks deep and is from right to left. But where's the weapon?"

"Huh? Right to left? What are you talking about?" Jean asked.

"It isn't of concern to you."

Jean scoffed. "I'd say those bodies are of concern to everyone. Wait a moment…" Jean took a few steps closer and looked at the faces of the dead men before turning to Helen. "Madame, is your husband Japanese?"

Helen looked toward the bartender in shock. "Of course not!"

"Then I don't think your husband is here."

"What? What do you mean?" Helen mustered up the courage to approach. Dread became relief when she saw the two men were Japanese, and most definitely not her husband. One of them was wearing a suit and when she studied the man, the color drained from her face. "That man! He's the one who was with my husband!"

"You know this poor soul, madame?"

"I … I think so. I believe his name was, oh what was it again? Tanoka? Tanaka?"

"I see." Jean turned to Kotaro and spoke in Japanese, "She thinks one of the men's name is Tanoka or Tanaka."

"Tanaka? That sounds familiar … ah!" Kotaro leaped up. "He worked for the home minister! Another death in the Home Ministry. This must be connected to Minister Ōkubo's and Watanabe's murders."

Jean raised an eyebrow. "Weren't they considered suicides?"

"Bah! The great and powerful Yamada Kotaro knows better! They were murdered. And this is further proof. But if that's the case, then…" Kotaro's eyes grew wide. "The acting home minister is in danger! I have to warn him!"

"But what about the other monsieur?" Jean asked.

"Huh?"

Jean pointed to the other dead man, who had a similar wound to his abdomen. In his excitement, Kotaro had completely forgotten about him. While more of the second man's body was burnt, a distinct fish tattoo covered a large portion of his skin.

Jean raised an eyebrow. "I doubt they'd let anyone with tattoos like that work at the Home Ministry."

As much as Kotaro hated agreeing with a foreigner, the bartender had a point. The elaborate tattoo was the telltale mark of a yakuza gangster. He definitely seemed familiar to Kotaro, but he couldn't place where he had seen the gangster before. His thoughts were interrupted when he heard a woman shout out, "Hello!"

Kotaro looked up and nearly fell over in shock. There was the man in black approaching the temple. He was accompanied by two women, both in Western-style maid outfits. One of the two women let out a gleeful shout and ran up to the American woman.

Helen's eyes grew wide when she saw Aki rushing up to her, with both the cowboy and the shrine maiden following behind. "Huh? Aki? What are you doing here?"

Aki ran up and clasped Helen's hands. "Ma'am. I'm so relieved. Why did you run off like that? I was so worried!"

Helen strained her memories about what had happened earlier since it was all such a blur. "Oh, right! You need not concern yourself on my account."

"But you were my responsibility, ma'am. Please forgive … what's going on back there?" Aki pointed toward the policeman and the bartender.

"They're looking for clues," Helen replied. "How do you know the cowboy?"

"What's a cowboy?"

"That man right there!" Helen said through gritted teeth, pointing at Makoto, who had caught up and was standing behind Aki. Emiko was standing at his side.

Aki turned around and looked over Makoto before turning back to Helen. "But … he doesn't look like a cow."

"That's … Oh never mind," Helen said. "How do you know him?"

"I don't," Aki replied. "I saw Miss Emiko and asked her and her friend to help me find you."

Helen glanced at Emiko, who made a respectful bow, and to Makoto, who gave a curt nod. She gave a weak smile. "I don't suppose any of you have seen my husband as of late?"

Makoto shook his head, relayed Helen's words to Emiko, and she shook her head as well.

Helen sighed. "You see, I thought he had died in the blaze, but thank heavens, it wasn't John."

Makoto's eyes grew wide. "Why was he here?"

"I don't know. He said business or something like that. There are a couple of bodies there, but neither one is my husband." Helen pointed toward the debris.

Aki gasped. "Bodies!? Dead bodies?" She staggered back. Emiko looked back and forth, not seeming to understand, until Makoto translated for her, prompting a gasp from her as well.

"There are bodies?" Emiko asked. "I only knew about Master Inzan's injury. But…"

"Man in black," Kotaro interrupted as he stepped in front of Makoto, drawing himself as tall as he could muster, which wasn't so impressive next to Makoto. "I thought you were responsible for this recent string of deaths, but now I realize that's not the case."

Makoto was surprised by Kotaro's words. "Why did you change your mind?"

Meanwhile, Helen displeased at her lack of understanding, went up to the bartender and asked to get on the fly translations, which the bartender was happy to oblige.

Kotaro continued. "That man in the Shinsengumi coat and the mask. I think he's responsible. And with this latest death, I am sure, now more than ever; he is the culprit."

Makoto gave a grim nod. "I see. And why are you telling me this?"

"Because I know who he is, and right now … I can't fight him."

"You know who it is?" Makoto asked, trying his best to remain composed.

Kotaro nodded. "Yes. He is my superior. Well, former superior, Lieutenant Sugimoto. He's the only one who could be responsible for all this."

Makoto heard Jean chuckle and mutter in English. "Figures that it's a policeman. They're all untrustworthy scum."

"Sugimoto? Wasn't he on the *Hiei*?" Makoto asked.

Kotaro blinked. "Y-Yes. How did you know that?"

Makoto rubbed his arm, which still pulsed from the night's escapade. "We've met before." Makoto's grip tightened on his arm. To think he had the Shinsengumi in his sights all day, and he hadn't even realized. But when he thought about it, it made sense a police officer would be able to get away with so much undetected.

"I think he's also responsible for the deaths here," Kotaro said.

Makoto nodded, walked over to the bodies, and knelt down to get a better look. He remembered seeing their outlines when he was rushing through the temple, but now he could see them clearly. Makoto could feel the eyes of everyone there boring into the back of his head, but he kept his focus on the two dead men.

Kotaro stepped forward and pointed to the one with the tattoos. "Have you seen him before?"

Makoto nodded. "Yes. He was one of the men in the brothel yesterday."

"Ah ha! I knew I recognized him from somewhere."

"It looks like they were both stabbed," Makoto said.

"That's what I said. Just like Watanabe, but there's no weapon in sight," Kotaro replied.

"It was probably lost in the fire," Jean chimed in. Everyone glanced the bartender's direction, who shrugged. "Or maybe they killed themselves."

"With the exact same cut in the same area?" Makoto asked.

"That doesn't make sense!" Kotaro said.

Jean let out a nervous chuckle. "Well, I never said I was a detective, monsieur."

"What are you all talking about?" Helen asked.

Jean gave Helen a quick translation as Makoto further studied the bodies. He knew he was no detective either, but here he was, investigating murders. But it was at least related to his goal. He had to find the Shinsengumi police officer, and it seemed that he had committed these crimes as well. He had a sinking feeling it was all a bit too convenient.

Makoto glanced at Kotaro. "What makes you so sure these men were killed by the Shinsengumi?"

"Because of their connection to the Home Ministry!" Kotaro replied.

"What?" Makoto asked.

"All of the men killed so far: Home Minister Ōkubo, Watanabe, and now Tanaka, are all connected to the Home Ministry. So naturally, the next victim will be the current home minister."

Makoto pointed to the man with the fish tattoos. "And him?"

"Well, uh, he was probably just at the wrong place and the wrong time."

"I see." Makoto stood up straight. "Is Sugimoto still on the *Hiei*?"

"The last I saw him was at the station where … we parted ways. But he'll definitely be on the *Hiei* for the ceremony tomorrow. Ah! The home minister and the emperor will be there. We have to stop him!"

"I agree. But I already tried that and they've increased their guards.

How do you propose to sneak in?" Makoto asked.

"Uh, well..."

While they were talking in words she couldn't understand, Helen glanced around at the burnt remains of the temple, observing the others standing around. Aki was nodding off due to the late hour, while Emiko was staring intently at the bodies.

Helen noticed some pieces of white cloth stained red with blood. She also saw a short, black stick with gold bands, which looked somewhat familiar. She bent down and picked it up. As Makoto continued speaking with Kotaro, Helen went up and tapped him on the shoulder.

He glanced her way with a frown. "If this is about your husband, I don't know where he is."

"I know," Helen replied. "But I think I've found the murder weapon."

"What?"

Helen showed the stick to him and the bartender. Both looked at her with confusion in their eyes. "Madame, I fail to see how a stick would cause stab wounds like that."

"It's not the stick, but the blade that was attached to the top. That nagi-thing from the temple."

Makoto's eyes grew wide. "The naginata?"

Helen nodded. "Yes, that's it."

Makoto took the stick and showed it to Emiko, while the others looked on. "Emiko, is this the base of the naginata from last night?"

Emiko scrutinized the base and gave Makoto an uncertain look. "I'm sorry, Makoto. I'm not sure. It's been heavily damaged by the fire."

"A naginata?" Kotaro asked. "But that doesn't match at all! They were killed with short blades. The wounds may have been deep, but there was no sign of a naginata. You can't just carry a weapon like that away. Besides, what killed them isn't important anymore!"

Jean shrugged. "Of course the police don't need evidence. Especially when it gets in their way."

Kotaro glared at Jean. "Bah! Like I need some foreign devil to help."

Jean sneered. Makoto ignored their little spat and took back the stick. Then Aki ran up in front of him, waving her hands. "Did any of you invite other people to some masked party?"

"What are you talking about?" Kotaro asked.

Aki pointed to the edge of the hill were several men were gathering, all wearing Noh masks. Everyone looked on nervously at the men, save for Makoto who stepped forward and readied the stick. He would have given just about anything for his sword, gun, or even a fully functional naginata. Just as the light of dawn began to illuminate the sky, the masked men pulled out their swords and rushed toward the group.

Chapter Thirty

The men waved their swords and charged toward the unarmed group. Makoto glanced back. "Run! I'll hold them off."

The three women didn't need to be told twice and dashed away at full speed. Kotaro hesitated, but breathed in and joined Makoto. "The great and powerful Yamada Kotaro doesn't run from criminals!"

"Do you have a weapon?" Makoto asked, keeping his eyes forward.

"Uh, well, I…"

Before they were assailed by the masked men, Jean yanked back on both Kotaro's and Makoto's collars. "The fight can wait! Living is a bit more important."

Makoto wasn't a fan of running away, but even he knew he couldn't fight off half a dozen men with just a stick. Another yank from Jean was enough to convince both him and Kotaro to retreat down the steep side of the hill, forgoing the steps and each dashing off in a different direction.

A couple of masked men approached Makoto, and he used the stick to whack one of them across the face and jab the other one in the gut. It would have been more effective with his sword, but as it was, Makoto's strikes were at least serviceable as the two men fell down, giving him ample time to escape.

He didn't know where Jean or Kotaro had gone, and after he put sufficient distance between himself and the temple, he slowed his pace and looked around. He kept his grip tight on his duffel which held the canister of gunpowder. Deciding that getting his gun ready was the best he could do at the moment, Makoto headed back to the doctor's office.

***

Makoto made it to Halifax's office quickly; the steadily growing light from the predawn sky helped him find his way. Despite being up all night, this latest attack kept him wide-awake. This was hardly the first time he had spent all night on the run. He banged on Halifax's door. After hearing a volley of muffled curses on the other side, the door opened.

The doctor rubbed some of the sleep out of his eyes and yawned. "What in the world? Do you know what time it is?"

"I am aware of the time," Makoto flatly replied.

Halifax gave Makoto a dirty look, but opened the door wider, letting Makoto inside. "Your caps are ready. Though if anyone asks, you didn't get them from me. The police already hound me enough as is." Halifax pointed toward the table with his chemistry set, and Makoto saw his gun and a row of copper caps. The powder that half-filled each cap was the dark red of highly refined mercury fulminate.

Makoto nodded and pulled up a chair next to the table. He took the gun and opened the cylinder out of the frame as Halifax approached.

"You're loading here?"

Makoto nodded. "I have to. It takes half an hour to load. And I'll need this soon." Makoto pulled on the thin rod which rested beneath the barrel of the gun. It pivoted to become a ramrod for packing shot and powder into the chambers of the cylinder.

Halifax shrugged and yawned. He collapsed into a chair and looked on as Makoto opened his duffel and pulled out the canister of gunpowder and a small scoop. "How is Inzan?" Makoto asked.

"The priest is still unconscious, but he probably made it through the worst," Halifax said. "Barring any infections, he may just recover."

Makoto glanced over to the other room, feeling a sense of relief that Inzan might live after all. However, he desperately wanted to know what in the world happened in the temple. "Would it be possible to wake him?"

Halifax snorted. "Absolutely not. He needs to heal, plus I have him on a sedative to help with the pain. He won't be waking up for many hours, if ever."

"I see." Makoto returned his attention to his gun as Halifax dozed off in his chair. Makoto carefully used a scoop to measure out the right amount of gunpowder into the first chamber. Even in his fatigued state, he was precise in his work. He had done this hundreds of times in America and it was second nature to him. After pouring in the powder, he tore a small piece of cotton from a wad he kept in his duffel and stuffed it into the chamber.

He then took out his chess set and pulled out one of the .36 caliber bullets, which previously formed the heads of the pawns. He inserted the metal ball into the chamber. He rotated the cylinder and used the loading lever to compress the bullet, wad, and powder to ready it for firing.

He repeated the process four more times, leaving one cylinder empty. The gun's hammer would rest on the empty cylinder, preventing an accidental misfire. Makoto's final step was taking Halifax's percussion caps and carefully placing them over the nipples on the back of the cylinder. Once finished, he rotated the cylinder so the hammer rested on the empty chamber.

He slid the gun into his belt. He only had five shots and needed to use them wisely. Hopefully, he'd get his hands on his sword or some other useful weapon before his bullets ran out, but he had to be ready for the worst.

The sun had cleared the horizon and if he was going to sneak onboard the ship, now was the time. Halifax was still sleeping, so Makoto decided not to disturb him. Before heading out, he also looked over to Inzan and hoped he would make it through, even if they were possibly enemies. He quietly opened the door, shut it behind him, and made his way to the harbor at a brisk pace, doing his best to fight back the encroaching fatigue. He wished coffee was more commonplace in Japan.

***

Helen dashed away from the masked men and split off from Aki and Emiko, who each ran off in a different direction. As she ran as fast as her legs could carry her, she tripped on something along the edge of the hill and toppled over. She looked back at what caused her to trip and paled at the sight of a curved blade attached to a short, black pole. It was the missing top half of the weapon that cowboy mentioned.

She slowly went to her knees, nervously picked up the weapon, and looked it over. As she brought the blade closer to get a better look, she saw it was stained with blood. Helen breathed in sharply and dropped the blade. As she bent down to pick it up again, she saw a piece of paper, half-charred from the flames. Helen picked it up, turned it around, and gasped. It was the letter to her husband from Watanabe, which disappeared from her room a few nights ago.

She looked it over a couple more times, but the red flower on the top and the bits of text that were still legible were definitely the same. She wondered how in the world it ended up near the burnt temple.

Before she could collect her thoughts, the bartender dashed up to her. "Madame! Why are you still here?"

Helen looked up as Jean yanked her upright. Aki was nervously standing next to the bartender wearing a worried expression.

"We have to go madame, before those ruffians come this way. Come on."

"But what about-" Helen began.

"Discussion can wait until after we leave! Come on."

"Let's go. Let's go!" Aki said.

Jean pulled Helen forward and Aki followed behind as they dashed away from the hill and back toward the bar. When they arrived, Jean pulled open the cloth and beckoned Aki and Helen to enter. They did, with Jean following. The bar was empty inside, save for Tora, who was dozing off behind the counter.

"Hey! Tora!" Jean said.

Tora snapped awake and gave a yawn. Jean gave Tora some instructions in Japanese, which Helen couldn't understand. "What did you just say? What are you going to do?"

Jean gave Helen a smile. "I'm just going to see what's going on with that silly battleship. You and the young mademoiselle should rest here."

Helen glanced at Aki, who was nodding off while standing up, but Helen shook her head. "No. My husband wasn't there, praise the Lord, but I have a feeling he's gotten himself involved in this somehow. I'm not going to just leave him. And also…"

Helen thought back to the temple and the letter she found next to the bloodied blade. "I think I may know who's responsible for the deaths of those two men."

Jean raised an eyebrow. "What are you talking about madame? Didn't that fat policeman say it was one of his cohorts? It must've been a police officer."

"But I saw that nagi-something or other back near the temple. It was covered with blood."

Jean shrugged. "Even if that's the case, madame, I can't in good conscious let you come along."

Helen gave the bartender her most intense, matronly gaze. "I *will* be coming. My women's intuition is telling me to go there and I will, whether you approve or not."

Jean returned Helen's hard gaze for a moment but let out a relenting chuckle. "Who am I to deny a woman's intuition?"

The bartender stepped aside and held open the cloth for Helen. Tora looked at the two with a confused look in his eye, while Aki collapsed into a chair and was dozing away. Jean gave some final instructions to Tora and followed Helen toward the *Hiei*.

***

Kotaro ran as fast as he could through the chaos and found himself following one of the young ladies. He believed the man in black addressed her as Emiko. She ran at a speed much faster than one would expect in a dress, as if those men in the masks were following her. Kotaro glanced back and was startled when he saw that, in fact, about four of the masked men were running after them.

He picked up his pace and the two dashed back into the well-lit harbor and ran into the fish market. The sharp stench of fish permeated the air, but there were many people at the market and it was unlikely the men would attack in so public a place. Kotaro turned back to see if the men were following, and sure enough, none seemed to be there. He sighed with relief and breathed hard from the sprint while the young woman, after a brief survey of their surroundings, began walking away.

"Where are you going?" Kotaro asked.

The young woman did not reply and continued walking. Kotaro felt the slap of a fish to the back of his head and staggered forward. He gave a dirty look as a fishmonger scooped up the rogue fish and tossed it into a bin with other flopping fish.

Kotaro trotted up behind Emiko and looked her up and down. He had to admit the maid was quite pretty, but now was not the time to get distracted. As they continued walking in silence, Kotaro realized where they were heading. "Wait a moment, if we keep going this way, we'll run into the *Hiei*."

Emiko nodded.

"But why are you going there?" Kotaro asked.

Emiko continued staring forward as she walked. "Because that's where Mako- I mean Master Mori will be going."

"Mori? Oh, you mean that suspicious man in black?"

Emiko gave Kotaro a disdainful glance. "You speak of him as if he was a criminal."

"Don't be ridiculous. I don't think that anymore."

Emiko returned her gaze forward and kept her pace. Kotaro had trouble keeping up. "Slow down. The ship isn't going-" Kotaro clammed up when the ship came into view and his eyes fell on the gangway. The area was almost devoid of people; most early risers were at the fish market. But three people stood at the foot of the gangway.

Standing in front of the two guards was a man in a bright blue Shinsengumi coat and a demon mask. It was the same man who nearly decapitated him at the warehouse. The guards parted ways and let him onboard. Emiko stopped and looked on.

"It must be Sugimoto! Quick, get out of sight," Kotaro whispered as he motioned her to follow him further back and hide in the space between a couple of buildings.

Emiko nodded and backed up into the alley behind Kotaro, and they both peeked their heads out.

"The emperor is supposed to tour first," Kotaro said. "The ministers will come after. That's when Sugimoto will probably try to kill the home minister. Where is that blasted man in black when you need him?"

"You stay here. I'll find Master Mori." Emiko stepped out of the alley and walked away from the *Hiei* before Kotaro could raise an objection. "Huh? No. Wait!"

But she was out of sight before Kotaro could run after her. Kotaro briefly wondered if she'd just said that to get away from him, but he dismissed the thought and focused back on the *Hiei*, wondering how to deal with Sugimoto and how in the world he could hope to explain all of this to Captain Fujita.

***

Makoto continued his brisk pace toward the harbor. It took longer than he had hoped to load his gun and a small crowd started gathering to get good viewing spots before the ceremony began. As he moved forward into the crowd, he felt his spirits rise when he saw Emiko.

She also seemed pleased to see him. "Ah, Makoto! There you are. We have to hurry. I saw the Shinsengumi board the ship!"

Makoto's eyes grew wide, he nodded, and he followed Emiko toward the harbor. As they neared the ship, he felt Emiko grab his hand. "This way," she said. "We don't want to be seen."

Makoto nodded and followed her. She took him around to the back of the ship. Toward the front, the crowd suddenly grew very thick, and it parted ways to make a path. Everyone made respectful bows as a carriage approached.

Emiko pointed toward the carriage. "It's the emperor's carriage. They're starting the ceremony early. After his tour, the ministers will board, including Home Minister Ito."

"How do you know that?"

"The policeman said so," Emiko replied.

"I see." Makoto briefly wondered where Kotaro had gone but shifted his attention back to the *Hiei*.

A military band struck up a loud fanfare as the carriage approached the battleship. Makoto knew once the emperor boarded the ship, it would be almost impossible to sneak aboard, so now was his best opportunity. As he glanced around for some way to get on the ship, he felt Emiko tug on his sleeve.

As he looked at her, she pointed toward several smaller boats which were being ignored further down the harbor. Makoto nodded, and they headed toward one. Makoto commandeered a small rowboat and they made their way to the water-facing side of the ship, which was unguarded.

Makoto formed a makeshift lasso from the rope that had tied the boat to the wharf. He was nowhere near as skilled as some of his old colleagues in America, but good enough to be useful. He threw the loop and caught one of the belaying pins on the side railings. He tightened the rope and gave it a tug. The rope held, and he glanced over to Emiko. "Stay on the boat."

"What? But-"

"No buts. Stay here."

Emiko let out a sigh and nodded. She grabbed the rope to keep the boat from floating away while Makoto heaved himself up the rope. In a few moments, he was hanging from the rails by his fingers. He lifted his head just above the railing to get a quick view of the deck.

The emperor, a stern-looking, bearded man in a black military uniform, stepped up the gangway. With all of the attention on him and the crowd of sailors partially blocking the view, Makoto silently crept over the side of the railing.

Not waiting to be spotted, he dashed to the right and grabbed the handle of the nearest hatch to go below deck. He opened it and slid inside, readying his gun should it be needed. He kept an eye on what was happening on deck through the small porthole in the door.

Fortunately for Makoto, the emperor and his entourage went to a different area of the ship. Makoto prepared to descend the stairs, but one of the sailors broke off from the group and walked toward the door Makoto was hiding behind.

Makoto's eyes grew wide when he saw the man roll up his sleeve, revealing a dragon tattoo. He was one of the goons from the brothel. Makoto took a couple steps back as the door opened and the dragon-tattooed man stepped inside. The moment the door shut, Makoto grabbed the tattooed man's collar, yanked him forward, and slammed him against the wall.

Makoto pointed his gun at him. "Talk. What's going on?"

The man's head slumped forward, unconscious. Makoto let out a frustrated sigh at his repeated mistake. He let go of the man's collar, and he crumpled to the ground.

"Someone there?"

Makoto was surprised to hear Togo's voice. He stepped further into the room. He soon realized he had found the brig and saw Togo, along with some British and Japanese sailors, and an American man that Makoto thought he had seen before were all locked inside.

As Makoto neared, Togo recognized him. "It's you. Get us out of here!"

Makoto put his finger to his lips to keep the men from shouting. He glanced around, but couldn't see any conveniently placed keys on the wall. He checked the tattooed sailor to see if he had any on him but again had no luck. He pulled out the hatpin he used the previous night, though it was very bent and crooked.

He kneeled in front of the lock and went to work. "What happened?"

"I'm not sure," Togo replied. "The moment I started questioning the captain, I was thrown in here by that Buddhist police officer."

"Why?"

"How should I know!?"

One of the British sailors being held in the brig spoke up. "They wanted us to show 'em where the boiler was, and after we did, they threw us in here, saying something about going down with the ship."

"Going down with the ship?" Togo asked. "Are these men trying to sink the ship? What do they want?"

"I'm not sure," Makoto replied as he worked on the lock. "But according to a policeman, they want to kill the home minister."

"What!? The home minister?"

The hatpin snapped in half and both pieces fell to the ground. Makoto heard a sinister voice behind him. "That idiotic patrolman is partially right."

Makoto pulled out his revolver, shifted the cylinder away from his safety round, and thumbed back the hammer so it was ready to fire, but felt a pressure on the back of his neck. He heard the click of the hammer of another gun and glanced back to see Lieutenant Sugimoto pointing a rifle at him.

Sugimoto gave a dark grin. "You'd best surrender. The ministers will be boarding the ship any moment, and I would hate to miss out on killing them myself."

Chapter Thirty-One

As Jean and Helen walked toward the pier, Helen saw a massive crowd quietly milling around. She noticed a large, black carriage parked next to the gangway of the ship and pointed it out to Jean.

"Ah, the emperor's carriage. He must be onboard, touring the ship," Jean said.

Helen looked up and let out a gasp. "But doesn't that mean the emperor's in danger?"

Jean raised an eyebrow. "Doubtful, madame. The emperor is like a god on Earth to these people."

"Don't be so nonchalant. We don't know their plan, but we know these masked villains have killed before and will do it again. You know, I performed with John Wilkes Booth and I couldn't believe it when I read that he shot President Lincoln only six years later."

Jean gave Helen a concerned look. But after a quick glance to the gangway, the bartender smiled and pointed. "It looks like your fears are unfounded, madame. There, see? He's coming out now."

Just as the bartender said, a man with a bristling beard and mustache, wearing a dark, military uniform descended the gangway with a small entourage of other men in military uniforms. The crowd immediately bowed respectfully toward the emperor, while the police made sure the people kept their distance.

The emperor gave a curt wave as he approached his carriage; inside were a couple of Japanese women wearing the latest European fashions. After the emperor entered the carriage, it pulled away with a few people following behind. Most of the audience looked back at the *Hiei* as a new group of men, all wearing European-style suits, walked up the gangway and entered the ship.

Helen frowned; the suits the men wore reminded her of her own husband's style of dress, as well as the Japanese man who had died at the temple. She thought back to the events so far and felt the answer was staring her in the face, but she had to confirm a few more things to be sure.

"Aha!" Helen and Jean turned to the sound of Kotaro's voice and saw him leap out of one of the alleyways and approach them, pointing his finger in their direction. He started yammering away in words Helen didn't understand while Jean replied. After they exchanged a few more words, she nudged Jean. "What are you two going on about?"

"The fat policeman has been here for some time, and he seems to have lost track of the girl from the temple. What was her name again?"

"Emiko?"

Jean shrugged. "I suppose. I don't recall her name. But it seems she was with the fat policeman here and decided to go off and find the cowboy. Not that I can blame the mademoiselle to want to find better company." Jean chuckled.

"The cowboy? Is he here?" Helen asked.

The sound of two gunshots erupted from the ship, causing the crowd to gasp and the trio to whip their heads back toward the *Hiei*.

***

Sugimoto kept his rifle trailed on Makoto. "Drop the gun."

Makoto glared and held his gun out to the side, the hammer still pulled back. He kept the revolver in his hand, which caused Sugimoto to prod the barrel of his rifle deeper into Makoto's neck. "I won't ask twice."

"If you insist." Makoto tossed the gun, and it landed on the ground. The impact jarred the trigger, allowing the spring to snap the cocked hammer onto the percussion cap, causing the gun to fire. Sugimoto lurched back as the bullet ricocheted around the metal plating of the ship.

The men in the brig dove down to avoid the ricochet, while Makoto spun around and charged forward, grabbed the rifle Sugimoto was holding and tried to twist it out of his hands. But Sugimoto held firm. In their struggle, his rifle fired as well, and Makoto felt the bullet whiz by his head.

Makoto staggered back and retrieved his revolver from the ground. Sugimoto used the lever repeater mechanism of the rifle to load another cartridge, but in his haste, he jammed the spent brass cartridge in the ejection port, and by the way he struggled with it, Makoto guessed he didn't know how to clear the rifle. Sugimoto retreated back, threw down his now useless rifle, forced open the door, and ran.

Makoto dashed after him, but before making it to the door, he heard Togo shout, "Wait! Let us out of here."

Makoto skidded to a halt. He wanted to run after Sugimoto, but he realized he was heavily outnumbered on this ship and could use all the help he could get. He ran up to the cell again.

Since there was no key and lock picking didn't work, he'd have to force it open. He glanced down at his revolver. As much as he hated wasting another shot, it seemed he didn't have a choice. "Stand back."

Togo and the other men in the cell backed away from the door as Makoto aimed his revolver at the lock. He fired, blowing it apart, and the door swung with ease.

Makoto pulled the door open. "Do you know where the weapons are stored?"

Togo nodded as he and the other men exited the cell. "Yes. I inspected it often."

"Arm yourselves and head for the deck. You'll need those weapons. I'm going after that policeman."

Togo nodded and directed the men down one of the corridors. Though before Togo left, Makoto stopped him. "If you happen to find my sword there, bring it to the deck. It has a black katana grip but the blade is a Western cutlass."

Togo gave Makoto a confused look, then nodded and led the men down the corridor. Makoto returned to the door through which Sugimoto fled and glanced out the small porthole. He knew better than to rush out into a possible ambush.

Through the window, Sugimoto appeared calm and gracious while talking to a group of well-dressed civilians Makoto didn't recognize on the deck. Sugimoto motioned the men toward the middle of the ship and signaled something to the other sailors, who nodded and moved in different directions.

Makoto was about to charge out and attack when he realized he wasn't alone. He spun around and pointed his gun at whoever was behind him. Makoto's eyes grew wide when he saw it was the portly American man from the brig.

The American held up his hands and took a step back; his face seemed nervous. "Wait. Wait. I mean no harm. Do you speak English?"

Makoto lowered his gun. "I do. Why are you here?"

The man frowned. "I want to get off this ship as soon as possible, not go further in. I've had enough of you backstabbing Japanese. I did as I was asked and in return, I was nearly killed at some wretched temple and thrown in the brig."

Makoto didn't want to deal with him and returned his attention back to what was going on outside the door, keeping his gun at the ready. He saw a sailor armed with a rifle step in front of the path to the gangway, blocking the exit.

Makoto cracked open the door just a sliver to see if he could hear what was going on, and at that moment, all of the armed sailors turned their guns on the ministers. Most of the ministers let out panicked shouts, but one stepped forward calmly and asked, "What's the meaning of this?"

"A return to glory for our country." A sailor handed Sugimoto a rifle and he aimed it at the minister's heart. "Which begins with the deaths of all foreign-loving ministers whispering poison into the emperor's ears."

Before Sugimoto could pull the trigger, Makoto burst out from the door, aiming his revolver right at the police officer, but held off on firing since he had only three shots left. The American man followed Makoto out the door and staggered back at the sight of the men with the rifles. The sailors all turned their attention to Makoto and aimed their rifles right at him. Sugimoto raised his rifle toward him as well.

Makoto couldn't wait any longer. He fired once toward Sugimoto, but his aim was off in the confusion, and he struck one of the enemy sailors. The ministers ducked low, and the sailors fired their weapons in Makoto's direction.

The American man dove toward the ground. "What in the blazes is going on!?"

***

As the shots rang out, the crowd started to panic and frightened whispers spread among them. The guards at the front exchanged glances and shouted out words Helen couldn't understand. She looked up at the bartender. "What are they saying?"

Jean chuckled. "They're saying it's only a weapons demonstration. That's ridiculous of course. And the crowd's not believing it either." Jean gestured toward the people in front of them, and even Helen could tell they seemed nervous.

However, among the nervous murmurs, she heard a man shout from the ship, "What in the blazes is going on!?" Helen gasped at the sound of her husband's voice and pushed forward through the crowd. Before she had taken a few steps, she felt Jean grab her arm. "Madame, most women should avoid gunfights."

"My husband is there! I have to go!"

Before Jean could raise any further objections, Kotaro pushed past them and charged forward, forcing his way through the crowd. Helen pulled away her arm and followed.

"Wait, madame. That's dangerous!"

Helen didn't reply to Jean's words and followed after the policeman as he dashed for the gangway. The two guards stepped in the way, preventing the two from passing.

Kotaro stepped forward and crossed his arms. "Clear the way! This is police business! You can't stand in the way of the great-" He stopped himself from finishing, realizing Sugimoto might have told the guards to look out for him. Kotaro stood up straight. "I'm here under direct orders from Sugimoto. For his … plan."

The guards gave Kotaro suspicious looks, but Kotaro continued his story, desperately trying to spin a convincing lie. "That's right! I'm a vital part of Sugimoto's plan. To do … what he's planning, of course! Now get out of the way!"

The guards hesitated. Kotaro let out a shout and pointed up the gangway when he saw Sugimoto dash by, a rifle in hand. He had a small entourage of sailors aiming their rifles at the man in black. "Don't you see? The plan's already started!"

The guards looked up toward the ship, and Kotaro took advantage of their distraction to shove them violently to either side. The guards stumbled, their guns spinning out of their hands. Kotaro ran up the now unguarded gangway.

Helen followed him up to the deck of the ship. The policeman pushed the man blocking the gangway forward and the sailor fell, creating an exit for the terrified ministers. Hampered by their morning suits, their rush for safety resembled the waddling of frightened penguins.

A police officer Helen vaguely recognized looked in their direction with fury in his eyes and shouted something she couldn't understand while pointing their way.

Helen and Kotaro froze as the sailors aimed rifles in their direction. Helen took a nervous step back and gasped when she saw her husband pressed against one of the walls of the ship. He also looked shocked to see her. "Helen? What in the blazes are you doing here? It's dangerous!"

Helen wanted to give him a witty retort, a slap, and a hug but dared not move with the rifles all pointing in their direction. Even the fleeing ministers froze as the guns were aimed their way.

But before the men could fire, one of the hatches to the lower deck opened and several men, led by Togo, streamed out and pointed their weapons at Sugimoto and his men. Their numbers were roughly even. In the chaos, Arkwright dashed forward, grabbed Helen by the arm, and pulled her out of the line of fire to behind the shelter of the wheelhouse.

"Surrender in the name of the Emperor!" Togo shouted as he tossed a sheathed sword toward Makoto. "Here, I found this in the weapons room, I think this is yours."

The weapon clattered to the ground and the blade partially stuck out of the sheath; clearly the sailors tried to force it into a random sheath which didn't fit. Makoto picked up the sword and tore away the sheath while holstering his gun, saving his last two shots. He gave Togo a nod. "Thanks."

Sugimoto gnashed his teeth, and Kotaro took a triumphant step forward, pointing at him. "That's right! You best surrender now Sugimoto, for I, the great and powerful Yamada Kotaro know that you are behind the deaths of Minister Ōkubo, Watanabe, and the two men at the temple. You stole my evidence. And I know you were the masked Shinsengumi in the Miyazaki District!"

Sugimoto snorted. "Me? A Shinsengumi? Don't be ridiculous."

"Agreed. Ridiculous."

Everyone glanced over at one of the doors as a masked man in a Shinsengumi coat stepped out, katana at the ready.

Chapter Thirty-Two

The mass of people on the ship looked on at the new arrival in confusion, save for Makoto, who immediately went on the attack. He swung his sword, but the Shinsengumi parried with his katana. The blades scraped against each other at a standstill.

"Wait! Stop! He's not the enemy," Togo shouted.

Makoto wasn't sure if Togo was speaking to him or the Shinsengumi, but it didn't matter. All Shinsengumi were his enemy. If he wasn't using both of his hands to hold his sword, he would have drawn his gun and ended the fight right there.

The masked man continued his attack. The blades eventually separated, and the two fighters circled each other. Makoto glanced around to see if anyone would come to the aid of the Shinsengumi and was surprised when no one stepped forward.

Sugimoto's sailors and Togo's men continued to tentatively aim their guns at each other. However, Sugimoto lowered his rifle and looked angrily at the Shinsengumi. "What are you doing here? You were removed from the *Hiei* mission."

The Shinsengumi kept his eyes on Makoto but appeared to be listening to the lieutenant's words. The masked man let out a scoff that made Makoto's blood boil even though it wasn't aimed at him. "I should have noticed it was you a long time ago, Sugimoto."

"What are you talking about?"

Makoto noticed the Shinsengumi's guard drop just a hair as he was talking to Sugimoto. In a quick movement, Makoto brought his sword over his head and swung down. The Shinsengumi was able to put up his sword in time to block Makoto's blade, but Makoto had the advantage now. He wouldn't let this chance slip away again.

As Makoto pushed his sword forward, the Shinsengumi went down on one knee while the intersecting swords inched closer to his face. As Makoto pressed further down, he felt a shove to his side, and he nearly tripped over. Makoto reached out his hand as he fell and inadvertently grabbed the mask of the Shinsengumi, tearing it off before barely regaining his footing. Makoto dropped the mask and readied his sword at whoever would dare shove him but was shocked to see Togo was the one responsible.

Makoto scowled and pointed his sword at Togo. "What are you doing?"

Togo gave the sword a nervous glance but held his ground. "He helped us get the weapons. This isn't the time to fight each other!"

Makoto glared, and his hand hovered over his holstered gun. He glanced toward the Shinsengumi and saw the man slowly stand upright. Makoto didn't recognize him but had a feeling he had seen him somewhere before.

Kotaro, on the other hand, let out a gasp. "C-Captain Fujita! Why are you-?"

Sugimoto also seemed surprised and staggered back, his hand going to the prayer beads hanging haphazardly from his pocket. "Captain? You were the swordsman?"

Fujita glared at Sugimoto. "I only played along to find out what your foolish little group was up to. And here I thought you were just typical smugglers. But it seems your plot was far more sinister. And to think I let you join the force despite you being a Buddhist."

Sugimoto flared up in anger. "It is because of your kind's treatment of my faith that I have been driven to this. You, these ministers, the foreigners, and this wretched government is driving my faith into extinction. I won't allow it!"

In a swift movement, Sugimoto aimed his rifle at Fujita and pulled the trigger. Fujita winced and grabbed his arm as it started to bleed, and he collapsed to his knees. This shot was the signal to unleash chaos as both sides began firing at each other. The British and Japanese sailors under Togo provided covering fire as the ministers scrambled down the gangway.

Sugimoto ducked behind the mast and called two of his men over. "The battle's turning against us. Destroy the ship!" The two men nodded and ran to the door to go below deck.

Kotaro noticed the two. "No, you don't! I, the great and powerful, Yamada Kotaro will stop you!" He gave chase.

Kotaro was quickly confused by the myriad of corridors in the large ship. But the sounds of the men's footsteps kept him on track, and he entered a large room that was blazing hot. He looked around and saw the two men were shoveling coals into the boiler. Kotaro noticed large stacks of barrels precariously positioned behind the men, which were labeled in an unknown language.

One of the barrels fell and spilled its contents of black granules, which Kotaro recognized as gunpowder. He stifled a gasp when he realized this was how they were planning to blow up the ship, which would kill everyone onboard along with many of the spectators on the dock.

The two men didn't seem to notice him, so he looked desperately around for some kind of weapon. He found a pile of rifles near the door next to an ax and three buckets of sand. Kotaro thought that was a strange array of weapons to have in the boiler room. Not thinking too much about it, Kotaro grabbed one of the rifles and pointed it at the two men. "Ha! Surrender now! Or, I the great and powerful Yamada Kotaro will shoot!"

The two men looked up in panic at Kotaro's boast. They glanced at his rifle and burst out laughing.

"What's so funny?" Kotaro asked.

One of the men laughed and pointed to the pile from which Kotaro had grabbed his rifle. "Those rifles aren't loaded." The two men pulled out their own rifles and aimed them at Kotaro. "These are."

Kotaro flinched and tried pulling back the hammer and then the trigger. The rifle clicked helplessly. He nervously chuckled. "Oh. I see."

The two men readied their rifles. There wasn't time to go back and retrieve the ax. Kotaro glanced at his rifle. It wasn't a sword, or even a baton, but at least it was a blunt object. Having nothing left to lose, he charged forward, madly swinging the butt end of the rifle.

Neither of the men seemed to expect this, and Kotaro landed several good whacks. One man fell backward and knocked his head hard against the steel bulkhead and slumped down, unconscious. The other fired his rifle. The bullet ricocheted around the room and knocked more barrels from the stack and caused them to burst open, spilling gunpowder everywhere. Kotaro recoiled in horror as he realized a trail of gunpowder was dangerously close to the flames and could carry the fire directly to the barrels stacked by the door.

***

Sheltered by the wheelhouse, Arkwright let his wife sit up, "What's going on, Helen? What are you doing here?"

"That's my line! What are *you* doing here?"

"I was dragged here by a tattooed thug. Tanaka brought me to some heathen temple with two of those bullyboys from the warehouse. He claimed there was something wrong with the guns I provided. Right after we climbed that accursed hill, Tanaka pulled a revolver on me! The bastard actually apologized for having to kill me! Then he said something about needing to silence me, a priest, and some girl."

"So I was right! Your life was in danger. I knew it," Helen said triumphantly, prompting an annoyed look from her husband.

"Er, I mean, what happened next?"

Arkwright shook his head and continued. "Then this little slip of a girl in some strange red and white outfit stepped out of the little building and started walking toward a larger one. I don't think she saw us. Tanaka said something, and one of the thugs grabbed me and put his hand over my mouth. Then Tanaka and the other thug pulled knives from under their jackets and moved toward her. The girl walked into the big building, and Tanaka and the other man followed her."

"Did you see what happened in the temple?"

Arkwright shook his head. "No. We were outside the whole time. Then some crazy old man, dressed in white robes, ran up to us and started yelling at the man in their nonsense tongue. He pointed down the hill and the big man picked me up and ran with me down the stairs like the Hounds of Hell were after him. He ran all the way to this ship and the captain threw me in the brig with the British sailors."

Helen frowned, "So you didn't see what happened to Tanaka and the other man?"

"No, the man ran away while they were inside the building. They probably killed the poor girl."

"I'm not so sure…" Before she could say anything else, a hail of bullets slammed into the deck near their feet. The battle had moved aft and the wheelhouse no longer provided enough cover. Arkwright pulled Helen back so the structure was mostly between them and the men firing rifles and pressed her to the deck, shielding her from the shots with his own body.

***

Makoto was at a loss. On the one hand, the Shinsengumi was right there on his knees, unable to attack. He could take his revenge right then and there. However, even though he despised the swordsman and what he represented, killing a wounded and defenseless man in cold blood just wasn't his way. He deeply wished it was, but he couldn't bring himself to strike him down.

"Makoto!"

Makoto froze when he heard Emiko's voice and saw her appear from one of the doors which led below deck. "What are you doing here? Go back!"

Makoto ducked low when a new hail of gunfire punched holes in the deck and superstructure. He dodged the incoming fire and made his way toward Emiko. When Makoto reached her, he grabbed her by the hand, threw open the door, and led her inside. "Why are you here? You have to leave now. It's dangerous!"

Emiko shook her head. "I can't. I have something I must tell you. That man, over there." Emiko pointed through the open door. Makoto followed her finger and saw she was pointing at Sugimoto.

"That man. He's a Shinsengumi. He was one of the ones who killed your family. Inzan recognized him and pointed him out to me."

"What do you mean? The Shinsengumi is there." Makoto gestured toward where Fujita was standing, but his eyes grew wide when he saw the man in the blue coat had moved out of sight.

He must have gone below deck or off the ship by now. Makoto felt his anger rise at losing his opportunity yet again, but a pleading look from Emiko snapped him out of it.

"I'm not sure what you mean, Makoto, but it's your duty to avenge your family with that monster's blood."

Makoto felt his grip tighten on the handle of his sword. He wasn't sure if Sugimoto was Shinsengumi or not, but he was certainly not defenseless. Besides, Makoto owed him back for the wound to his arm the previous night. It still ached, but not enough to slow him down. Makoto drew his gun and handed it to Emiko.

She gasped. "What are you…?"

"Stay hidden. There are only two shots left, but if someone tries to hurt you, pull the hammer, aim, then pull the trigger." Makoto pointed to the respective parts of the gun while he spoke.

Emiko stared for a moment, but slowly nodded and took the gun. She backed away further inside, and Makoto stepped back out, sword at the ready. However, before he had the chance to attack, Helen approached, keeping low to avoid the gunfire, the American man hovering near her. Makoto let out a frustrated sigh as she approached.

"Now's not the time for that attitude!" Helen half-shouted as she ducked.

Makoto ducked as well. He saw the tide of battle was starting to turn in favor of the men under Togo. As a trained naval officer, Togo seemed to know how to direct and lead men in the heat of battle.

Helen shouted under the deafening gunfire. "I found my husband." She motioned toward the American man, who was keeping low but made the effort to be at his wife's side.

"Then get off the ship. It's not safe here," Makoto replied as he scanned the deck for Sugimoto.

"Yes, that's what I've been saying! Helen, listen to the man," her husband shouted.

"We will! But I have something important to tell you, about that girl from the temple, Emiko."

This grabbed Makoto's attention, and he turned to face her. "Emiko? What about her?"

All of them ducked low again as another hail of gunfire rained nearby. When Helen straightened from her crouch, she continued, "Can't you see? She's using you. She's the one who killed those two men back at the temple!"

Chapter Thirty-Three

Kotaro frantically kicked away at the stray gunpowder which was closest to the boiler, but no matter how much he kicked, there always seemed to be some left. He did manage to move most of the barrels out of the boiler room and behind a steel bulkhead, but there were still a couple that were dangerously close.

The coals in the boiler let out some small flicks of flame which landed near the gunpowder. As Kotaro tried to shoo them away, he didn't notice one of the sailors regain his senses and reload his rifle.

A gunshot rang out, and Kotaro flinched. He looked behind to see the sailor drop his rifle and collapse, a small pool of blood forming underneath him. Kotaro looked around for the shooter and saw Captain Fujita grasping the door with one hand and holding a rifle with the other. His arm was bleeding heavily. He dropped the rifle and staggered inside.

Kotaro froze. He knew Captain Fujita was the same Shinsengumi from a couple of nights ago who tried to kill him, and he didn't know if he would try again. However, Fujita dragged himself forward, clutching his injured arm, and headed for the boiler. "We have to move the rest of the gunpowder out of the way."

Kotaro put aside his doubts and followed the captain. Fujita tried to push one of the barrels away from the boiler, but in his injured state ended up knocking it over and spilling out more gunpowder.

"There's no time for that!" Kotaro said. "We should put out the fire in the boiler instead."

Fujita gave Kotaro a dark look, which made him wince. "I mean. If you think it's a good idea, sir."

"How do you propose to put out the fire?" Fujita asked.

"Huh? Uh, well…" Kotaro looked around; he had never been on a ship like this before. He ran up to the boiler and glanced around for any sort of door to cover the flaming coals. Lying next to the boiler was a small piece of metal. Kotaro picked it up and realized it was the missing door that had been torn from the boiler. He tried to place it back where it belonged, but it immediately fell off again.

"That doesn't seem very effective, patrolman."

As Kotaro looked around, he saw the empty rifles from before, and his eyes drifted to the buckets of sand. "Ah! The sand!" Kotaro grabbed two buckets and struggled to heave the sand to the furnace.

"What are you doing?" Fujita asked.

"The sand, sir. We can use it to suppress the fire."

Fujita nodded. "That's true. Better than I expected from you, patrolman." He grabbed the remaining bucket with his good arm and headed to the boiler.

Kotaro dumped his sand on the burning coals, and Fujita did the same. The fires seemed to be suppressed by the sand, but there were still some embers flying out.

"It's not enough. We need more." Fujita staggered around and looked for other means to subdue the flames, while Kotaro grabbed the door to the boiler and held it in place to prevent the embers from escaping. However, the metal grew hot, Kotaro let out a yelp, and he dropped the door. He blew at his hands to cool them down.

They heard someone running toward the room, and both glanced nervously toward the door. They were in no condition to fight any more of Sugimoto's men. They were both relieved when Lieutenant Togo entered the room.

After briefly looking over of the situation, the lieutenant paled at the sight of the gunpowder and the furnace. He slammed shut the hatch to the corridor where Kotaro and Fujita had been stacking the barrels. "Get away from there! The embers!"

Kotaro looked and nearly jumped out of his skin as some of the glowing embers fluttered right toward the loose gunpowder scattered on the floor.

***

Makoto could only stare at Helen for a few moments before he could find even the simplest words. "What? What are you talking about?"

Helen grew annoyed. "That girl, Emiko. She killed those two men last night at the temple and lord knows who else. She used the nagi-thing to kill them!"

"That's ridiculous! Why?"

"I'm not sure, but if I had to guess, those two men tried to kill her first. But she definitely killed them and lied to us afterward. My husband saw her!"

"Helen, I didn't see anything like that," Arkwright said. "I saw two men go into the doorway after the girl, but that's all."

"Don't interrupt, John. Who else could have killed two armed men? Not that doddering old man." Helen paused for a moment, trying to find the right words. "She seemed odd at the temple, like her mask was starting to come undone. Especially when she lied about the staff of her weapon. We only saw it once and could recognize it immediately. Her real intentions are starting to show."

Makoto found himself glancing at the area where Emiko was supposed to be hiding, and he stiffened when he saw her standing out in the open. She was as calm and poised as ever as if she'd been through the heat of battle before.

Makoto noticed she was staring intently ahead, an expression he hadn't seen on her before. He followed her gaze and saw the subject she was focused on: Sugimoto. By now, he had tossed away his rifle and was using his sword to fight while directing his steadily dwindling force.

He glanced around the deck with a wild-eyed look. "What's taking so long!? The boiler and the gunpowder should have been prepared by now." As he glanced around his eyes landed on Emiko, and the wild-eyed look took on a murderous rage. "You! You're responsible!"

Sugimoto readied his saber and charged straight at Emiko. She didn't seem fazed by the sudden attack and readied the gun Makoto had given her. But before she could fire, Makoto charged forward, sword at the ready, and intercepted Sugimoto. Their swords clashed. Makoto was the superior swordsman, but Sugimoto's blind rage gave him an undeniable edge in the fight as he swung his sword wildly and didn't leave any openings.

After a few blows, Makoto glanced back at Emiko, who had lowered the gun and returned to a more innocent look. "Now's your chance to avenge your family!" she said.

Makoto didn't know whether to believe her, but another strike from Sugimoto brought him back into the fight. Makoto regained his footing and struck back at Sugimoto, which startled the police officer. He took several steps backward until he hit the mast of the ship.

He saw Makoto approach and after letting out a curse, ran to the side of the deck, and grabbed the rigging to climb up the ratlines to the main spar. Makoto followed, gripping his sword in his teeth like a pirate from the Spanish Main. Sugimoto maintained his lead, while Makoto struggled with the ropes.

Emiko ran below the two as Makoto pursued Sugimoto. "Remember, you're better than the Shinsengumi. Claim your revenge!"

Helen could only look on as the cowboy followed the policeman. She heard gasps and shouts coming from the onlookers and looked over the ship's rail. She saw several of the hundreds of onlookers pointing toward the two men scaling the ropes. Helen looked warily at Emiko, who returned her look with an innocent smile that seemed faker than those Noh masks, as she held firmly to the gun.

Sugimoto stepped off on the main yard and had his sword at the ready. Makoto swung from the rigging and stepped onto it as well, grabbing his sword from his teeth and shifting to an attacking stance. Balancing on the rounded wood was perilous, but Sugimoto didn't seem to care. He swung his sword, while Makoto struggled to block the blows.

"Are you Shinsengumi or not?" Makoto asked.

Sugimoto paused for a moment, raising a confused eyebrow, but resumed swinging his sword. "The Shinsengumi are a relic of the past. I'm only concerned for the future; one where the people of my faith are secure, rather than being sold out by these kowtowing ministers whispering poison into the Emperor's ear."

"So you were the one who killed the old man at the inn with the Shinsengumi coat?"

Sugimoto snarled. "That wretch. She dares to copy my methods?"

"What?"

"That traitorous shrine maiden was the one who killed Watanabe. She had the gall to copy my method for getting rid of that accursed foreign-lover, Ōkubo."

"Shrine maiden? You mean Emiko?"

"And that treacherous woman dares to double-cross us again. I'll make certain she pays for this."

Makoto frowned and shifted from defensive blocks to offensive attacks. Sugimoto and Makoto both struggled to maintain their balance on the main yard while striking at each other.

A sudden explosion rattled the ship and black smoke started billowing from below. Makoto grabbed a nearby rope to avoid falling, and Sugimoto fell over the side. He reached out and was able to grab onto the canvas furled beneath the yardarm, saving himself from a fall to certain death.

Makoto glanced down below and heard the screams of several onlookers as they pointed toward the smoke. Despite the noise, it seemed the explosion hadn't done any significant damage. Makoto looked down at the smoke billowing from an open hatch, where a few coughing men ran out from below deck. One of them was a very charred Kotaro, who staggered out and collapsed face first on the deck. The screams of the onlookers were replaced with loud chatter as he saw several of them pointing toward both the smoke and him.

All of the men under Sugimoto were either dead or had surrendered. Sugimoto had held onto his sword but didn't seem to have the strength to pull himself back up. Makoto inched out to just above Sugimoto's precarious position and stood over him.

Sugimoto glared up at Makoto. "Go ahead. Finish me."

Makoto hesitated. The regrets of not killing the Shinsengumi a few minutes ago still weighed on him and his rage told him to just go for the kill. Shinsengumi or not, Sugimoto deserved no better.

However, after everything that had happened, something told him it would be better for the police lieutenant to face justice instead. The thought made Makoto pause further. He had never thought about seeing justice served or sparing anyone who got in the way of his vengeance. But now he was no longer sure about his revenge. How much was true, and how much was a lie?

He couldn't rely on Emiko or Inzan. He couldn't even rely on his own memories. His eyes drifted toward Emiko, who was staring up at him with those same eyes that he'd grown to trust. Breathing in sharply, Makoto thrust his sword through his belt, kneeled down, and stretched out his hand. "Take my hand."

Sugimoto looked up at him with confusion in his eyes. He seemed to debate internally whether to take up Makoto's offer. However, before he could decide, two shots rang out, one hitting the mast and the other piercing Sugimoto through the back. He let go and nearly fell, but Makoto reached down and grabbed his hand.

Makoto nearly fell off the crossbeam but held fast to the rigging and ropes with his other hand. He struggled to hold both his and Sugimoto's weight. The bloodstain on Sugimoto's back was growing.

He looked up at Makoto with a weary, melancholic glare. "What are you doing?" he asked weakly.

Makoto wasn't too sure himself. He normally wouldn't go so far to help someone who had just tried to kill him. He looked down at Sugimoto. "Better you face justice than death."

Sugimoto scoffed. "Death's preferable. And inevitable." Using the last of his strength, Sugimoto swung his sword toward Makoto, forcing him to let go. Sugimoto fell, calling out, "Long live the Crimson Chrysanthemum!"

Makoto stared as the police lieutenant fell, wincing when Sugimoto hit the wooden deck. The Buddhist officer landed with a sickening thud, prompting several screams from onlookers. Makoto scanned the deck for any sign of the shooter, and his eyes rested on where Emiko had stood. But she was nowhere to be seen. Only Makoto's revolver remained behind on the deck, a thin wisp of smoke curling from its barrel.

Chapter Thirty-Four

As soon as things were under control, official government spokesmen made their best efforts to assure the public that everything was fine, though the populace knew better. That afternoon, Makoto, Kotaro, and Helen found themselves sitting in the waiting room of the home minister, on the top floor of an elaborate, Western-style building which had clearly been built in the last couple of years.

All three were sitting in their own wooden chairs, spaced apart. Kotaro, much worse for wear, seemed to be nodding off, but each time he nearly fell from his chair, he jerked awake and sat upright before repeating the process. His uniform was blackened from the gunpowder explosion. A hasty washing had removed much of the soot from his face, though large streaks of black persisted on his neck and behind his ears. His head was bandaged.

The police confiscated Makoto's gun and sword after he descended the rigging. At that point, he was too exhausted to protest. His clothes were less stained and more intact than Kotaro's, but there were several new holes and tears in his duster. He remained awake but had to occasionally rub his eyes from fatigue.

Helen's clothes were in the best state, though a little frayed. Her husband had been taken to another room to speak with the Minister of the Navy, and she hoped everything would be all right. She glanced at Makoto and opened her mouth to say something but closed it and looked down.

After a couple of minutes, Makoto broke the silence and spoke in English, "How?"

Helen's head popped up. "Huh?"

"How did you know it was Emiko?"

Helen blinked and gave him a confused look. "Emiko? Oh! Well…" She reached into her purse and pulled out a half-charred letter. She handed it to Makoto.

It was too damaged for him to read the text, but he did recognize the symbol at the top; that same red flower which seemed to keep following him wherever he went.

"This letter disappeared from my room a few days ago. And I found it again near that nagi-weapon. The only ones who have easy access to the rooms at that hour are the maids. Aki and Emiko were the ones assigned to my room. Aki was with me at the time of the deaths, and it was Emiko who owned the weapon."

"But what about Inzan?" Makoto asked. "He would be more likely to kill than a woman of Emiko's stature."

"Don't underestimate a woman under attack. My husband saw the two men go after her, and they ended up dead. He also saw her wearing 'strange robes,' which must have been that red and white outfit, but when we saw her, she was wearing the hotel maid uniform, probably because her regular clothes were covered in blood."

"And that's how you figured it out?" Makoto asked with a bit of disbelief in his voice.

Helen gave a smug smile. "Well, that's not all. Any proper actress can spot someone playing a role. I knew Emiko wasn't as pure and innocent as she pretended. Her pretty face and sighs didn't fool me like they did you. She's clearly an accomplished little liar. It's elementary, my dear cowboy."

Makoto was surprised, but the American woman's logic made sense. And as much as he didn't want to admit it, it seemed all the more likely Emiko was responsible, especially with what happened on the ship. He couldn't help but wonder what could have driven her to do such things. Also, Sugimoto's words rang in his head. Just what was the Crimson Chrysanthemum? He glanced once more at the red flower at the top of the letter before handing it back to Helen.

The large wooden door to the inner office swung open, and Fujita stepped out, irate as usual. One of his uniform sleeves was cut open to the shoulder and his arm was in a sling. He glared darkly toward the three. As Fujita held the door open with his good hand, Togo stepped out, his formerly pristine uniform now tattered and frayed from the fight. There were a few small smatterings of dried blood along the sleeves. As he stepped by, Togo bowed toward Makoto, who stood up and reciprocated.

Togo held out his hand. "Thank you for your help. I am forever in your debt."

Makoto took his hand, and after they shook, Togo left.

"Inside. Now," Fujita said with an icy tone.

Kotaro jolted at the sound of the captain's voice and immediately stood up at the order, while Makoto stayed still, his fists clenched. He and the police captain exchanged glares. While he may not have been wearing the bright blue coat anymore, Fujita was still the same masked Shinsengumi he fought in the warehouse.

"What is it?" Fujita asked, his tone having an impatient edge.

Makoto stared at Fujita. The police captain had his katana by his side while Makoto did not have any of his own weapons, but at this point, that didn't matter to him. "That coat you wore. It was a Shinsengumi coat."

"Why does that matter to you?"

"They murdered my father, my mother, my brothers, and my sister."

They stared each other down. Kotaro nervously took a step back, while Helen looked on, not certain what either of the men were saying.

"Are you Shinsengumi?" Makoto asked with an edge to his voice.

Fujita chuckled. "Of course not. The Shinsengumi are long gone."

"Then why-?"

"I owe you no explanation."

"Uh, sir?"

Fujita cast his dark glare to Kotaro, who flinched at his gaze. "Not now, patrolman."

"But sir, maybe you could explain why you were wearing a coat like that? I would like to know too, especially after what happened at the Miyazaki District."

Fujita let out an annoyed grunt. "If you must know, I used it infiltrate that traitorous group, the Crimson Chrysanthemum. Using a relic of the old government was an easy way to gain their trust. I knew there were potential traitors in the police force and formed this plan in secret with the home minister. That is all there is to it."

"But you were about to cut my head off!" Kotaro protested. "I could have died!"

Fujita's glare retained its steely edge. "That was a sacrifice I was willing to make."

Kotaro let out something between a grumble and a whimper and lowered his head. Makoto listened to Fujita's explanation, which made sense but wasn't very satisfying. "Where did you get the coat?"

"It wasn't mine," Fujita replied.

"Whose is it?"

"I'm not at liberty to say, but if you wish to speak with its former owner, he's already dead."

Makoto frowned. "You seem very skilled with a sword for a policeman."

"When you've survived as many wars as I have, you pick up a thing or two. Now get going." The police captain's expression did not waver, and Makoto did not see any sign he was lying.

Kotaro didn't need to be told twice and trotted to the door, leaving a small trail of soot behind him. Makoto followed Kotaro inside, exchanging suspicious looks with Fujita. Helen didn't understand the exchange and looked around for some sort of guidance, but a dark stare from Fujita prompted her to stand up and follow after Makoto.

The three entered the room, with Fujita following behind and closing the door. The office was quite large, and the walls were decorated with memorabilia from Europe and the Americas.

The many shelves were lined with books in several different languages. Sitting in the center of the office behind a large, ornately carved wooden desk was a man in his late-thirties in a well-tailored European-style suit. Makoto recognized him as the minister on the *Hiei* who spoke up against Sugimoto, and whom the police officer threatened with a rifle.

The well-dressed man motioned for the three to sit on some chairs stationed in front of his desk. Kotaro walked up and sat down immediately, though his head started to droop from fatigue. A dark look from Fujita snapped him awake. Makoto also took one of the seats, studying the minister.

That left Helen looking back and forth between everyone, not sure what to do next. The man in the suit smiled and spoke to Helen in English. "Please have a seat, Mrs. Arkwright."

Helen was startled but pleased by his ability to speak English. She nodded and sat down. "Since you seem to already know my name, may I ask yours?"

The man nodded. "Of course. Forgive my rudeness. I am Ito Hirobumi, the acting Home Minister of Japan."

Helen turned to Makoto and whispered, "What's a home minister?"

Makoto could only shrug. Kotaro frowned at the two. "That blasted devil's tongue again. What are you saying?"

"He says he's the home minister."

"What!? We're in the presence of the home minister?" Kotaro stood up and made a salute. "Forgive my rudeness, sir. The great- I mean, Patrolman Yamada Kotaro is at your service."

Ito chuckled and spoke in Japanese, "That's good to hear, but what I need from the three of you is information about the *Hiei* incident this morning. Captain Fujita and Lieutenant Togo provided their accounts, but we were hoping you three could fill in some of the details."

Ito pulled out a few papers and gave them a brief looking over. "According to the captain, it's not clear how you came to be involved in this incident. Would you care to inform me about what brought you to the *Hiei* this morning, starting with you, Mrs. Arkwright?" Ito repeated the phrase in English for Helen, who was a little startled at being put on the spot.

"Well, to be honest, John, I mean my husband, Mr. Arkwright, was getting a bit secretive and disappearing for these long meetings. So I did what any wife would do and started looking through his things. I first found this strange letter." Helen pulled out the letter she had shown Makoto and handed it to Ito. He took it and looked it over.

Helen continued, "After that, I looked for him while running into the cowboy over here a few times." She pointed to Makoto. "And before I knew it, I ended up on that strange battleship, and finally here."

Ito nodded before calling Fujita over and showing him the paper. The two exchanged whispers and nods before Ito spoke to Helen, "Would it be all right if we kept this as evidence?"

Helen gave a shrug and nodded. "I don't see why not."

"Thank you, Mrs. Arkwright." Ito turned to Kotaro and spoke to him in Japanese, "I heard from your captain you were intent on finding the true cause of Minister Ōkubo's and Mr. Watanabe's deaths, correct?"

Kotaro nodded. "Yes, sir. I didn't think they committed suicide, and I first thought the man in black was responsible." Kotaro glanced at Makoto. "But I never would have thought Sugimoto was behind it. I just followed the leads, realizing that members of the Home Ministry seemed to be targets, and, uh, ended up on the *Hiei*, sir."

Ito nodded. "Your bravery and determination are admirable. However, based on what I've heard, you still need a little work on sobriety, decorum, and obedience."

He finally turned to Makoto. "And you, Mr. Mori? I heard you were seen with the body of Mr. Watanabe."

Makoto nodded. "I found him dead."

"But why did you try to solve the case on your own instead of going to the police?"

"It wasn't my intention."

Ito's eyebrows went up a little. "Oh?"

Makoto glanced at Kotaro and Helen. "I wanted to maintain a low profile and avoid contact with the police since I was searching for a certain group of people. I simply ended up involved in the case because I happened to run into these two a few more times than I would have liked."

"Is that so?" Ito paused, seemingly lost in thought. He looked up at the three with conviction in his eyes. "A few weeks ago, my predecessor, Home Minister Ōkubo Toshimichi, died under mysterious circumstances."

Fujita stepped forward, concern in his voice. "Sir, you intend to tell them everything?"

Ito nodded. "After what's happened, it only seems right."

Fujita frowned, but nodded and stepped back.

"Once I took office, Captain Fujita came to me and informed me there may have been foul play involved with Minister Ōkubo's death. And it involved the *Hiei*. He chose to keep it a secret from his men, brushing the death off as a suicide, but he initially suspected Mr. Arkwright."

"And despite my best efforts, the patrolman nearly exposed my plans," Fujita said, which made Kotaro shrink in his seat.

Ito repeated what he said in English for Helen, who was taken aback. "John!? Involved with murder? That's ridiculous. He may be slow, but he'd never be involved in a scheme of that sort! True we had already been in Japan at the time, but…" Helen trailed off, seemingly lost in her own thoughts.

Ito continued in English, "We also found out that Mr. Arkwright was heavily involved in a plot to smuggle American weapons into the country. So the captain deduced the home minister's murder had something to do with the deal."

"But John would never help rebels. He hated the Confederates in the Civil War."

"I understand your confusion, Mrs. Arkwright," Ito replied. "We realized we were incorrect in our assumptions when we intercepted a few telegrams and realized a certain group was posing as the government, instructing Mr. Arkwright how to smuggle the weapons into Japan."

Ito pulled out some papers from a folder. "It's understandable your husband was fooled. The European nations have imposed severe limits on our access to modern weapons, and your husband hasn't been the only person to try and profit by offering access to contraband. The paperwork we found shows he fully believed he was providing the weapons for our military. It seems Minister Ōkubo's assistant, Mr. Watanabe, was involved in this subterfuge, as was his replacement, Mr. Tanaka."

Ito repeated his words in Japanese. After he was finished, Fujita chimed in. "The group calls themselves the Crimson Chrysanthemum, and their symbol was the one on that letter." He pointed to the letter on Ito's desk.

Makoto remembered Sugimoto calling that name as he fell. "What is this group?"

"To put it simply," Ito said, "they hate the new government and hate foreigners even more. They keep to the old mantra, 'Revere the Emperor; expel the barbarians.'"

Makoto vaguely recalled hearing that chant back in the warehouse in the Miyazaki District.

Kotaro cocked his head. "So they still claim to revere the emperor? Even though they want to overthrow *his* government?"

Fujita scoffed. "No one ever said they were sane, which made it all the more important to figure out what they were planning."

Ito nodded. "To try and figure out their plans, the captain infiltrated their ranks, posing as a former member of the Shinsengumi."

"Was this Watanabe a Shinsengumi?" Makoto asked.

Ito seemed surprised at Makoto's question, while Fujita groaned. "The Shinsengumi again? You have a one-track mind."

"While my association with Mr. Watanabe was brief, I knew his background," Ito said. "He's from a minor samurai family but was never Shinsengumi. Although he did have a cousin who was part of that group, but his cousin died several years ago during the early part of the Restoration. I suppose Watanabe must have felt the government was responsible for his cousin's death and his family losing their samurai status. But why are you interested in the Shinsengumi?"

"I'm … searching for them." Makoto didn't elaborate further.

"Ah, so that's the group you were looking for when you arrived?" Ito asked.

Makoto nodded.

Kotaro scratched his head. "But why was poor ol'- I mean, Mr. Watanabe, killed?"

"We believe he had a falling out with the Crimson Chrysanthemum when he realized their true intentions with the *Hiei*," Fujita said.

"True intentions?" Makoto asked.

Ito's face became grave. "Thanks to Captain Fujita's efforts, we realized they intended to smuggle American rifles into the country, with both the *Hiei* and Mr. Arkwright's ship, the *Abraham Lincoln*, but we weren't sure if there were other plans as well. Because he was new, they didn't trust the captain enough to reveal their true intentions or their identities."

Ito continued, "Captain Fujita and the other members of the Crimson Chrysanthemum were told the smuggled guns were to drive out the foreigners and would never be used against the emperor or the Japanese people. When searching Watanabe's home we found a letter addressed to Lieutenant Togo. In it, he explained the Crimson Chrysanthemum promised him that he would be an officer in a reconstituted Shinsengumi once the barbarians had been expelled. However, he had been dragged into the killing of Minister Ōkubo, and he feared he would be the next victim."

Fujita nodded. "I tried to find out more, but many of my efforts were thwarted, particularly when you and I crossed blades, as we did in the shipbuilding district when you took the telegram and the card." Fujita glared at Makoto. "After questioning the members we captured, we found out their plan was to hijack the ship and kill the ministers during the tour of the *Hiei*, using the weapons smuggled aboard. Then they would blow up the ship to kill as many bystanders as possible and discredit the military."

Kotaro nodded. "Yes, but thanks to *my* efforts, that was averted!"

Ito smiled. "Really? I heard things didn't go according to plan, and I can see the results." He gestured toward Kotaro's charred uniform.

"Well, the reason for that is … uh…"

Fujita interrupted. "I already informed the home minister about your little debacle in the boiler room."

Makoto looked at them in confusion. "I saw the smoke. What happened?"

"Apparently, there was just enough gunpowder for the embers of the boiler to set off a small flash fire, which was very noisy and produced lots of smoke, but not enough to actually trigger a full explosion. This foolish patrolman just got a light scorching, like *yakitori* left too long on the grill," Fujita said.

Ito chuckled and translated for Helen, who also laughed. "I see. So that's where the smoke came from. But… I still don't understand why my husband was involved."

"Mr. Arkwright informed us he was promised the next several shipbuilding contracts for the Japanese Navy so long as he provided the weapons secretly. Apparently, he did something similar in his own country," Ito said.

Helen nodded. "That's true. During the Civil War, he secretly armed several of his ships to protect California. One actually drove off a Confederate raider. But still…"

Ito continued. "Apparently, Mr. Arkwright wanted to meet up with Minister Ōkubo, the navy minister, and the finance minister to close the deal, which was why he came to Japan since he had only been working with Watanabe to that point. However, we know Ōkubo wasn't part of this Crimson Chrysanthemum."

"So the home minister was killed to buy time?" Makoto asked.

Ito nodded. "We believe so. Though it was staged to look like a suicide to throw off the police. We believe Lieutenant Sugimoto was responsible for this death with the assistance of Mr. Watanabe. Captain Fujita pretended to accept the determination of suicide to keep their guard down and make it easier to sneak into the Crimson Chrysanthemum."

Fujita nodded. "I was able to use some old contacts in Osaka to get the right people to vouch for me and infiltrate the group as a reactionary from Kyoto. I was able to hide my identity because when different sections of the Crimson Chrysanthemum meet, it's customary to wear Noh masks to keep identities as secret as possible. Sugimoto was wearing that fox mask back at the warehouse behind the brothel."

"Then Sugimoto was the one who used the fan blade?" Kotaro asked. "No wonder he seemed so surprised when I opened it."

"Fan blade?" Fujita asked.

"Uh, yes sir. I think it's still in the evidence room."

"We'll discuss it later," Fujita said.

"Lieutenant Togo informed us he was good friends with Mr. Watanabe and that he telegraphed him to inform him of his arrival on the *Hiei*. And we believe it was this friendship which contributed to Watanabe's faltering resolve. Since if the lieutenant was on the *Hiei* during the attack…" Ito started.

"He would have been killed," Makoto finished.

Ito nodded again. "From his unsent letter to Lieutenant Togo, we believe Mr. Watanabe was planning to ask Mr. Arkwright to go to the American ambassador, and the ambassador could then warn the Foreign Ministry."

"Why? Why not just go the police directly?" Kotaro asked.

"If he was aware of the plan, he probably knew about Sugimoto's involvement and knew that members of the Crimson Chrysanthemum were in the police force," Fujita replied.

"Oh, I see," Kotaro said.

"It seems the Crimson Chrysanthemum became aware of his plan and decided to silence him. We initially thought Sugimoto killed him as well, but he was at the police station at the time. For now, we think it must have been another member of the Crimson Chrysanthemum, possibly Mr. Tanaka, but that then leaves the question of who killed Mr. Tanaka and the other man at the temple. Do any of you have an idea who might be responsible?" Ito asked.

Makoto hesitated to bring up her name but decided it would be best to let them know. "While we fought, the policeman claimed a shrine maiden was copying his methods. Her name is Hayashi Emiko."

Chapter Thirty-Five

"Hayashi Emiko?" Ito asked.

Fujita scoffed. "It couldn't have been a girl. The wounds on all of the men were far too deep for a woman's strength."

"For a tantō, that's true. But not for a naginata," Makoto replied.

"A naginata?" Fujita asked.

Makoto turned to Helen, who was doing her best to keep up with the conversation, but with only the occasional phrase being repeated to her in English, she was struggling. "Didn't you say that Emiko used the naginata to kill those men at the temple?" Makoto asked her in English.

"Huh? Oh! Yes. I found the blade of the weapon covered in blood and figured either the priest or the girl from the temple must have used it. Then I saw she was wearing the hotel uniform and not her shrine maiden outfit even though my husband saw her wearing it before, probably because it was drenched in blood. Based on the evidence, what my husband saw, and that girl's strange behavior, I deduced that she must have been the killer."

"What kind of strange behavior?" Ito asked.

"She didn't seem too upset about the destruction of the weapon, which she said was an important family heirloom. I think it's meant to unscrew into pieces."

Makoto nodded and translated the information to Fujita and Kotaro. Fujita frowned. "A naginata which can be taken apart? It sounds a bit farfetched."

Ito rubbed his chin. "But it would explain the depth of the wound, which even a woman can easily achieve with the leverage of a naginata. And when she escaped, she could break the weapon into pieces, put it into a bag, and walk away unnoticed. Did they find the naginata at the temple?"

Fujita shook his head. "No. But I'll send some men to look into it."

"But why?" Kotaro asked. "Why would that pretty girl and Sugimoto do all this?"

Ito and Fujita paused and didn't seem to want to answer, so Makoto spoke, "I think Emiko wants revenge for her family, and Sugimoto mentioned something about his faith being wiped out."

"His faith? But surely it's not that bad," Kotaro replied. "He was allowed in the police force, after all."

"While Buddhism hasn't been outlawed," Ito said, "its close ties to the shogun and the old government makes it a threat. As a result, certain measures needed to be taken against several temples and monasteries."

"What kind of measures?" Makoto asked.

Ito didn't reply and glanced downward. Makoto tightened his fists, remembering his own quest for revenge. Possibly he, Emiko, and the police lieutenant weren't so different.

"Moving on, there are a few things we would like to clear up," Ito said, repeating his words in English for Helen. "There was a great fire in the Miyazaki District a couple of nights ago. Captain Fujita informed me it started in a warehouse, which was serving as a temporary headquarters for the Crimson Chrysanthemum. He also informed me you two were there."

Ito gestured toward Makoto and Kotaro before turning to Helen. "And Mr. Arkwright informed me he may have heard your voice in the Miyazaki District when he was there to get his payment from Tanaka."

Helen felt herself shrink a bit. "That fire might have been a teensy bit my fault. You see, I was being pursued by some tattooed ruffian and dropped my lantern. And it was in an area where they were storing weapons."

"Ah, I see," Ito said. "A fire in a room filled with weapons and ammunition would create the dramatic explosion we saw."

"I-I'm sorry. Was anyone … hurt?" Helen pensively looked down.

"Hurt? Yes. Many people were hurt badly and the entire district is in ruin," Ito said frankly.

Helen shrank further into her chair.

"However, the deaths were kept to a minimum thanks to the fire brigades. And it seems the only casualties were a few of the conspirators, and to be frank, they're no great loss in our eyes."

Helen looked up. "So, will I be getting into trouble? And what about my husband?"

"It's a little complicated. Even though it was unintentional, you did cause a fair amount of destruction, and your husband was involved in a treasonous plot," Ito said.

Helen flinched at his words.

"However, as far as the government is concerned, everything which happened on the *Hiei* this morning never occurred."

Helen cocked her head in confusion. "Huh?"

"The official story is that everything was part of a weapons demonstration gone awry. The last thing the government wants to do in these tumultuous times is look weak to the people. And as for the fire, it was simply caused by a rouge lantern. So we're willing to show leniency to you and your husband, provided you both leave and stay out of this country … for a long time."

"Really?" Helen sat up in excitement when she heard the words 'leniency,' but her mood dropped when she realized it meant getting kicked out of the country. "Oh. I see."

Ito smiled. "Captain, could you take the lady to see her husband in the other room? And you should go as well, patrolman. Your captain would like to have a few words with you."

Fujita nodded, and Kotaro squirmed a little in his seat. Helen stood up and looked at Makoto with a slightly sad smile as she followed Captain Fujita out the door. Kotaro hesitated to leave, but after one dark glare from Fujita, also followed him, leaving Makoto alone with Ito.

After Kotaro shut the door, Makoto and Ito stared at each other across the desk for a moment. Ito broke the silence. "Those clothes are quite … unique."

Makoto glanced down at his duster. "They weren't in America."

"America? I see," Ito said. "I heard you had entered the country recently, though I'm guessing with forged papers?"

Makoto stiffened at the accusation and said nothing.

Ito chuckled. "There's no need to worry. I also left Japan when it was illegal to study in England. I even visited America for a brief period." Ito gestured toward the British and American memorabilia along the shelves. "How long were you in America?"

"Fifteen years. I arrived after the raid on the Mori family household."

Ito's eyes widened. "The Mori family? Ah, I take it you're from the Yokohama branch of the family?"

Makoto nodded. "Yes. You've heard of the raid? Do you know anything about it? Such as why it happened and who was involved? I thought I knew, but now … I'm not so sure."

Ito shook his head. "I only heard about it after the fact and that the Shinsengumi carried it out. Though I don't know why. But you must have been a child at the time. How did you survive?"

"I snuck aboard a ship which took me to America. While there, I did odd jobs until I could save enough to get back here."

"For revenge? You may not be aware, but four years ago, the laws were changed to forbid *katakiuchi*. You can't use blood vengeance as a justification to kill anymore."

Makoto didn't reply. He had no intention of justifying his revenge with some outdated loophole, but if he was not careful with his words, he could easily find himself in prison.

After a couple of moments of silence, Ito continued, "The Shinsengumi have been disbanded for many years. However, I've heard there are some fragments that still exist. Plus, there are others who miss the old days and want to emulate them, like Mr. Watanabe."

Ito appeared to be thinking about something before making a decision. "What if I could grant you access to the Imperial Archives, which may have the information you seek?"

"Why would you do that?" Makoto asked.

"Even though most of the Shinsengumi have been killed in the conflicts over the years, especially last year's rebellion, remnants are still out there, plotting against the new government they fought so hard against, whether it's with the Crimson Chrysanthemum or acting on their own. I can't officially condone hunting them down, but I wouldn't mind lending a hand in your quest to pursue them, assuming you'd be willing to do me a favor as well."

Makoto had a feeling there would be a catch, but this could be his first real lead in finding the Shinsengumi. "What is this favor?"

Ito smiled. "I have a proposition for you. You understand foreign ways, and you've lived among them longer than any other Japanese I know. Japan is at a crossroads. It is now more important than ever for us to prove ourselves as an equal to the other nations. To put it simply, I want to hire you."

Makoto was astonished. "Hire me? For what?"

"To help the Home Ministry whenever there are *incidents* which involve foreigners."

"What kind of incidents?"

"Anything involving foreigners, but based on your skills, I think you would be most helpful in solving crimes. I saw your skills in person, and Lieutenant Togo informed me of your assistance in helping him escape from the brig. I also heard of your fighting prowess in the Miyazaki District from Captain Fujita."

The memories of that fight flowed through Makoto's mind, and he would have hardly called his defeat a skillful display. "I'm not sure you've got the right person. I'm no detective."

"We already have plenty of detectives in the police force. What we need is someone who understands foreigners and can handle their incidents quickly and discreetly."

"I don't know them any better than anyone else and as you mentioned, my clothes are hardly discreet."

"Based on what I've seen and heard, I disagree. And while your clothes are interesting to the average pedestrian, it is the investigations I want to be discreet. I appreciate that you've not publicized what happened this morning to those sensationalist newspapers, though I'm sure you had ample opportunity."

Makoto actually hadn't run into any reporters, and it didn't occur to him to speak to others about what happened. He tended to keep to himself; it kept him alive in America, and it seemed it would be the case here as well.

Ito continued, "If you agree to this position, I will personally make certain you will have access to any records you may need. And also…" Ito reached down and placed two items on the top of his desk.

Makoto breathed in sharply when he saw both his sword and revolver.

"Since you will be working for the Home Ministry instead of the police, I can authorize you to have your weapons back," Ito concluded.

Makoto contemplated. He didn't have any idea just what kind of tasks this "job" would entail, but it may help him find and destroy the Shinsengumi. He might even find out the reason for his family's deaths. He couldn't afford to say no. "Very well. I accept."

***

The next day, Helen walked down to the harbor, escorted by her husband.

"Really, the nerve of these people. Blaming me because they can't get their own people in order. It's ridiculous. This whole trip was a waste," he grumbled.

"I don't know about that. It certainly had its moments," Helen replied.

Arkwright gave his wife a confused look. "I thought you were bored."

Helen chuckled. "I think I've had enough excitement to last quite a while. Getting on a boat, I mean a ship, for a few weeks sounds delightful right about now."

Arkwright scratched his head. "Helen, I believe I may owe you a bit of an apology."

Helen cocked her head. "Hmm? What for?"

"For calling your book a 'flight of fancy.' It seems all of that detective mumbo jumbo did seem to help you find your way around when I wasn't available. So in that regard, I may have been a little misinformed."

Helen chuckled again. "I suppose I could say the same. I was looking for trouble and wasn't quite ready when I found it. And you were so brave on that horrid ship, like a knight in shining armor. Far better than anything in a book."

The two exchanged smiles as they walked down the harbor, her arm through his. As Helen glanced around the area, she noticed the familiar sight of Sakénomi's. "Let's go in here a moment. There's someone I'd like to speak to."

Arkwright seemed less than pleased with the run-down nature of the place, but didn't argue and followed Helen. She lifted the cloth and poked her head inside. Unlike in the late hours of the previous night, the bar was filled with customers, all clamoring to get drinks. She caught sight of the bartender rapidly pouring saké into several boxes and handing them out. Even the doorman was helping.

Helen walked up to the bar, her husband reluctantly following behind.

Jean gave a smile as she approached. "Ah, madame, a pleasure to see you again. And this must be your dead husband. He seems to be well, all things considered."

"Dead? What?" Arkwright asked with confusion in his voice.

Helen laughed. "Indeed. It turns out he was fine. I found him on the *Hiei*."

"Oh? Well, I apologize for trying to stop you," Jean said, making another over-the-top bow.

"No apologies necessary," Helen said. "By the way, have you seen the cowboy? You seem to know what's going on better than most."

Jean gave a smile and poured another box of saké. "I haven't seen him recently."

Helen gave a disappointed look. Jean noticed and beckoned her to come closer. She did and the bartender whispered, "Though he'll probably be back. He asked me about renting one of the rooms upstairs."

Helen perked up. "Will he be here soon?"

Jean shrugged. "Most likely."

Helen reached into her purse and handed the bartender an envelope. "Then could you give this to him when he gets back?"

Jean raised a curious eyebrow and took the letter. The bartender gave the envelope a brief looking over before sliding it under the counter. "If I see him, I'll hand it to him."

Helen smiled. "Thank you. For your help. Oh, and his too." Helen motioned toward Tora, who was busy slamming boxes of saké onto unsuspecting patrons' tables, making them jump.

"Thanks are not necessary, madame. We honestly didn't do much," Jean said.

"Well, it's still worthy of thanks! And you know…" Helen leaned low, motioning Jean to come closer; the bartender obliged. "You don't have to keep pretending."

Jean grew pale, took a startled step back, and looked away. This caught the attention of Helen's husband, and he gave his wife a curious glance.

"I-I don't know what you're talking about," the bartender stammered.

Helen chuckled. "When you've been in as many plays as I have, you can see through the masks people wear … well, most of the time."

Jean didn't reply, but the bartender's gaze hardened.

"Don't bother the man, Helen," Arkwright interjected. "He's clearly busy."

Helen ignored her husband. "You know, you would do well in a Shakespeare play. A modern-day Cesario, or maybe you're closer to Ganymede?"

Jean scoffed, turned away, and poured another box of saké. Helen briefly wondered if she had gone too far when the bartender spoke again, "Are you making fun of me, madame?"

Helen shook her head. "Not at all. But here's some friendly advice … lies tend to come to light no matter what. It's better to expose them on your own terms. Either way, thank you for your help, and I wish you the best."

Jean turned around and gave Helen a confused look. "You speak as if we will never see each other again."

"Well, my husband and I will be leaving on the *Abraham Lincoln* tomorrow. And, well, we've been told not to come back."

Jean's hard look softened. "My oh, my. The madame and her dead husband must have caused quite the scandal. I'll keep your advice in mind. Bon voyage." Jean made one, last over-the-top bow, and Helen smiled. She led her husband out of the bar.

Once they left, Arkwright let out a disgusted grunt. "What a filthy bar. Why in the world did you know anyone there? And what did you tell the bartender that made him go so pale?"

Helen chuckled and grabbed her husband's arm with confidence. "Oh, it's nothing, just another flight of fancy."

The Arkwrights continued their stroll down the harbor.

***

Kotaro stood nervously in front of the closed door to Fujita's office in a fresh, new uniform that stretched uncomfortably around the waist. After speaking to the home minister the previous day, Fujita had peppered him with questions about the case, and Kotaro answered them to the best of his ability, of course leaving out the events that weren't quite so flattering about himself.

While he was grilling Kotaro, the captain received a notice from the home minister and told Kotaro to leave and not come back to the station until he was summoned. By then, the captain would have decided what to do with him.

When one of the lieutenants came to retrieve him from the barracks, Kotaro thought the officer would have the same smug look on his face the others did when they knew Kotaro was in trouble again, but his face was grim. He was probably still in shock over Sugimoto. Kotaro guessed all of the department, officers, and patrolmen alike, were now under investigation to root out potential traitors.

Though he didn't have to fear an inquiry on that account, Kotaro still felt nervous, the memories of the scuffle in the Miyazaki District fresh in his mind, and he hesitated when he reached Fujita's office. He took a deep breath and knocked on the door.

"Enter."

Kotaro nervously opened the door and peeked inside Fujita's all too familiar office. The walls and shelves were bare and the desk was the same plain style used by the other officers. Fujita's razor-sharp katana occupied a place of honor on a side table, and Kotaro made an effort to avoid stepping too close.

Fujita was working his way through a mountain of paperwork so high that just staring at it made Kotaro a little dizzy. Without looking up from his papers, Fujita motioned Kotaro to sit in one of the two chairs in front of his desk. Kotaro sat in the chair to the right. He had been there enough times to know that one had a slightly more comfortable cushion.

After the chair groaned a little under Kotaro's weight, Fujita looked up from his papers and placed them to the side. "I'll cut to the chase Yamada. You're in serious trouble."

Kotaro shrank down into the chair, which groaned louder. He should have known he would be chewed out.

Fujita continued, counting off Kotaro's transgressions on his fingers. "You disobeyed direct orders, drank on duty, involved yourself in cases you were ordered to stay away from, lost evidence, jeopardized a mission of colossal importance, and are an embarrassment to the Yokohama police department, to your family, and to the Empire. It would be perfectly reasonable of me to demote you and send you to freeze in Abashiri prison."

Each accusation felt like a direct blow. Kotaro wanted to raise objections, but each time he opened his mouth, his eyes darted to the katana on the side table. And the memories of the Miyazaki District as well as the "sacrifices" that the captain was willing to make echoed through his mind.

"That being said," Fujita continued, his tone shifting a little, "you did show surprising competence and what some may even call bravery on the *Hiei* yesterday. You even impressed Minister Ito, despite your obvious shortcomings."

Kotaro perked up a little at these words. This was the only time he had ever heard the captain praise him, even if they were backhanded compliments. However, as his spirits rose, a dark look from Fujita made him shrink back again.

"So it's been determined that you should be given a special assignment."

"Special assignment?" Kotaro asked.

"You remember the foreign-dressed man who you kept calling the 'man in black?'"

Kotaro nodded.

"I was informed yesterday he'll be working for the home minister. And since you two seem to work together so well when it comes to making my life difficult…" Fujita looked at Kotaro with annoyance. "You will be working with him from now on as the representative of the police in incidents involving foreigners. Hopefully, you can make their lives difficult instead of mine. Who knows? You may even get a promotion out of it."

Kotaro's excitement rose at the possibility of a promotion, but then he realized what that would entail. "F-Foreigners? But I don't want to deal with them! They're loud, obnoxious, rude, and they smell weird!"

Fujita snorted. "Sounds like a perfect match. You and they will get along just fine. Though I suppose you could always refuse."

Kotaro breathed a sigh of relief.

"And be sent to Abashiri prison instead."

Kotaro froze.

"Your choice," Fujita finished.

Kotaro swallowed a lump in his throat, stood up, and made a salute. "Those smelly foreigners should be no problem for the great and powerful Yamada Kotaro!"

Fujita smiled sourly and returned the salute. "That's what I wanted to hear."

Chapter Thirty-Six

Makoto knocked on Halifax's door. The doctor opened it and looked at the cowboy. "I see you're looking as terrible as ever. I was almost worried you weren't coming back after hearing about that little debacle in the harbor yesterday."

"How is Inzan?"

Halifax gestured inside. "See for yourself."

Inzan was sitting in bed, a thick wrapping of bandages around his abdomen. Once Inzan saw Halifax, he started complaining. "Blast these Jesuit contraptions! I must have been contaminated. Where is my *nusa*? I need to perform a purification ceremony."

However, when he saw Makoto enter, Inzan's eyes grew wide. "Master Mori! What are you doing here?"

"I'm glad to see you're all right," Makoto said, feeling relieved.

Inzan smiled. "I'm also glad to see you as well Master Mori. This blasted Jesuit doctor wouldn't let me go out to find you."

Halifax rubbed his temple and spoke to Makoto in English. "He's been complaining incessantly since he woke up. One wouldn't think he was on the edge of death last night, but I didn't want him going out and reopening his injuries. Despite what he claims, he still has several weeks of recovery ahead."

Makoto nodded and glanced toward Inzan, who seemed frustrated at not understanding the conversation. Makoto's eyes then drifted to the nearby table and he saw Inzan's smiling Noh mask. He picked it up and went to Inzan, holding the mask in front of him. "What can you tell me about this?"

Inzan tensed up and looked toward Halifax. Makoto spoke to the doctor in English, "Sorry. He wants to speak in private."

Halifax shrugged and went into the other room. Makoto turned his attention back to Inzan. "Are you and Emiko involved with this … Crimson Chrysanthemum?"

Inzan sighed and looked down. "To think you've already learned so much. I suppose there's no point in denying it. Yes, I was involved."

"And Emiko?"

Inzan nodded. "Her, too."

"But why did you join them?"

Inzan sighed again. "After the attack on the Mori family … life was difficult. First, the Shogun converted the Mori lands to a Buddhist shrine, but when the government changed, the emperor's men closed the shrine and dared to convert the land to a stable! A shrine is at least respectable, but a stable? So after that, I…"

Inzan avoided looking at Makoto. "I hated the Shogun, but I also hated the new government. I found myself with like-minded people, and they led me to the Crimson Chrysanthemum. They helped me plant weeds which made the horses sick and spread rumors that the land was cursed with angry ghosts and demons. The soldiers were easy enough to frighten."

"Haunted? So you were the source of those rumors?"

Inzan let out a sad chuckle. "Yes. And thanks to the Crimson Chrysanthemum's government connections, the land was converted to a Shinto temple with me in charge. Granted I knew next to nothing about being a priest at the time and my knowledge is still a bit rudimentary."

Inzan gave a half-hearted smile. "All they asked in return was to use the temple for storage and for the occasional meeting. The temple's location made it isolated and not many visitors came to pray … or donate. I had trouble keeping the temple up on my own and a bad storm last year damaged the worship hall. So this year, they sent me Emiko to help out."

"What's her role in all of this?" Makoto asked. "I've heard so many things. I was told she's responsible for the death of that man at the inn and the men at the temple. Is it true?"

Inzan didn't reply. Makoto glanced at Inzan's bandages. "Did she do that, too?"

"Yes. She did all you said. Including this." Inzan touched the bandages at his side.

"But how did she do it?" Makoto asked.

"You saw her naginata, right?"

Makoto nodded.

"That naginata is designed to be taken apart so it can be carried without being noticed. She was tasked with killing Mr. Watanabe since he was going to betray the plan."

"And she carried it out?"

Inzan nodded. "She was sparse with the details but told me she just used the top third of her weapon to rush him. He never had a chance. Then after, she placed one of our daggers by the side of the body, both to make it look like a suicide and to let the members involved within the police know the death was mandated by the Crimson Chrysanthemum, so it wouldn't be investigated further. The same technique was done to the home minister a few weeks ago, but I don't know which member was responsible for that slaying."

Makoto remembered exploring the inn with Emiko, and how she had been eerily calm in the room despite the blood on the ground. The "note" she found came to mind. "I went back to the inn with her."

"Huh?"

"I was looking for some sort of lead on the Shinsengumi and decided to go back to the room. She claimed to find a note there, which led me to the shipbuilding district. I saw Fuji-" Makoto stopped himself, remembering Ito's emphasis on being discreet. "I saw a masked member of the Crimson Chrysanthemum there; he wore a Shinsengumi coat."

"She did that? And he wore a Shinsengumi coat you say?" Inzan seemed lost in thought for a moment. "Ah, that makes sense."

"What does?"

"I think Emiko was against the plan to attack the *Hiei*. She told me after she killed Watanabe that it was foolish and jeopardized the true mission of the Crimson Chrysanthemum. Emiko believes foreigners are the cause of past and current strife in Japan and wants nothing more than to drive them all out."

"How would attacking the *Hiei* drive out foreigners?" Makoto asked.

"The ministers were the target. By killing as many as possible, they were hoping to cause chaos. The Crimson Chrysanthemum had already maneuvered some of their members into positions as deputies. When the ministers were dead, these deputies would take their place and guide the emperor properly. Emiko thought it wouldn't work and expected there were other traitors in the group besides Watanabe. So she used you to disrupt their plans."

"Used me? How?"

"I think Emiko was directing you so that you'd cause the plan to fail."

Makoto thought about it. If she did fabricate the note and sent him to the shipbuilding district to fight Fujita, it would make sense she was trying to derail the plan. But if she knew Fujita was a traitor, as Inzan implied, then it would seem like she was trying to help the plan.

But another possibility was she had planned even further ahead and calculated that no matter who won in the fight, the ensuing chaos would create doubts in all parties and make them more suspicious, a distrust she could direct to suit her needs. He saw her persuasion skills first hand when she goaded him to kill Sugimoto, even if she had to finish him off herself. He wondered if she'd ever cared for him, or had she always been manipulating him?

"But what about those men at the temple?" Makoto asked. "And you? Why did she attack you?"

Inzan rubbed at the wound. "The man in charge of the plan, I never found out his name…"

"Sugimoto?"

"Possibly. Emiko was a bit vocal about her displeasure with the plan. And he didn't like anyone, especially a woman, questioning his authority. He arranged a meeting at the temple a couple of nights ago, and he told me to be there, but not tell Emiko about it. Those kinds of meetings have happened before so I thought nothing of it. Apparently, it was the final weapons exchange with that accursed foreigner."

Makoto guessed the "accursed foreigner" was Helen's husband.

"They didn't inform Emiko about the meeting because the two extra men that came along had another mission. They had been sent to kill her."

Makoto tightened his fists and didn't say anything. The American woman was right after all.

Inzan continued, "I stayed near the temple to make sure those men didn't steal anything. But I saw them approach Emiko and attack her in the temple. I suppose she expected something like that because she pulled out the shortened naginata and, in one movement, slashed both of them. Once they were down, she shoved the blade into one of the man's gut and then the other one. Her shrine maiden outfit was covered in their blood."

Makoto felt his eyes grow wide; he couldn't imagine Emiko pulling off such a deadly move.

"I didn't want more blood spilled, so I ran and shouted at the third man to flee for his life. He grabbed the foreigner and ran."

"She defeated two armed men? That's … impressive."

Inzan nodded. "Her family was well known for their ability to wield the naginata, using secret techniques that were deadly even if the weapon was broken in half. It only makes sense that she is so skilled. As for me…"

Inzan rubbed his wound again. "I had the bad luck to be seen by her. I'm not sure if she thought I had also been sent to kill her or didn't want anyone alive who had seen her, but she turned her blade on me."

Inzan stopped rubbing the bandages and gripped the armrests of his chair. "I was surprised by the attack and dropped the lantern I was carrying on the floor. The fire quickly spread along the tatami mats and up the walls. I suppose she thought that would finish me off and went to hide the blade. But how could you not know? Her miko outfit was covered in blood."

"She had changed into her maid's uniform."

"Ah, that makes sense," Inzan replied. "Is she still alive?"

"I assume so. She disappeared from the *Hiei* after killing Sugimoto."

Inzan's eyes grew wide before he sighed. "It seems she is far more dangerous than I realized. To think I once thought such a woman would be a good match for you, Master Mori. I thought you and she could heal each other. That was before I found out she killed Watanabe. Please forgive me."

Makoto shook his head. "You weren't the only one she fooled."

Inzan gave a sad smile and bowed his head.

"Were you the masked man who showed me the way out of the warehouse back in Miyazaki?" Makoto asked.

"Yes. I was lucky to find you in that chaos. I feared you would have been trapped in the fire."

"But you also led the American woman to safety. I thought you hated foreigners."

Inzan let out a sigh. "I seem to be getting soft-hearted and soft-headed in my old age. Everywhere I go, murder seems to follow. I suppose I was just tired of seeing so much death, so I helped her, even if she was a Jesuit." Inzan chuckled half-heartedly. "And as a reward, she polluted the shrine, which probably made the gods angry, and why it's now only ashes."

"If you hadn't helped her, you wouldn't have been there for me and the policeman, and we would have all perished."

Inzan gave Makoto a wide-eyed look, which softened into a smile. "Well, I can handle any spirits or even the wrath of the gods themselves if it means even one member of the Mori family lives."

Makoto nodded. "What will you do now?"

Inzan cast his eyes downward. "Knowing you and the Mori family name are both alive changed something in me. I'll … turn myself in for what I've done."

"Are you sure?" Makoto asked.

Inzan nodded. "It is only right. I have a lot I need to atone for."

Makoto stared at him for a moment but gave a solemn nod. "I understand."

"But what about you, Master Mori? What do you intend to do?"

"The home minister offered me a position to help the government in return for giving me information about the Shinsengumi."

"And you accepted?"

Makoto nodded.

"I wish I could offer you a place to stay while you worked," Inzan said, "but the temple is in no state to be lived in, especially with me not there."

"I have already made arrangements somewhere else. I'll see if I can convince the home minister to show you leniency."

"I appreciate your kindness, Master Mori, but it is unnecessary."

"Let me be the judge of that."

Inzan looked surprised and then smiled warmly. "Well, if I may ask one inconvenience of you Master Mori, would you be willing to accompany me to the police station? I'm a bit too weak to do it on my own."

Makoto nodded. "Of course."

***

The next afternoon, Helen paced about the edge of the gangway to the *Abraham Lincoln*. There was a small crowd of people gathered to see the ship leave, but it was nowhere near as large as the crowd that saw it coming in. Helen guessed the excitement surrounding the *Hiei* was the talk of the town instead.

Her husband impatiently tapped his foot, holding a couple of their bags, while Aki held many more bags than one would expect of a woman of her small size: two Gladstone bags in her hands, and two more carpet bags tucked under her arms.

"Come on, Helen," John complained. "We don't have time to waste. The ship will be leaving soon and this strange maid is probably getting tired."

Helen glanced back at Aki and saw her bouncing up and down. If anything, she had more energy to spare than ever. "Go on without me. I'll be right there."

Arkwright shook his head and started up the gangway. He looked back and saw Aki hadn't followed him.

"Don't just stand there, girl. Get up here!"

Aki nodded once and sprinted up the gangway, nearly running right into Arkwright, who had only made it up halfway. He let out a yelp and tried scurrying up before Aki ran him down, but ended up tripping over his own feet and fell face-first on the gangway. Aki screeched to a halt before tripping over Arkwright. She looked down at him with a large, goofy grin on her face.

Arkwright picked himself up with what little dignity he had left and took his bags up the remainder of the gangway to the deck of the ship, with Aki closely following behind. After reaching the top, Aki flopped down all of the bags she was carrying and skipped her way back down the gangway.

She approached Helen with a friendly wave. "Have a good trip and come back soon."

Helen smiled sadly. "Take care of yourself, Aki."

Aki nodded and headed back to the hotel, or at least Helen thought she did. Helen looked around nervously, wondering if the cowboy wasn't going to show up after all. She let out a sigh of relief and waved when she saw Makoto show up on the pier. He walked up to her.

"Oh good! You got my letter?"

Makoto nodded, pulled out the envelope, and showed it to her. "You said you wanted something from me?"

"Not from you, but to give to you." Helen started digging through her side-bag.

Makoto glanced up at the ship, which was billowing smoke from its smokestack. "Heading back to America?"

"Yes. We were always planning on returning on the *Abraham Lincoln*, but it looks like we won't be back for a long time."

"I see."

Helen stopped digging through her bag and looked up at Makoto. "You know, you could probably get onboard if you wanted to return to America."

Makoto shook his head. "I still have things I need to do."

"Those Shinsen-whatever they're called?"

Makoto nodded.

"Just so you know," Helen said, "I've been in a lot of plays. And most of the ones about revenge usually end with everyone dying. You still have your whole life ahead of you, do you really want to spend it chasing ghosts from the past?"

Makoto didn't respond to that since he wasn't entirely sure himself.

Helen shrugged and continued digging into her bag. "Oh, well. I suppose that's your business. Though based on how much trouble likes to follow you around, I probably shouldn't be encouraging you to get on the ship and … ah! Here we are."

Helen pulled out a book and handed it to Makoto. He only stared at it with confusion.

"It's a gift!" Helen said. "You should accept it. In fact, it would be impolite not to take it!"

Makoto hesitated, but reached forward and took the book.

Helen smiled. "It's one of my favorites. And while you and the detective in that book have almost nothing in common, it just seems right to give it to you. I've always found these books to be helpful when I'm bored, but this one may even help you in your quest."

Makoto tipped his hat toward Helen. "Thank you."

Helen smiled and picked up her bag. The bell of the ship sounded. "Ah, that's my cue. Exit stage left!" She trotted halfway up the gangway. She turned around and waved toward Makoto. "Best of luck to you! Remember everyone wears masks, but I'm confident you'll be able to see past them, even that young lady's."

Makoto nodded.

She walked up the remainder of the gangway to meet her husband at the top. She waved from the deck as the ship's bell rang again, and the gangway was pulled up. The ship headed out into Tokyo Bay.

Makoto watched as the ship slowly pulled out into the water. He thought about Emiko and everything that had happened. How many masks did she wear? Did she have any feelings for him at all, or was he just a pawn to her? He reached into his pocket and pulled out the dragon king shogi piece Emiko had given him. He contemplated tossing it into the water, but couldn't bring himself to do so and stuck it back into his pocket. He looked down at the book Helen gave him, the title read *A Study in Scarlet: Reminiscences of John H. Watson, M.D.*

"Hey! Mori! Over here!"

Makoto looked toward Kotaro, who was jogging toward him and was already out of breath. Kotaro stopped in front of him. "I just got word from the captain! There are some foreigners acting strangely. Come with me, right now!"

Makoto glanced out at the *Abraham Lincoln* as it pulled away. The people on the deck were only dots now. He smiled when he saw one of the dots was bright purple. He tucked the book under his arm and followed Kotaro into Yokohama.

THE END

The adventure continues in the next novel in this exciting series:

Notorious Ninja

Meiji Mysteries Book Two

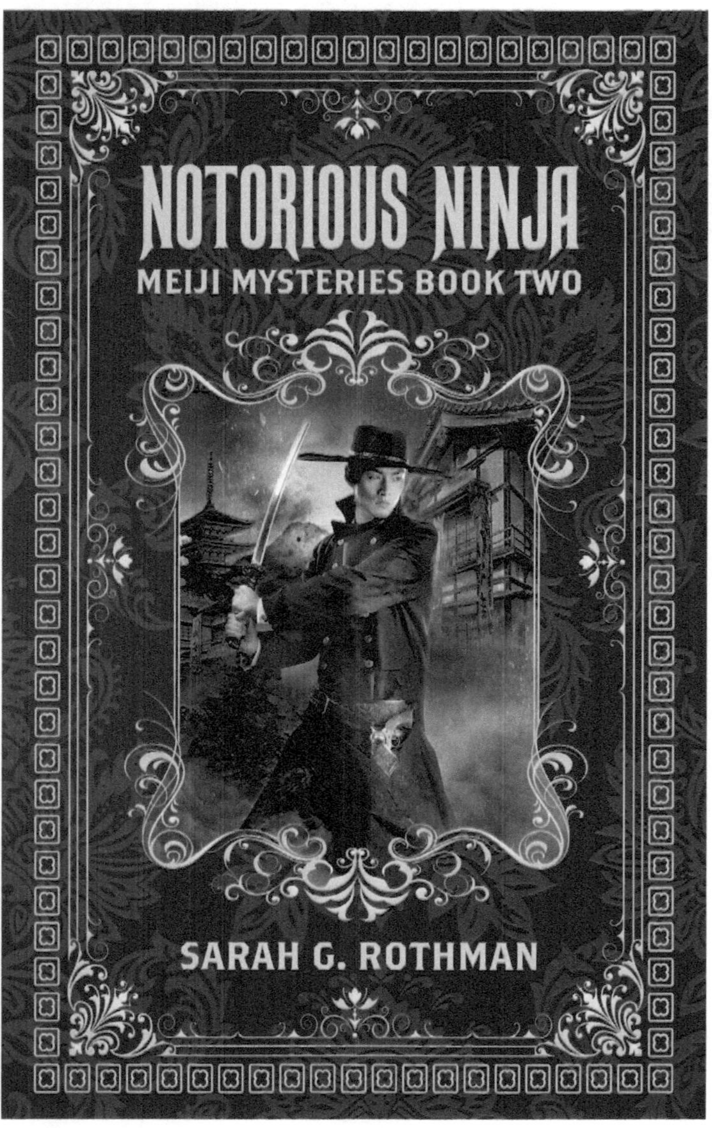

Want More Meiji Mysteries?

Visit **meijimysteries.com** and sign up to download the first episode of a FREE serial about Mori Makoto's adventures in the American Wild West before the events of Suicidal Samurai. You'll also find the latest news about Meiji Mysteries plus some cool information about the characters and locations in the story.

Author's Note

Thank you for reading Suicidal Samurai! I hope you had fun traveling back in time to Victorian Japan. If you have the time, I'd really appreciate it if you could leave a review. It doesn't have to be long, just a sentence or two about what you did (or didn't) like about the book. I'm always open to feedback! If you did enjoy the book, feel free to share it with your friends.

I'd love to hear from you, so feel free to e-mail me with your opinions, critiques, questions, concerns, and corrections, or just to say hello. My e-mail is sgrothman@rozfire.com. If you want to find out more about Meiji Mysteries, be sure to check out the website, meijimysteries.com, for the latest news about the series. That's all for now, and I hope to see you in Meiji Mysteries Book Two, Notorious Ninja!

Other ROZFIRE Titles

Thinking about traveling to Japan? *An Otaku Abroad* is a handy travel guide aimed at anime and manga fans which will teach you how to plan your trip. It also includes tips and tricks for keeping your costs under control.

For more information, visit otakuabroad.com.

WWW.ROZFIRE.COM

Other ROZFIRE Titles

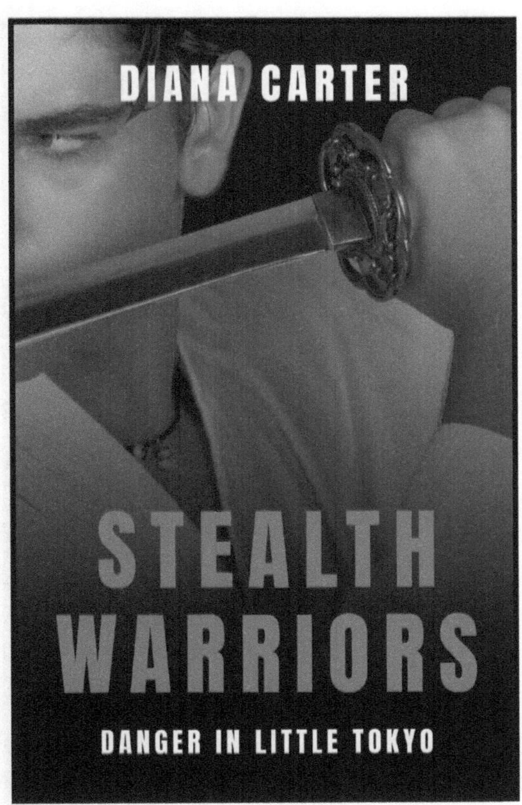

Her boss told her it was a simple job ...

Now Valerie's on the run from a gang of ruthless thugs who want her dead. And she has no choice but to depend on a mysterious stranger with no past. Together, they must dodge assassins, and unmask a powerful conspiracy as they race across Los Angeles.

For more information, visit rozfire.com.

WWW.ROZFIRE.COM

OTHER ROZFIRE TITLES

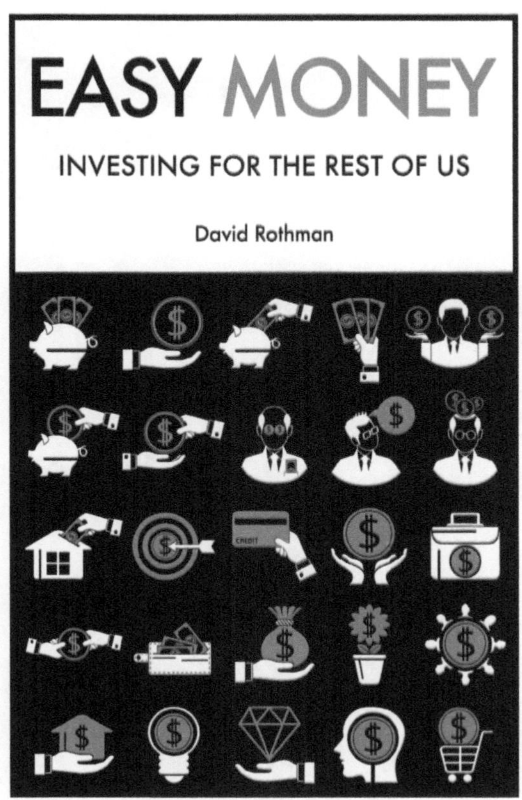

Want to learn about investing? *Easy Money* goes over a straightforward, low risk, step by step procedure you can use to build your own fortune. Once you've mastered this technique, you will see your wealth grow as your money works for you.

For more information, visit rozfire.com.

www.ingramcontent.com/pod-product-compliance
Lightning Source LLC
Chambersburg PA
CBHW020322030826
48979CB00022B/816
* 9 7 8 0 9 9 8 9 6 4 7 1 3 *